T0355392

Here in Our
Auschwitz and
Other Stories

Here in Our Auschwitz and Other Stories

TADEUSZ BOROWSKI

FOREWORD BY TIMOTHY SNYDER

TRANSLATED FROM THE POLISH
BY MADELINE G. LEVINE

YALE UNIVERSITY PRESS ■ NEW HAVEN & LONDON

A MARGELLOS
WORLD REPUBLIC OF LETTERS BOOK

The Margellos World Republic of Letters is dedicated to making literary works from around the globe available in English through translation. It brings to the English-speaking world the work of leading poets, novelists, essayists, philosophers, and playwrights from Europe, Latin America, Africa, Asia, and the Middle East to stimulate international discourse and creative exchange.

Yale University Press books may be purchased in quantity for educational, business, or promotional use. For information, please email sales.press@yale.edu (U.S. office) or sales@yaleup.co.uk (U.K. office).

Set in Electra type by Newgen North America. Printed in the United States of America.

Library of Congress Control Number: 2020951855
ISBN 978-0-300-11690-8 (hardcover : alk. paper)

A catalogue record for this book is available from the British Library.

This paper meets the requirements of ANSI/NISO z39.48-1992 (Permanence of Paper).
10 9 8 7 6 5 4 3 2 1

CONTENTS

FOREWORD

TIMOTHY SNYDER

"Crematorium Esperanto." When I first read that phrase, de-
cades ago, I put my thumb on the page, let the book close on my
hand, lay down in the grass, and stared at the sky. I knew that I
would never forget it. With the words come a scene: men awaiting a train by a ramp, some assuring others, in a pidgin of Nazi
terms and Indo-European monosyllables, that the work ahead was
light. Nothing to offload, just people, Jews to be selected for labor
or death who will walk down the ramp and into the trucks themselves. They will give up their belongings and their clothes. The
narrator has come to assist in that selection and to take a few things
for himself. That was Auschwitz in 1944, the mass murder of the
Jews of Europe, as mercilessly retold in the short story "Ladies and
Gentlemen, Welcome to the Gas" by Tadeusz Borowski.

Thanks to Madeline Levine's marvelous translation, we now
have in English the most important work of the most challenging
chronicler of Auschwitz. Though the abysmal grace of phrases such
as "crematorium Esperanto" suggests distance, Borowski's narration
is as close as a last breath. In this story as in others, the narrator is a
participant, and shares a name with the author. As he waits for the
train, a fellow prisoner buys water from an SS man on credit, to
be paid back with money to be taken from Jews who have not yet
arrived. When the train halts, a young mother, clever and pretty,
separates herself from her little daughter in the hope of being selected for labor. The child runs after her, screaming "Mama!" An

vii

inmate angrily beats the woman with a shovel, then throws her into the death transport with her child.

Tadeusz Borowski was a young and sensationally gifted Polish poet. He was never not young: he gassed himself to death at the age of twenty-eight as a leading writer in Stalinist Poland. The poet began to write prose in 1945, after surviving Auschwitz and Dachau. He was not his narrators, the kapos and Vorarbeiters who share his name, but he could see the camp from a variety of perspectives. He understood other inmates, their habits and speech; and he made friends. Borowski grew up poor in provincial Soviet Ukraine and in a tough Warsaw neighborhood, generally apart from his parents, both of whom were incarcerated for long periods. He knew about camps and about the Holocaust before he was deported to Auschwitz.

Unlike most Auschwitz writers, Borowski could not see deportation as exceptional. Concentration camps were a kind of family regularity: the father was imprisoned in one from 1926 to 1932, the mother from 1930 to 1934, and the son from 1943 to 1945. Borowski's first known poem, composed when he was nine, was recorded by a hand, his father's, that had just ceased laboring in the Gulag. When Tadeusz wrote to his parents as a young man from Auschwitz, not so very many years thereafter, he relied on shorthand: "You know what I mean."[1] The Holocaust was part of his coming of age in Warsaw. More Jews had lived in Poland than anywhere else, and most were dead before Auschwitz became a killing facility. His milieu was partly Jewish, and he spent anxious nights worrying that his girlfriend would be arrested by the Gestapo on her way home from the warehouse where he lived. He went to Auschwitz as a result of an attempt to shelter someone fleeing the ghetto. Days before his deportation he saw the ghetto burn.

In Auschwitz, Borowski was determined and brave, although he always portrayed himself as mean and cynical. Arrested by the Gestapo as a student, he applied his classical education to what he saw. He worried that the literary and philosophical canon he cherished was a residue of dominion. So he turned the writers he loved to the creation of something new, a literature of apocalypse that would analyze power and outlast it. He was scornful of his own stories, disparaging them, ascribing them to imaginary authors, and eventually, as a Stalinist, denouncing them. And yet they will last, as the Polish writer Jerzy Andrzejewski said, as long as Polish literature lasts. We might add, as long as the memory of the Holocaust lasts.

Borowski's Auschwitz is not set apart from the world; it is a natural part of the world. It is not a mechanism but a society. Rather than straining to show the abnormality of the camp, Borowski portrays it as normal. Then comes a moment, a juxtaposition, in which the normality is too thick, and the reader's own ability to normalize is exposed. In "The People Who Were Walking," the selection of Jews at the ramp and their transport to the gas chamber is in the background. In the foreground is a soccer game being played by inmates. The narrator is now the goalkeeper. Fetching a ball kicked behind him and out of bounds, he sees Jews walking to the gas chambers. Then he returns to the field and plays on. Another ball goes out of bounds, and the goalie turns around again to get it. The people who were walking are gone: "Behind my back, between one corner kick and the next, they had gassed three thousand people."[2]

A typical writer seeks the exceptional in a concentration camp: the decent, the heroic, the patriotic, the revolutionary. This authorizes us to associate the camp with something we feel, or feel we ought to feel. We look away from the reality of Auschwitz and into some metaphysical middle distance. Borowski is more demanding of us, and tougher on himself. What is universal, he wants us to understand, is our capacity for degradation. Auschwitz does not ennoble anything, nor does it affirm our prior commitments. Borowski was an exceptional writer in that he sought out the typical. He did once go to the ramp to await a transport: not to steal from Jews but to observe it for himself, and at risk to himself.

Auschwitz was a consequence of choices Borowski knowingly made. His girlfriend Maria Rundo, of Jewish origin herself, was arrested in Warsaw while trying to help a Jewish friend, and he was arrested because he followed her. Much of his poetry desired Maria; all of his prose required her. She is the imagined reader of his very first story. He described an everyday life he knew she would understand. Unlike other imaginable readers, she knew Auschwitz as well as he. In one important sense she knew it better: unlike Maria, Tadeusz did not have to worry about being denounced as a Jew and gassed.

When asked to write an autobiographical sketch after the war, Borowski said that he lacked the balance. From a childhood amid terror in the Soviet Union, through deportation to Auschwitz at twenty, his life had no fulcrum.

His father and mother, Stanisław Borowski and Teofila (née Karpińska) Borowska, were Poles who grew up in the southwest of the Russian Empire, in Ukraine. They were married in Zhytomyr in 1917, the year of the Bolshevik Revolution. In the three years that followed, Ukraine was the site of chaotic struggle. Five armies— Reds who wanted world revolution, Whites who wanted imperial restoration, Ukrainians who wanted national independence, anarchists who wanted anarchy in Ukraine, and Poles who wanted territory and a Ukrainian ally—fought in various configurations. All committed pogroms against Jews, for whom the year 1919 was the most murderous in all modern history up to that point.

Stanisław Borowski played a small part in the war for Ukraine. Its final act, in 1920, was an intervention by the Polish Army to support the Ukrainian government against the Red Army. The Poles were hoping to create an east European federation or alliance with an independent Ukraine; the Soviets hoped to control Ukraine, destroy the young Polish state, and spread the revolution to Germany and Europe. The Polish Army was aided in Ukraine by the Polish

Military Organization, locals who served as couriers, scouts, and agitators. Stanisław Borowski was one of these.

The Polish Army got as far as Kyiv in May 1920, and the Red Army reached the outskirts of Warsaw that August. In the end, the Poles were victorious but exhausted, and the peace treaty of 1921 did not create an independent Ukraine. It left Zhytomyr, where the Borowskis resided, on the Soviet side of a new Polish-Soviet border. The defeat of the Red Army ended Lenin's dream of spreading revolution westward to Europe by force, and forced the Bolsheviks to found a state.

In December 1922, a few weeks after Teofila Borowska gave birth to Tadeusz, the Soviet Union was established. It was a one-party communist regime, but it took the form of a federation of national units: Russia, Belarus, Ukraine, and so forth. The Borowski family found themselves members of a Polish minority in the Soviet republic of Ukraine. This was not an enviable position. Poles were among the ethnic minorities most subject to terror in the Soviet Union, and Ukraine was among the territories most wracked by Stalinism.

In 1926, when Tadeusz was three, his father, Stanisław, was arrested by the Soviet secret police for his earlier activity in the Polish Military Organization. Stanisław was sentenced to hard labor at a concentration camp in Karelia, in the far north of European Russia. He worked on the first grandiose project of the Gulag, the construction of a canal from the White Sea to the Baltic Sea. He was among the 170,000 or so prisoners who labored with primitive tools in the bitter cold. Some twenty-five thousand of them perished. The canal, dug shallow by sick people with shards and spoons, was of little economic significance. In 1930, Tadeusz's mother, Teofila, was arrested in her turn and deported to Siberia. Her crime was her marriage.

Tadeusz was separated from both of his parents at the age of seven. This was no unusual situation for Polish children in the USSR. The expectation was that such orphans of terror would sovietize and forget their parents' culture. His older brother Juliusz was indeed sent to an orphanage. Tadeusz, however, was taken in by an aunt in the town of Marchlewsk, which at the time was part of a Polish cultural district. Pedagogues there created a communist version of Polish culture, including egalitarian forms of address and a simplified orthography. As a result, Tadeusz had two years of elementary schooling in Polish and early exposure to a form of Polish communism. The autonomous region was dissolved in 1935, and its activists executed. But by then the Borowski family was no longer in the Soviet Union.[3]

In 1932, as a result of a prisoner swap, Stanisław Borowski was allowed to leave the Gulag and emigrate to Poland. This was probably bad luck for the Polish communists freed from Polish prison and sent to the Soviet Union; almost all such people were executed by Soviet authorities by the end of the 1930s. It was good luck for the Borowski family. Thanks to the Red Cross, Tadeusz and Juliusz were able to join their father in Poland. Their mother followed in 1934. By leaving Soviet Ukraine when they did, the boys were spared the worst of the *Holodomor*, the political famine of 1932 and 1933 that took nearly four million lives. The Zhytomyr region was hard hit. In 1932, the year the boys left, about one in a hundred of its inhabitants died of starvation or related disease. The next year it was one in ten.

Stalin had consolidated power in the Soviet Union, and the famine in Ukraine was a result of his First Five-Year Plan. Beginning in 1930, agriculture was collectivized: farmland was seized by the state and farmers became state employees (or were deported). When yields dropped in fertile Ukraine, Stalin blamed local party members, Polish spies, and the Ukrainian peasants themselves. Claiming that the famine was about national resistance, Stalin ordered measures that ensured that millions died unnecessarily. Party members who reported the facts were punished; the world of experience succumbed to the party line. So began Stalinism.

Its next phase was the Great Terror. Had the Borowski family remained in the Soviet Union (and survived the famine), Stanisław would almost certainly have been executed. In 1937 and 1938, some seven hundred thousand Soviet citizens were shot to death by the authorities. More than a hundred thousand were killed in the Polish Operation, the pretext for which was a Stalinist fabrication about the Polish Military Organization. The lie that Polish spies had provoked the famine in Ukraine was extended to a new boundary of the absurd. In the fantasies of the interrogators, a local Polish paramilitary that had been defunct for fifteen years became a vast conspiracy penetrating the heights of Soviet power. Poles in the Gulag were tried a second time, and often executed. In the Marchlewsk and Zhytomyr regions, Soviet units went from village to village as mobile killing squads. Secret policemen surrounded villages at night, seized Polish men, and shot them in nearby woods after a perfunctory trial. Their wives and children were deported to Kazakhstan.[4]

The Borowski family escaped alive to Poland, although Tadeusz's parents between them spent ten years in the Gulag. Yet life in Warsaw, where they settled, was not simple. The family was regrouping in a poor country in the midst of the Great Depression. Their circumstances were extremely modest, proletarian at best. The parents, from peasant backgrounds themselves, worked to equip their sons for an excellent Warsaw high school (*gymnazjum*). To save money, Tadeusz and Juliusz resided in a Franciscan dormitory for five years, until 1937. Tadeusz did live with both of his parents in Warsaw for a couple of years after that—until the Germans invaded Poland on 1 September 1939.

As the Luftwaffe bombed the undefended capital, the house where the Borowskis rented a room burned to the ground. Tadeusz went east on his bicycle when the bombing started, following the evacuation instructions of the Polish government. This put him

right in the path of the Red Army, which invaded Poland on 17 September. He returned to Warsaw to find his parents living in a tent.
In those weeks, Poland ceased to exist: the Wehrmacht and the Red
Army rushed to meet, and Nazi and Soviet leaders consulted about
the division of the spoils. According to the agreement by which Hitler and Stalin began the war, the Molotov-Ribbentrop pact, Warsaw
was to fall on the Soviet side of the border. The German-Soviet
Treaty of Borders and Friendship of 28 September, however, placed
Warsaw in the German zone. This was perhaps good luck for the
Borowskis. Had the family once again come under Soviet rule, they
would all likely have been deported to the Gulag, or worse. In 1940
and 1941 the Soviets deported about half a million Polish citizens
and executed tens of thousands.

At first, the German and Soviet occupations were comparable
in their scale of murder and deportation. Following different ideologies, each apparatus of power targeted Poles, especially educated
elites, for deportation and murder. With time a difference emerged,
one that was particularly striking in Warsaw, Europe's most important Jewish city. Hitler's worldview demanded the removal of Jews
from the planet, and Nazi policy was seeking a Final Solution.
In Warsaw, where a third of the population was Jewish, a ghetto
became part of everyday life, and the deportations were known to
all. Tadeusz studied, became a poet, and fell in love with a Polish
(Jewish) girl in this time and place.

Tadeusz Borowski was sixteen years old in late September 1939,
when Warsaw surrendered to the Germans. He could not return to
his high school that autumn, since the German plan was to ex-
ploit Poles as colonial *Untermenschen*. Like many young men and
women in Warsaw, Tadeusz continued his studies illegally, conspiring with other students and their professors.[5] His parents sacrificed,
in dreadful wartime conditions, to pay for his lessons and his clothes.

He graduated from high school in spring 1940 by this method, on a day when the Gestapo carried out roundups in Warsaw to hunt for Polish laborers—a juxtaposition he later described in a story.

He began university studies that fall. The seminars in private apartments created intimacy between students and professors. The central figure, Professor Jerzy Krzyżanowski, taught students that studying literature required history—and also that critique and mockery were part of scholarship. Tadeusz was happily absorbed by his courses in Polish literature, European intellectual history, and Shakespeare, led by outstanding scholars, people risking their own lives to teach. He read constantly, in bed, on the tram, during lectures. The impoverished son of political refugees found a circle of bright friends who shared a secret and a love of learning.

Following his father, Tadeusz worked for a building supply firm, as a stock boy and a night watchman. He lived in its warehouse. He covered a wall with bookshelves, "nailed together clumsily out of unplaned boards," as he wrote in "Farewell to Maria." His school colleagues visited him there, argued about philosophy, and read poetry. The job provided papers that made deportation to a camp less likely. The economy under German occupation, as Tadeusz learned, was thoroughly corrupt; no building firm could function without cooperation with Germans, who were themselves stealing and breaking rules. Tadeusz distilled vodka on the site and traded on the black market.

In autumn 1940, as Tadeusz Borowski and Maria Rundo began their university studies, German authorities transformed a large section of northern Warsaw into a ghetto for Jews. As of November, Jews found beyond its walls were to be shot. For the Nazis, Jewishness was defined by ancestry. For many people in Warsaw, it was a matter of personal choice: one could be of Jewish origin and regard oneself (and be regarded) as Polish. Such people might disobey the German order to move to the ghetto and remain where they were—

so long as they were not denounced. Maria Rundo was Jewish by Nazi reckonings, although her forebears had seen themselves as Poles for generations. The Rundo family did not go to the ghetto.

The following spring the Wehrmacht massed in its occupied Polish territories. In June 1941, Hitler betrayed Stalin, and Germany invaded the Soviet Union. That summer the Germans began the murder of entire Jewish communities. They killed Jews face to face by gunfire: more than 23,000 Jews in Kamianets' Podils'kyi, more than 33,000 in Kyiv, more than 28,000 in Riga . . .[6] By the end of 1941, about a million Jews had been shot to death over pits. The Final Solution took shape as an extermination campaign.

The Holocaust took a different form in the Polish territories the Germans had occupied in 1939, where Jews were already concentrated in ghettos. In 1942, the Germans transported them by rail to Chełmno, Bełżec, Sobibór, and Treblinka, where they were gassed to death with exhaust fumes. In 1942, as Tadeusz and Maria fell in love, most of the Jews of Warsaw were deported from the Umschlagplatz in the ghetto and murdered at Treblinka. In "Farewell to Maria," Polish traders report in the warehouse on what they have seen inside the ghetto walls: "Pan Tadek, what I saw there, Pan Tadek, you wouldn't believe. Children, women . . . It's true, they're Jewish, but still, you know . . ."

On 24 February 1943, the day described in "Farewell to Maria," a schoolfriend of Maria's left the ghetto. Irka's parents had been deported to Treblinka, and she was alone and had nothing. Tadeusz and Maria had been saving money to rent an apartment, and Maria decided on the spot that Irka would live with them. This was to put their own lives at risk and to set aside their youthful vision of permanent intimacy. The first order of business was to get false identification papers identifying Irka as a non-Jewish Pole.

Maria had connections. She worked in a laundry, where she did favors for Czesław Mankiewicz, a good friend of hers and of Tadeusz. Just two years older than they, he was very active in the communist underground, editing an illegal newspaper and helping to organize a paramilitary. He would leave packages with Maria at the laundry to be picked up by other comrades. Communists would come to the laundry to use the telephone; Maria would do the dialing, since she was the one entrusted to know the numbers. Mankiewicz had helped Jews escape from the ghetto before, and Maria knew that he could forge documents for Irka. She told Tadeusz of her plan, and then went to Mankiewicz's apartment. She did not return. Mankiewicz had been arrested a few days earlier, and the Gestapo had staked out the place. She was arrested and taken to Pawiak Prison.

In the story "Farewell to Maria," the narrator "hadn't the faintest idea what to do," and Maria was gassed. In reality, Tadeusz went after her. Once Maria had disappeared, conspiratorial protocol dictated that Tadeusz, for his own safety, avoid the places she had been, especially clandestine meeting points. He did the opposite. The next day he rang the bell at Mankiewicz's apartment, and was arrested in his turn by the Gestapo. Expecting this, he had emptied his briefcase of any material that could compromise others. On his person the Gestapo found a copy of Aldous Huxley's *Brave New World* and a few poems. Tadeusz arrived at Pawiak Prison a day after Maria. When she saw him there, head shaven, she burst into tears. He smiled at her and said: "Don't worry. I wanted us to be together."[7]

He had good cause to fear that she would die. Had her Jewish background been discovered at Pawiak, she would have been shot. As luck would have it, she was sent to prison at the same time as an elderly aunt who also bore the surname Rundo. The relative, who had been denounced as a Jew by her landlady, sought out Maria in the prison, not understanding the danger. The aunt was shot at the ghetto wall before she found Maria. Later, some of Maria's cellmates decided that she was a Jew because she received nice food packages from her mother. Before that could take a sinister turn,

Maria was transported to Auschwitz as a communist, and therefore as a Pole. Tadeusz was transported to Auschwitz at about the same time, in late April.

In their absence, Tadeusz and Maria's friends published his love poems to her. A fragment of one reads:

> Will you come back to me? A wave
> in the dark catches legs from below,
> heavy sky abreast. You are like that:
> like my shadow beside me,
> as real as my body; elusive
> and as deep as the reflection
> of my unlit face in a pane already
> black from night

At the time, the typical Auschwitz laborer was Polish. Auschwitz had been founded by the Germans in 1940, in occupied southwestern Poland, as a punishment camp for Poles. Some seventy-five thousand non-Jewish Poles lost their lives there. About twenty-three thousand Roma and Sinti were deported to Auschwitz, most of whom perished. Borowski describes the Gypsy camp in his stories. In 1941, after Germany invaded the Soviet Union, Soviet prisoners of war were also sent to Auschwitz. About fifteen thousand were killed, some of them in experimental gassings. One finds such men in Borowski's stories, speaking Russian. One of them wielded that shovel in "Ladies and Gentlemen, Welcome to the Gas." Another, in "Here in Our Auschwitz," asked Tadeusz to visit his mother in Siberia to tell her how he died.

By 1943 most Polish Jews were dead, and the Nazi policy of extermination was shifting to Europe as a whole. Tadeusz and Maria were witnesses to this transition. From his cell in Pawiak Prison, Tadeusz saw the suppression of the Warsaw Ghetto Uprising. The Germans were going house to house with grenades and flamethrowers, burning out any survivors. "The ghetto burned," he remembered, "and smoke blocked out the sky." This was a late stage in the murder of the Jews of Warsaw, who were resisting deportation to Treblinka. Just before Tadeusz and Maria arrived in Auschwitz, the Germans opened two gas chambers in the Birkenau part of the complex. In the second half of 1943 and the first half of 1944, Auschwitz became the center of the Holocaust. Most of the Jews murdered came from Hungary or Poland; significant numbers also came from France, the Netherlands, Greece, and the territories of Czechoslovakia. Maria could see the smoke from the crematoria from the women's camp. For much of his time in Birkenau, Borowski had a direct view of the ramp and the crematoria. He said after the war that he had seen a million people die. This was only a minor overstatement.

Borowski was twenty years old and physically fit when he arrived in Auschwitz on 29 April 1943. Assigned to labor in Birkenau, he dug ditches and carried telegraph poles. "A Day at Harmenze" is about this period. He made friends, as he did at all points in his life. He caught pneumonia that fall and was treated at the infirmary. He was popular there, befriended a doctor, and stayed on as a night watchman. He was bad at this job, since he spent his nights thinking about Maria and composing poems. One night a thief got in, and by way of apology Borowski recited the poem he had composed. In March 1944 he was trained as a Pfleger, an assistant or orderly in the infirmary. This was lighter work physically, although he watched hundreds of patients die inside every day (and thousands more outside). His physician friend remembered Borowski's good spirits, and said that he improved the mental health of his colleagues.

When Auschwitz was founded, German criminal inmates, often veterans of other camps, held the positions of responsibility. Subordinate to the SS men who directed the camp, they oversaw its daily operations. With time, as Poles came to outnumber Germans, they gained the upper hand in these positions, which they called "functions." As a Pfleger, Borowski found himself in the middle of the "hierarchy of fear," able to look upward toward the kapos and the SS men, and downward toward other prisoners, Gypsies, and Jews.[8] He was not the Vorarbeiter or the kapo who figure as narrators in his stories, but he was privileged enough (in camp terms) and worldly enough (in personal experience) to imagine them.

Tadeusz missed Maria. His love for her became a kind of legend among the prisoners who knew him. After almost a year, he found a way to make contact. One day a German criminal inmate, someone with a good function, arrived in the infirmary with an illness. The Poles in the infirmary wanted to finish him off; this was the normal way to assert dominance and claim the functions. Tadeusz defended the German, even sharing food. Kurt was a journalist sentenced for smuggling. Once he was well, he found Maria in the women's camp and then delivered nine letters to her in March 1944.

Soon thereafter Tadeusz got himself assigned to a roofing crew that was at work in the women's camp. In this way he got to see Maria several times. She was living in far worse conditions than he. She was very ill, had lost her hair, and her skin was disfigured. He sent her medicine and a pair of boots. He was cheerful with her; and they sat, holding hands, talking about literature and philosophy.

Tadeusz and Maria both survived Auschwitz. Strange though it might seem, he was probably in less danger there in late summer 1944 than he would have been in Warsaw. The Warsaw Uprising, the struggle of the Polish Home Army against the German occupation of the city, began that August. It was a hecatomb for students of their generation.

In June 1944 the Red Army won a major battle in Belarus, and seemed poised to march through Poland. German soldiers were seen retreating through the streets of Warsaw. The Polish government, in exile in London, wanted to raise the flag in the capital before the Red Army arrived. Believing that the Germans would withdraw from Warsaw before the Soviet advance, the Polish government ordered an uprising for 1 August. Yet the Germans managed to hold a defensive line on the Vistula River, and the Red Army halted. The insurgents fought the Germans in Warsaw on their own for eight long weeks. Stalin blocked American and British attempts to supply the Poles by air.

Young men and women of Tadeusz and Maria's cohort, too young to have been called up in 1939, were eager to fight, or felt bound by honor to do so. Talented writers and scholars threw themselves upon the barricades and were killed. The Germans murdered some two hundred thousand civilians while defeating the uprising. Beginning in October, they demolished what remained of the city, dynamiting building after building. Himmler and Hitler's idea was that Warsaw would never rise again. The Red Army arrived in the rubble in January 1945.

For Tadeusz and Maria, the approach of the Red Army meant separation, as the Germans sent inmates from Auschwitz to camps farther west. In August 1944 Tadeusz was sent to the Netzweller-Dautmergen camp, near Stuttgart, where "The Death of an Insurgent" is set. Maria was transported from Auschwitz to Ravensbrück five months later. In early 1945, as the Germans retreated and supplies were cut off, hundreds of thousands of prisoners perished in the camps. Maria had a terrible first two weeks at the *Jugendlager* at Ravensbrück, where all she ate was snow, and that only at the urging of her friends. Once she was in the main camp, her conditions were better: it was a "sanatorium" by comparison with Auschwitz.

Tadeusz had a harder time in Dachau, where he was sent from Netzweller-Dautmergen in January 1945. When the U.S. Army came upon the camp on 1 May 1945, soldiers found piles of skeletal corpses. "Liberation" is not really the word; as an American nurse remarked, the prisoners "couldn't be liberated. What they needed was medical care, lots of it and as soon as possible."[9] Borowski had nearly starved to death. He weighed less than eighty pounds when the Americans arrived. He wrote poetry the entire time, even when he was too weak to stand.

He spent an unhappy summer in a displaced persons camp run in a former SS garrison by the Americans. In September 1945, he was released and made his way to Munich. As a free man in the American occupation zone of Germany, he considered whether or not to return to Poland, now under the control of the Red Army. Stalin claimed the eastern half of the country for the USSR, as he had in his 1939 accord with Hitler. The new Poland, shifted westward at the expense of Germany, fell into a Soviet zone of influence. Borowski was frustrated that the Polish officers he encountered in the displaced persons camp had no answer to this strategic predicament.

For Borowski, though, separation was more important than politics. His only clear plan in Munich was to find Maria Rundo. With the help of Anatol Girs, a charismatic editor he knew from Netzweller-Dautmergen, he was put in charge of a Red Cross office that sought missing family members and learned that she was in Sweden. Tadeusz and Maria began corresponding in early 1946 but could not easily meet. He could not travel to Sweden, nor she to Germany. She wanted to emigrate to a West European country, and he said he would follow her. In the meantime, he sent her a story.

In Warsaw and in the camps, Borowski was a poet. In Warsaw he wrote poems about catastrophe in hexameter, and about his love for Maria in loose modern verse. His catastrophist poetry of 1942, which he self-published in the warehouse just after his twentieth birthday, describes the whole world as a concentration camp. The last quatrain of "Song," the final poem in the collection, is exemplary.

> Night above us. The stars on high
> Violet putrefacting sky

> Our legacy is scrap iron
> and the mocking laugh of generations

His poetic style did not change in Auschwitz; details of the apocalypse just clarified, as in "Night in Birkenau."

> Like a shield cast down in battle
> blue Orion amid stars supine
> Through the dark an engine rattles
> And the eyes of a crematorium shine

Although most of his wartime poems were lost during transports, inspections, and disinfections, he published thirty-seven of them in Munich, thanks to Anatol Girs. It was Girs who persuaded Borowski to take part in a group project, a collection of writings by three Polish inmates of Auschwitz. Borowski had never written prose and had no wish to do so, but he owed Girs some favors, and agreed. As the only true writer among the three former prisoners, Borowski took charge of the effort. He learned from the other inmates, both of whom were in Auschwitz longer than he. Editing their texts, recording their oral accounts, he began to write prose himself.

In Munich, Borowski also learned from former inmates who were not participating in the writing project. One Auschwitz survivor he met was Stanisław Wygodzki, a Polish-Jewish communist poet who had been transported with his family from Będzin in 1944. Unlike Jews from elsewhere in Europe, Polish Jews knew what a transport to Auschwitz meant. In a collective suicide attempt that went awry, Wygodzki poisoned his wife and little daughter on the train, but survived himself. In the story "Ladies and Gentlemen, Welcome to the Gas," Borowski is describing precisely that Będzin transport, full of Polish Jews who know what awaits them.

Maria Rundo was on his mind as he wrote. As soon as he located her in Sweden, he mailed her a draft of "A Day at Harmenze." She was "shaken. Horrified by this picture of Auschwitz, even though I knew it myself. The moral side of it all, the strange form that humanity takes in those conditions." His contact with Maria was essential to his prose. Indeed, his earlier correspondence with her in Auschwitz is where it began. To write "Here in Our Auschwitz," his first story, he reconstructed the nine letters he wrote to her in March 1944. This broke the barrier, and he wrote three more stories in Munich: "Ladies and Gentlemen, Welcome to the Gas"; "A Day at Harmenze"; and "The People Who Were Walking."

Borowski's first Auschwitz story thus took the form of a long letter from someone called Tadeusz to someone called Maria. He is close to autobiography here; the cynical narrators appear in the stories to follow. "Here in Our Auschwitz" alternates between descriptions of the camp and memories of time with Maria in Warsaw, for which he tenderly thanks her. "I think about this and smile indulgently when people talk to me about morality, law, tradition, duties . . . Or when they renounce all tenderness and sentimentality and, making a fist, talk about an age of firmness. I smile and think that man is always discovering man anew—through love. And that this is the most important and the most enduring thing in human life."

In "Here in Our Auschwitz," Tadeusz shifts from gentle nostalgia about one woman to the present reality of the women he sees in the camp: those who lean out the window of the experimental block. He casts his eye upon the masses of men altered by the denial of contact with women. Men fit enough to think about sex are bestialized by generic desire: they cannot think of a particular woman, but need "a woman" in general. They see unclothed women: those on their way to the gas chambers. The mass murder of women exposes the uniform helplessness of men. Tadeusz describes a truck full of naked women screaming for help. "And they drove past us to the profound silence of ten thousand men. Not one man moved, not one hand was raised."

Food was a source and symbol of control. By 1943, some prisoners were permitted to receive packages from the outside. Jews could not. Many prisoners had no one on the outside to help them. As Maria remembered, "It was really only Poles who got packages." The Germans otherwise controlled the food supply in the camp through the kapos. In "Ladies and Gentlemen, Welcome to the Gas," his second story, Borowski describes a meal. "All eyes are fixed on the kapo's face. Two more cauldrons [of soup]: seconds. Every day the kapo delights in this moment. He is owed this complete power over people for his ten years in the camp. With the end of his ladle, he points out who has earned seconds; he never makes a mistake. The better workers, the stronger and healthier, get seconds." Those who waste away do so in the company of those who eat. Everyone is in some way complicit.

Even gassing was a social process, opening the moral black hole at the center of everyday life, and creating a vertical of human emotion that reinforced the hierarchy of the camp. The overall German policy to kill all Jews meant that they were valued only insofar as their bodies could deliver labor or portable wealth. If life is only about possessions, someone will find a way to extract both. After the Jews not selected for labor at the ramp are murdered in the gas chambers, their bodies become excavation sites. "Professional, well-practiced people will rummage in their insides, extract the gold from under the tongue, diamonds from the womb and rectum. They'll tear out the gold teeth. They'll send them to Berlin in tightly sealed boxes."

Before this happens, prisoners take from the still-living. In "Ladies and Gentlemen, Welcome to the Gas," the narrator Tadeusz is describing the plunder of the doomed. Prisoners might rebel internally against the horror of mass extermination, but they can only direct that rage against its victims. In raising his shovel against the young mother, the prisoner is affirming the line of power in the camp, showing how it runs through him. As a veteran inmate explains to the narrator, such a reaction is "normal, foreseen, and calculated. The ramp tortures you, you revolt, and it's easiest to unload your rage at those who are weaker. It's even desired that you should unload it."

Crematorium Esperanto is a language we can all learn. Dehumanization, as Borowski shows us, is a human process. The meaning of death is that we organize our actions around it. Fascism is not limited to a certain time and place; it is a certain orientation of life toward death. Extermination does not sanctify a victim or dignify a cause. It only instructs us about human possibility.

In Borowski's poetry all the world is a camp. Characters in his stories imagine Auschwitz and the Warsaw ghetto as models for the future of all humanity. In "Ladies and Gentlemen, Welcome to the Gas" the narrator fantasizes about a vast concentration camp covering half of Poland, holding millions of prisoners. In "Farewell to Maria," young people in occupied Warsaw discuss what the future holds. By that point three hundred thousand Warsaw Jews have been murdered at Treblinka. In the story, a Jewish woman who has escaped the ghetto predicts that "there'll be a ghetto on the Aryan side, too." And then: "Only there will be no way out of it."

In such a total Nazi triumph, prisoners labor to create a material order that will erase all memory of their suffering. In "Here in Our Auschwitz," Tadeusz asks, "What will the world know about us if the Nazis are victorious? Gigantic edifices will arise, highways, factories, towering monuments. Our hands will be placed beneath every brick, the railroad ties and concrete slabs will be carried on our backs. They will slaughter our families, the sick, the old. They will slaughter the children. And no one will know about us. The poets, lawyers, philosophers, priests will drown out our voices. They will create beauty, goodness, and truth."

These stories, although set in 1943, 1944, or 1945, were written after the Nazis had been defeated. For Borowski, the specter of a global Nazi victory was a special case of a general problem, one that surfaces throughout his work. Perhaps the values in which we are raised, our sense of beauty, goodness, and truth, are just an echo of earlier violence. If this is true, a writer chooses between defiance now and significance later. If he sides with power he is inhuman; if he resists it he is irrelevant. In "Farewell to Maria," as Gestapo raids take place outside, and as the hours pass since Maria's departure, her friends debate the issue. One position: what we call the classics is a record of extermination. Nothing honorable can endure, and nothing enduring can be honorable. The other: the writer should labor on despite war, because literature will survive and transcend.

Though he was haunted by the problem, Borowski's position as a writer in 1945 seems clear. He chose explication over adaptation, resisting power's thrust into the future by creating something absolutely new. Embedded in "Here in Our Auschwitz" are the mottos: "I do not know if we will survive, but I wish that some day we will be able to call things by their proper names, as courageous people do." With the proper names comes the proper analysis, which aims to "disentangle from daily events their quotidian essence, discard revulsion, disgust, and contempt, and find a philosophical formula for all of this." He was doing what he was calling for when he wrote that "we will have to give the living a report from this camp, from the time of deceptions, and stand up in defense of the dead."

This did not mean sentimentalizing death, or attaching to it a meaning beyond its immanent one. On the contrary, defending the dead meant recording the truth about their lives, down to the end: "I don't know why later on people in the camp said that the Jews on the way to the gas sang a heartrending Hebrew song that no one could understand."

Borowski returned to Poland in May 1946. He knew what the Red Army would mean for his country's future. His childhood had been ruined by Soviet terror. On the other hand, he had no faith in European civilization, of which he understood Auschwitz to be a part. He wanted a renaissance and expected none from the west. He liked seeing Germany in ruins. Paris, which he visited from Munich, was louche and depressing. He seems to have despised the Americans who guarded his displaced persons camp, as some of these stories suggest.

His missed Poland. He wrote to his mother from Munich that homesickness was worse than hunger. This is a strong sentiment, when conveyed by someone who nearly starved to death, or from one survivor of the Ukrainian famine to another, or from one former camp inmate to another.

Tadeusz wrote Maria one last letter from Munich to apologize for breaking his word; he could no longer stay away from Poland. From Warsaw he pleaded with her to join him. Maria was exhausted and traumatized, and discouraged that none of her plans to find work in Western Europe were working out. She gave in, returning to Poland that November to marry him. She told an uncle that the return was "humiliating."[10] But she was concerned about Tadeusz's mental health, and wanted to take care of him.

The only place Borowski really knew in Poland was Warsaw, which no longer existed as such. The Germans had totally destroyed the city: by the bombing of 1939, the burning of the ghetto in 1943, and then the demolition of the city's remaining structures after the Warsaw Uprising of 1944. In 1946 Warsaw was a city in reconstruction, a mood Borowski relished. He wrote to Maria that the ruins, "also the moral ones," were a chance for a new Poland. He told her, in very patriotic terms, that reconstruction was an expression of love for country. He wanted to do "good things." From his peers he demanded a new form of writing: "The apocalypse has come and gone, and nothing changed in literature." He dedicated stories to writers who sentimentalized the camps—as we see in this collection.

In January 1947 he started a debate about the meaning of Auschwitz by attacking Zofia Kossak-Szczucka. She was a famous novelist of an older generation who had been in Auschwitz for a few months; one of her sons died there. In Warsaw she had founded an organization to support Jews in hiding. Borowski was nevertheless ruthless with her, reviewing her book about the camp under the heading "Alice in Wonderland." Chroniclers who survived Auschwitz, he said, must explain how they had done so. Kossak-Szczucka had failed to do this, and so was not to be trusted.[11] Borowski's view was that everyone who lived through Auschwitz bore some responsibility for its crimes. No one was exempted: not by class, not by nation, not by piety, not by artistry. And if responsibility was shared in Auschwitz, it is also shared everywhere else. It mattered that Kossak-Szczucka expressed antisemitic views and belonged to antisemitic milieux.

The deeper issue between the writers was Polish Romanticism. Were Poles ennobled by their suffering? Did they have a right to define themselves as innocent because of the war? In "Here in Our Auschwitz," Tadeusz writes to Maria of "the usual path of human thought": "the birth of messianism amid all this destruction and death." He wanted to break the grip of violence upon values. He wanted to cast aside the Polish writer's traditional role as an alchemist who transforms others' wrongs into Polish rights. The killers and the victims, the killing and the dying, should be denied metaphysical status. In stories about Auschwitz, SS men should be described as human, as should the Jews, as should the Poles, as should everyone else.

Borowski was not a nihilist, as his Catholic critics claimed. He was a moralist. He was a man of mercurial emotions, who his whole life long found equilibrium only in Auschwitz. "In the camp," as Maria remembered, "he was psychologically mobilized, he had no black thoughts, none of the depressions he experienced both before and after. Just courage." He imagined that in politics, as in literature, a complete renewal was possible. Destruction and death had not made Poland holy, but they had, he thought, created the possibility for a revolution. In early 1948, as he was finishing "The World of Stone," he joined the communist party.

Stalin still ruled the Soviet Union when Borowski joined the Polish communist party at the age of twenty-five, just as he had when Borowski had left the Soviet Union at the age of nine. The intervening sixteen years had been bloodily eventful: famine in the Borowskis' native Ukraine, terror in the Soviet Union, a German-Soviet alliance that began a world war, Nazi and Soviet terror in occupied Poland, a German invasion of the Soviet Union, the Holocaust of the Jews of Europe, the suppression of the Warsaw Uprising, the return of the Red Army, the establishment of a Polish communist regime.

The neophyte communist was quickly trapped by Stalinism. Borowski was a working-class writer, but that mattered not at all. In the Leninist interpretation of Marxism, which Stalin inherited, the working class is represented exclusively by the party, which speaks scientific truth through its politburo. Whoever wins the bureaucratic battles for control of the party's heights pronounces in the name of the working class as an infallible interpreter of history. The party line is objectively correct—even as it contradicts the line of yesterday, and even though it will be changed tomorrow. Party discipline, framed as resignation to the demands of history, meant the willingness to denounce comrades and issue public self-criticism.

One can date the beginning of Stalinism in Poland to 31 August 1948. The central committee plenum that began that day pronounced that socialist realism was now the obligatory style for all cultural production. Writers were to produce stony references to the classical heritage, clunky descriptions of class conflict, and moralizing narrators who were identifiable with the author. This was everything that Borowski was not. His descriptions of Auschwitz were irreconcilable with a myth of Polish national virtue because they resisted the metaphysical undertow: that death confirms the values of the living. For the same reason, they were incompatible with socialist realist blood redemption, in which death in the camps heralds the coming revolution. His stories had not changed, but the line had. He was now a deviationist; he was in trouble.

Just as socialist realism became mandatory, Stalinism became antisemitic. This turn also began in summer 1948, after the establishment of the State of Israel. Once Israel had failed to become a Soviet ally, as Stalin had expected, he initiated an "anti-cosmopolitan campaign" against comrades and writers of Jewish origin. The Holocaust was a problem for Soviet ideology. It was impossible to explain as class struggle; its victims extended beyond the borders of the USSR; and many of the collaborators, especially in the shootings, had been Soviet citizens. Portrayals of the Holocaust were treated as disloyal particularism, and as disrespectful of the suffering of other civilians.

In Poland, Stalinist antisemitism reinforced pressure from below to present the war as national martyrdom. Few Polish Jews had survived the Holocaust, and most of these emigrated amid postwar violence. Communist Poland also expelled millions of Germans and hundreds of thousands of Ukrainians, creating by 1948 an ethnically homogenous country. Well over a million (non-Jewish) Poles had been killed during the war. Hundreds of thousands more had been deported from formerly Polish lands annexed by the Soviet Union. Millions of Poles were living in houses and apartments that had once belonged to Germans, Jews, or Ukrainians. Since communism was seen as an external imposition, communists had good reason to make compromises with national feeling. Although a number of its leading figures were Jewish, Stalinism in Poland became ethnic and Polish.

Jakub Berman, as the politburo member responsible for culture, would try to guide Borowski as a writer. He was himself Jewish; one of his brothers had been murdered at Treblinka, the other would soon depart for Israel. Berman's own power was threatened by ethnic Polish comrades who were, in Stalinist terms, less "cosmopolitan" than he. Berman helped to construct the victimhood consensus. Now that non-communist parties had been eliminated or tamed, there was no harm in claiming their issues. This was good Stalinist practice. Berman was partially responsible for the myth, still current today, that Poles and Jews suffered equally in the war. And thus Borowski was deviating from the line in another way: his stories were too Jewish.

In January 1949, Borowski was denounced as a decadent cosmopolitan beholden to Western literature. But his was a talent worth salvaging for the cause. Offered a chance to earn his living as an apparatchik, he took it. He went to Berlin that June to work as a press officer for the military mission of the Polish embassy and, it seems, as a spy. His job required him to pass between the Soviet and American sectors of Berlin. Suddenly Borowski was part of the greater game of the Cold War and the division of Europe. While he and Maria lived in Berlin, the Soviet occupation zone of Germany became a new country, the German Democratic Republic. In Berlin he issued his self-criticism. He cast aside his Auschwitz stories, declaring, "I wasn't able to parse the camp in class terms; even as I experienced the camp, I did not really know what I was experiencing. I was playing around in narrow empiricism, in behaviorism, or whatever it's called. I had the ambition of showing the truth, but I ended up in an objective alliance with fascist ideology."[12]

In Hitler's former capital, a Polish survivor of Nazi camps takes the blame for fascism. Just how had matters reached this point? How did the author of one of the best analyses of fascism come to say that his work aided it? Borowski had a painful question: If the truthful is always transient and the timeless is always tainted, how can a writer be honest and significant? Stalinism offered a kindred analysis: all culture was scarred by capitalism. It also proposed a solution.

A socialist revolution, a Stalinist could say, is not one historical event among others. It is not just one more victory that leaves behind one more set of arbitrary values. The working class, unlike any social group before it, is the bearer of both power and rectitude. Its misery permits it to understand human exploitation, which its triumph will undo. The way forward to socialism, visible to the party, is the only meaningful truth. Writers who serve the party need not choose between truth and power, because truth is whatever allows communists to take power. Just follow the line.[13]

For a few months after his return from Berlin to Warsaw in March 1950, Borowski was euphoric. He worked as a regime journalist, "a little propaganda factory." Still in his twenties, he presented himself as a member of a young generation that had everything to learn from the party. His last major writing project, in early 1951, was a celebration of Feliks Dzierżyński, the founder of the Soviet secret police, on the occasion of the twenty-fifth anniversary of Dzierżyński's death. It was also the twenty-fifth anniversary of his father's Gulag sentence, carried out by that secret police. His father pleaded with him not to abuse his "divine spark," and not to trust his new friends.

Yet Borowski's mind was not entirely in captivity, and he had not forgotten his old friends. In spring 1951, the Polish secret police arrested Czesław Mankiewicz on suspicions of espionage. Mankiewicz was not only a friend but an axial figure in Borowski's life. Back in 1943, it had been Mankiewicz's arrest by the Gestapo that led to Maria's arrest, and thus to Tadeusz's arrest. In 1946, when Tadeusz was trying to persuade Maria to return to Poland, he sent her greetings from Mankiewicz, as from one of their closest friends. Now the insinuation was that Mankiewicz, in the meantime a colonel in the Polish army, had collaborated with the Nazis rather than working against them.

The charge was a move in an internal party struggle, in which those controlling the politburo used the party line to protect their position. Tito's Yugoslovia had departed the socialist camp dominated by the Soviet Union, which led Stalin to speak of right-wing, nationalist deviation. The line set in Moscow was then interpreted by local East European rulers to their own advantage. Poland's ruling Stalinists, Berman and his group, seized upon the right-wing deviation to eliminate rivals, usually non-Jewish Poles who had remained in Poland during the war. The Berman group had to do this before they themselves were attacked as left-wing cosmopolitan deviationists. That was how Stalinism worked. When the line held that both a right-wing and a left-wing deviation were possible, all communist leaders were at risk from one another at all times.

Borowski had been willing to say that his own writing was somehow fascist. But the idea that Mankiewicz had been working for the Nazis and not against them, a slippage archetypical of Stalinism, was too much. He sought a meeting with Berman, who was responsible for security as well as culture in the Polish politburo. An intermediary, a member of the central committee of the communist party, asked Borowski whether it was not suspicious that Mankiewicz had survived the war in Germany (in fact he spent it underground in Warsaw and then in Auschwitz and Majdanek). In the struggle for power, some communists insinuated that others were German spies simply because they had survived the German occupation. Berman's group, having spent the war in the USSR, was immune to any suggestion of Nazi collaboration.

Borowski asked in return whether it was not suspicious that the comrade himself had survived the war in the Soviet Union without being slaughtered. In Stalinist Poland, among communists, such a direct reference to Soviet terror, and in particular to the Soviet murder of Poles, was shocking. Perhaps even more so was the implicit comparison between collaboration with Nazi Germany and collaboration with the Soviet Union. Borowski might also have been understood to be suggesting that Berman and his allies were too close to Moscow: in other words, to be taking a side in an ongoing struggle for power.

Borowski got his conversation with Berman, and spoke up for his friend. Berman's reply might have been interpreted as a threat: comrades in the security services would take Borowski's position under advisement, and summon him for questioning if necessary.[14] Borowski faced the reality that Stalinism could turn against a communist survivor of Auschwitz.

In 1943, in the infirmary of the women's camp in Birkenau, Maria Rundo listened as a Jewish woman gave birth. The mother was separated from her child immediately. The infant lay in the bed long enough to get lice. When it was time for the collection of corpses from the infirmary, the baby was thrown alive into the crematorium.

In 1951, in a Warsaw hospital, Maria (née Rundo) Borowska gave birth. Her doctor was troubled that she seemed unable to sleep. She was having visions at night: "I am looking at the door the entire time and thinking: what would happen if an SS man in a green uniform came in now and took my child away."

Tadeusz visited every day. On 1 July, six days after the birth, he left the hospital in the evening, promising Maria that he would bring diapers. She never saw him again. Their housekeeper found him the next morning, unconscious. He had apparently left the gas on. Barbiturates were found in his bloodstream. He died the following day. He was twenty-eight years old.

As Madeline Levine notes in her introduction, it is tempting to attach meaning to this. Those who associate Borowski with Auschwitz might be drawn by the ironic symmetry: the author of stories about the gassing of others gasses himself. Surely he meant to tell us something, surely he wanted us to know that he was killing himself from survivor's guilt. Of course, domestic gas was the standard method of committing suicide in postwar Europe. The technique means nothing.

To be sure, his interactions with others revealed a wound. Not long before his death, Borowski paid a visit to Aleksander Wat, a Polish poet of Jewish origin of an older generation. Wat had abandoned communism and played the role of confessor to doubting communists. They were joined by the poet Stanisław Wygodzki, the survivor of the Będzin transport, now working for Polish radio. Wygodzki was distraught: a friend of his, another Auschwitz survivor, had just committed suicide in Wygodzki's apartment. Borowski screamed at Wygodzki to pull himself together: "If we're here now together, it's only because there in Auschwitz we took bread from the dying."[15] There was more in that vein, and worse.

Screaming about Auschwitz six years after the fact to a grieving Jewish survivor might reveal more about the pressures of Stalinism than about survivors' guilt. Borowski's Stalinist euphoria was giving way to its opposite. Aleksander Wat's wife, the perceptive and wise Ola Watowa, remembered him as "defeated." He himself confided to friends that he had "stepped on the throat of his own song."[16] Czesław Miłosz later explained his death as a case of disappointed love. Those who associate Borowski with communism might be drawn by the ironic symmetry: the boy who escaped Stalinist terror became the man who followed Stalinism to the end.

Auschwitz and Stalinism both figured in Borowski's predicament. His life was writing, and he feared that a writer must choose between the true and the durable, between fidelity and immortality. A humanities education amid Nazi atrocity led him to fear that the culture we inherit is a result of violence, that present ideas of good arise from past evil. A writer might set himself the mission of breaking this pattern by sheer force of truth and grace, as Borowski did after Auschwitz, but how could he know that he had succeeded? How could he know the future? Stalinism had an answer. All prior culture was indeed tainted, including Borowski's own stories about Auschwitz. Yet a revolution was a new start, allowing writers to orient themselves toward a predictable socialist future in which evil would be banished. Rather than creating freely at the risk of being ignored by an unknown future, the Stalinist writer submits today to a known future. It never arrives.

If we heed the strictures of the earlier Borowski, the chronicler of the camp, we hesitate to separate life under totalitarianism from life in general. Borowski's reaction to fascism was to emphasize individual responsibility, beginning with his own. His participation in Stalinism was of another quality: self-criticism demanded by a party line that, once accepted, demanded the condemnation of others. Hysterical conformism feels like participation in a grand transformation, at least for a time. But if he had misunderstood Auschwitz, as his self-criticism indicated, what about his own decision to go there? Auschwitz and love were connected. Revolution and marriage were also connected; in 1946 he persuaded Maria to return to Poland to rebuild. And Stalinism and extramarital affairs were connected: at the moment Tadeusz was screaming at Wygodzki, he was sleeping with one of his employees.

Before he visited Maria in the hospital on 1 July, Tadeusz had spent the afternoon with his lover, Dżennet Połtorzycka. Perhaps he was trapped between promises to two women. He had already tried to kill himself once during the affair and the pregnancy. Or perhaps it was all of this at once. Maria knew about Dżennet and had given him permission to leave. She needed the kind of husband he wasn't just then. Not being needed by Maria nullified the sense of going to Auschwitz, the central decision of his life. He had not passed through Auschwitz to a new world by embracing Stalinism. Their friend Mankiewicz was being interrogated and tortured despite his time in Auschwitz, indeed in some sense because of his time in Auschwitz. This nullified the sense of another major decision.

Borowski's life lacked balance. But his decisions had had a clear line: Maria, Auschwitz, communism. Now the clarity was fading.

Of course, these meditations are only relevant if Borowski's death was a suicide. Perhaps it was not. His lover thought that it was an accident.[17] He had an article due the next day, he put on water for tea, and he fell asleep. That was it. In Dżennet's recollection, Borowski was neither disenchanted with communism nor wracked by guilt. She believed that he was planning to leave his family for her. Right or wrong, she makes a telling point by calling his suicide a "legend." Of course the lover does not want the death to be deliberate. But is it not equally predictable that we the readers *do* want the death to be a suicide? A dramatic ending to a writer's life empowers us to drown his work in the flush of our own emotions. As Borowski put it in "Here in Our Auschwitz," "the living are always in the right as opposed to the dead."

The night when Tadeusz gassed himself, the first of July, Dżennet stood outside his apartment building and saw the light on. She decided not to ring the bell. What if she had done so? She was a courageous person, she had faced death in the Warsaw Uprising, she would have acted.[18] What if help had been summoned earlier, what if he had lived? The two women in Borowski's life that night, the one brooding in the dark, the other obsessing about infanticide, both lived into the twenty-first century. Collectively the women outlived the man by one hundred and twenty years. One wonders whether such longevity was possible at his side.[19]

Maria agreed with Dżennet that Tadeusz's death was not caused by the circumstances. She believed that he did kill himself, but not in connection with challenges in his public or private life. He had her permission to leave. He had not, thought Maria, drawn any conclusions about the system from his failure to protect Mankiewicz. He was manic-depressive, and his dark thoughts had their own logic. Only in Auschwitz was his mood calm, his feelings mastered, his courage directed. Afterward he had tried to take his own life at least twice; the difference this time was that he succeeded. He had tried drugs; he had tried gas; this time he tried both. That was it.

Assuming that Borowski died for reasons, they were his, not ours. If we heed Borowski's better writing, we will not seize upon his death as a buttress for our own prior commitments. When we ballast our worldview with the weight of another's death, we invite more death to supply more gravity. The ability to kill then becomes the ability to signify, and the clouds of human smoke fill our heaven. That was Borowski's aching fear about civilization: that all we hold to be beautiful, good, and true is an echo of earlier violence: the mocking laugh of generations.

There is an exit from Borowski's dilemma, a way to marry truth with endurance. The proof is in your hands, as it was in mine. He was able to write about Auschwitz thanks to his love for Maria and the sense of responsibility he felt for her. He followed her to the camp because he loved her. In "Here in Our Auschwitz," he says that he would do it again. His letters to her cleared the passage from poetry into prose. He was true to her in the camp, as true as any man could be; he told the truth about the camp, as well as any man could. Love may not last, but it is an honorable source of art that does.

I first read Borowski a long generation ago as a student of twenty, his own age when the Gestapo cut short his studies. His words reached me then not through some matrix of power, not because of the way things turned out: in the war, in the Cold War, for the Nazis, for the Stalinists, or for Borowski himself. They reach us because he puts us inside that matrix of power, shows how we can normalize anything, makes fascism everyday life—and then shakes us free from the spell.

NOTES

1. For this and correspondence cited below, see Tadeusz Drewnowski, ed., *Postal Indiscretions: The Correspondence of Tadeusz Borowski*, trans. Alicia Nitecki (Evanston, Ill.: Northwestern University Press, 2013).

2. I quote Madeline Levine's translations of the stories. Here and there in this text I have translated a few lines of poems or other texts myself.

3. Biographical detail and a few quotations are drawn from Tadeusz Drewnowski, *Ucieczka z kamiennego świata (o Tadeuszu Borowskim)* (Warsaw: Państwowy Instytut Wydawniczy, 1972); and Anna Bikont and Joanna Szczęsna, *Lawina i kamienie. Pisarze w drodze do i od komunizmu* (Wołowiec: Wydawnictwo Czarne, 2021). I thank Anna Bikont for allowing me to read this revised edition prior to publication, and for reading an early draft of this text. Irena Grudzińska-Gross, Susan Laity, Leah Mirakhor, Antony Polonsky, Jason Stanley, and Leora Tanenbaum also kindly commented on drafts. Marci Shore reminded me of the Wygodzki connection.

4. See Timothy Snyder, *Bloodlands: Europe Between Hitler and Stalin* (New York: Basic, 2021), chap. 1 on the famine; chap. 3 on the Polish Operation; chap. 4 on German and Soviet repressions in Poland from 1939 to 1941 (below); and chap. 11 on Stalinist antisemitism (below).

5. See Jadwiga Biskupska, *Survivors: Warsaw Under Nazi Occupation* (Cambridge: Cambridge University Press, 2021), chap. 6.

6. On the origins of the Holocaust in the western Soviet Union, see Timothy Snyder, *Black Earth: The Holocaust as History and Warning* (New York: Tim Duggan Books, 2015).

7. For this and other details of Maria's life between 1943 and 1945, including quotations, see Maria Borowska, "Pożegnanie z Tuśką. Notowali Krystyna Bratkowska i Michał Cichy," *Gazeta Wyborcza*, 28–29 January 1995.

8. The phrase is from Tadeusz Borowski, "Alicja w krainie czarów," *Pokolenie* 1 (1947): 9. This article is discussed below, and in the sources cited in note 11.

9. Cited in Dan Stone, *The Liberation of the Camps: The End of the Holocaust and Its Aftermath* (New Haven: Yale University Press, 2015), 61.

10. Her uncle (in fact her first cousin once removed) was Mieczyław Grydzewski, the celebrated editor of *Wiadomości Literackie*, the leading

literary journal of interwar Poland. See Marci Shore, *Caviar and Ashes: A Warsaw Generation's Life and Death in Marxism* (New Haven: Yale University Press, 2006).

11. On the debate that followed see Dariusz Kulesza, *Dwie prawdy. Zofia Kossak i Tadeusz Borowski wobec obrazu wojny w polskiej prozie, 1944–1948* (Białystok: Trans Humana, 2006). As Justyna Kowalska-Leder has established on the basis of witness accounts, Borowski's intuitions about Kossak were exactly right. See her "Skaza na portrecie—postać Zofii Kossak w relacjach byłych więźniarek Birkenau," *Acta Universitatis Lodziensis: Folia Litteraria Polonica* 1, no. 47 (2018).

12. Tadeusz Borowski, "Rozmowy. Dla towarzyszy: Jerzego Andrzejewskiego i Wiktora Woroszylskiego," *Odrodzenie* 7, no. 8 (1950): 6.

13. This is nicely explained in Richard Wright's essay in Richard Crossman, ed., *The God That Failed* (New York: Harper, 1949). Borowski acquired this book in Berlin.

14. Borowski's defense of Mankiewicz failed. He was sentenced and imprisoned as a Polish nationalist and an agent of Nazi Germany. Later released and rehabilitated, he returned to the armed forces, reached the rank of major general, and commanded Poland's air defenses. Then he was purged again, this time as a Zionist and an agent of Israel.

15. Ola Watowa, *Wszystko co najważniejsze* (Warsaw: Agora, 2011), 228–229. This scene is reconstructed in Shore, *Caviar and Ashes*, 296.

16. Jan Kott, "Afterword," *American Poetry Review* 4, no. 6 (1975): 29.

17. Given his intelligence work, foul play cannot be entirely excluded.

18. Dżennet Połtorzycka's recollections of the war can be found in the Archiwum Historii Mówionej of the Museum of the Warsaw Uprising. She worked as a writer for radio and television. In later life she was an animal rights activist. She died in 2020.

19. Maria Borowska married again, turned against communism, and took part in the Solidarity movement of the 1980s and then in projects concerning the history of Jewish veterans and the Holocaust. She died in 2001.

TRANSLATOR'S ACKNOWLEDGMENTS

Initial work on this translation was begun during a semester's leave as a faculty fellow at the Institute for the Arts and Humanities at the University of North Carolina, Chapel Hill. I am grateful to the Kenan Foundation of Chapel Hill for providing research funds in support of this project. Special thanks are owed to Professors Tomasz Hueckel, Janusz Kasperkiewicz, and Daria Niedźwiedzka, who identified for me a specific type of brick mentioned by Borowski in one story; to Piotr Sommer, who generously offered to be there when dictionaries failed me; and to Anna Panszczyk, my attentive research assistant. Dan Heaton and Susan Laity at Yale University Press were attentive readers of the manuscript, catching errors and offering helpful improvements. I owe the deepest debt of gratitude to Professor Halina Filipowicz, who made the case for a new translation of Borowski's stories and prodded me to undertake it. And heartfelt thanks to Jonathan Brent, who was convinced that it was time for a new translation and made sure that my own commitment to the project did not flag. Any errors and infelicities are mine, of course.

When a writer dies young, and by his own hand, the circumstances of his death become a final text that can lead critics and commentators away from the work that ought to be at the center of our attention. Tadeusz Borowski's posthumous fame rests, as it should, on the brilliance of his disturbing stories, whose impact is powerful in whatever language they are translated into. He is universally recognized as one of the most influential authors of Holocaust literature, and for many who know his work only through the stories that have been available in translation, he is a kind of martyr, a writer whose suicide was indisputably the direct result of his experience in Auschwitz. Those who know his later writings as well and are familiar with the postwar Polish context, however, see him as far more complicated than that—as an extraordinarily gifted writer who conveyed his experience of Auschwitz in brutally effective short stories and then, in willing service to Poland's Stalinist regime, began churning out one heavy-handed political feuilleton after another, eventually destroying himself along with his art.

Let us begin with his death: on July 1, 1951, Tadeusz Borowski took an overdose of barbiturates and turned on the gas in his kitchen stove. It was not his first suicide attempt, but this third try was successful, and he died in hospital on July 3. He was twenty-eight years old, a survivor of sixteen months' imprisonment in Auschwitz and another eight months' slave labor in the Dautmergen and Dachau-Allach concentration camps. After Dachau was liberated, he spent four months behind the barbed wires of an American-run displaced persons camp in Freimann. He had contemplated remaining in western Europe, but after living in Munich for nine months, he returned to bombed-out Warsaw in the late spring of 1946 to begin his life anew. All things considered, he was lucky, and perhaps he should have been pleased with his good fortune. His family had come through the war unscathed; he had survived the camps and had been spared the suffering and death experienced by so many of his contemporaries during the Warsaw Uprising. Maria, his fiancée, had just as miraculously survived Birkenau and Ravensbrück; they were married at the end of 1946. In one of his stories, the first-person narrator fantasizes about how wonderful it would be, should he survive, to have a little daughter of his own to love. His and Maria's baby girl, their only child, was born five days before he died.

Armed with this bare outline of Borowski's biography, some commentators have noted a satisfying symmetry: guilt-ridden at having escaped the gas chambers of Auschwitz-Birkenau, the writer who became famous for his Auschwitz stories repaid his debt in kind by using gas to end his life. Even Sidra DeKoven Ezrahi, one of the most astute commentators on the literary representation of the Holocaust and the concentration camp universe, a critic who does not make the all too common mistake of identifying Borowski with the narrators of his carefully crafted stories, is among those who have been drawn to this neat explanation. "For a writer like Borowski," she insists, ". . . there can be no post-Holocaust existence; the only logical 'solution' to survival beyond liberation is suicide—and, in 1951, at the age of twenty-nine [*sic*], having outlived the Nazi gas chambers, Borowski chose to gas himself."[1] But Borowski didn't "outlive" the gas chambers; he wasn't slated to go to them, because he was "just" a Polish political prisoner, and by the time he arrived at Auschwitz, the gas chambers were reserved for Jews. Nor was he then a world-famous author of Holocaust literature; that acclaim came later, through the impact of translations from the Polish, well after his death. There is no record of his having felt guilty about "exploiting" his Auschwitz experience for the sake of art and thus having to pay for that presumed exploitation with his life.

To question whether Borowski chose to die by gas because he had escaped the gas chambers at Auschwitz is not, of course, the same as arguing that there was no connection between his experience of the Nazi camps and his death. There is no doubt, as the stories collected in *Here in our Auschwitz* demonstrate, that Borowski emerged from the camps with the grim knowledge that there is no limit to human depravity within a social order that denies the value of human life. Like so many war-exhausted Europeans, he saw no promise of stability and a better world to come as the postwar evolved rapidly into the Cold War. Czesław Miłosz, conceiving of Borowski as a "disappointed lover," would have us look to an even earlier period to understand him, to the stony hopelessness expressed in the poems Borowski wrote in occupied Warsaw well before he entered the concentration camp universe. Borowski's "lack of any sort of vision led him to see the world as a place in which nothing existed outside of naked force," Miłosz tells us, and quotes these lines from one of Borowski's pre-Auschwitz poems: "There will remain after us only scrap-iron and the hollow, jeering laughter of generations."[2] (It should be noted, with a nod to Theodor Adorno, that Tadeusz Borowski entered Auschwitz as a poet; he emerged as a writer of unflinchingly brutal, controlled prose, but prose that reveals here and there a suppressed impulse toward tender lyricism. He did write poetry after Auschwitz, but not for long, and no poems that could be called lyrical.)

In one of the essays in *The Captive Mind* Miłosz sketched a portrait of Borowski, thinly disguised as "Beta," as an example of an East European writer whose wartime experiences propelled him toward an embrace of the Stalinist version of Marxism. Indeed, by early 1948 Borowski had joined the Polish communist party (known formally as the Polish Workers' Party) and had begun his transformation into the officially lionized, strident anti-American propagandist and hack writer of feuilletons that he soon became. This Borowski is not known to English readers; the present volume, by introducing several stories that point to this evolution, begins to address this gap. By 1949 Borowski was writing little of lasting value. In early 1950 he shocked the Polish literary world by denouncing his concentration camp stories as "an objective alliance with fascist ideology" and *The World of Stone* as "a cycle of pessimistic little tales." "I don't see any possibility of social value in what I have written up till now," he wrote.[3] He had, then, deliberately rejected the narrative posture that makes his concentration camp stories so powerful—a refusal to adopt the position of moral arbiter in a world given over to naked survival and deprived of moral norms. What he replaced that stance with was the role of scathing critic and loud-voiced purveyor of agitprop calls for a literature that would serve the cause of state and party.

And so we have another, competing reading of his death according to which, like the Russian poet Vladimir Mayakovsky, who wrote that he had "stepped on the throat of my song," Borowski killed himself when he could no longer prostitute his gift for the sake of a political regime that he had come to view as just as brutally culpable as the fascists and Nazis of the West. Thus the noted Polish critic Jan Kott could write about Borowski in his introduction to *This Way for the Gas, Ladies and Gentlemen*, "Borowski was the greatest hope of Polish literature among the generation of his contemporaries decimated by the war. He was also the greatest hope of the communist party, as well as its apostle and inquisitor; many years had to pass before many of us realized that he was also its martyr."[4]

Each of these competing explanations, in which Borowski is seen as ultimately a victim of either the Nazis or the Communists, no doubt contains some truth, although both ignore as unimportant the writer's personal life, the state of his marriage, and all the unknowable private demons that may have driven him to his death. Instead, Borowski is made into one of those iconic figures of writers who are seen as encompassing in their tragic fates the incomprehensible horrors of the twentieth century. Primo Levi, Paul Celan, and Jean Améry, along with others less well known, are our iconic witnesses to the Holocaust who died by suicide; Mayakovsky and Sergei Esenin, along with those like Osip Mandelstam who did not live to take their own lives, stand as martyrs of the Soviet regime. Tadeusz Borowski may well have had the dubious honor of being a victim of both totalitarianisms of the twentieth century, but he lent his powerful prose to the unmasking of only one of them.

What he bore witness to in his writings about the Holocaust and the concentration camp universe was the complicity of *everyone*, victim and victimizer alike, in the social system of the camps that left no room for ethical responses. Unlike other survivor-witnesses, women authors especially but also, notably, Primo Levi in *If This Is a Man* (published in America as *Survival in Auschwitz*), Borowski as a rule chose not to describe instances of human solidarity. His narrator is enmeshed in the camp system; he is a victim whose cleverness and cynicism, only occasionally yielding to moral revulsion, are what allow him to survive. The narrator is, or strives to appear, hardened and indifferent. But not always. He may record his pleasure in being better off than other prisoners and casually narrate one brutal act after another committed not just by German guards and SS officers but by prisoners whose disgust with what they have become can be expressed only through violence directed against their fellow prisoners. Borowski's fame as a writer who has reached the limits of literature, "the writer with whom . . . Holocaust literature begins and ends," "whose art does not transfigure brutal reality," derives from his insistence on the unaverted gaze that characterizes almost every one of his concentration camp and labor camp stories.[5] And yet a careful reading of the stories reveals, after the shock of what is narrated subsides, a deeply moral sensibility within the brutalized psyche of the narrator. Tenderness does find its way into the barbaric world of the camps and into Borowski's representation of that world. Usually, in his stories, it is linked with

love, with a man's love for a woman. The narrator of "Here in Our
Auschwitz . . ." relies on a fellow prisoner to deliver his letters to his
girlfriend in the women's camp; the "Jew with rotten teeth" in "The
People Who Were Walking" focuses all his energies on buying eggs
for Mirka, the kindly young female block elder he adores.

These glimpses of kindness, of openings for love, appear also
in Borowski's stories about the war's end and the immediate postwar
period. Mostly, however, the tone of the later stories—later, that is,
with regard to the narrated events and not necessarily to the time
of composition—is harsh. The narrator of the lengthy story "*The
Battle of Grunwald*" can hardly contain his loathing for his newly
liberated fellow inmates, his disgust at the corruption that continues
even in freedom. That moralistic tone, with no attempt to restrain
or disguise it, marks several of the short-short stories of *The World
of Stone*. In others, primarily those set in Poland, Borowski moves
closer to the journalistic style he would soon commit to and that
he had first explored in a series of sketches in the form of letters to
the editor, written from the Freimann DP camp. Yet in "The Girl
from the Burned-out Building," as in "Here in Our Auschwitz . . . ,"
Borowski reveals himself as a writer who could still write lyrically,
in the softest of voices, about loss and inconsolable grief.

Readers may wonder what a new translation of Borowski's writings has to offer them. Borowski's reputation in the English-speaking
world has been based largely on the stories gathered under the title
This Way for the Gas, Ladies and Gentlemen, the 1967 translation
by Barbara Vedder. More than fifty years after its initial publication,
This Way for the Gas remains in print and is widely read, taught,
and admired as one of the most powerful literary representations of
the concentration camp universe. Borowski's characteristic use of
understatement, his technique of evoking his reader's horrified response with his terrifyingly affectless narration of brutal facts, comes
across powerfully in Vedder's translation. What is missing from *This*

Way for the Gas, however, is "the other Borowski"—the author of the richly detailed descriptions, the dense sentence structure, the overlay of synchronous events, as in the story "Farewell to Maria," which appears here for the first time in English. "The Death of an Insurgent" and *"The Battle of Grunwald"* also appear here for the first time in English, revealing Borowski's loathing for the nationalist aspirations of many of his fellow Poles. Borowski's return to Poland and his enthusiastic embrace of a Marxist-Leninist interpretation of history become more understandable in the light of these stories. *The World of Stone* is presented here in its entirety; all twenty of the ministories or "pictures" that make up the whole are included.

A translation, of course, is never the thing itself. Translations are verbal performances, interpretations of meaning and style, approximations of the narrative voice heard in the original text. The translator who attempts a new version of a work believes that she can offer a better (even if in places deliberately rougher) performance of the original. She hears different resonances in the author's, or his narrator's, voice and attempts to render them in her language, but she does so with the understanding that no translation is ever definitive and there is always the possibility of yet another, more satisfactory interpretation.

Here in Our Auschwitz and Other Stories is based on the first scholarly edition of Tadeusz Borowski's writings, *Pisma w czterech tomach* (Writings in four volumes).[6] All the stories collected in this translation appear in the order established in volume 1 of that edition, *Proza* (Prose), and adhere to the editors' practice of restoring Borowski's original texts where later editions, published posthumously, inserted subtle and not so subtle changes largely for political reasons.

The book opens with two stories written in Munich and contributed by Borowski to the collectively composed volume *Byliśmy w Oświęcimiu* (We were in Auschwitz)—"Here in Our Auschwitz . . ."

and "The People Who Were Walking."[7] These are followed by the
complete texts of *Pożegnanie z Marią* (Farewell to Maria) and
Kamienny świat (The world of stone). In the section "Uncollected
Stories" the translation diverges from the Polish edition of *Proza*.
One story from that volume, "Zostawcie umarłych w spokoju"
(Leave the dead in peace), begun in 1948 and never completed, has
been omitted; it is a fragment of what was to be a much longer work
and demands of the reader detailed knowledge of the political and
artistic aims of Borowski's contemporaries in occupied Warsaw.

The final entry in *Here in Our Auschwitz* is a glossary of terms
that Borowski and his coauthors appended to *We Were in Auschwitz*.
It lists German words specific to the camps, invented words that
matched the new realities of camp life, familiar words that had acquired new meanings. Readers who come across unfamiliar terms
in the stories may wish to consult the "Auschwitz Lexicon." The
occasional footnotes in the text are mine.

NOTES

1. Sidra DeKoven Ezrahi, *By Words Alone: The Holocaust in Literature*
(Chicago: University of Chicago Press, 1980), 111.

2. Czesław Miłosz, "Beta, the Disappointed Lover," *The Captive
Mind*, tr. Jane Zielonko (New York: Vintage, 1953), 108.

3. Cited in Tadeusz Drewnowski, *Ucieczka z kamiennego świata. O
Tadeuszu Borowskim*, 2nd ed. (Warsaw: PIW, 1977), 306.

4. Jan Kott, Introduction, tr. Michael Kandel, in Tadeusz Borowski,
This Way for the Gas, Ladies and Gentlemen, tr. Barbara Vedder (New York:
Penguin, 1976), 11.

5. Ezrahi, *By Words Alone*, 52, 53.

6. Tadeusz Borowski, *Pisma w czterech tomach*, ed. Tadeusz Drewnowski, Justyna Szczęsna, and Sławomir Buryła (Kraków: Wyd. Literackie,
2004), vol. 1, *Proza*, ed. Sławomir Buryła.

7. Janusz Nel Siedlecki, nr 6,643; Krystyn Olszewski, nr 75,817;
Tadeusz Borowski, nr 119,198, *Byliśmy w Oświęcimiu* (Munich: Oficyna
Warszawska na Obczyźnie, 1946).

Here in Our
Auschwitz and
Other Stories

We Were in Auschwitz

HERE IN OUR AUSCHWITZ . . .

I

. . . so, I'm already taking the course for medics. They chose about a dozen of us from Birkenau and they're going to train us to be doctors almost. We have to know how many bones a person has, how the blood circulates, what is the peritoneum, how to combat staphylococci and streptococci, how to perform a sterile appendectomy, and when a pneumothorax is required.

We have a very lofty mission: we are going to be treating our colleagues, whom "bad luck" has afflicted with illness, apathy, or loss of interest in life. We—yes, we, a little over one dozen individuals for the twenty thousand men in Birkenau—are supposed to lower the mortality rate in the camp and elevate the prisoners' spirits. Such were the parting words of the camp doctor, the Lagerarzt. He also asked each of us about our age and profession, and when I answered, "Student," he raised his eyebrows in amazement.

"What did you study?"

"The history of literature," I replied modestly.

He nodded, disappointed, got into his car, and drove off.

Later, we walked to Auschwitz along a lovely road. We saw a lot of the countryside, then someone assigned us somewhere, to some kind of hospital block, as guest Flegers, or paramedics, but I wasn't particularly interested in this because I went with Staszek (you know, the guy who gave me the brown pants) to the camp—I, in search of someone who would carry this letter to you, and Staszek to the kitchen and storehouse to organize white bread, a brick of margarine, and at least one sausage for supper, because there are five of us.

Naturally, I didn't find anyone, because my number is higher than a hundred thousand and here there are only old numbers and they look down on me. But Staszek promised he'd send the letter through his connections, only it mustn't be long "because it must be boring to write like this to a girl every day."

So when I learn how many bones a man has and what the peritoneum is, perhaps I'll prescribe something for your pyoderma and your bunkmate's fever. Only I'm afraid that even though I know how to treat an *ulcus duodeni*, I won't manage to steal that stupid Wilkinson's salve for your scabies because there isn't any at present in all of Birkenau. What we do is pour mint tea over the sick person while reciting certain extremely effective incantations which, unfortunately, cannot be repeated.

As for reducing deaths: one of the big shots in my block was sick, he was doing poorly, had a fever, was talking more and more about death. Once, he called me over. I sat down on the edge of his bed.

"I was well known in the camp, wasn't I?" he asked, nervously looking me in the eyes.

"Could there be someone who wouldn't know you . . . and remember you?" I answered innocently.

"Look," he said, pointing to the windowpanes that were red with fire.

They were burning on the other side of the woods.

"You know, I'd like them to lay me down separately. Not with the others. Not on the pile. Do you understand?"

"Don't be afraid," I told him sincerely. "I'll even give you a sheet. And I'll have a word with the corpse squad, too."

He squeezed my hand without saying a word. But nothing came of it. He recovered and sent me a brick of margarine from the camp. I grease my boots with it, because it's the kind that's made from fish. So that's how I contributed to the reduction of mortality in the camp. But enough about this; it's too camp-centered.

It is almost a month now since I've had a letter from home . . .

II

Blissful days: no roll calls, no duties. The entire camp is standing at roll call, but we are looking at them from our window, witnesses from another world. People smile at us, we smile at them, they address us as "Colleagues from Birkenau" with a certain amount of sympathy because our fate is so miserable, and with a certain amount of shame because theirs is so good. The view from our window is innocent; there isn't a cremo in sight. The people here are in love with Auschwitz; they say proudly, "Here in our Auschwitz, we . . ."

And they really do have something to brag about. Picture for yourself what Auschwitz is. Take that hideous prison building, Pawiak, add the women's wing that people call Serbia, multiply it by twenty-eight, and place it all so close together that there is only a little space between each of these Pawiaks, surround it all with a double row of wires and a cement wall on three sides, pave over the mud, grow some anemic little trees, and in the midst of all this plant ten or fifteen thousand people who have each been in the camp for several years, have suffered fantastically, endured the worst of times, and now wear trousers pressed with a stylish crease and strut around, swaying their hips; do all this and you will understand why they hold us in contempt and pity us—us, the people from Birkenau, where there are only wooden stables for barracks, no sidewalks, and, in place of a bathhouse with hot water, four crematoriums.

From the infirmary, which has very white, rather village-like walls, a concrete prison floor, and many, many three-tiered plank beds, one has an excellent view of an open road on which sometimes a person is walking, sometimes a car drives by, sometimes a hay cart, and sometimes a bicyclist, probably a laborer going home from work. In the distance, very far away (you have no idea how much space can fit inside such a small window; after the war, if I survive, I would like to live in a tall building with windows looking out onto a field), there are a few houses and then a dark blue woods. The soil is black and is probably moist. As in that sonnet by Leopold Staff. Do you remember his "Springtime Walk"?

But there are very civilized things in our infirmary: a tile stove clad in colorful majolica tiles, like the ones that were stored in our warehouse. The stove has a cunningly designed grill for roasting; it looks useless, but we should try roasting a piglet on it. There are blankets from "Canada" on the plank beds, as fluffy as cats' fur. There are white, wrinkle-free sheets. There is a table that is some-times covered with a tablecloth, but only for special occasions and for meals.

One window looks out on the birch road, the Birkenweg. It's a pity that it's winter now and the leafless weeping birches droop like ragged brooms, and that there's sticky mud under them instead of lawns, probably just the same as in that "other world" on the other side of the road, only we have to knead it with our feet.

In the evening, after roll call, we stroll along the birch path solemnly, with dignity, greeting acquaintances with a nod of the head. At one of the intersections there's a street sign with a bas-relief that represents two people sitting on a bench and whispering into each other's ear, and a third person who is leaning toward them, pricking up his ears and eavesdropping. A warning: your every con-versation is overheard, noted, and reported to the proper authori-ties. Here, everyone knows everything about someone else: when he went through a Muselmann phase, what he has organized and from whom, whom he strangled and whom he has squealed on, and everyone smiles derisively when praising someone else.

So, picture Pawiak multiplied many times over and sur-rounded by a double row of barbed wire. Not like in Birkenau, where the watchtowers really do stand like storks on tall, long poles, and there are lamps glowing on every third post, and there is only a single wire fence, but there are so many sectors that you can't count them on your fingers!

Here, it's not like that at all; there are lamps on every second post, and the watchtowers have solid brick foundations, the wire is double, and there's also a wall.

So we walk along the Birkenweg in our civilian clothes, straight from the sauna, the only group of five not wearing *pasiaki*, the striped uniform of the camp prisoner.

We walk along the Birkenweg shaved, fresh, and without a care. A small crowd, clustered in smaller groups, is standing in front of Block Ten where the girls who are guinea pigs sit behind bars and firmly shut windows, but more often the crowd gathers in front of the Schreibstübe where the records are kept, not because there's a symphony hall there, a library and museum, but simply because upstairs is the Puff. I'll write to you some other time about what the Puff is; in the meantime, you can be curious . . .

Do you know how strange it is to be writing to you, whose face I haven't seen in so long? Your image is fleeing my memory, and even with an immense effort of will it cannot be called back. There's something amazing about dreaming; you appear so clearly and graphically in my dreams. You know, a dream is not like a picture, but rather like an experience in which there is space, and the weight of objects, and the warmth of your body is palpable . . .

It is hard for me to picture you on a camp plank bed, with your hair shorn after typhus . . . I remember you in Pawiak: a tall, slender young woman with a slight smile and sad eyes. You were sitting with your head bowed at Gestapo headquarters on Aleja Szucha, and I saw only your black hair that has now been cut off.

And this is the most powerful thing that has remained in me from there, from that other world: your image, even though it is so hard for me to recall you. And that's why I write you such long letters; they are my evening conversations with you, just like then, on Skaryszewska Street.* And that's why these letters are cheerful. I have preserved a lot of cheerfulness in myself, and I know that you, too, haven't lost any. Despite everything. Despite your bowed head at the Gestapo, despite typhus, pneumonia, and closely cropped hair.

But these people . . . You see, they have passed through the terrible schooling of the camp, this camp that's existed from the very beginning, that is legendary. They weighed thirty kilos, they were beaten, selected for the gas—do you understand why they now wear ridiculous jackets, narrow in the waist, adopt a peculiar swaying gait, and praise Auschwitz at every step?

That's how it is . . . We walk along the Birkenweg, elegant men in civilians' suits. But with numbers above a hundred thousand! One hundred three thousand, one hundred nineteen thousand, black despair that we didn't arrive here in time to get earlier numbers! Someone dressed in pasiaki approached us, a twenty-seven thousand, such an old number that one's head spins. A young guy with the dull look of an onanist and the walk of an animal sniffing out danger.

"Colleagues, where are you from?"

"From Birkenau, if you please."

"From Birkenau?"

He examined us critically.

"And looking so good? But it's terrible there . . . How do you stand it?"

Witek, my tall friend, an excellent musician, replied while straightening his cuffs, "We don't have a piano, unfortunately, but it's possible to stand it."

---

* Before he was arrested, Borowski worked as a night watchman and warehouse hand for a building supplies firm on Skaryszewska Street.

The old number looked at us as if through a fog.

"Because here we're afraid of Birkenau . . ."

III

Our classes keep being postponed because we're waiting for Flegers from the surrounding camps, from Janina, Jaworzno, Buna. There are also supposed to be Flegers from Gliwice and Mysłowice, more distant camps but still belonging to Auschwitz. In the meantime, we've listened to a couple of lofty speeches by the black-haired director of our courses, a little dried-up Adolf who recently arrived from Dachau and is up to his ears in Kameradschaft, that camaraderie he puts so much stock in. He is going to raise the state of health in the camp by educating the Flegers and lower mortality by teaching about the nervous system. Adolf is unusually likable and not of that world, but as a German he doesn't understand the relationship between things and appearances and clings to the meaning of words as if they can become reality. He says "Kameraden" and thinks that we really are comrades; he says "to lessen suffering" and thinks that this is possible. On the camp gates are letters formed in iron: "Work makes one free." They seem to believe in this, these SS men and the prisoners who are Germans. The ones who were raised on Luther, Fichte, Hegel, Nietzsche. So for the time being there are no classes, and I roam around the camp on ethnographic and psychological excursions. Actually, we roam around together: Staszek, Witek, and I. Staszek usually hangs out near the kitchen and storeroom, seeking out those to whom he once gave something and who are now obligated to give something to him. Indeed, a parade begins in the evening. Various types arrive who have an evil look about them; they smile ingratiatingly with their naked jaws, and one of them pulls out a brick of margarine from under his fitted jacket, another pulls out white hospital bread, yet another produces a sausage, and someone else cigarettes. They throw it all on the bottom bunk and vanish as in a film. We divide the loot, add to it from our parcels, and cook it in the stove with the colorful majolica tiles.

Witek hangs out near the piano. There's a black box in the music room in the block where the Puff is located, but it's forbidden to play during work hours or Arbeitszeit, and after roll call the musicians who give classical concerts every Sunday have to practice. I will definitely go to hear them.

Across from the music room we discovered a door with a sign saying "library," but the initiated assured us that it held just a few detective novels for Reichsdeutsche only. I didn't check this out because the door is shut tight.

Next to the library in this culture block is the political division, and next to it the museum hall. There are photographs there that were confiscated from letters and apparently nothing else. It's a shame; they could have placed that undercooked human liver there that my Greek friend got twenty-five lashes on his a— for eating.

But the most important thing is located one floor up. It's the Puff. The Puff is the windows that are half open even in winter. In the windows after roll call women's little heads in various shades lean out, and arms as snowy as sea foam emerge from little robes of blue, pink, and willow green (I like that color very much). There are about fifteen little heads, it seems, and thirty arms if we don't count old Madame with the powerful, epic, legendary bosom who watches over the little heads, necks, arms, etc. . . . . Madame does not lean out the window but, like Cerberus, administers the upper floor at the entrance to the Puff.

In the vicinity of the Puff stands a crowd of camp bigwigs. If there are ten Juliets, then there are around a thousand Romeos (and not just any sort). So there is a crush and competition near each Juliet. The Romeos stand in the windows of the blocks that face the Puff; they yell, signal with their hands, seduce. There are representatives of prisoner officialdom: a Lagerältester and a Lagerkapo; there are doctors from the hospital and kapos from the kommandos. More than one Juliet has a steady admirer, and in addition to assurances of eternal love, of a happy life together after the camp, in addition to rebukes and bantering, one can hear more concrete details concerning soap, perfume, silk panties, and cigarettes.

There is a good deal of camaraderie among the men; they don't compete disloyally. The women in the windows are very affectionate and alluring, but inaccessible, like goldfish in an aquarium.

That's what the Puff looks like from the outside. One can get inside only through the Schreibstübe with a ticket bestowed as a reward for good and diligent labor. True, as guests from Birkenau we have priority, but we declined; we have red triangles as politicals, so we let the criminals make use of what is for them. Sorry, but this description will only be secondhand, though based on such good witnesses and such old numbers like Fleger (honorary, to be sure) M from our block, whose number is almost three times lower than the last two digits of my number. You understand: a founding member! Therefore, he sways like a duck and wears wide trousers with a crease down the legs, fastened in front with a safety pin. In the evening, he returns excited and jolly. He's going to the Schreibstübe, and when they read the number of the "permitted ones" he'll be waiting for a no-show; then he'll shout "*hier,*" he'll grab a pass and pursue Madame. He'll press a couple of cigarette packs into her paw; she'll perform a number of hygienic measures around him, and the well-spritzed Fleger will bound upstairs. The Juliets from the window are strolling in the corridor in robes wrapped carelessly around their bodies.

Occasionally, one of them will walk beside the Fleger and ask indifferently, "What number do you have?"

"Eight," the Fleger will answer, checking his ticket to be sure.

"Oh, that's not for me; it's for Irma, the blonde," she'll mutter, disappointed, and walk languidly over to the window.

Then the Fleger goes over to number eight. On the door he reads that it is forbidden to perform such and such depraved acts, or you'll get the isolation cell; that only this and that are permitted (a detailed list), and only for so many minutes each; he sighs in the direction of the Judas-hole through which the woman's colleagues occasionally watch, or sometimes Madame or the Kommandoführer of the Puff, or even, on occasion, the camp commandant himself; he places a pack of cigarettes on the table and . . . aha, he also notices that two packs of English cigarettes are lying on a small cupboard. Only then does it happen . . . , after which the Fleger leaves, distractedly slipping those two packs of English cigarettes into his pocket. He submits to disinfection a second time and, jolly and happy, tells us about everything.

But sometimes the disinfection fails; that was the cause of an epidemic that broke out in the Puff the other day. The Puff was closed; they determined who had been there by their numbers, summoned them in accordance with regulations, and administered a cure. Since there is widespread trading in passes, people were treated who didn't need to be. Ha, such is life. The women from the Puff had also made trips into the camp. Dressed in men's clothing, they climbed down ladders and went off to drinking bouts and orgies. But the sentry from a nearby watchtower didn't like this and everything came to a stop.

There are also women in other places: Block Ten, the experimental block. There, they are artificially impregnated (so people say), injected with typhus and malaria, operated on. I caught a glimpse of the man who directs this work: dressed in a green hunting suit, wearing a Tyrolean hat with sports badges pinned onto it, and with the face of a kindly satyr. They say he's a university professor.

These women are protected by bars and boards, but men often break in there, too, en masse and impregnate them not at all artificially. The old professor must be furious.

Understand: these are not depraved men who do this. The whole camp, once it has sufficient food and sleep, talks about women; the whole camp dreams about women; the whole camp tries to get at them. The Lagerältester went sailing out of here in a punishment transport because he repeatedly climbed into the Puff through a window. A nineteen-year-old SS man caught the orchestra conductor, a fat, pompous gentleman, and several doctors inside the ambulance in unambiguous positions with their lady partners who had come to have their teeth pulled, and he laid into them with a stick he was holding in his hand, summarily dealing out appropriate rations in the appropriate spot. Such an occurrence doesn't disgrace anyone: they were simply unlucky.

A psychosis about women is on the rise in the camp. That is why the Puff women are treated like normal women to whom one speaks of love and domestic life. There are ten of these women, and the camp numbers some fifteen thousand men.

That is why they are so eager to go to the women's camp, the Frauenkonzentrationslager or FKL, in Birkenau. These people are sick. Think about it: there isn't just this one Auschwitz. This is what goes on in the hundreds of "great" concentration camps, the Oflags and Stalags, the . . .

Do you know what I am thinking about as I write to you about all of this?

It is late at night; separated by a wardrobe from the large ward which is full of sick men breathing with difficulty in their sleep, I sit in my little room near a black window that reflects my face, the willow-green lampshade, and the white sheet of paper lying on the table. Franz, a young lad from Vienna, came to an agreement with me the very first night, and now I am seated at his table, using his lamp, and writing to you on his paper. But I won't write to you about what we talked about today—about German literature, the culpability of Romantic philosophy, the problems of materialism.

Do you know what I am thinking about as I write to you about this?

I am thinking about Skaryszewska Street. I look at the dark window, see my own face reflected in the glass, and outside the glass is the night and the sudden flashes of the searchlights from the watchtowers, carving out fragments of objects in the darkness. I watch and think about Skaryszewska Street. I remember the sky, pale and star-spangled, the burned-out building across from us and the grill of the window frame that cut up the image as in a stained-glass window.

I think about how I used to yearn for your body in those days, and sometimes I smile a little when I think about what a great crisis must have ensued when, after our arrest, they discovered alongside my books and poems your perfumes and your bathrobe, red as the brocade in a Velázquez painting, heavy, long (I loved it passionately; you looked magnificent in its frame, though I never told you so).

I am thinking about how very mature you were, how much good will and—forgive me for writing this to you now—devotion you invested in our relationship, how you voluntarily entered my life in the tiny room without running water, the evenings with cold tea, a couple of half-wilted flowers, a dog who gnawed constantly, and the kerosene lamp in my parents' home.

I think about this and smile indulgently when people talk to me about morality, law, tradition, duties . . . Or when they renounce all tenderness and sentimentality and, making a fist, talk about an age of firmness. I smile and think that man is always discovering man anew—through love. And that this is the most important and the most enduring thing in human life.

I am thinking about this and remembering my cell in Pawiak. The first week I couldn't comprehend a day without a book, without an evening circle of lamplight, without a sheet of paper, without you . . .

But just look what it is to grow accustomed: I walked back and forth in the cell and composed poems to the rhythm of my footsteps. One of them I inscribed in a cellmate's Bible, but from the others (they were songs à la Horace) I remember only random stanzas, like this one from a poem to my friends from the days of freedom:

> Friends from freedom! I bid you farewell with this prison song
> So you will know that I am not departing this world in despair.
> I know that there will remain after me both love and my poetry,
> And, as long as you live, memories of me among my friends.

IV

Today is Sunday. In the morning we went for a walk, looked down on the women's experimental block (they stick their heads out through the bars just like my father's rabbits—you remember, they were gray with one floppy ear), then we carefully observed the Straffkommando block (in its courtyard there is a black wall against which they used to shoot people in the past, but now they do it more quietly and discreetly—in the crematorium). We saw a couple of "civilians": two terrified women in fur coats and a man with a crumpled, sleep-deprived face. An SS man was escorting them, but don't be afraid, only to the temporary city lockup which is located precisely in this punishment block. The women, terrified, looked at the pasiaki-garbed people and the sturdy camp installations: the multistoried buildings, the double wires, the wall beyond the wires, the solid watchtowers. And if they only knew that the wall, so people say, goes two meters down to keep us from digging out! We smiled at them, because it's a trifle: they'll sit there for a couple of weeks and get out. Unless it can really be proved that they were black marketeers. In that case, they'll go to the crematorium. These civilians are funny. They react to the camp like savages at the sight of a gun. They don't understand the mechanics of our life and smell something improbable, mystical, beyond human strength in all of this. Do you remember how you sank into terror when they arrested you? You wrote me about this. I read *Steppenwolf* at Maria's (she also chose what to read), but I don't have a clear idea of what and how.

Today, on familiar terms with the improbable and the mystical, having the crematorium as a daily fact, cases of phlegmon and tuberculosis by the thousands, having learned what rain and wind are, and sun, and bread, and rutabaga soup, and working so as not to arouse suspicion, and slavery, and power—existing, so to speak, under the hand of the beast, I look on all this with a certain amount of condescension, the way a learned person looks at a layman, or someone who's already initiated at one who's still in the dark.

Disentangle from daily events their quotidian essence, discard revulsion, disgust, and contempt, and find a philosophical formula for all of this. For the gas and the gold, the roll calls and the Puff, the civilian and the old number.

Had I said to you as the two of us danced in my little room with the orange light, "Listen, you have one or two, or maybe three, million people, kill them in such a way that no one knows anything about it, not even they, imprison several hundred thousand, shatter their solidarity, set one man against another, and . . . ," why, you would have thought I was a madman, and who knows, we might have stopped dancing. But I am certain I would not have said that even had I known about the camps, because I would not have wanted to spoil the mood.

But look here: first of all, one country barn painted white and—they're suffocating people in it. Then four larger buildings— it's nothing to suffocate twenty thousand people. Without magic, without poisons, without hypnosis. A couple of people directing traffic to prevent a jam, and the people flow like water from a pipe when the faucet is turned on. This goes on amid the anemic trees of a smoke-covered woods. Ordinary trucks deliver the people, drive back as if on a conveyor belt, return with another delivery. Without magic, without poisons, without hypnosis.

How is it that no one cries out, no one spits in a face, no one hurls himself at someone's chest? We doff our caps in front of the SS men returning from the woods; when they read out our numbers, we go with them to our death—and nothing? We starve, get drenched in the rain, they take our loved ones from us. You see—it's mystical. Behold the wondrous possession of one man by another. Behold the terrible passivity that nothing can break. And our only weapon is our numbers, which the gas chambers cannot accommodate.

Or, here's another way: the handle of a shovel across a throat and one hundred people daily. Or nettle soup and bread and margarine, and then a young, fully grown SS man with a crumpled slip of paper in his paw, a number tattooed on an arm, then a truck, one of those . . .

Do you know when "Aryans" were last selected for the gas? April fourth. And do you remember when we came to the camp? April twenty-ninth. What would have happened to you with your pneumonia had we arrived at the camp three months earlier?

. . . I know that you lie on a shared bunk with friends who are no doubt astounded by my words. "You said this Tadeusz is cheerful, but look, he writes only depressing things." And they are probably very angry at me. But, after all, we can also speak about these things that are happening around us. We are not conjuring up evil for no reason, irresponsibly; after all, we're embedded in it . . .

You see, it is late evening once again after a day filled with bizarre events.

In the afternoon, I set out to see a boxing match in the large Waschraum barracks, the place from which the transports used to leave for the gas. We were admitted with great ceremony, even though the hall was filled to the brim. A boxing ring had been set up in the large waiting room. Overhead lighting, a referee (nota bene, a Polish Olympic referee), internationally renowned boxers, but only Aryans, because Jews were not allowed to participate. And these same people, who have been knocking out dozens of teeth day after day, many of whom have no teeth left in their own jaws, went crazy over Antoni Czortek, Walter from Hamburg, and some young fellow who, trained in the camp, had matured, as they say, to a first-rate talent. Also connected with this is the memory of number 77, who in bygone days used to box against Germans if he felt like it, taking revenge in the ring for what others received outside. The hall was dense with cigarette smoke, and the boxers pounded each other, getting in as many blows as they could manage. But they did it unprofessionally, although with real doggedness.

"That Walter," said Staszek. "Just look at him! At a command, if he feels like it, he can floor a Muselmann with a single blow! But here, look at this, three rounds already, and nothing! They've even beaten up his face. Obviously, there are too many spectators, don't you think?"

Incidentally, the spectators were enraptured, and we were in the front row, you know, as guests.

Right after the boxing matches, I went to see a competition, a concert. You people over there in your Birkenau don't have the faintest notion of what miracles of culture take place here, just a couple of kilometers from the chimneys. Picture it: they're playing the overture to *Tancred* and something by Berlioz, and also some Finnish dances by a composer who has a lot of a's in his name. Warsaw can't even dream of such an orchestra! But I'll tell it to you in order, and you pay attention, because it will be worth it. So, I left the boxing match, ecstatically excited, and immediately entered the block that also houses the Puff. Beneath the Puff is the music room. It was crowded and noisy; the audience lined the walls, the musicians, seated throughout the room, were tuning their instruments. Opposite the window was a dais; on it stood the kitchen kapo (who is also the conductor), and the potato peelers and the *Rollwage*, the carters' kommando (I forgot to write you that during working hours the orchestra peels potatoes and pushes carts), began to play. I just managed to squeeze myself in between the second clarinet and the bassoon. I crouched down next to the unoccupied chair of the first clarinet and abandoned myself to listening. You would never guess how powerful a symphony orchestra of thirty people sounds in a large room! The conductor waved with restraint so as not to bang his hand against the wall and clearly threatened the players who hit a wrong note. He'll give it to them during potato peeling. The men in the corners of the room (a drum in one, a double bass in the other) did the best they could. The bassoon drowned out every-thing, perhaps because I was standing right beside it. But what a double bass! The fifteen listeners (there wasn't room for more) were expertly engrossed in the music and rewarded the orchestra with meager applause.

—— someone once called our camp *Betrugslager*, camp of de-ceptions. A meager hedgerow in front of a small white house, a yard that resembles a farmyard, signs that say "bath," are sufficient to dupe millions of people, to deceive them to death. A boxing match, some lawns in front of the blocks, two German marks a month for the most diligent prisoners, mustard in the canteen, weekly lice control and the overture to *Tancred* suffice to deceive the world— and us. People on the outside think it is monstrous, but after all it's not so bad since there's an orchestra, and boxing, and lawns, and blankets on the beds . . . What's deceitful is the bread ration, which we have to supplement by theft in order to live.

What's deceitful is work time during which it is forbidden to speak, sit, take a rest. What's deceitful is each partly filled shovelful of earth that we fling onto the bank of a ditch.

Observe all of this attentively, and don't lose strength when things are going badly for you.

For it may be that we will have to give the living a report from this camp, from this time of deceptions, and stand up in defense of the dead.

Once, we were walking to the camp in kommando groups. The orchestra was playing and setting the beat for the marching columns. The kommando assigned to the DAW firm and dozens of others had assembled and were waiting in front of the gate: ten thousand men. And then, trucks arrived from the FKL, filled with naked women. The women stretched out their arms and shouted, "Save us! We are going to the gas! Save us!"

And they drove past us to the profound silence of ten thousand men. Not one man moved, not one hand was raised.

Because the living are always in the right as opposed to the dead.

v

First of all, we've already been attending classes for a long time, only I haven't written you anything about it because it's in a garret and very cold. We sit on stools that have been rounded up for us and have a wonderful time, especially with the large models of the human body. Those who are curious observe what it is like, but Witek and I toss a sponge back and forth and fence with rulers, which drives black-haired Adolf to despair. He flaps his hands at us and speaks about Kameradschaft and the camp.

We sit quietly in a corner, Witek pulls out a photograph of his wife, and asks in a hushed voice, "I wonder how many he killed in Dachau? Otherwise, he wouldn't be advertising himself like this . . . Could you strangle him? . . ."

"Umm . . . what a pretty woman. How did *you* win her?"

"Once, we were taking a walk in Pruszków. You know, greenery, little side lanes, woods on the horizon. We're walking along, pressed close to each other, and suddenly an SS dog jumps out from the side . . ."

"Come on, don't tell lies, that was in Pruszków, not Auschwitz."

"It was really an SS dog, because there was a villa nearby that was occupied by the SS. And that beast goes after the girl! What would you have done? I unload my revolver at the beast, grab my wife by the hand, and say, 'Irka, march!' But she's standing there like she's glued to the ground, looking at my piece. 'Where'd you get that?' I almost tore her away, because voices could be heard from the villa. We ran across the fields like two hares. For a long time I had to explain to Irka that that piece of metal is necessary in my line of work."

In the meantime, one of the many doctors is babbling on about esophaguses and similar things that are inside a person, but Witek continues his reporting without a care.

"Once I had a fight with a friend. It's either he or I, I thought. He had the same thought, of course; I knew him well. I tailed him for about three days and kept looking to see if someone was following me. I lay in wait for him one evening on Chmielna Street and slashed him, but I didn't manage to do the job right. The next day, I walk over; his hand is bandaged and he's scowling at me. 'I fell down,' he says."

"And what did you do?" I ask, because this is a very contemporary story.

"Nothing, because they arrested me right afterward."

It's hard to say if it was that friend of his who caused his arrest, but Witek did not give in to fate. In Pawiak he was either a section head or a bath attendant—one of those errand-boy Pipels for that Kronszmidt person who, along with a certain Ukrainian, would torture Jews on every shift. You know the Pawiak cellars? Those iron floors? Well, naked Jews, their skin steaming after a bath, crawled back and forth on them, back and forth. Have you ever seen the bottom of a soldier's boots? How many nails are in them? Well, Kronszmidt would mount a naked body with those boots on and go for a ride on the crawling man. Aryans had an easier time of it; it's true I crawled too, but in a different section, and nobody mounted me. And not on principle but for my bad reputation. We had gymnastics: one hour every other day. An hour: running around the yard, then "Fall down!" and pushups, good exercise from school.

My record: seventy-six times in a row and pain in my arms until the next time. The best exercise that I know is "Airman, take cover!" performed in a group. A double row of people, lined up chests to backs, carry a ladder on their shoulders, supporting it with one hand. At the cry, "Airman, take cover!" they drop to the ground without letting the ladder fall off their shoulders. Anyone who drops it either dies under a club or is hunted down and killed by a dog. Next, an SS man starts walking on the rungs of the ladder that is lying on these people—back and forth, back and forth. Then they have to stand up and, without breaking ranks, fall down again.

You see, everything is unbelievable: doing somersaults for kilometers as in Sachsenhausen, rolling on the ground for hours, doing hundreds of knee bends, standing in one spot for whole days and nights, sitting for months in a concrete coffin, in a bunkier, hanging suspended by one's arms from a post or on a pole slung between two chairs, jumping like a frog and creeping like a snake, drinking buckets of water to the point of suffocating oneself, being beaten by thousands of the most varied whips and sticks, by thousands of the most varied people . . . Look, I listen insatiably to the stories of prisons that no one knows about, provincial prisons in Małkinia, Suwałki, Radom, Puławy, Lublin, stories of the monstrously developed technology of torturing a man, and I cannot believe that it emerged suddenly from the head of a human being, like Minerva from the head of Jupiter. I cannot understand this sudden reveling in murder, this outpouring of an atavism that ostensibly had been forgotten.

And then there's this, too: death. I have been told of a camp in which transports of new prisoners arrived daily—scores of people at one time. But the camp had a set number of rations, I no longer remember how many, maybe two or three thousand, and the commandant didn't want his prisoners to starve. Each prisoner had to receive a ration. Every day, therefore, there were scores of excess people in the camp. Every night in every block they drew lots with cards or with ballot balls made out of bread, and the men who drew the lots did not go to work the next day. They were escorted outside the wires at noon and shot.

And in this flood of atavism stands a man from another world, a man who conspires so that there may be no more conspiracies among men, a man who steals so that there may be no pillaging on earth, a man who kills so that people will not be murdered.

So, Witek was from this other world, and he was a Pipel for Kronszmidt, the worst executioner in Pawiak. And now he is sitting beside me, listening to what's inside a person and how to repair it with home remedies should something go wrong. Then there was a scandal during class. A doctor turned to Staszek, who organizes things so well, and ordered him to repeat the liver. Staszek repeated poorly.

The doctor said, "You are answering very stupidly, and in addition you could stand up."

"I'm sitting in a camp, so I might as well sit during class," Staszek responded, turning red. "Furthermore, please don't insult me."

"Be quiet, you're in class."

"Oh, you'd certainly like me to be quiet, because I could say too much about what you've done in the camp."

At that, we began banging on our stools and shouting, "Yes! Yes!" and the doctor flew out the door. Adolf came in, called us names out of Kameradschaft, and then we went back to our block, right in the middle of the digestive system. Staszek immediately went running around to his friends to make sure that the doctor wouldn't attempt to stick his foot out and trip him up. Most likely he won't trip him up, because Staszek has good shoulders. We have learned this one fact from camp anatomy: it is not easy to trip up someone who has broad shoulders. As for that doctor, people really had various experiences with him; he was studying surgery on the sick. It's hard to determine how many people he slashed for the sake of science, and how many out of ignorance. Probably quite a lot, because the hospital is always crowded and the morgue is always full.

You will think, as you read this, that by now I have totally cast off that other world, the one from home. I write and write to you only about the camp, about every little event, and I extract meaning from these events as if nothing else awaits us . . .

Do you remember our little room? The one-liter thermos that you bought for me? It couldn't fit in my pocket, and finally, to your annoyance, it wound up under the bed. And the roundup in Żoliborz, which you gave me reports about by telephone all day long? That they were pulling people out of streetcars, but you got off one stop before they started; that they cordoned off the block, but you walked away through the fields all the way to the banks of the Vistula? And what you said to me when I complained about the war, about the barbarity, about the generation of uneducated fools that would emerge from among us: "Think about the people who are in the camps. We are only wasting time, but they are suffering."

There was a great deal of naïveté, immaturity, and a search for comfort in what I used to say then. But I think that probably we were not wasting time. Despite the passions of war, we were living in a different world. Perhaps for the world that is to come. If these words are too bold, forgive me. And our being here now is probably also for that other world. Do you think that were it not for the hope that that other world will come and the rights of man return, that we would survive in this camp for even a single day? It is hope that makes people go apathetically to the gas chambers; it makes them not risk rebellion, it entraps them in torpor. It is hope that severs family bonds, that makes mothers deny their children, makes wives sell themselves for bread and husbands kill people. It is hope that makes them struggle for every day of life because perhaps that very day will bring liberation. Oh, not even hope for another, better world, but simply for a life in which there will be peace and rest. Never in human history has a stronger hope existed in man, but also never has it caused as much evil as in this war, as in this camp. We were not taught to relinquish hope, and that is why we are perishing in the gas.

Look at what an original world we are living in: how few people there are in Europe who have not killed a man! And how few people there are whom other people would not wish to murder!

But *we* are longing for a world in which there is love for one's fellow man, peace from other people, and respite from instincts. Apparently, such is the law of love and youth.

P.S.—but before that, you know, I would like to slit one man's throat and then another's, so as to unburden myself of the camp complex, the complex of doffing one's cap, of passively observing the beaten and the murdered, the complex of fear of the camp. I am afraid, however, that this complex will weigh heavily upon us. I do not know if we will survive, but I wish that some day we will be able to call things by their proper names, as courageous people do.

VI

For several days now we have had a regular entertainment at noontime: a column of people marches out of the *für Deutsche* block and makes several circuits around the camp singing "Morgen nach Heimat." The Lagerältester acts as conductor and signals them with a stick to keep in step, Schritt und Tritt.

These are criminals, so-called "volunteers" for military service. All the green triangles, the prisoners convicted of real crimes, have been pulled out and the least vicious ones are being sent to the front. Someone who has slaughtered his wife and mother-in-law but let the canary go free into the fresh air so that the little bird shouldn't suffer in a cage is lucky, because he will stay here. For the time being, however, they are all together.

They are drilling them on how to march while waiting to see whether they will also display any understanding of communal life. But they display a sense of community in their own way. They have been together for only a couple of days and already they have broken into the storehouse, stolen parcels, vandalized the canteen, and demolished the Puff (in connection with which it has once again been closed down, to universal disappointment). "Why," they say very sagely, "should we have to go and fight, and stick out our necks for the SS, when we're doing all right here? Talk about the Vaterland all you like, but it's going down without us, and who is going to clean our boots at the front, and are there young boys there?"

So, a band of thugs walks along the road and sings "Tomorrow, we'll go home."* All the famous brawlers, each more famous than the next: Seppel, the terror of the roof kommando, the Dachdecker, the one who mercilessly orders people to work on the roofs in rain, snow, and frost, who will throw a man off a roof for a badly hammered nail; Arno Böhm, number 8, a long-term Block Elder, kapo, and Lagerkapo, a guy who killed room orderlies for selling tea and administered twenty-five blows for every minute late and every word spoken after the nighttime gong, the same man who wrote his elderly parents in Frankfurt short but moving letters about separation and reunion. We recognize all of them: this one beat people at the DAW works, and this one is the terror of Buna; that

---

* Having given the popular Nazi song its proper German title, "Morgen nach Heimat," at the beginning of this section, Borowski chose to render the title in Polish, employing the simpler possible translation of "Heimat": "home" (*dom*) rather than "homeland" (*ojczyzna*).

one's a sluggard, but when he was sick he made so many trips to the block guardhouse for tobacco that they threw him out into the camp beaten black and blue, and he got some unfortunate kommando in his criminal paws. Known pederasts march in their ranks, alcoholics, drug addicts, sadists—and at the very end marches Kurt, elegantly attired; he surveys the scene, falls out of step, and does not sing.

At the last minute, I realized that he's the one who found you for me and carried our letters, so I dashed downstairs at full tilt, grabbed him by the neck, and said, "Kurt, you must be hungry; come up here, you criminal-volunteer," and I pointed to the window that belongs to us. Somehow, he managed to show up toward evening, just in time for the dinner we'd cooked up in the stove with the majolica tiles. Kurt is very nice (that sounds exotic, but it would be hard to come up with a different description), and he's good at telling stories. He wanted to be a musician once upon a time, but his father, a rich shopkeeper, threw him out of the house. Kurt went to Berlin, met a girl there, the daughter of another shopkeeper, began living with her, wrote for sports newspapers, landed in the clinker for a month for brawling with a helmet-wearing thug, and after that he never showed up at the girl's home. He acquired a sports car and smuggled foreign currency. He ran into his girl once when he was out for a walk, but he didn't dare remind her of his existence. Then he went back and forth to Austria and Yugoslavia until they caught him and put him in prison. And since he was a recidivist (that unfortunate month), from prison he was sent to the camp: wait there until the end of the war.

It's growing dark. In the camp, roll call is over. A couple of us are sitting at the table and telling stories. People tell stories everywhere: while walking to a kommando assignment, returning to camp, over a shovel and in a truck, in the evening on the bunks, while standing at roll call. We tell stories about stories and we tell stories about life. Both this life and the other one, the one outside the wires. Today we were focused on the camp, maybe because Kurt will soon be leaving it.

"Actually, no one knew anything definite about the camp. Some nonsense about aimless labor—tearing up and laying asphalt, for example, or collecting sand. And, of course, that it was awful. Rumors were circulating. But as God is my witness, no one was particularly interested in all this. We knew, after all, that if you get caught, you'll never get out."

"If you came here two years ago, the wind would certainly have blown you out of the chimney," Staszek, who is such an accomplished organizer, interjected skeptically.

I shrugged, unsure of this.

"And maybe not. It didn't blow you out, so it wouldn't have blown me either. But you know, there was a fellow from Auschwitz in Pawiak."

"He probably came for interrogation."

"Exactly. We questioned him, but he didn't say a word; he kept his mouth shut. All he'd say was, 'When you come, you'll see. What's the point of telling you now? Like talking to children.'"

"Were you afraid of the camp?"

"I was. We left Pawiak in the morning. In trucks to the train station. A bad sign: the sun was at our backs. That meant we were going to the Western Station. To Auschwitz. They loaded us into the freight cars at breakneck speed, and what a trip! We traveled in alphabetical order, sixty men to a car; it wasn't even crowded."

"Did you take your things?"

"Of course I did. A blanket and a smoking jacket that my fiancée had given me, and two sheets."

"Sucker. You should have left them for your friends. Didn't you know they'd take everything away?"

"I hated to leave them. Then we pulled all the nails out of a wall, tore out the boards, and out we went. But there was a machine gun on the roof; it finished off the first three men instantly. The last one stuck his head out of the carriage and caught a bullet in the nape of the neck. They stopped the train immediately, and boy, did we back up into a corner! Screaming, shouting, hell! We shouldn't have tried to escape! Cowards! They'll kill us! And curses, you should have heard them!"

"No worse than from the women's camp."

"No, no worse. But always strong ones. And I was sitting under a pile of people, at the very bottom. I'm thinking: Good, if they shoot, they won't hit me first. And it was a good thing, because they did shoot. They fired a round into the pile, killed two men and wounded a third in the side. And '*Los, aus,* leave your stuff!' Well, I'm thinking, now I'm kaput! Nothing, just a bullet in the head! I felt a little sad about the smoking jacket because I had a Bible in it and, you understand, it was from my fiancée."

"The blanket was also from your fiancée, I think?"

"It was. I felt sad about it, too. But I didn't take anything because they threw me off the step. You have no idea how big the world is when a man goes flying out of a sealed freight car! The sky is high . . ."

". . . and blue . . ."

". . . exactly, it's blue, and the trees smell so good, the woods, you want to take them in your hands! There are SS everywhere, machine guns in their hands. They led four men over to the side and herded the rest of us into another car. A hundred twenty of us traveled together, including the three dead and the one wounded. We almost suffocated in that car. It was so close in there that water was pouring from the ceiling, literally. Not a single little window, nothing, everything was boarded up. We shouted for air and for water, but when they started shooting, we calmed down immediately. Then we collapsed on the floor and lay there like slaughtered pigs. I took off my sweater and then my two shirts. My body was swimming in sweat. Blood was trickling from my nose. There was a ringing in my ears. I yearned for Auschwitz, because it meant fresh air. When they opened the doors to the loading platform, I got my strength back completely with the first gulp of air. It was an April night, starry, cold. I didn't feel the cold even though I put on a thoroughly wet shirt. Someone embraced me from behind and kissed me. 'Brother, brother,' he whispered. In the black darkness that lay low on the ground, the lights of the camp shone in rows. A restless red flame flared above them. The darkness was flowing toward it. It looked as if it were burning on top of a towering mountain.

"'The crematorium.' The whispered word flew through our ranks."

"Boy, do you pile it on; it's obvious that you're a poet," Witek said appreciatively.

"We walked to the camp, carrying the corpses. Behind me I heard people's labored breathing and I thought that my fiancée was walking behind me. Time and again, muffled blows. Right in front of the gate I got a bayonet blow in my thigh. It didn't hurt, it just felt very warm. The blood was flowing down my thigh and calf. After a couple of steps my muscles went into spasms and I started limping. An SS escort struck a couple of men in front of me and announced as we walked through the barred gate of the camp, 'You'll have a good rest here.'

"That was Thursday night. And on Monday I went out to a kommando, seven kilometers from the camp. To Budy, to carry telegraph poles. My leg hurt like hell. But we had a rest, and a good one!"

"That's nothing," said Witek. "The Jews travel in even worse conditions. You have nothing to brag about."

Opinions were divided as to the traveling conditions and the Jews.

"Jews! You know what Jews are like!" Staszek suddenly spoke up. "You'll see, they'll even make *gesheft* in their own camp! Even in the ghetto, in the crematorium, they'll sell their own mother for a bowl of rutabagas! Once, we're standing in the Arbeitskommando since early morning, the Sonderkommando is nearby, guys like bulls, contented with life, and why not? One of my friends is with me, Moishe. He's from Mława and I'm from Mława, you know how it is, we're friends and traders, we trust and respect each other. 'What's up, Moishe? Why are you in such a bad mood?' 'I got photographs of my family.' 'So what's there to worry about? It's good.' 'Go to hell with your "good"; I sent my father to the chimney!' 'That's impossible!' 'It's possible, because I did it. He arrived on a transport, caught sight of me in front of the gas chamber where I was herding the people, threw himself on my neck, started kissing me and asking what was going to happen, and telling me that he was hungry because they'd been traveling for two days without eating. And meanwhile the Kommandoführer is screaming at us not to stand there, that we have to keep working! What could I do? "Go on, Father," I said, "wash up in the bathhouse, and then we'll talk, you can see that I don't have time now." And my father went off to the gas chamber. Afterward, I pulled the photos out of his clothes. So tell me, what's good about my having photographs?'"

We burst out laughing. Come to think of it, it's a good thing that they're not gassing Aryans now. Anything but that.

"They used to gas them in the old days," said the "local" Fleger, who always sits with us. "I've been in this block for a long time and I remember a lot. How many people have passed through my hands to the gas, friends and acquaintances from the same city! A person doesn't even remember their faces any more! That's the way it is—a mass. But one incident I think I'll remember all my life. At the time I was a Fleger in the walk-in clinic. I don't dress wounds too delicately; obviously, there's no time to talk nonsense. You dig around in a hand or a back or wherever, cotton wool, a bandage, and out of here! Next! You don't even look at a person's face. And no one thanks you, because there's nothing to thank you for. But once, I dressed an abscess and someone said to me in Russian from the doorway, '*Spasibo*, Fleger!' He thanked me! He was so pale, thin, barely able to stand on his swollen legs. I went to see him and brought him some soup. He had an abscess on his right buttock, then the whole thigh got infected, a pocket of pus. He was in terrible pain. He was crying and talking about his mother. 'Be quiet,' I said to him; 'we have mothers, too, after all, and we're not crying.' I comforted him as best I could, because he kept complaining that he wouldn't be going home. What could I give him? A bowl of soup and occasionally a slice of bread. I hid Tolechka from the selections the best I could, but once they found him, they wrote down his number. I went to him immediately. He was feverish. He said, 'It doesn't matter to me that I'm going to the gas. That's obviously the way it has to be. But when the war ends, and if you should survive . . .' 'I don't know if I'll survive, Tolechka,' I interrupted him. 'You'll survive,' he insisted stubbornly, 'and you'll go to my mother. After the war I'm sure there won't be any borders, there won't be any states, there won't be camps, people won't kill each other. *Ved' eto poslednii boi*,' he said emphatically. 'It's the final battle. *Poslednii, ponimaesh'?*' 'I understand,' I said; 'the final battle.' 'You'll go to my mother and you'll tell her that I died. So that there shouldn't be any borders. Or war. Or camps. You'll tell her?' 'I'll tell her.' 'Remember: my mother lives in the Dalnyvostok region, in the city of Khabarovsk, at 25 Leo Tolstoy Street. Repeat it.' I repeated it.

"I went to Szary, the Block Elder, who had the power to remove Tolechka from the list. He lashed me in the face and threw me out of his room. Tolechka went to the gas. A couple of months later Szary left in a transport. Before their departure, he asked for cigarettes. I made sure that no one would give him any. And no one did. Maybe I did wrong, because he was going to be finished off at Mauthausen. But I've memorized Tolechka's mother's address: Dalnyvostok region, the city of Khabarovsk, 25 Leo Tolstoy Street . . ."

We were silent. Kurt, disturbed, asked what had happened, because he couldn't understand anything in our conversation. Witek summarized it for him: "We're talking about the camp and about whether the world will be better. You could tell a story, too."

Kurt looked at us, smiling, and said slowly, so that we could all understand:

"I'll tell a very short story. When I was in Mauthausen, two escapees were caught, right on Christmas Eve. A scaffold was erected in the square next to a large Christmas tree. The entire camp was brought together for a roll call when they were hanged. They had just lit the lights on the Christmas tree.

"Then the Lagerführer stepped out, turned to the prisoners, and gave the order to remove our hats: '*Häftlinge, Mützen ab!*'

"We took off our caps. For his traditional Christmas Eve speech the Lagerführer said, 'He who behaves like a pig will be treated like a pig. *Häftlinge, Mützen auf!*'

"We put our caps back on.

"'Disperse!' We dispersed.

"We lit up cigarettes. We didn't talk. Everyone was thinking his own thoughts."

VII

If the walls of the barracks were to collapse, thousands of people smashed and jammed together on the bunks would be left hanging in the air. It would be a sight more abominable than medieval pictures of the Last Judgment. What shocks a person most is the sight of another man sleeping on his share of the *buksa*, the stacked-up bunk, in the space he has to occupy because he has a body. They have made use of his body in every way possible: they tattooed a number on it to avoid spending on dog tags, allowed just enough sleep at night for a man to be capable of working, and just enough time in the day for eating. And enough food to keep him from dropping dead unproductively. There is only one place for living: his space on the wooden bunk; the rest belongs to the camp, to the state. But not even that space, not even your shirt or your shovel, is yours. When you get sick they'll take everything away from you: your clothing, your cap, the scarf you smuggled in, your handkerchief. When you die, they'll rip out your gold teeth, which have already been entered in the camp ledgers. They will burn you and scatter the ashes over the fields or use them to fill in ponds. True, they waste so much fat, so many bones, so much meat, so much warmth by this burning! But elsewhere they make soap out of people, lampshades from human skin, ornaments from their bones. Who knows, perhaps for export to the Negroes whom someday they will subjugate?

We work underground and on the ground, under a roof and in the rain, with shovels, gondola cars, pickaxes, and crowbars. We carry bags of cement, we lay bricks and train tracks, we fence off arable land, we tamp down the earth . . . We are constructing the foundations of some kind of new, monstrous civilization. Only now do I recognize the cost of antiquity. What monstrous crimes those Egyptian pyramids, temples, and Greek monuments are! How much blood must have spilled onto Rome's roads, onto the ramparts and the buildings of the City! Antiquity, a gigantic concentration camp where slaves had the mark of property branded onto their foreheads and were crucified for attempted escapes. Antiquity, a great conspiracy of free people against slaves!

You remember how I loved Plato. Today, I know that he lied. Because it's not a reflection of the ideal that's contained in the things of this earth but the hard, bloody labor of man. It is we who built the pyramids, cut the marble for the temples and the stones for the imperial roads; it is we who rowed in the galleys and dragged the plows, while they wrote dialogues and dramas, justified their intrigues by referring to the fatherland, fought over borders and democracies. We were filthy and we died for real. They were aesthetic and debated imponderables.

There is no beauty if injustice done to a human being is at its core. There is no truth that ignores this injustice. There is no goodness that tolerates it.

What does antiquity know about us? It knows the crafty slave from Terence and Plautus; it knows the Gracchi, the tribunes of the common people, and the name of only one slave—Spartacus.

They made history and no matter if they were criminals (Scipio) or lawyers (Cicero or Demosthenes), we remember them perfectly. We go into raptures over the extermination of the Etruscans, the destruction of Carthage, treasons, crimes, and pillage. Roman law! Today, too, there is law!

What will the world know about us if the Nazis are victorious? Gigantic edifices will arise, highways, factories, towering monuments. Our hands will be placed beneath every brick, the railroad ties and concrete slabs will be carried on our backs. They will slaughter our families, the sick, the old. They will slaughter the children.

And no one will know about us. The poets, lawyers, philosophers, priests will drown out our voices. They will create beauty, goodness, and truth. They will create religion.

Three years ago there were villages and hamlets here. There were fields, dirt roads, and pear trees in the boundary strips between the fields. There were people who were no better or worse than other people.

Then we came along. We drove out the people, destroyed their houses, leveled the earth, pulverized it into mud. We erected barracks, fences, crematoriums. We brought with us scabies, phlegmon, and lice.

We toil in factories and mines. We perform gigantic labors from which someone derives incredible profit.

The history of Lenz, a local firm, is astonishing. This firm built our camp, barracks, halls, warehouses, bunkiers, chimneys. The camp lent the firm prisoners, and the SS gave it supplies. When the accounts were drawn up, the bill turned out to be so fantastically in the millions that not only Auschwitz but Berlin itself clutched its head. Gentlemen, they said, this is impossible, you have earned too much, way up there in the millions and millions! Nonetheless, the firm replied, these are the charges. All right, said Berlin, but we can't meet them. Then half, the patriotic firm proposed. Thirty percent, Berlin continued to haggle, and that's what they agreed on. Since then, all the charges from the Lenz firm are reduced accordingly. Lenz, however, doesn't worry; like all German firms, its investment capital is growing. It made a huge profit on Auschwitz and is calmly awaiting the end of the war. The same is true of the Wagner and Continental firm that installed the water system, the Richter firm that drilled the wells, Siemens of the lighting and electrical wires, the suppliers of bricks, cement, iron, and wood, the makers of parts for the barracks and striped clothing. The same is true of the Union motor vehicle company, the DAW scrap demolition works. The same for the owners of the mines in Mysłowice, Gliwice, Janina, Jaworzno. Whoever among us survives must some day demand the equivalent of that labor. Not in money, not in goods, but in hard, stony labor.

When the sick and the men who have returned from work assignments go to sleep, I converse with you from afar. I see your face in the darkness, and although I speak with bitterness and hatred that are alien to you, I know that you are listening intently.

You are harnessed to my fate. But you have hands not made for the pickax and a body unaccustomed to scabies. We are united by our love and the boundless love of those who remained behind. Those who live for us and are our world. The faces of our parents, friends, the shapes of objects that remained behind. And this is the dearest thing that we can share: survival! And even if all we had left were our bodies on a hospital bunk, we would still have our thoughts and our feelings.

And I believe that man's dignity truly resides in his thoughts and in his feelings.

VIII

You have no idea how happy I am.

First of all—the tall electrician. I go to him every morning with Kurt (because he's his friend), and we hand him the letters for you. The electrician, a fantastically old number, just a bit over a thousand, loads himself down with sausages, little sacks of sugar, ladies' underwear, and slips a bunch of letters down into his boot. The electrician is bald and cannot understand our love. The electrician makes a face at every letter that I bring him. When I try to give him some cigarettes, the electrician says, "Friend, here in our Auschwitz we don't take anything for letters! I'll bring the answer when I can manage it."

Indeed, I go to see him in the evening. The reverse procedure ensues: the electrician reaches into his boot, pulls out a card from you, hands it to me, and scowls. Because the electrician cannot understand our love. And he certainly doesn't like the bunkier, which measures one by one-and-a-half meters. Because the electrician is very tall and he would be uncomfortable in the bunkier.

So, first of all, the tall electrician. Second—the Spaniard's wedding. The Spaniard defended Madrid, escaped to France, and then was sent to Auschwitz. Just like a Spaniard: he had a French woman, and they had a child. Since the child had gotten quite big and the Spaniard was still in the camp, the Frenchwoman began yelling that she wanted a wedding! So she petitioned H. himself. H. was indignant: Such disorder in the new Europe! Give them a wedding immediately!

The Frenchwoman and her child were dragged off to the camp, the Spaniard was forcibly stripped of his pasiaki, was fitted with an elegant suit ironed by the laundry kapo himself, matching socks and a tie were carefully selected from the rich camp stores, and they were given a wedding.

Then the newlyweds went to have their picture taken: she with their little son and a bouquet of hyacinths in her arms, and he with her on his arm. Behind them, the orchestra *in corpore*; and behind the orchestra, a furious SS man from the kitchen: "I'm going to report you! I'm going to submit a Meldung; you're playing during work time instead of peeling potatoes! My soup is standing there without potatoes! I don't give a shit about your weddings . . ."

"Shh," the other dignitaries calmed him down. "Berlin ordered it. The soup can be without potatoes."

In the meantime, the newlyweds were photographed, and an apartment in the Puff, from which the inhabitants were exiled to Block 10, was vacated for them for their wedding night. The next day, the Frenchwoman was sent back to France, and the Spaniard, in pasiaki to his kommando.

But the entire camp is walking around ramrod stiff.

"Here in our Auschwitz they even provide weddings."

So first of all—the tall electrician. Second—the Spaniard's wedding. And finally, third—we are finishing our course. Recently, the women Flegers from the FKL finished theirs. We bade them farewell with chamber music. They were all seated in the window of Block 10, and a few members of the orchestra played for them from our windows: the drum, the saxophone, and the violin. The saxophone is wonderful: it sobs and cries, laughs and sparkles!

It's a pity the poet Słowacki didn't know it; he would certainly have become a saxophone player because of the richness of its expression.

First the women, and now us. We assembled in the attic; Lagerarzt Rhode (the "decent" camp doctor, the one who makes no distinctions between Jews and Aryans) arrived, took a look at us and our dressings; he said he was very satisfied, and that now it would certainly be better here in our Auschwitz. And he left very quickly, because the attic is cold.

Here in our Auschwitz people have been saying good-bye to us all day long. Franz, the guy from Vienna, gave me a final lecture on the meaning of the war. Stumbling somewhat over his words, he talked about people who work and people who destroy. About the victory of the former and the defeat of the latter. About the fact that comrades of our own generation from London and Uralsk, from Chicago and Calcutta, from mainland and island, are fighting for us. About the coming brotherhood of working people. Here it is, I thought, the birth of messianism amid all this destruction and death, the usual path of human thought. Then Franz laid out the contents of a parcel he had just received from Vienna and we drank our evening tea. Franz sang Austrian songs and I recited poems which he did not understand.

Here in our Auschwitz they gave me some medicines and a couple of books as a parting gift. I stuffed them into a package underneath the food. Imagine: the reflections of Angelus Silesius. So I am happy, because everything came together: the tall electrician, the Spaniard's wedding, our completing the course. And finally, fourth—yesterday I received letters from home. They'd been on my trail for a long time, but they did find me.

For almost two months I haven't had a sign of life from home, and I was terribly worried, because the news here about conditions in Warsaw is fantastic; I had already started writing despairing letters and then yesterday of all days, think about it! two letters: one from Staszek, and one from my brother.

Staszek writes in very simple words, like a man who yearns to convey the contents of his heart in a foreign language. "We love you and we remember you," he writes, "and we also remember Tuśka, your fiancée. We live, we work, and we create." They live, they work, and they create, except that Andrzej perished and Wacek "is no longer alive."*

What a blow it is that those two most talented men of our generation, with the greatest passion for creative work, had to have been the ones to perish!

You know how sharply I opposed them: their imperialist notion of constructing an insatiable state, their lack of decency in social understanding, their theories of a national art, their philosophy as murky as their master Stanisław Brzozowski himself, their poetic practice that kowtowed before the wall of the avant-garde, their style of conscious and unconscious lying.

And today, when the threshold between two worlds separates us, the threshold that we, too, will cross, I resume this argument about the meaning of the world, about how to live, and the nature of poetry. And today I accuse them of yielding to the seductive ideas of a powerful, aggressive state, of admiration for an evil whose sole defect is that it is not our evil. And today, too, I accuse them of a lack of ideas in their poetry, the absence in it of man, the absence in it of the poet.

But I see their faces across the threshold of the other world, and I think about them, these boys of my own generation, and I feel that the emptiness around us is growing ever larger. They departed so incredibly alive, right from the center of the work that they were building. They departed belonging so very much to this world. I bid them farewell, my friends from a different barricade. May they

---

* Andrzej Trzebiński (1922–1943) and Wacław Bojarski (1921–1943), colleagues of Borowski's from the underground university they all attended, were two of the four coeditors of a slim, mimeographed literary-political monthly, *Sztuka i Naród* (Art and nation). Their group, inspired in part by the writings of Stanisław Brzozowski (1878–1911), combined devotion to avant-garde poetics with right-wing nationalist politics. Bojarski was shot while laying a wreath at the statue of Copernicus—a symbolic patriotic act. A few months later, Trzebiński was caught in a street roundup and executed.

find in that other world the truth and the love that they did not encounter here!

. . . Ewa, the woman who recited such beautiful poems about harmony and the stars and the fact that "it's still not so bad," was executed, too. Emptiness, ever greater emptiness. Loved ones and acquaintances are departing, and now may those who are able to pray, pray not for the meaning of our struggle but for the lives of their loved ones.

I thought it would stop with us. That when we'd return, we'd return to a world that was unacquainted with the horrible atmosphere that is choking us. That we alone had descended to the depths. But people are departing from there—right out of the center of life, struggle, love.

We are as insensitive as trees, as stones. And we remain silent like felled trees, like split stones.

The second letter is from my brother. You know what heartfelt letters Julek writes to me. And now he writes that they are thinking about us, they are waiting, they've hidden all my books and poems . . .

When I return, I will find my slender new volume on my book shelves. "They are the poems about your love," writes my brother. I think that our love and poetry are symbolically intertwined, and these poems that were written for you alone, and with which you were arrested, now are definitely a victory from afar. They have been published—perhaps as a memento now we're gone? I am grateful to people's friendship for preserving after us poetry and love, and for recognizing our right to them.

And my brother also writes to me about your mother, that she thinks about us and believes that we will return and we will be together always, because that is a human right.

. . . Do you remember what you wrote in the first card I received from you a couple of days after our arrival at the camp? You wrote that you were sick and in despair because you had "dragged me" into the camp. That if it weren't for you, then I, etc. But do you know what really happened?

I was waiting for your prearranged telephone call from Maria's. In the afternoon the secret class met at my place, as it usually did on Wednesdays; I think I spoke about my paper on language, and it seems the carbide lamp had gone out.

Then I waited for your phone call. I knew you would call, because you promised. You didn't call. I don't remember if I went to dinner. If I did, then after I came back I sat by the telephone again; I was afraid I might not hear it from the next room. I read some newspaper items and a Maurois story about a man who weighed souls so that, having learned how to seal human souls in everlasting vessels, he could seal up his own soul with the soul of the woman he loved. But he sealed up only the souls of two chance circus clowns, and his soul and the woman's soul had to dissolve through the universe. Toward morning I fell asleep.

Early in the morning I went home as usual with my briefcase and books. I ate breakfast, said I would be back for dinner and that I was in a great hurry, twisted the dog's ear, and went to see your mother. Your mother was worried about you. I took a streetcar to Maria's. I looked intently for a long time at the trees in Łazienki park because I am very fond of them. To calm my nerves, I walked along Puławska Street. There was an unusual number of cigarette butts on the stairs and, if I remember correctly, traces of blood. But maybe that was my imagination. I went up to the door and rang according to our prearranged signal. The door was opened by men with guns in their hands.

A year has passed since that day. But I am writing this so you should know that I have never regretted that we are together. And I never think that it might have been otherwise. But I often think about the future. About the life we will live, if . . . About the poems I will write, the books we will read, the things we will have in our home. I know that this is foolishness, but I think about them. I even have an idea for our ex libris. It will be a rose tossed onto a thick, locked tome with large medieval clasps.

IX

We're back already. I went to my own block just as I used to, smeared mint tea over the men who are sick with scabies, and early this morning we washed the floor together. Then, with a sage expression on my face, I stood next to the doctor as he lanced abscesses. Then I took the last two syringes of Prontosil and sent them to you. Finally, our block barber Heniek Liberfreund (in civilian life the owner of the restaurant under the Kraków post office) proclaimed that now I will surely be the best Fleger among all men of letters.

Other than that, I've spent the entire day roaming around with this letter to you. My letter to you is these pages, but to reach you they must have legs. I'm working on finding those "legs." At last, I found one pair—in tall red boots with laces. The "legs" also have dark glasses; they have broad shoulders and they go to the FKL every day to pick up the corpses of male children. Those corpses, you see, have to pass through our Schreibstube and our morgue, and our sanitarian in the Sanitätsdienstgrade has to inspect them with his own hands. The world rests upon order or, less poetically, *Ordnung muss sein.*

So, the "legs" go to the FKL and are very well disposed toward me. They, too, they say, have a wife in the women's section, and they know how hard it is. Therefore, they will take the letter just like that, for the pleasure of it. And me, too, if the occasion should arise. So I'll send the letter immediately, and I shall try to come to you myself. I'm even in the mood for traveling. My friends advise me to take a blanket—and tuck it in where I'll need it. Given my good luck and camp ingenuity, they reason correctly that I'll be caught on my first outing. Except that I'll be going under some-one's protection. I advised them to smear themselves with Peruvian balsam to protect against scabies.

And I also survey the landscape. Nothing has changed, only, amazingly, even more mud has piled up. It smells of spring. People are going to drown in the mud. From the woods the smell of pine trees reaches us, and then the smell of smoke. First, trucks drive past transporting rags, then Muselmänner from Buna. First, dinner to the storehouse, then SS men changing shifts.

Nothing has changed. Yesterday was Sunday, so we were in the camp for louse control. The camp blocks are hideous in the winter! Filthy bunks, swept dirt floors, and the stale smell of human beings. The blocks are packed with people, but there's not a single louse. It's not for nothing that the delousings take all night.

Just as we were leaving the blocks after the control was com-pleted, the Sonderkommando came back from the cremo. They were coated with smoke, swimming in fat, bent low under heavy bundles. They are permitted to bring back everything but gold, but that is what they smuggle most often.

Small groups of people erupted from the blocks, fell upon the marching ranks, and tore at packages that caught their eye. Shouts, curses, and blows swirled in the air. Finally, the Sonderkommando disappeared through the gate of their own courtyard, which was separated from the rest of the camp by a wall. Immediately, how-ever, the Jews began to slip away stealthily to trade, to organize, and to visit.

I stopped one of them, a friend from our former kommando. When I fell sick, I went to the Krankenbau. He was "luckier" and went to the Sonderkommando. It's better than working for your bowl of soup with a shovel. He shook hands warmly.

"Oh, it's you? Do you need something? If you have apples . . ."

"No, I don't have any apples for you," I replied in a friendly way. "So you haven't died yet, Abramek? What's new?"

"Nothing interesting. We gassed the Czech women."

"I know that without you. And personally?"

"Personally? What can be 'personally' about me? The chimney, the block, and again the chimney? Do I have anyone here? Oh, you want to know personally: we've devised a new method for burning in the chimney. Do you know how?"

I was very politely curious.

"Here's how: we take four tots with hair, put their heads together, and set their hair on fire. Then it burns on its own and it's *gemacht.*"

"Congratulations," I said drily, without enthusiasm.

He burst out laughing in a strange way and looked me in the eyes.

"Hey, Fleger, here in our Auschwitz we have to amuse ourselves as best we can. You think there's another way to stand this?"

And putting his hands in his pockets, he walked off without saying good-bye.

But this is a lie and a monstrosity, like the whole camp, like the whole world.

THE PEOPLE WHO WERE WALKING

First of all, in an open field behind the hospital barracks, we built a soccer field. The field was well situated: on the left was the Gypsy camp with the kids running around, the women sitting in the latrines, and the lovely women Flegers decked out in their finest; at the rear was the wire fence, and beyond it the loading ramp and the wide train tracks that were always filled with railway cars, and beyond the loading ramp the women's camp. Actually, there wasn't a women's camp. That's not a term we used. We said FKL, for Frauenkonzentrationslager, and that was enough. To the right of the field were the crematoriums, some beyond the loading ramp, next to the FKL, and others closer, right next to the wire. Solid buildings, firmly planted in the ground. Beyond the crematoriums was a little woods one walked through to reach a small white building.

We built the soccer field during the spring, and even before it was completed we started planting flowers under the windows and laying out red crushed-brick paths around the blocks. We planted spinach and lettuce, sunflowers and garlic. Small lawns were laid down, cut from the turf near the playing field. All this was watered every day with water brought over by the barrelful from the camp washroom.

By the time the watered flowers came up, we had completed the playing field.

Now the flowers grew on their own, the sick lay by themselves in their beds, and we played soccer. Every day after the evening rations were distributed, whoever felt like it came to the field and kicked the ball around. Others walked over to the wires and chatted with the FKL across the entire width of the loading ramp.

One day, I was the goalie. It was Sunday, a sizable crowd of Flegers and almost-cured patients surrounded the field; someone was running on the field, chasing someone else and, probably, the soccer ball, too. I was playing goalie with my back to the ramp. The ball went out of bounds and rolled right up to the wires. I ran after it. As I picked it up off the ground, I glanced at the loading ramp.

A train had just pulled in alongside the ramp. They had started unloading people from the freight cars, and they were walking in the direction of the little woods. From a distance, only the colors of dresses could be seen. Apparently, women were already wearing summer clothing, the first time this season. The men had removed their suit jackets, and their white shirts glistened. The procession moved slowly; new people from the freight cars kept joining it. Finally it came to a stop. The people sat down on the grass and looked in our direction. I brought the ball back and kicked it onto the field. It passed from foot to foot and returned in an arc to the goal. I kicked it toward the corner. It rolled onto the grass. Again I went after it. And as I picked it up off the ground I froze: the loading ramp was empty. Not a single person from that colorful summer crowd was left on it. The freight cars were also gone. There was a perfect view of the FKL blocks. The Flegers were standing by the fence again and shouting greetings to the girls, who shouted back at them from the other side of the ramp.

I came back with the ball and aimed at the corner. Behind my back, between one corner kick and the next, they had gassed three thousand people.

Then people began walking toward the woods along two roads: the one that led directly from the ramp and the other one, on the other side of our hospital. Both led to the crematorium, but some people had the good luck to walk farther, all the way to the Zauna, which for them meant not only the bath house and delousing, the barbershop and new rags with their numbers marked in oil paint, but also life. Life in the camp, to be sure, but still—life.

When I got up in the morning to wash the floor, the people were walking—along the one road and the other. Women, men, and children. Carrying bundles.

When I sat down to dinner, a better dinner than I used to eat at home—the people were walking, along the one road and the other. There was a lot of sunlight in the block; we opened the doors and windows wide, sprinkled the floor to keep the dust down. In the afternoon I would bring in from the storeroom packages that had been delivered that morning from the main post office in the camp. A clerk handed out letters. The doctors applied dressings, gave injections, and lanced abscesses. Actually, they had one syringe for the entire block. On warm evenings I sat in the doorway of the block and read *Mon frère Yves* by Pierre Loti—and the people kept walking and walking, along the one road and the other.

At night, I would go outside to the front of the block; lights were shining above the wires in the darkness. The road lay in darkness, but I distinctly heard the distant babble of many thousands of voices—the people were walking and walking. Flames rose from the wood and lit up the sky, and a human scream rose with the flames.

I peered into the depths of night, stupefied, speechless, motionless. My whole body shuddered and seethed inside me without my doing anything. I had no control over it, although I felt each of its shudders. I was completely calm, but my body was in revolt.

Not long afterward I left the hospital for the camp. The days were filled with great events. Allied troops were landing on the coast of France. The Russian front was about to move and march as far as the outskirts of Warsaw.

But here, day and night, rows of trains packed with people waited at the station. The freight cars would be unlocked, and the people would start walking—along the one road and the other.

Next to our workers' camp was the uninhabited and unfinished sector C. Only the barracks and the electrified wire were ready. But there was no roofing paper on the roofs, and some of the blocks had no bunks. With three-tiered bunks installed, the horse-stable blocks of the Birkenau camp could hold up to five hundred people. In sector C, more than a thousand young girls were packed into each of these blocks, selected from among the people who were walking. Twenty-eight blocks—more than thirty thousand women. These women were shaved to the skin and dressed in sleeveless summer frocks. They were given no underwear. No spoons, no bowls, no washrags. Birkenau was situated in marshland near the foothills of the mountains. During the day the mountains could be seen very clearly in the transparent air. In the morning they were shrouded in fog and seemed to be covered with frost, because the early mornings were unusually cold and foggy. These early mornings invigorated us men before the hot days, but the women, who had been standing at roll call twenty meters to our right since five A.M., were blue from the cold and huddled together like a flock of partridges.

We named that camp the Persian Market. In fair weather the women would come out of the blocks and gather in groups on the wide street between the blocks. From a distance, their colorful summer dresses and the bright kerchiefs covering their bald heads gave the impression of a gaudy, animated, noisy market. Because of its exoticism—a Persian market.

From a distance, the women had neither faces nor ages. Only white spots and pastel shapes.

The Persian Market was not a finished camp. The Wagner kommando was building a road inside it from stone that they crushed with a huge roller. Others were tinkering with the plumbing and washrooms that were newly installed in all sectors of Birkenau. Still others were laying the foundations of the sector's well-being: they carted over quilts, blankets, tin pots, and pans, and busily unloaded them in the storehouse under the direction of the SS man in charge. Naturally, a percentage of these things immediately went into the camp, stolen by the people who were working there. After all, so much profit could be had from these quilts, blankets, and pots and pans that it was okay to steal them.

All the roofs of the block elders' shacks throughout the entire Persian Market were installed by my friends and me. We weren't ordered to do this, nor did we do it out of pity. We covered the roofs with organized roofing paper and glued it down with organized tar. We also didn't do it out of solidarity with the old numbers, either—the women Flegers from the FKL who held all the posts there. The block elders had to pay for every roll of roofing paper, every bucket of tar. They had to pay the kapo, the Kommandoführer, the kommando's "prominents." They paid in various ways: with gold, provisions, women from the block, themselves. How depended on the woman.

In the same way as we patched the roofs, electricians installed lights, carpenters built shacks and furniture for the shacks out of organized wood, and masons brought in stolen iron stoves and installed them as needed.

It was then that I came to know the face of this strange camp. We would arrive at the gate on foot early in the morning, pushing our cart with roofing paper and tar. Female SS guards, wide-hipped blondes in tall leather boots, stood watch at the gate. The blondes searched us and let us go inside. Later, they went to inspect the blocks. Not a few of them had lovers among the masons and carpenters. They gave themselves to them in the unfinished washrooms or the block elders' shacks.

Then we would ride into the heart of the camp between various blocks, and we would make a fire and heat the tar right there on the square. A crowd of women would immediately besiege us. They would beg us for a penknife, a handkerchief, a spoon, a pencil, a piece of paper, a shoelace, bread.

"You are men, after all, and you can do anything," they said. "You've been living in this camp for so long and haven't died. You must have everything. Why don't you want to share with us?"

We gave them all the odds and ends we had; we turned our pockets inside out to demonstrate that we had nothing left. We took off our shirts for them. Finally, we started arriving with empty pockets and didn't give them anything.

These women were not all alike, as they had appeared to be from the perspective of the second sector, twenty meters to the left.

Among them were little girls whose hair had not been shaved off, trapped little cherubs in a painting of the Last Judgment. There were young girls looking with amazement at the crowd of women around us, and with contempt at us coarse, brutal men. There were wives who asked us tearfully for news of their lost husbands; there were mothers seeking from us a trace of their children.

"It's so awful for us here, it's cold, we're hungry," they wept. "Are they at least better off?"

"They are definitely better off, if a just God exists," we replied solemnly, without our usual mockery and derision.

"They haven't died, have they?" the women asked, looking anxiously into our eyes.

We walked off in silence, hurrying to our work.

The block elders in the Persian Market were Slovak girls who knew the language these women spoke. Each of these girls had a couple of years of camp life behind her. They remembered the early days of the FKL, when women's corpses lay next to all the blocks and in the hospital beds where they were left to rot, and human feces piled up in monstrous heaps inside the blocks.

Despite their external roughness they still had a woman's softness and kindness. Certainly, they had their lovers and they, too, stole margarine and canned food to pay for the blankets or frocks brought to them from the warehouses, but . . .

. . . but I remember Mirka, a sturdy, short girl in pink.

Her shack was also decorated in pink, and she had pink curtains in the window that looked out on the block. The air in the shack touched her face with a pink reflection, and the girl seemed to be swathed in a delicate veil. A Jew from our kommando, who had bad teeth, was in love with her. The Jew purchased fresh eggs for her which he collected from the entire camp, and threw them, carefully wrapped, across the wires. He spent long hours with her, paying no attention to the SS women's inspections or to our boss, who walked around with an enormous revolver strapped to his white summer uniform. We called the boss Peter Rabbit because he kept popping up where he wasn't supposed to be.

One day, Mirka ran over to where we were laying tar paper on a roof. She beckoned to the Jew and shouted at me, "Get down! Maybe you can help, too!"

We slid off the roof over the barracks door. She grabbed our arms and pulled us toward her. She led us between the bunks and, pointing at a pallet piled with colorful quilts and a child lying in the middle of them, declaimed in an affected manner, "Look, she's going to die soon! Tell me, what am I to do? Why did she have to fall sick so suddenly?"

The child was sleeping very fitfully. She was like a rose in a gold setting: flushed cheeks and a golden halo of hair.

"What a pretty child," I whispered softly.

"Pretty!" Mirka shrieked. "You know she's pretty. But she might die! I have to hide her so she won't go to the gas. An SS woman might find her. Help me!"

The Jew placed his hand on her arm. She shuddered violently and began sobbing. I shrugged and walked out of the block.

In the distance freight cars could be seen moving alongside the loading ramp. They were bringing new people who would soon be walking. On the road between the sectors, one group on the way back to Canada from the freight cars passed another going to take its turn. Smoke was rising from the woods. I sat down near the boiling cauldron and mused for a long time while I stirred the tar. At one point the thought came to me that I would like to have just such a child with cheeks rosy from sleep and tousled hair. I smiled at the inappropriate thought and went up on the roof to fasten down the tar paper.

I also remember another block elder, a sturdy, tall, red-haired girl with wide feet and red hands. She didn't have her own shack; just a couple of blankets spread on her bed and, instead of a wall, a couple of blankets draped over strings.

"They shouldn't think," she said, indicating the women lying head-to-head on the bunks, "that someone is avoiding them. I can't give them anything, but I won't take anything away from them."

"Do you believe in life beyond the grave?" she asked me during one of our jocular conversations.

"Sometimes," I said, hesitantly. "I believed once when I was in prison, and once when I was close to death in the camp."

"And if a person does something evil, he'll be punished, right?"

"I think so, as long as there are no higher norms of justice than human norms. You know—revelation of impulses, interior motives, the insignificance of guilt in relation to the essential meaning of the world. Can a crime committed on a level plane be punished in space?"

"But in human terms, normally!" she shouted.

"It ought to be punished, that's obvious."

"And would you do good if you could?"

"I'm not seeking a reward; I cover roofs and I want to survive the camp."

"And do you think that they," she indicated an indefinite direction with her head, "should not be punished?"

"I think that for people who are suffering unjustly, justice alone will not suffice. I want the perpetrators to suffer unjustly, too. They'll experience that as justice."

"You're a smart guy! But you wouldn't be able to distribute the soup justly and not give any to your lover!" she said ironically and walked into the main section of the block.

The women were lying stacked up on bunks, head-to-head. Huge eyes glittered in their immobile faces. Hunger was already setting in in the camp. The red-haired block elder moved among the bunks and chatted with the women to keep them from thinking. She pulled out singers from the bunks and ordered them to sing. Dancers, and ordered them to dance. Declaimers, and ordered them to recite poetry.

"They're constantly, constantly asking me where are their mothers, their fathers. They ask me to write to them."

"They ask me, too. It's tough."

"You! You come and go, but what about me? I ask them, I beg them, anyone who's pregnant, don't go to the doctor; anyone sick, stay in the block! Do you think they believe me? After all, I only want what's good for them. But how can I help them if they themselves are in a hurry to get to the gas!"

A girl was standing on the stove, singing a popular song. When she finished, the women in the bunks began clapping. The girl smiled and bowed. The red-haired block elder clutched her head.

"I can't stand it any more! It's vile," she hissed, and jumped up onto the stove.

"Get down!" she screamed at the girl.

The block became quiet. The block elder raised her hand.

"Quiet!" she screamed, although no one had said a word. "You asked me where your parents and your children are. I didn't tell you, because I feel sorry for you. I'm going to tell you now so that you'll know, because they'll do the same with you if you get sick! Your children, husbands, and parents are not in a different camp.

They were pushed into a cellar and asphyxiated with gas! You understand, with gas! Like millions of others, like my own parents! They were burned on pyres and in crematoriums. The smoke that you see above the roofs is not what you've been told, it's not from the brickworks. It's from your children! Now, you may continue singing," she said calmly to the terrified singer, jumped down from the stove, and left the block.

It's well known that Auschwitz and Birkenau went from bad to good. At first, they beat and murdered people in the kommandos routinely; later, only sporadically. At first, people slept on their sides on the floor and turned over on command; later, they slept in bunks in whatever position they wanted to, and even singly in beds. Originally, people stood at roll call for two days at a time; later, only until the second gong, until nine at night. During the first years, it was forbidden to send parcels; later, they permitted up to five hundred grams, and in the end, as much as someone wanted to send. It was forbidden to have pockets; later, even civilian clothing was allowed in Birkenau. In the camp it was "better and better." After three or four years no one believed it could again be the way it was in the past, and everyone was proud to have survived. The worse it was for the Germans at the front, the better it was in the camp. And it will be worse and worse for them . . .

In the Persian Market time was running backward. Once again, we were looking at Auschwitz from 1940. The women greedily slurped down soup that no one in our blocks would eat. They stank of sweat and female blood. They stood at roll call from five in the morning. By the time they were all counted, it was almost nine. Then they got cold grain coffee. At three in the afternoon the evening roll call began and they got supper: bread and something to put on the bread. Since they didn't work, they didn't receive a Zulage, the bonus for working.

Sometimes they were driven out of the blocks for an unscheduled roll call. They lined up close together by fives and entered the block, one after the other. Wide-hipped blondes, SS women wearing tall boots, pulled the thinner, uglier women, the women with swelling bellies, out of the ranks and shoved them into the center of the "eye." The eye was a circle of hall elders holding hands. They formed a closed circle. Filled with women, the eye moved like a macabre dance to the camp gate and got sucked into a general eye. Five hundred, six hundred, one thousand selected women. They all were walking—down that road.

Sometimes an SS woman entered a block. She surveyed the bunks, a woman looking at other women. She asked, who wants to go to the doctor? Who is pregnant? They'll give you milk and white bread in the hospital.

Women left the bunks and, corralled by the eye, walked over to the gate, and out to that road.

We spent our free time (we took breaks to make the day pass, because there was very little material) with the block elders in the Persian Market, either next to the blocks or in the latrine . . . At the block elders' we drank tea or went into their shacks for an hour's nap on a hospitably offered bed. Outside the blocks we conversed with the plumbers and masons. Women hovered around them, already wearing sweaters and stockings. If you bring them any kind of rag at all, you can do with them what you will. Since the camp became a camp, there has never been such a Canada of women!

The latrine is for both men and women. It's just divided by a board. On the women's side, there's crowding and loud voices; on ours, quiet and the pleasant coolness of the concrete fixtures. One can sit here for hours on end and engage in lengthy romantic dialogues with Katia, the short, neatly dressed latrine attendant. No one is embarrassed, and the situation doesn't disturb anyone. People have already seen so much in the camp . . .

And so, June passed. Day and night the people were walking— along the one road and the other. From dawn until late at night the entire Persian Market stood at roll call. The days were warm and the tar melted on the roofs. Then the rains came and a sharp wind blew. Early mornings became piercingly cold. Then good weather returned. Freight cars kept arriving without a break at the loading ramp, and the people were still walking. Frequently, we would get up in the morning and be unable to go out to our work site because the roads were blocked by them. They walked slowly, in loosely formed groups, holding each other's hands. Women, old men, children. They were walking on the other side of the wires, turning their silent faces toward us. They looked at us with pity and tossed us bread through the wires.

The women removed their watches and threw them at our feet, showing us with gestures that we should take them.

The orchestra played fox-trots and tangos near the gate. The camp looked on at the people who were walking. Man has a narrow range of reactions to great emotions and violent passions. He expresses them with the same ordinary, tiny responses. He uses the same simple words.

"How many of them have gone by already? It's almost two months since the middle of May, so counting twenty thousand a day . . . Around a million!"

"They didn't gas that many every day. But who the hell knows, with four chimneys and a couple of pits."

"Figure it this way: from Kosice and Munkács, almost six hundred thousand, what's the use of counting, they brought them all, and what about from Budapest? That'll be around three hundred thousand?"

"Do you even care?"

"*Ja*, but then it'll probably end soon? They're exterminating all of them."

"There won't be a shortage."

You shrug and look at the road. Behind the mass of people the SS men walk ever so slowly, smiling kindly and urging the people to keep moving. They indicate that it's not far now, and pat an old man on the shoulder when he runs over to the ditch, hurriedly pulls down his trousers, and squats.

The SS man shows him the crowd disappearing into the distance. The old man nods, pulls up his trousers, and hobbling in a funny way, runs after them.

Amused, you smile, seeing another man who is in such a hurry to reach the gas chamber.

After that we went to the warehouse to once again tar the leaking roofs. There were mountains of clothes piled up there and backpacks that were still in good shape. The treasures collected from the people who were walking lay on top, not protected from sun or rain.

We lit a fire under the tar and went to do some organizing. One of us brought over a bucket of water, another a sack of dried cherries or prunes; someone else brought sugar. We cooked up a compote and carried it up to the roof for the men who were pretending to work. Others fried up bacon and onions and chewed on cornmeal bread.

We stole everything we could get our hands on and brought it to the camp.

From the roofs there was a clear view of the burning pyres and the working crematoriums. A crowd would go inside, undress, then the SS men would quickly shut the windows, screwing them down tight. After a couple of minutes, not long enough to coat a sheet of tar paper properly, they would open the windows and side doors and air the place out. The Sonderkommando would arrive and drag the corpses onto the pyre. And so it went from morning to night, beginning anew every day.

Sometimes, after a transport had been gassed, trucks arrived late with sick people and their nurses. It didn't pay to gas them. They were stripped naked and Oberscharführer Moll either shot them with a small-caliber rifle or shoved them alive into the burning pit.

Once, a young woman who didn't want to leave her mother arrived by car. They were both undressed in the chamber; the mother went first. The man who had to lead the daughter stopped, struck by the wondrous beauty of her body, and scratched his head in amazement. Seeing this simple, human gesture, the woman relaxed. Blushing, she clutched his arm.

"Tell me, what are they going to do to me?"

"Be brave," replied the man, not trying to free his arm.

"I am brave! You see, I'm not ashamed in front of you! Tell me!"

"Remember, be brave, and go on. I'll take you there. Just don't look."

He took her by the hand and escorted her, covering her eyes with his other hand. The crackling and stench of burning fat and the heat rising from the pit frightened her. She jerked away. But he delicately bent her head down, revealing her neck. At that moment, almost without taking aim, the Oberscharführer fired. The man pushed the woman into the burning ditch, and as she fell, he heard her horrible, broken scream.

When the Persian Market, the Gypsy camp, and the FKL filled up with women selected from among the people who were walking, a new camp, Mexico, was opened across from the Persian Market. It was just as unfinished, and in just the same way the block elders' huts were fitted out with electricity and windows.

One day was like another. People emerged from the freight cars and walked, along one road and the other.

The people in the camps had their own worries: they were waiting for parcels and letters from home, they were organizing for their friends and lovers, conspiring with other people. Nights followed days, rains came after dry spells.

Toward the end of summer, the trains stopped coming. Fewer and fewer people were walking to the crematorium. The people from the camp felt an emptiness at first. Then they grew accustomed to it. After all, other important events were happening: the Russian offensive; Warsaw taking up arms and burning; transports departing the camp every day to the west, to the unknown, to new sickness and death; the revolt in the crematoriums and the Sonderkommando's escape, which ended with the execution of the escapees.

Then people were flung from camp to camp, without a spoon, without a bowl, without a rag for their bodies.

Human memory retains only images. And today, when I think about the final summer in Auschwitz, I see the endless, colorful crowd of people, ceremoniously heading down one road and the other, the woman standing with her head bowed over the burning ditch, the red-haired girl against the background of the dark interior of that block, screaming at me impatiently:

"Will men be punished? But in a human way, normally!"

And I still see before me the Jew with rotten teeth walking over to my bunk every evening and, lifting his head, asking the same thing:

"Did you get a parcel today? Maybe you'll sell some eggs for Mirka? I'll pay you in marks. She is so fond of eggs . . ."

Farewell to Maria

FAREWELL TO MARIA

I

Behind the table, behind the telephone, behind the cube that contained the office ledgers, there's a window and a door. In the door there are two panes of glass, black and lustrous from the night. And also the sky, the window's backdrop, covered with fluffy clouds that the wind nudges down toward the windowpanes, toward midnight, beyond the walls of the burned-out building.

The burned-out building looms black on the other side of the street, directly opposite the narrow gate in the metal security fence topped with silvery barbed wire along which the violet reflection of a blinking streetlight glides like a musical note along a string. Against the backdrop of a stormy sky, to the right of the building, swathed in milky clumps of floating smoke from the locomotives, a leafless tree is silhouetted pathetically, motionless in the fierce wind. Loaded freight cars pass it by, clattering as they press on to the front.

Maria lifts her head from her book. A streak of shadow lies across her forehead and her eyes and flows along her cheek like a transparent scarf. She rests her hands on the mushroom-shaped lamp that stands among the empty bottles, the plates with leftover salad, the round-bellied, crimson wineglasses with their dark blue stems. As if sinking into a carpet, the bright light refracted in the edges of these objects sinks into the blue smoke that fills the room, splashes off the delicate, fragile rims of the glasses, and glitters inside the wineglasses like a golden leaf in the wind; it streams into her hands while they, like an illuminated rosy dome, close firmly over it, and only the even rosier lines between her fingers pulse almost imperceptibly. The dim little room fills with an intimate darkness converging in her hands and becomes as small as a shell.

"Look, there's no boundary between light and shadow," Maria whispers. "Shadow creeps up to our feet like the incoming tide, surrounds us, and contracts the world so there's just the two of us—and here we are, you and I."

I bend down to her lips, to the tiny cracks concealed in their corners.

"You pulse with poetry like a tree with sap," I say jocularly, shaking an insistent, drunken noise from my head. "Watch out, or the world will wound you with an ax."

Maria parts her lips. The dark tip of her tongue trembles gently between her teeth; she's smiling. As she tightens her fingers around the lamp, the gleam deep within her eyes dims and goes out.

"Poetry! For me, it's as incomprehensible as hearing a shape or touching a sound."

She leans back, deep in thought, against the arm of the settee. In the half-shadow her close-fitting red sweater acquires a crimson lushness; it shines bright red and fluffy only where the light slides along the edges of its folds.

"But only poetry can faithfully depict a man. I mean, a complete man."

I drum my fingers on a wineglass. It responds with a faint, fleeting sound.

"I don't know, Maria," I say doubtfully, shrugging my shoulders. "I think that the measure of poetry, and perhaps of religion, too, is the love they awaken in man for man. And that is the most objective test of all."

"Love, yes, of course, love!" says Maria, narrowing her eyes.

Outside the window, behind the burned-out building, on the wide street divided by a plaza, the streetcars are screeching. Electric flashes light up the violet of the sky; they cut through the darkness like flakes from a dark blue magnesium fire; they bathe the building, the street, and the gate in moonlight and, grazing the black windowpanes, flow down the glass and silently burn out. A moment later the high, thin song of the streetcar wheels also fades away.

Behind the door, in the other room, they've cranked up the phonograph again. The muffled melody that sounds as if it's being played on a comb merges into the insistent shuffling of dancing feet and the throaty laughter of young women.

"As you see, Maria, there's another world in addition to us," I laughed, and got up from the settee. "It's like this, you know. If it were possible to understand the whole world, to feel the whole world, to see the whole world, as one understands one's own thoughts, feels one's own hunger, sees a window, the gate outside the window and the clouds above the gate, if it were possible to see everything simultaneously and definitively, then," I say pensively, circling the couch and stopping beside the hot stove between Maria and the majolica tiles and the sack of potatoes that we'd purchased during the autumn for the winter, "then love would be not only a measure but the definitive instantiation of all things. Unfortunately, we rely on the method of trial and error, on lonely, misleading experience. What an incomplete, what a false, measure of things that is!"

The door to the room with the phonograph opened. Tomasz entered, swaying to the beat of the music and leaning on his wife's shoulder. Her slightly pregnant-looking belly, the same matronly size for many months now, was the focus of their friends' unceasing curiosity. Tomasz walked up to the table and swayed above it with his shaggy, round head, massive as that of an ox.

"You're not trying hard enough, there's no vodka," he said reproachfully but gently after carefully inspecting the dishes, and sailed away toward the door, propelled by his wife. He looked at her blankly, as if appraising a painting. People said that that was his professional gaze since he traded in forged Corots, Noakowskis, and

Pankiewiczes. He was also the editor of a syndicalist biweekly and was considered a radical leftist. They stepped out onto the squeaking snow. Clouds of icy vapor swirled over the floor like fluffy skeins of white cotton.

Following on Tomasz's heels, dancing couples staggered majestically into the office, spun dreamily around the table, the tiles, and the potatoes, carefully avoiding the damp spots under the windows, and then, leaving behind red stains from the freshly waxed parquet floor, returned to where they'd come from.

Maria jumped up from the table, straightened her hair with her characteristic gesture, and said, "I've got to go now, Tadeusz. The manager asked us to get started earlier."

"You still have at least an hour," I replied.

The round office clock with its bent metal face, suspended on a long string between a partially unrolled poster, a drawing of an imaginary horizon, and a charcoal composition depicting a keyhole through which a fragment of a cubist bedroom could be seen, ticked off the minutes.

"I'll take the Shakespeare; I'll work on *Hamlet* tonight for our Tuesday class."

She went into the other room and knelt in front of the books. The bookcase had been nailed together clumsily out of unplaned boards. The boards sagged beneath the weight of the books. Blue and white stripes of smoke hung in the air, and there was a heavy odor of vodka mixed with the reek of human sweat and the smell of whitewash from the damp, moldy walls. Brightly painted cardboard panels hung from them, fluttering like laundry in the wind and, like the ocean's depths, projected colorful outlines of jellyfish and coral. In the black window, separated from the night by a pane of glass and entangled in the fine lace of the curtain that a railroad thief had been tricked into selling for pennies, a despondent, drunken violinist (who believed that he was impotent) was struggling in vain to drown out the phonograph's wheezing with the moaning of his instrument. He was hunched over as if under the weight of a sack of cement, and kept extracting a single passage from his violin with gloomy obstinacy. He'd been practicing for two hours for the Sunday poetry and music concert. He always appeared at those concerts freshly bathed, in his best striped suit; his face was melancholy and his eyes sleepy, and he seemed to be reading the notes from the air.

On the table, on the red-flowered tablecloth that we'd obtained by swindling a woman thief who worked the railroad, surrounded by wineglasses, books, and half-eaten sandwiches, lay the naked, dirty feet of Apoloniusz. Half-drunken people, gasping like fish on sand, lounged on the wooden settee, which had been painted with lime to repel bedbugs. Apoloniusz, rocking back and forth in his chair, turned to face the settee and said in a loud voice, "Would Christ have been a good soldier? No, probably a deserter. At least the early Christians ran away from the army. They didn't want to oppose evil."

"I oppose evil," said Piotr lazily. He was sprawled out between two disheveled girls, pawing their hair. "Either take your feet off the table or wash them."

"Wash your feet, Polek," said the girl next to the wall. She had big fat thighs and red, fleshy lips.

"But you'd have wanted to! You know, there was once a very cowardly tribe of the Vandals," Apoloniusz droned on, pushing the plates into a pile with his foot. "Everyone slaughtered them, and they were driven out of either Denmark or Hungary to Spain. There, the Vandals boarded ships, sailed to Africa, and reached Carthage on foot, where the bishop was Saint Augustine, the one who was Saint Monica's son."

"And then the saint rode out on an ass and turned back the Vandals," said a young man who was sitting beside the stove, smoking a pipe. He puffed out his chubby pink cheeks, covered, just like peaches, with golden fuzz. He had large black-and-blue bruises under his eyes. A pianist, he had been living for a long time with a woman pianist who had enchanting dimples and a predatory, passionate gaze. We had baptized him that summer (because he belonged to the independent Polish National Catholic Church) in front of burning candles, bunches of flowers, and a basin of cool water from the chapel, with which a prescient priest carefully bathed his head, and then immediately after his baptism, on the busiest stretch of Grójecka Street, we managed to escape a roundup. We took our time marrying them; that happened only in late winter. Her parents refused their blessing, considering it a mésalliance. True, they relented and gave the musicians a room to sleep in and a piano to practice on, along with a kitchen in which to produce homemade spirits, but they weren't willing to invite the couple's friends to the wedding, so the friends arranged the wedding celebration themselves. The bride, wearing a stiff, blue dress, sat motionless in an armchair, looking as if she had swallowed a poker. She was sleepy, exhausted, and drunk.

"It's nice here, very nice, you know?" A Jewish girl who had escaped from the ghetto and had nowhere to sleep that night knelt down beside Maria near the books and put her arm around her. "It's strange, I haven't held a toothbrush, a sandwich, a glass of tea, or a book for so long. You know, it's hard even to describe it. And that constant feeling that you have to get away. I'm terrified!"

Maria silently stroked her birdlike head, crowned with shining waves of slicked-down hair.

"You were a singer, weren't you? You probably didn't lack for anything."

The girl was wearing a yellow frock with a chrysanthemum pattern and a provocative décolleté. The cream-colored lace of her slip peeked out of it coquettishly. A gold cross dangled from the long chain between her breasts.

"Lack? No, I didn't lack a thing," she replied, with a glint of astonishment in her teary, cowlike eyes. She had broad, wide-set hips, good for giving birth.

"You have to understand, even the Germans treat artists differently. . ."

She stopped abruptly and grew pensive, staring dully at the books.

"Plato, Thomas Aquinas, Montaigne." She fingered the frayed spines of the books, which had been purchased from peddlers and stolen from used-book stores. Her nails were painted with dark red polish.

"Only, if you had seen what I saw behind the walls . . ."

"Augustine wrote sixty-three books! When the Vandals laid siege to Carthage, he was in the middle of correcting proofs and he died working on them!" Apoloniusz declared maniacally. "Nothing of the Vandals has been preserved, but Augustine is read today. Ergo," he raised his hand toward the ceiling, his fingers outstretched, "the war will pass, poetry will remain, and so will my vignettes!"

Beneath the ceiling, draped over ropes, the covers for a slim volume of poetry were drying. Thick printer's ink dripped from them. Light shone through the black and red layers of wrapping paper and became entangled among the sheets of paper as if in a wooded thicket. The covers rustled like dry leaves.

The Jewish girl went over to the gramophone and changed the record.

"Yes, but I think there'll be a ghetto on the Aryan side, too," she said, casting a sideways glance at Maria. "Only there will be no way out of it."

She floated away, swept into the dancing by Piotr.

"She's upset," Maria said softly. "Her family remained inside the walls."

The needle hit a crack in the record and began playing the same note over and over. Tomasz stood in the doorway, red-faced. His wife smoothed her dress over her slightly rounded belly.

"'Only a few more heavy clouds remain, not yet snorted away by a horse's nostril,'" he declaimed, quoting Norwid. And pointing at the gate beyond the window, he cried out with feeling, "A horse, a horse!"

In the circle of golden light from over the door the blindingly white, smooth snow lay like a plate on a gray tablecloth; farther off, in shadow, it looked gray and dark blue, as if reflecting the sky, and finally, right next to the wicket, it was transformed in the glow of the streetlight. Loaded up like a hay cart, a wagon was standing there motionless in the darkness, like a mountain. A red lantern swayed under its wheels, casting swaying shadows on the snow and illuminating the legs and belly of a horse that seemed taller and more muscular than normal. Clouds of steam rose from the horse, making it seem as if he were breathing through his skin. His head drooped; he was exhausted.

The driver stood beside the wagon and waited patiently, slapping his hands against his chest. When Tomasz and I dragged open the two halves of the gate, he reached for his whip without undue haste, shook the reins, and clicked his tongue. The horse lifted its head, strained with its entire body, but the wagon didn't move. The front wheels were caught in the gutter.

"Whip him, damn it, and back up," I said knowingly. "I'll lay a board across the gutter in a minute."

"Back up!" the driver yelled, pressing on the shaft.

A gendarme in a blue coat who was guarding the building next door, a former public school now crammed full like a prison with "volunteers" for labor in Prussia, walked over to us from the direction of the streetlamp, his hobnailed boots resounding dully on the stones of the sidewalk. He had a searchlight dangling from a strap across his chest. He switched it on and politely shone the light for us.

"There's too much stuff in this load," he said matter-of-factly. From under the deep shadow cast by the peak of his helmet his eyes glittered sharply like a wolf's above the beam of light. He came into the office every morning to use the telephone after his shift was

over, and he always reported the same thing: that nothing important had happened during the night.

The horse snorted, settled its weight on its hind legs and pushed
backward, and the wagon moved back onto the cobblestones. Now
the horse strained forward. The wagon, rocking like a flat-bottomed
boat and loaded to the brim with suitcases, bundles, bedding, furniture, and jangling aluminum pots, drove over the boards and into the
courtyard. The gendarme switched off his searchlight, straightened
his straps, and walked off with measured steps in the direction of the
school. Usually, he would walk past it, go as far as the little church of
the Pallottine Fathers (partially burned down in September 1939 and
painstakingly, continuously, under repair throughout the season with
materials from our firm), and turn back near the decaying wall of the
shelter for the unemployed, which was housed in the vacated factory
depots alongside the railroad track. It was a busy transfer port for,
singly or by the bale, blankets, supply vouchers, warm clothing, slippers, canned goods, dinnerware, curtains, tablecloths, and towels all
flowed through there, as well as all sorts of goods that had been stolen
from the freight trains headed for the front or had been purchased
from the staffs of the ambulance trains, which, returning from the
front with watches, food, the wounded, linen, and machine parts,
furniture and grain, often stopped at the station as if at a wharf.

The driver cracked his whip again for the fun of it, got the
horse to back up, and backed the wagon into the wooden shed.
The horse's sides were heaving, and steam was rising from him.
Unhitched with a kind of rough affection by the coachman, he
stood inside the shafts for a while looking utterly exhausted, then
finally, urged on harshly, he moved slowly to the faucet and dipped
his face into a bucket. He drank it down to the bottom, then slurped
water from a second bucket and, dragging his harness behind him,
headed over to the open doors of the stable.

"You've brought us a lot, Olek," I said, after looking over the
stuff on the cart.

"She told me to take everything," said the coachman. "Look, I even loaded up the kitchen stools and the bathroom benches. The old lady was standing over me like an executioner over a good soul."

"She wasn't afraid to do it in broad daylight?"

"Her son-in-law got his colleague to authorize her," said Olek. He had a bony face, thin, pinched by the frost. He threw his cap down. His shaggy hair, stiff with lime, stuck up above his forehead.

"And her daughter?"

"She stayed with her husband. She had a fight with the old lady about having to stay another day."

He spat into his sinewy, twisted hands, corroded by cement, lime, and gypsum.

"All right, I'll start unloading."

He climbed onto the cart, untied the ropes, and began handing down, one after the other, chairs, vases, pillows, baskets of bed linens, old-fashioned boxes, books tied together with string. Tomasz and I caught them, and the two of us carried them into the moldy, dark shed, setting the goods down on the concrete floor amid sacks of half-calcified cement, a stack of black roofing paper that stank of pitch, and a pile of dry lime intended for retail sale to peasants. The lime rose into the air as a fine dust and burned our nostrils excruciatingly. Tomasz was gasping for breath. He had a weak heart.

"Tell me, sir, why has the manager taken her in?" the coachman asked after he finished unloading.

"She made him a man; it's to express his gratitude."

I slid the shed door shut and locked it with a padlock.

"Gratitude is a beautiful thing," said Tomasz. He took measured breaths, drawing the air down deep. He grabbed a fistful of snow and washed his hands with it, then wiped them on his trousers.

"Man . . . , did I work today," the driver said as he climbed down from the cart. It was hard for him to move in his stiff sheepskin, which was covered with a layer of lime, pitch, and wood tar.

He leaned against the cart, blew his nose with relief, and wiped his forehead with his hand.

"Pan Tadek, what I saw there, Pan Tadek, you wouldn't believe. Children, women . . . It's true, they're Jewish, but still, you know . . ."

"But somehow you managed to drive out without incident?"

"The engineer saw us in the street. Will it be a problem?"

"What can those nincompoops do to us?" I said disdainfully. "If the manager wants to buy a branch office, he's got to treat them well, doesn't he? You'll set off on your route in the morning. A meter of lime under the counter. You'll come back before seven."

"All right then, in the morning I'll have to muck out the pit. I'll go groom the horse now."

He shuffled to the stable, following in the animal's traces. As he passed the office, he tipped his hat.

Maria was standing inside the golden circle of light as if in a halo, embraced by the hands of dark blue night sparkling with its ring of stars. She had closed the door behind her, shutting out the music and the people, and was peering expectantly into the darkness. I brushed the dust off my hands.

"How are you going to handle the bottling and distribution tomorrow?" I took her arm and accompanied her to the narrow gate along the creaking, brittle snow of the trampled-down path. "Can you wait till noon? We'll distribute it together."

We stood in the open narrow gate. Along the empty street, opened up by the flickering light of the streetlamp, the gendarme in his blue overcoat was pacing with a heavy tread, guarding the school. Above the street, above the streetlamp's light, above the steep roof of the shed nestled into the wall, the wind noisily carried smoke from the trains and chased the feathery clouds, while above the wind and the clouds the sky trembled, as deep as the depths of a dark torrent. The moon shone through the clouds like a golden tract of sand.

Maria smiled tenderly.

"You know very well that I'll distribute it myself," she said re-provingly, giving me her lips to kiss. Her large black hat shaded her face like a wing. She was half a head taller than me. I didn't like her kissing me in front of strangers.

"You see, you poetic solipsist, what love can do," Tomasz said cheerily. "Because love is sacrifice. I speak from profound experience, since I've had many lovers."

Twilight, which erases a man's features, lent him solidity and weight, as if Tomasz were a rough-hewn rock. The black mole under his left eye looked playful on his monumental face, which seemed to have been carved from gray sandstone.

"Of course it's love!" Maria burst out laughing happily, and making us a dignified curtsey, she set off down the street along the wire fence, in the direction of the clouds which the wind was chasing above our heads. She passed the black marketeer's shop, where I purchased bread and blood sausage for my breakfast, and where peasants redeemed their children who were locked up in the school. She disappeared around the corner without looking back. I kept watch for a while longer, as if tracking her footsteps in the air.

"Love, of course it's love!" I said, smiling at Tomasz.

"Give the driver some vodka, if you've got any under your bed," said Tomasz. "Go on; you should fraternize with the common people."

II

It snowed a little that night. Having sent my drunken guests on their way and straightened up the room, I officially opened the gate as a sign that the trading day had begun. The driver, who had risen at dawn, had already shoveled the lime out of the pit, transported it to the construction site, returned from that trip, unhitched the horse, and smoothed over the wheel tracks in the plaza. This early in the morning it was still dark blue outside, and the street was empty. We could hear the clatter of trains on the railroad tracks. The gendarme on patrol grew grayer and smaller in the retreating darkness that left him behind like a strand of forgotten seaweed on the shore of a street that was emptied of people. Heads of the imprisoned people started appearing in the windows of the former school. In the black marketeer's shop, near the storeroom, two blue policemen* were warming themselves near the red-hot stove. Blinking his red eyes drunkenly, the shopkeeper, his hands trembling, was laying out cheese, kasha, and bread on the glass-enclosed counter. A peasant woman was pulling loops of kielbasa out of her basket; they disappeared inside a double wall beneath the counter. Gray dawn was seeping in through the frozen windowpanes. Filthy drops flowed down the rusty grates, dripped monotonously onto the windowsill, and trickled onto the floor.

Day after day, in summer, autumn, winter, and spring, the street—a blind alleyway paved with cobblestones, stinking from the filth in the open gutters, and lost between a field as boggy as a rotted corpse and a row of decaying two-story buildings that housed a laundry, a barber shop, a soap factory, a couple of grocery stores, and a pitiful bar—swelled with a surging, weaving crowd that flowed up to the concrete walls of the school, craned to look at the modern windows, at the roof covered with red tiles, lifted its head, waved its hands, and yelled. From the open windows of the school, people shouted and signaled with their white hands as if they were on a ship moving away from the shore. The crowd, trapped as in a dam between the two rows of policemen, flowed away through the trough of the street, walked as far as the square at the street's outlet from where there was a pleasing view of the river's litter-strewn sandbars, dotted with clumps of tattered reeds and covered here and there with mangy patches of snow, the bridge above the fog that

---

* "Blue policemen"—Polish policemen employed by the German occupying authorities.

rested on the twinkling current, and the yellow and pastel houses of the city dissolving in the peaceful, clear, azure sky. Desperate, the crowd surged in the square and turned back again with a cry.

The black market shop was a small cozy bay. At the counter, policemen fraternized with peasants over a glass of home brew distilled from beets and came to terms on the price of the people in the school. The police would shove the goods out the school windows at night, and the people would either vanish immediately into recesses along the street or, cutting themselves painfully, would crawl through the barbed wire into our construction firm's yard, where they would wander around until morning since the office was closed, of course. As a rule, the goods were girls. They roamed aimlessly through the courtyard, checking out the piles of sand, mounds of clay, cubes of stacked bricks, piles of sawdust, leather splits, firebricks; they walked over to the mounds of crushed gravel, various shades and sizes of which were used for stairs and gravestones, and relieved themselves there unabashedly. I would show them the other side of the gate very altruistically when I woke up, and other than the policemen (and probably also the unapproachable gendarme, who had no understanding of simple human needs) the only person who profited from this procedure was my neighbor, the shopkeeper. However, he felt neither a sense of obligation nor the need to be grateful. Day in and day out, I would drop into his shop for a quarter loaf of dark bread, a hundred grams of blood sausage, and twenty grams of butter. He made a habit of not giving me the full weight and he rounded off the price for his own benefit. He gave me an embarrassed smile, but his hand trembled when he took the money.

Furthermore, he always poured out less than a full measure of home brew, he never weighed out a full ten grams of butter, he cut the bread into uneven pieces, and he squeezed money mercilessly out of the peasants for every girl released illegally, since he himself wanted to live, he had a wife, a son in the second year of high school, and a young daughter—a student in an underground lyceum class who was experiencing the seductive allure of clothing, the attractiveness of boys, the taste of knowledge, and the enchantment of conspiracy. The construction firm, in contrast, sold wet potter's clay and calcified cement to peasants and engineers alike; it mixed water into the lime, and sand into the adhesive, and also, whenever it accepted freight-car loads of goods, it declared serious shortages which were immediately entered into the ledgers with the warehouse clerk's unspoken understanding. The official purveyor kept his mouth shut; he had personal accounts with the firm that were not entered into any books.

The construction firm! Like a patient milk cow it distributed sustenance to everyone. In order to support his fanatically religious wife, who squandered money on beggars, churches, and monks, and his erotomaniac son, the firm's legal owner—a potbellied man encased in a tight-fitting checked vest and a watch chain, a patriarchally gray-haired, apoplectically nervous engineer with a goatee— squeezed from the firm like milk from udders many thousands of zlotys during periods of great hunger (when we were eating potato peels and rationed bread with salt); he built more warehouses at his headquarters, rented a yard from a firm that burned down in September and established a branch of his own business there, bought a carriage fit for a nobleman, a team horse with a docked tail, hired a coachman, acquired an estate on the outskirts of the capital for half a million though, to be sure, it was somewhat neglected and run-down but suitable for hunting (it included a large forest tract) and industrial development (it had clay), and finally, in the third year of the war, initiated and successfully conducted negotiations with the German Eastern Railway about purchasing and constructing his own railway siding and erecting transshipment warehouses next to it.

The fates of the engineer's workers turned out just as auspiciously. True, the occupation laws prohibited the engineer from paying wages of more than seventy-three zlotys a week; the engineer, however, on his own initiative gave a dozen or so of his people almost one hundred zlotys a week without deducting costs, taxes, and services. In emergencies, such as the deportation of a family to a concentration camp, illness, or a street roundup, he never shirked his duty. For three months he financed my studies at the underground university, setting only one condition: that I should study for the Fatherland.

The branch office was run differently. The drivers sold lime on the street, carting short measures to the building site. They developed their own private routes. They stole from the railroad. At first, I used to carry clay and chalk from the warehouse in a basket and sell it in the neighboring soap works; however, as I developed closer relations with the manager, I entered into a partnership with him, shared my sales territory, and came to an agreement with him on the bookkeeping. We were also bound to each other by the production of home brew, which took place in the manager's apartment, but at my cost. Having given me the lion's share of the retail sales, the manager immersed himself in far-flung business deals, using the firm as a transit point and the warehouse telephone as a reliable means of communication. The manager was knowledgeable about gold and jewelry, bought and sold furniture, knew the addresses of apartment brokers, and even dealt in apartments himself; he had ties with the railroad thieves and arranged contacts for them with consignment stores; he befriended drivers and people who sold automobile parts, and he also carried on a lively exchange with the ghetto. He engaged in trade with great fear, as if forcing himself, despite his own sense of what was right. He felt bitterly nostalgic for the safe, prewar times. He had worked as a warehouseman then in a Jewish enterprise. Under the eye of the vigilant proprietress he doggedly improved his lot at other people's expense, purchased a sports car and earned up to three hundred zlotys a day from this taxi, not counting the driver's wage. He soon acquired a building site adjacent to the highway and close to the city, and a couple of months before the war, another site in a nearby suburb. He understood that he was doing this in accordance with a human right, and he lived life to the full, without any gnawing spiritual doubt. He had managed to salvage some of his possessions from those days: his properties and hard currency, as well as a deep attachment to the elderly doctor's widow.

The old lady was sitting in Maria's place at the foot of the wooden settee. Her face was sallow, worn, empty, like a depopulated city. She wore a black silk dress, threadbare, its elbows shiny. She had a wide velvet ribbon around her neck, and on her head was an old-fashioned hat adorned with a bouquet of violets from beneath which protruded strands of thin, gray hair. She held on her knees a carefully folded overcoat with a mangy collar. She was dressed too poorly to have been the prewar owner of an enormous store of building supplies, a couple of trucks, her own railway siding, dozens of workers, and an inexhaustible account in Polish and Swiss banks; too poorly even to be the owner of a cart for transporting all sorts of baggage, or the many precision adding machines that had been hastily and farsightedly handed over to the Swiss consulate for safekeeping, not to mention the gold and diamonds that—according to what people on the Aryan side imagined—every Jew carried out of the ghetto. She was dressed like a poor woman; she sat modestly in a corner. Her gaze was fixed just below the ceiling, on a spiderweb on the top bookshelf. The spiderweb was swaying because the spider was climbing higher.

"Jasieńku, they'll telephone, won't they?" the old lady said to the manager after a long silence.

Surprised, I raised my head from a book about medieval times and superstitions. She spoke in a hoarse whisper, like a rock grating against a rock. A whistling whisper escaped from her throat with every breath. Two massive gold rows of teeth sparkled in her mouth; it seemed as if they were snapping closed, almost even clanging.

"Because they ought to let us know if they're coming. Isn't it true that they ought to?" She turned her faded, dead, seemingly frozen eyes on him.

"The best thing to do would be to wait a while, ma'am," the manager said decisively. He diligently blew on the ice-covered pane to create a clear area, and tilting his head, looked sideways out of one eye at the square, the open gate, the street, which was already teeming with crowds of people. He drummed his fingers on the window frame; he was waiting for a customer.

"After all, the director promised he'd telephone. He'll probably come out today together with your daughter."

"You're only saying that, Jasio. But what if they don't make it, Jasieńku?" She transferred her gaze once more from the ceiling to the window. She placed her withered, gnarled, wormlike hands on her yellow kerchief, clenched her fingers as if she wanted to rip the kerchief from her shoulders, then weakly let them drop onto her knees.

"What can you possibly be saying, ma'am!" the manager whistled incredulously. He smoothed his thick, golden, wavy hair, tossing it back with an impatient movement of his head. As a result of this gesture, a gold Longines wristwatch—elongated, convex, fitted to the circumference of his wrist, a souvenir from the good times in the firm on Towarowa Street—emerged from under his poplin cuff.

"What can you be thinking?! Your son-in-law, a director in the workshops, can come out when he feels like it! He'll take care of whatever needs to be done, a wallet into a pocket, and that's that! You'll see! Why are you so worried about them getting out?"

He pulled over a chair and sat down, comfortably stretching out his legs in their tall officer's boots.

"You have to think instead about where can you buy an apartment. Do you know what they're asking, ma'am? Fifty thousand! It's a good thing a person bought himself a little corner during the first year of the war, or what would he do now? Live as a tenant in someone else's apartment? Become a lodger?"

"You know how to manage, Jasio!" the doctor's wife whispered and gave a slight smile with the corners of her mouth.

"A person, praise God, has hands and feet, he thinks how and where he can snap up something, and therefore he's alive! Pan Tadzik," he leaned over to me, "your fiancée prepared twenty-five liters. A frugal girl! I could kiss her! And she burned only half the coal. She's hardworking, there's no denying it!"

"She phoned," I stammered from behind my book. "She went into town to distribute the spirits. She ought to be back soon."

It was quite dark, but warm between the stove and the coat tree. My back tickled deliciously in the warmth. My head felt heavy and there was a buzzing noise inside it. I was feeling the effect of the vodka and eggs. The book about medieval monasteries provoked daydreams about dark cells where, among the superstitions of the common people, the slaughter of tribes, and conflagrations of cities, the work of saving the human spirit was taking place.

"Jasieńku, are the suitcases in good order?" the old lady whispered hollowly, as if from the bottom of a well. "You know that's all that my daughter owns now. She's so lacking in resourcefulness. She was accustomed to being taken care of by her mother."

Warming myself beside the stove, I stared at the floor. The blanket draped over the settee didn't reach the red-polished floorboards. The black cover of the Remington could be seen underneath it. I had taken the typewriter from the shed to keep it from getting wet and had placed it under the settee, just in case.

"Everything has to be just so here, ma'am." The manager rubbed his hands out of habit and looked over at me for a moment. "In the most proper order, just like in an insurance company. Don't you know me?"

"But what if they can't find me here? The street is so tiny and located in the outskirts."

The old lady was suddenly getting anxious.

"I'll phone them," she decided, and bestirred herself on the settee.

"Have you gone mad in your old age?" the manager erupted and angrily narrowed his sincere blue eyes, almost covering them with his straw-colored eyelashes. "Bring the Germans down on our heads? Let them eavesdrop? Go ahead, but not from here!"

The old lady took fright and puffed up like a suddenly awakened owl. She crossed her arms over her chest as if she was cold. She mechanically fingered the brooch on her dress.

"How did you make your way to us, ma'am?" I asked, in order to keep the conversation going.

The office door slammed. The customer stamped his feet, knocking the snow off his boots. The manager kicked his chair and went out to greet the customer. The old lady fixed her empty eyes on me.

"I have been in a street blockade twenty-seven times. Do you know what a blockade is? You aren't sure? Never mind," she said in a voice hoarse with emotion, waving her hand in a friendly way. "We had a hiding place in a special niche behind a wardrobe. Twenty people! The little children were trained, so when the soldiers came and banged their rifle butts against the walls and when they fired their guns, the children just kept silent and watched with wide-open eyes, you know? Will they manage to get out?"

I walked over to the bookshelf. I slipped my book in among the medieval books. I looked around at the old lady.

"The children?" I asked, astonished.

"No, no, no! The children are over there! What about the children? My son-in-law and daughter, will they come out? He's great friends with the boss. Since his university days in Heidelberg."

"Why didn't he come out with you?"

"He's got business there. Another day, two days . . . Everything's coming to an end there. *Aus, aus, aus* all the time! The buildings are empty, there are feathers in the streets, and they keep taking the people away, taking them away . . ."

She ran out of breath and fell silent.

From the other side of the door, raucous, bantering voices could be heard. The customer and the manager had agreed on a price for the delivery of wood from the vacated Jewish houses in the Otwock ghetto, which the local Kreishauptmann had sold as a single lot to the Polish entrepreneur. The door creaked and they went across to the store to seal the transaction with a drink. The manager was a teetotaler, but he allowed himself to be seduced on particularly profitable occasions.

"I'd like to get at my things," the old lady said suddenly. She swept the coat off her knees and hastily stumbled outside.

The office clerk smiled at me from behind her desk. Petite and lean, she fit comfortably on her stool. She read popular romances all day long. The engineer had sent her to watch the cash register. His calculations showed that the firm was producing too little profit. During the second week she was in the office, two thousand zlotys were missing from the cash register. The manager covered the shortage out of his own pocket, and the engineer lost faith in the clerk. In fact, she came into the office for only a few hours at a time, never once looked in at the warehouse, did not know the difference between adhesive and asphalt, but with the regularity of a post office she kept me supplied with conspiratorial leaflets adorned with the emblem of the Sword and Plow organization.* I envied her her access to the underground; I myself had to be contented with my semiprivate duplicating of bulletins, with wide-ranging reading, poetry writing, and performances at poetry matinées.

---

* The Sword and Plow movement (*Miecz i pług*) was a Christian-nationalist, anti-Nazi, and anti-Communist underground organization, most of whose original leaders had been killed by 1941.

"What's with that old lady? Does she have a lot of furniture?" the clerk asked ironically. Her head was coiffed into an upsweep of unruly, piled-up hair.

"Everyone saves himself however he can."

"With the help of his fellow human beings."

She screwed up her eyes maliciously. She was very carelessly powdered. Her narrow nose shone as if it had been cleaned with tallow.

"Hey, Mister Warehouseman, how are the poems? Has the cover dried?"

The manager led the old lady into the office by the hand. The driver came in to warm up. He squatted near the stove and, wheezing, held out his wind- and frost-cracked hands toward the fire. His sheepskin coat emitted steam and stank of damp leather.

"There are big trucks in the city," the driver said. "I was at headquarters. The streets are empty; it's terrifying to drive there. People say that once they're done with the Jews, they'll be deporting us. They're carrying out roundups on our streets, too. Near the Orthodox church and at the station it's practically green from all the gendarmes."

"How lovely," the little clerk snapped. She stood up nervously from her desk. She shuffled her feet in their too deep felt slippers, unconscious of how charmingly she rotated her bony hips which protruded through her thin frock. "How am I going to get home?"

"*Per pedes*," I said acidly, and hastily pulling on my jacket, I walked out of the office. A biting wind mixed with snow slashed at my face. A worker was swaying rhythmically over a barrel of lime. Stamping his feet from the cold like a sleeping horse, he was stirring the slaked lime with a hoe. Clouds of white steam rose above the boiling mixture and shrouded his face. The slaker worked all winter long without a break, readying the lime for the summer season. Working in the frost, he prepared up to two tons of dry lime every day.

The manager pulled the warehouse gate to. Whenever a roundup surrounded our street, we locked the gate with a padlock. The drunken policemen would sweep the street of whatever remained of the crowd that had fled toward the fields. The German gendarme, above the crowd and its worries, but alert to the policeman's every move, apathetically pounded his iron boots on the pavement. In the square next to the walls of the buildings it was still noisy and crowded. Under the windows and parapets the peddlers' knees were shaking; they stamped their feet in their straw clogs and squabbled hoarsely over their baskets of rolls, cigarettes, blood sausage, doughnuts, white and dark bread. It seemed as if the black wall of the building itself was shaking and yelling. Inside the various entryways fresh pork was being weighed on crude scales and home brew was dispensed in haste. A fair was still in progress on the lot behind the school. A carousel with one stupefied child on a horse was revolving majestically to the accompaniment of shrill music. Empty wooden cars, bicycles, and swans with wings spread wide drifted peacefully in the air, rocking as if on the crest of a wave. Workmen walked on the treadmill underneath the carousel, hidden from view by the floorboards. Near the garishly painted shooting gallery and under a tent in the zoo (in which, as a snow-bleached sign announced, there were supposed to be a crocodile, a camel, and a wolf) it was hopelessly empty. A few newspaper vendors from the shelter, with piles of German newspapers under their arms, loitered indecisively at the streetcar stops. Streetcars with no passengers turned around at the terminus in the square and, their chains clanging, lumbered down the avenue. The trees were snow-covered, sparkling in the sharp sunlight as if they were carved from fragile crystal. The sky was calm, pale, high. It was an ordinary market day.

At the far end of the street the stone blocks of apartment houses and clumps of bare, skinny trees closed off the open space. Beyond the viaduct, which was protected by wooden barricades, tangles of wire, and signs on the tracks, and surrounded by a cordon of gendarmes, the crowd moved in waves, flowing toward the viaduct. Bulging, canvas-covered trucks emerged from the crowd and headed toward the bridge, their wheels struggling against the snow. As the last truck passed, a woman ran out from the crowd. She didn't make it. The truck gathered speed. The woman lifted her arms in a gesture of despair and would have fallen were it not for the helpful arm of a gendarme. He shoved her into the crowd.

"It's love, obviously, it's love," I thought with a rush of emotion, and fled to the warehouse because the square was emptying ahead of the approaching roundup.

"Your fiancée telephoned," the manager said. He was in a good mood; he was humming beneath his red moustache and tracing dance steps with his feet. "She's on her way from Ochota, but she can't go any faster, because they're rounding up people everywhere. She'll be here by evening."

The lean clerk with the upswept hair cast a quick, malicious glance in my direction.

"They'll start treating us just like the Jews, don't you think? Are you worried?"

"She should be able to manage somehow," I said to the manager. I was frozen to the bone. I raked the ashes in the stove and added some peat. Smoke billowed into the room through the open stove door. "It seems we won't be getting any freight cars this month? They'll surely place a hold on freight cars?"

The manager made a disgusted face. He sat down on a chair and tapped the table with his delicate fingers, like a pianist's.

"And what good will it do if they let the freight cars through?" he said bitterly. "The engineer is afraid of stocking cement and gypsum, he keeps lime on hand only for the Germans for their work at Fort Bem, so what do you want? That we should flourish? The Grochów Works got three carloads of cement, Borowik and Srebrny have whatever their hearts desire, and what do we get?

Ridge tiles, tongue-and-groove boards, crushed gravel, adhesives, reed matting!"

"Don't exaggerate," said the clerk. "If they were to poke around in the sheds, they'd find a thing or two . . ."

"That's right, a thing or two! Because I'm doing my own wheeling and dealing! Would anyone come to the warehouse otherwise? Of course, the shopkeeper would, to borrow our weights!"

The telephone rang. The manager turned around on his chair and grabbed the receiver half a second before the little clerk could reach it. He handed it to me with a silent gesture.

"Our truck," I whispered, shielding the mouthpiece with my hand. "What should I say?"

"Charge him fifty."

"*Fünfzig*," I said into the mouthpiece. "*Abends?* All right, then; in the evening."

"Splendid; in that case, let's get something to eat." The director rubbed his hands.

The old lady was sitting motionless on the settee like an animal that's been chased into a corner. The manager fussed around the room, put some bouillon on the hot plate, and cleared the table.

"When the engineer starts making less of a profit from us, number one, he'll throw out that *shiksa*, and number two . . . So, have you made up your mind?"

"What have I got compared to you?" I said despondently. "We invested everything in our home brew. You know how it is; we bought some books, some old clothes, and so on. The paper also costs money."

"Will you at least sell the poems?"

"I don't know if I'll sell them. I didn't write them for sale. They're neither hollow bricks nor asphalt," I replied, offended.

"If they're good, people should buy them," the manager said amicably, biting into a roll. "You should put those couple of thousand into our partnership. You've got a good head."

The old lady ate slowly, but with a good appetite. The massive golden row of teeth sank into the soft interior of the roll with pleasure. I stared at their brilliance, instinctively calculating the weight and the value of the whole jaw.

The door slammed and a customer entered. A Pallottine Father from the neighboring church, he wore horn-rimmed glasses and smiled timidly. After informing us about the roundup, he ordered a couple of sacks of cement and yellow crushed gravel. He paid in advance with zlotys tied together to form a small packet.

"God be praised," he said, and putting on his black hat, he walked out, his soutane swishing.

"For ever and ever," the clerk replied. She cranked the stove and wiped her fingers on a scrap of newspaper.

"What do you think, what's the old lady going to do?"

"The manager will find her an apartment. The old lady has too much dough for him to let her slip through his fingers," I said in a half-whisper.

She snorted contemptuously.

"So, you don't know anything? When the manager went out, the old lady telephoned her daughter. They can't get out of the ghetto. It's too late already. The whole place is under *Sperre*; it's locked down."

"The old lady will grieve for a while and then she'll stop."

"Very likely."

She wrapped her worn fur coat around her, arranged herself more comfortably on the stool, and returned to her book. She didn't betray any desire for further conversation.

III

In the evenings I remained alone in the warehouse among the covers for my volume of poetry that were hung up to dry like wet linen. Apoloniusz had cut them out of paper in an *in folio* format adapted to the dimensions of the screen of the hand-cranked duplicating machine that had been lent to me so I could copy priceless radio communiqués and valuable advice (accompanied by diagrams) on how to conduct street battles in large cities; it also served to print the sublimely metaphysical hexameters that expressed my disdainful attitude toward the apocalyptically blowing wind of history. The cover was decorated on both sides with black-and-white vignettes, thanks to a sensational new duplicating technique: individual sheets of an egg white–based stencil were pasted onto the screen to produce the white areas, while the screen itself produced the black parts. The technique was really clever, but it soaked up way too much ink, and the covers had been drying for a week—without result. So I carefully removed them from the strings, wrapped them in thick parchment, packed them up securely, and placed them under the wooden settee. The blanket, pulled down to meet the floor, covered a broken radio, which was awaiting a mechanic; the portable duplicating machine, flat as a cigar case; the sturdy Remington typewriter, which I had brought inside from the shed so it wouldn't get wet; and a complete set of a certain imperialist organization's publications that had been left for safekeeping in the warehouse by a friend who had to leave his house but couldn't muster the strength to get rid of his antiquarian collector's passions.

Also in the evenings, not sparing my back or my knees, I would diligently polish the floor, wipe the table, and more or less clean the window, and when I felt that the little room was as snug and cozy as could be, I would cover the glowing mushroom-shaped lamp with a willow-green lamp shade and carefully close up the room to get some warmth into it. I usually sat near the stove in the office. I was making detailed bibliographical notes with which I stuffed special boxes; I wrote down on separate note cards profound thoughts and apt aphorisms that I found in books, and then committed them to memory. In the meantime, dusk would be gathering and sprinkling the pages of my book. I'd glance up to watch the door and wait for Maria.

Outside the window the snow had lost its azure hue, mixing with the dusk as if with gray cement. The towering wall of the burned-out building, russet-colored like damp brick, was becoming engorged with blackness; it stood motionless, as if it had fallen silent. A silent wind was sweeping up puffs of rosy smoke from the tracks, tearing them to shreds, and flinging them into the dark blue sky like snowflakes into clear water. Ordinary objects—the firm's mountain of sand, mushy as a rotten melon, the winding path, the gate, the sidewalks, the walls and buildings on the street—were disappearing in the darkness as if swallowed up by rising floodwaters. All that remained was the imperceptible sound that echoes in the deepest silence, the burning pulse that beats in a human body, and the profound longing for objects and emotions that one will never experience.

People were still moving about in the courtyard. The coachman was carrying packages out of the dark interior of the shed as if he were pulling them out of a sack and flinging them into the cart. The old man who did the slaking was standing in the cart, his feet planted wide apart. Groaning, he caught the baggage and skillfully rammed it into the wagon as if he were arranging sacks of gypsum or slaked lime. The effort caused him to thrust out his cheek with his tongue.

The manager was standing behind the wagon next to the old woman. He had grabbed one of the boards on the wagon and was mechanically digging out a splinter from it with his fingernail.

"I know nothing about it, I've been taught differently," he said to the old woman angrily, curling his lips. "But the way I see it, it shouldn't have been done this way from the beginning. Where's your head? Your common sense? What was the point of all this commotion?"

The old woman tilted her head in its flower-bedecked hat toward her shoulder. The frost had brought out beet-colored splotches on her ashen cheeks. Her lips were quivering from the cold. Her gold teeth glittered from behind her lips.

"Be very careful with the packing," she said sharply to the old man. Her face quivered with every hurled package, as if it were she who was being flung into the cart.

"Forgive me, Jaś, for causing you trouble," she addressed the manager. "You have made it worth your while, haven't you, Jaś?"

"What can you possibly be thinking, ma'am," said the manager, shrugging his shoulders. "I used the money I took to pay for the apartment, and as for those few old clothes that you left with me, you can always . . . I'm not going to grow rich on them."

Beside the gray wall of the shed, the hunched-over old doctor's widow, her feet shod in thin, worn-down slippers, shifted from one foot to the other in the cold; she blew her nose and, as near-sighted people do, looked at the manager with teary eyes, blinking her reddened lids. She kept silent and smiled.

"You're protecting a lot of them there. Either way, it's a bloody mess," the manager continued, looking at the ground, at the spokes of the wheel, and the mud beneath the wheels. "Don't you know what's going to happen? They'll kill them, burn them, destroy them, crush them, and that's that. Isn't it better to live? It's my belief that there will come a time when they'll allow a man to do business in peace."

A diesel-powered tractor trailer rolled into the street, spewing smoke, and drove up to the gate. The manager smiled with relief and rushed to open the other shed, while I jumped up and ran straight across the snow to the gate. The tractor backed up onto the opposite sidewalk and, like a beetle crawling out of a gutter and into the courtyard, drove up to the open shed. The driver, wearing a dirty coverall and a German forage cap that sat jauntily on his shining, raven-black hair, jumped out of the cab.

"*Abend.* Fifty?" he asked, and slapping his hands together with a flourish, walked into the shed, his hips swaying. He looked around with interest.

"Oh, ho ho! So you've cleared out everything?" he said, smacking his lips. "A large turnover, a large profit. But now it's ten zlotys more for a sack. Thirty-five each?"

"Can't do," said the manager, spreading his hands wide in an eloquent gesture.

"Thirty-two. On the market they're fifty-five and even higher," the soldier said patiently.

"Does he have people to do the unloading?" the manager asked me. "We'll have to get some."

"*Keine Leute,*" the soldier smiled broadly. "No people." He had healthy horse teeth and gleaming, carefully shaved cheeks. He walked over to the trailer, untied the tarpaulin, and issued a command: "*Meine Herren, raus!* I'm asking you nicely, *ausladen!*"

Two workmen, who had been napping on sacks of cement, flung aside the coats they had covered themselves with and, terrified by his shout, jumped out of the truck and lowered the cover. One dragged the sacks to the edge of the truck bed; the other caught them in his arms one by one, hugged each flat sack to his chest, carried it into the warehouse, and threw it with a crash onto the floor. I explained to him the right way to stack cement, tying down the bags so the damn pile won't collapse.

The driver's assistant, who was napping in the cab of the trailer, leaned out the window.

"They have to hurry, Peter. We've got to get moving."

He propped himself up on his elbows and gazed sleepily into the shed. A woman's gold bracelet hung loosely around his wrist. He had hairy hands and a swarthy face that looked black because of his unshaven beard.

"Faster, faster, *du alte Slawe,*" he muttered through clenched teeth. Meeting my inquiring gaze, he smiled amiably.

Inside the shed, one of the workmen, covered with powdery cement (someone who doesn't know how to handle the goods will always rip a couple of sacks while unloading them and cause damages), raised his silvery, cement-covered face to me and asked in a whisper, pretending to rub his eyes with the back of his hand, "There are five extra sacks. Will you take them today?"

"At twenty each," I mumbled without moving my lips. "*Komm* to the office. We'll settle accounts," I said to the soldier. He blew out a match and carefully ground it under his sole. He greedily inhaled the smoke. The faint rosy glow illuminated his cheeks and was reflected in his eyes.

"*Fünfzig* sacks? Fifty?" He showed the laborer five widespread fingers.

"*Ja, ja, chef,* I'm counting! Not one sack more!" the man who was handing down the cement shouted enthusiastically from under the tarpaulin.

The driver had finished loading the wagon. The lime slaker was stuffing in the last pieces of baggage and tightening the ropes. They tied down the load as carefully as if it were a package containing glass. They were masters at packing. They concealed the more valuable pieces in the center, the leather suitcases and canvas sacks filled with linens, while on top and on the sides they placed woven baskets, tables, dilapidated pots and pans. The wagon stood there as patiently as an ark. The old lady shuffled over to the shed, keeping her hands in her muff. Catching sight of the soldier approaching, she panicked and hid behind the warehouse door.

"A move?" the truck driver asked in passing.

"Of course, a move; what else could this be?"

The sky seemed to huddle together, settling down onto the darkness without so much as a rustle, like a falling bird. The leafless tree above the track struggled furiously with the wind, like a man who has decided not to give himself up.

"You certainly lead a peaceful life," the soldier said with good-natured contempt. "And our men are fighting for your peace."

The manager asked him to sit down. He was talking with his wife on the telephone.

"So was the dinner a success, or not? Beets—no. Take cabbage." He smiled knowingly. "The kid? He's sleeping? Wake him up, he's been sleeping for two hours."

"You've got a load of books, eh?" said the soldier, opening the door to my room. "Oh, what a setup! All you need is to turn on the record player! A little lady, eh, a little lady?" He pointed to the red robe on the coat hanger. He glanced at Apoloniusz's paintings—the woman beggar beneath the rough wall, holding the hand of a child with protruding eyes, and the still life with yellow jug. He brought his soldier's mud and stench into the room.

The manager dug out of his briefcase a carefully wrapped packet of banknotes, counted them out in a prayerful whisper, and handed them to the truck driver.

"Wednesday again, next week, *ja?*" the driver asked.

"*Ist gut,*" the manager said, "*ist sehr gut.* You see, Tadzik, if a man had his own warehouse, he wouldn't have to hide his goods. He could hold onto it for a couple of days and make a guaranteed profit."

"Our clerk will run immediately to the engineer to report on us."

"He won't believe her if he doesn't find anything . . . We'll pass it on to the Czerniaków works right away. Even then, the engineer has to treat us well. He's put a lot of dough into that siding, and he's having a rough time with it," the manager boasted.

"Do what you can to buy the building. I'll invest whatever I have."

"And what if they absolutely forbid any construction?"

"It's forbidden now, but people are still building. If you survive, you'll survive on what you've got in that drawer. The yard and the sheds will still be here after the war. As you found them. All right, let's go and see the old lady off."

"She left some machines in your room," the manager said. He combed his hair with his hand and with a touch of elegance placed a streetcar driver's cap on his head. In the street he pretended to be a streetcar driver. He traveled by streetcar without having to pay and felt protected in the event of a roundup.

"The typewriter will come in handy for the firm."

"*Ja, ist gut.*" The soldier finished counting the money, tucked it into a pocket in his coveralls, shook our hands warmly but not effusively, and went outside, crunching the snow under his boots.

The wagon driver removed the horse's feedbag, lit the lantern, hooked it beneath the wagon, gathered up the reins, smacked his lips ceremoniously, and the cart, illuminated with a flickering bloody glow like a carnival wagon, moved out, creaking, past the gate, and plunged into the street as into a shaded avenue.

Between the bulging suitcases and a purple quilt the color of chapped lips that was securely tied down with a white curtain cord, protected above by a table that was propped at an angle, sat the old Jewish lady, curled up into a ball like a dog, with her feet tucked under her. The table's legs, jutting up toward the sky like dead stumps, bounced along with the tabletop with every jolt of the wagon, and seemed to be threatening the sky with vengeance. The old lady's eyes were closed, her head buried in her fur collar. Evidently, she had dozed off. A couple of ragged brats chased after the cart, hoping they'd be able to steal something.

The street was coming back to life with the evening. In the dark blue sky a yellow moon sailed toward the feathery clouds like a slice of pineapple, and its metallic glow fell on the roofs of the street, the shutters on the walls, the snow on the sidewalk that crunched like silver sheet metal. In front of the school, the handsome gendarme walked back and forth, all blue in the twilight. The laundry girls slipped past under the violet lantern and vanished in the shadow of the burned-out building. Policemen, fortified for their nighttime duty, were emerging from the shopkeeper's store. The bell in the chapel that had been renovated with our cement and lime began to chirp joyfully, like a child at play, startling the sleeping pigeons on the bell tower's parapet; with much beating of wings, they soared above the tower and drifted sleepily onto the rooftop like chrysanthemum petals.

The tractor with the cement carefully avoided the lime pits and left the courtyard, sounding its horn in farewell. I jumped into the trailer and pressed money into the laborer's outstretched hand.

"There were ten, ten!" he cried. The tarpaulin closed behind him.

"We had an easy time of it today," the manager said, belting his streetcar driver's coat. He tightened the belt firmly, exerting force, because he liked to appear thin. "You're going to be alone. What's keeping your fiancée?"

"I'm worried about her," I replied. "The roundup's gone on all day. They must have caught a lot of people."

"There's nothing you can do." The manager gave a deep sigh. "Your fiancée probably can't get here."

He put the piece of meat that he'd selected for tomorrow's dinner into his briefcase.

"Wait; I'll go buy something for supper. I feel like eating after this stupid day."

We walked out into the street, slamming the gate. The German tractor was blocking the end of the street; it shuddered and smoked. Pedestrians were crowding the sidewalk and looking at the square. A cart loaded with bedding was stopped near the gutter. The driver was waiting patiently for a chance to cross.

The evening was growing ever more dense. Beyond the black band of the field, over the silvery current of the river, the stone bridge stretched taut as a bow against the backdrop of the sky. On the opposite shore the black mass of the city was sinking into a boggy darkness. Above it, the high columns of search beams plunged their mercury light into the sky, flashed across it, and, like the arms of a marionette, dropped weakly to the ground. For a moment the world was reduced to a single street that pulsed like an open vein.

With a clanking noise, their headlights burning brightly, trucks crammed full of people came rolling down the street, almost spilling their loads as they hit the potholes. People's faces appeared from under the canvas, as white as if sprinkled with flour, and then disappeared in the darkness as if extinguished by the wind. Motorcycles, with soldiers in helmets astride them, emerged from under the viaduct, and like monstrous moths flapping their shadow wings, disappeared with a roar behind the trucks. The asphyxiating smoke of combustion engines hung over the roadway. The column was heading toward the bridge.

"They grabbed them near the Orthodox church," the shopkeeper said behind me. He placed his heavy hands on my shoulders. He gave off a smell of vodka and the stench of cheap tobacco. "May the earth open up and swallow them!"

"They're getting around to us," the policeman said gloomily, his strap fastened formally under his chin. He removed his cap and wiped his forehead with his sleeve. The red stripe imprinted on his bald head by his cap turned white in the cold. "Yes, that's how it is," he said through clenched teeth.

"Is that Jewish woman moving out of your place?" the shopkeeper asked confidentially. "So soon?"

"She's moving somewhere else."

"Then what will happen to the apartment?" the shopkeeper asked nervously. He bent over to my ear. "I've already spoken with people. The manager was supposed to make a down payment today."

"Then go find the manager," I replied impatiently, and shook his paws off my shoulders.

"Excuse me," the shopkeeper whispered. The light from a headlight passed over his face. He screwed up his eyes, fending off the glare. The headlight lit up the center of the street, and the shopkeeper's face was clothed in darkness.

"She's going back to the ghetto. She has a daughter there who can't get out."

"That's right," the shopkeeper said with conviction. "At least she'll die with her, like a human being . . ." He sighed deeply and stared at the street.

A traffic jam had developed where the avenue makes a turn. The column halted, the trucks pulled up close behind one another. Guttural pleas could be heard. The motorcycles pulled out from behind the trucks and illuminated the roadway with their search-lights—the streetcars, the sidewalk, and the crowd. The searchlights skimmed over people's faces as if they were moving over bleached bones; they peered into the black, blind windows of apartments; they took in the carousel with its green lanterns glowing, halted in midbeat with its gaudy rocking horses swaying on their cables, its swans with their gently outstretched necks, its wooden cars and bicycles; they probed the recesses of the horse plaza; they rubbed up against the zoo pavilion with its crocodile, wolf, and camel; they inspected the interiors of the streetcars halted there with their lights turned off; they swung left and right, like the head of an infuriated serpent; they turned back to the people, blinded them once again, and took aim at the trucks.

Maria's face, framed by the wide brim of her black hat, was white as lime. She raised her corpse-pale, chalk-white hands spas-modically to her breast, as if in a farewell gesture. She was standing in a truck, squeezed into the crowd, right next to a gendarme. She was looking intently at my face, like a blind woman, directly into the searchlight. She moved her lips, as if she wanted to cry out. She swayed, almost fell down. The truck shuddered, roared, and suddenly jerked forward. I hadn't the faintest idea what to do.

As I learned later, Maria, as an Aryan-Semitic Mischling, was deported in a Jewish transport to a renowned seaside camp and gassed, and her body most likely was turned into soap.

A DAY AT HARMENZE

I

The shade of the chestnut trees is green and soft. It sways gently across the still damp, freshly dug-up earth and, fragrant with morning dew, rises above our heads like a willow-green cupola. The trees form a tall row alongside the road and their crowns blend into the colors of the sky. An overpowering boggy smell rises from the ponds. The grass, green as plush, is still silvery with dew, but the earth is already steaming in the sunshine. It will be a hot day.

But the shade of the chestnut trees is green and soft. Covered in shade, I sit on the sand and tighten the connectors of the narrow-gauge railway with a large monkey wrench. The wrench is cool and fits comfortably in my hand. Every so often I strike the rails with it. A metallic, harsh tone resounds throughout Harmenze and returns from afar as a different-sounding echo. The Greeks are standing around me, leaning on their spades. But these people from Salonika and the vineyard-covered slopes of Macedonia are afraid of the shade. So they stand in the sunshine with their shirts off and bake their incredibly thin shoulders and arms that are covered with scabies and open sores.

"You're certainly working energetically today, Tadek! Good morning! Are you hungry?"

"Good morning, Pani Haneczka! Absolutely not. But I am pounding away on the rails because our new kapo . . . Forgive me for not standing up, but you do understand: the war, Bewegung, Arbeit . . ."

Pani Haneczka smiles.

"But of course I understand. I wouldn't have recognized you if I didn't know it was you. Do you remember how you ate the potatoes with their skins that I stole for you from the chickens?"

"Ate them? Pani Haneczka, I gobbled them up! Watch out, SS man behind you."

Pani Haneczka scatters a couple of handfuls of grain from her sieve for the chicks that come running toward her, but after looking around she waves her hand dismissively.

"Oh, it's only our boss. I've got him wrapped around my little finger."

"Around such a little finger? You're an amazingly resourceful woman."

And with a sweep of my arm I strike the wrench against the rails, drumming out a melody in her honor: *"La donna è mobile."*

"Don't make such a racket! Maybe you'll eat something after all? I'm on my way to the manor house now; I'll bring you something."

"Pani Haneczka, I thank you most kindly. I think you fed me enough when I was poor . . ."

". . . but honest," she retorts with gentle irony.

". . . or at the very least, not helpless," I parry as best I can. "But à propos helplessness: I had two beautiful cakes of soap for you, with the most exquisite name imaginable — 'Warsaw,' and . . ."

"And . . . they were stolen, as usual?"

"And they were stolen, as usual. When I had nothing, I slept peacefully. Now, no matter how I tie up my packages with string and wire, they're always untied. A couple of days ago someone organized a bottle of honey I had, and now the soap. But the thief's going to be in poor shape when I catch him."

Pani Haneczka bursts out laughing.

"I can imagine. What a child you are! As for the soap, you don't have to worry about it at all; I got two lovely bars from Ivan today. Oh, I almost forgot. Give this little package to Ivan. It's lard," she says, placing a small bundle under the tree. "Take a look, what lovely soap."

She unwraps the paper; it's surprisingly familiar. I walk over and take a closer look: etched into both pieces, which are as large as bars of Schicht soap, is a column and the inscription: "Warsaw."

Not saying a word, I hand her back the bundle.

"Indeed, it's lovely soap."

I gaze at the field in the direction of the scattered groups working there. In the farthest one, over by the potatoes, I catch sight of Ivan; like a sheepdog circling its flock, he is vigilantly patrolling his group of people, now and then shouting something that is inaudible at a distance, and brandishing a large peeled stick.

"Oh, but that thief's going to be in poor shape," I say, not noticing that I'm speaking to the air, because Pani Haneczka has already moved away and only calls out to me from a distance, turning around for a moment. "Dinner as usual, under the chestnut trees."

"Thank you!"

And I return to striking the wrench against the rails and tightening the loosened bolts.

Pani Haneczka creates quite a stir among the Greeks because sometimes she brings them potatoes.

"Pani Haneczka *gut*, *extra prima*. Is she your madonna?"

"What kind of a madonna!" I bristle, striking my finger with the wrench by accident. "She's an acquaintance, *camerade*, *filos*, *compris*, Greco bandito?"

"Greco niks bandito. Greco *gut* man. But why don't you to eat nothing from her? Potato, *patatas?*"

"I'm not hungry; I have enough to eat."

"You niks *gut*, niks *gut*," the old Greek, a porter from Salonika who knows twelve languages from the south, shakes his head. "We are hungry, eternally hungry, eternally, eternally . . ."

He stretches his bony arms. Under skin that is crusted with scabies and running sores, the muscles move amazingly clearly, as if detached from each other; a smile softens the strained facial features but fails to extinguish the fever lurking in the eyes.

"If you're hungry, ask her. Let her bring you something. But now get to work, *laborando, laborando,* because it's boring here with you. I'm going somewhere else."

"But the fact is, Tadeusz, you've done wrong," says an old, fat Jew, stepping out from behind the others. He lays his spade on the ground and, standing over me, declares, "After all, you, too, were hungry, so you are capable of understanding us. It wouldn't cost you anything if she brought a bucket of potatoes."

He draws out the word "bucket" slowly and dreamily.

"Bug off with your philosophy, Beker, and get busy with the ground and your spade, *compris?* But for your information: you're gonna be croaking, and I'm gonna finish you off, understand? You know why?"

"Why?"

"For Poznań. Or maybe it's not true that you were the Lagerältester in a Jewish camp outside of Poznań?"

"So, what of it?"

"And you didn't kill people? And hang them on a post for a stupid stolen bar of margarine or a loaf of bread?"

"I hanged thieves."

"Beker, they say your son's in quarantine."

Beker's hands convulsively clasp the handle of the spade, and his eyes begin to carefully measure my torso, neck, head.

"You, let go of that spade, and stop looking so menacing. Maybe it's not true that it's your son who put out an order to kill you for those people in Poznań?"

"It's true," he says dully. "And I hanged my other son in Poznań, only not by the arms but by the neck, because he stole bread."

"Beast!" I burst out.

But Beker, an elderly gray-haired Jew, somewhat given to melancholy, is already calm and self-controlled. He looks down at me and says, almost contemptuously, "How long have you been in this camp?"

"Oh, a couple of months."

"You know, Tadeusz, I really like you," he says unexpectedly, "but you haven't experienced real hunger, have you?"

"It all depends on what hunger is."

"Hunger is real when one person looks at another as something to be eaten. I have already experienced such hunger. Do you understand?"

And when I don't answer and only strike the rails with the wrench from time to time, glancing mechanically right and left to see if the kapo is coming, he continues.

"Our camp, over there, was a small one . . . Right beside a road. Well-dressed people walked along that road, women, too. On their way to church on Sunday, for example. Or young couples. Down the road was a village, an ordinary village. There, people had everything, just half a kilometer from us. And we had rutabagas . . . among us, man, people wanted to eat each other alive! And was I not supposed to kill the cooks who traded butter for vodka and bread for cigarettes? My son stole, so I killed him, too. I'm a porter, so I know life."

I look at him intently, with curiosity, as if he's some new person.

"And you, did you eat only your own portion?"

"That's different. I was the Lagerältester."

"Watch out! *Laborando, laborando, presto!*" I bellow suddenly, because an SS man on a bicycle has emerged from around a bend in the road and is riding past, peering at us intently. Instantly, backs bend lower, spades held at the ready are raised with difficulty, the monkey wrench strikes the rails.

The SS man disappears behind the trees, the spades drop and are still, the Greeks fall back into their habitual torpor.

"What time is it?"

"I don't know. It's still a long time till dinner. But you know, Beker, I'll tell you something in parting: there's going to be a selection in camp today. I hope that you and your running sores will go to the chimney."

"A selection? How do you know there's going to be one?"

"Why are you so terrified? It will happen, and that's that. You're afraid, eh? A taste of your own . . ."

I smile maliciously, delighted by the idea, and walk off humming a popular tune called "The Crematory Tango." The man's vacant eyes, from which all contents have suddenly disappeared, stare motionlessly straight ahead.

II

The rails of my little railroad stretched across the length and breadth of the field. I had extended one end of it to the pile of burned bones hauled in by truck from the cremo and submerged the other end in the pond where the bones are finally dumped; elsewhere, I rode them up a mountain of sand that will be spread evenly over the field in order to create a dry foundation for the overly boggy soil; in yet another spot, I laid them along an embankment of grassy earth that will be placed on the sand. The tracks run every which way, and where they intersect there is a gigantic iron turntable that turns now this way, now that.

A crowd of half-naked people is surrounding it, bent over, digging their fingers into it.

"*Hoch*, up!" I bellow, raising my arm encouragingly like a conductor for a better effect. The men tug once and then again, someone collapses heavily across the turntable, unable to remain standing, unsupported, on his feet. Kicked by his comrades, he crawls out of the circle and, raising his tear- and sand-stained face from the ground, groans, "*Zu schwer, zu schwer* . . . It's too heavy, colleague, too heavy . . ." He sticks his torn hand in his mouth and sucks at it greedily.

"To work, *auf*! Get up! Once more! *Hoch!* Up!"

"*Hoch-AHP!*" the crowd repeats in unison, bends down as low as they can, straining the muscles of their torsos and the arcs of their protruding backbones, jagged as a fish's spine. But their hands, in contact with the iron plates, hang loose and powerless.

"Up!"

"Hoch-AHP!"

Suddenly, onto this circle of strained backs, onto the bowed necks, the heads bent almost to the ground, onto the flaccid arms, a hail of blows rains down. A spade handle drums against foreheads, breaks the skin over bones, and groans hollowly against a stomach. There's a flurry of activity around the turntable. A hideous human scream suddenly erupts and then breaks off, and the turntable moves upward and hangs heavy over the men's heads, rocking back and forth, and then moves off, threatening to fall at any moment.

"You dogs," the kapo shouts at the people as they move away, "you'll see how I'm going to help you."

Breathing heavily, he wipes his hand across his swollen red face with its yellow spots, and follows them with a distracted, vacant gaze, as if seeing these people for the first time. Then he turns to me.

"You, railway man, it's hot today, isn't it?"

"Yes, hot. Kapo, we have to place the turntable near the third incubator, right? And what about the rails?"

"Run them straight out to the ditch."

"But there's an earthen wall there across the road."

"Then dig it up. It has to be done before noon. And you'll make me four stretchers for the evening. It's possible someone will have to be carried back to camp. It's hot today, isn't it?"

"Yes, hot. But, Kapo . . . Keep going, keep going with that turntable! To the third hut! The kapo is watching!"

"Railwayman, give me a lemon."

"Send me your Pipel. I don't have one in my pocket."

He nods a few times and walks off, limping. He's going to the manor house, to stuff himself. But I know that they won't give him anything there because he beats people. We put the turntable down. We extend the rails by dint of horrendous effort, pry them up with a pickax, tighten the bolts with bare fingers. Hungry, feverish figures, feeble, herded together, bloodied, drag themselves along. The sun rises high in the sky and bakes us more and more painfully.

"What time is it, colleague?"

"Ten," I say, not raising my eyes from the rails.

"My God, my God, still two hours till dinner. Is it true that there's going to be a selection in camp today, that we're going to the crematorium?"

Everyone knows about the selection by now. They are stealthily tending to their wounds to make them cleaner and smaller, ripping off bandages, massaging their muscles, sprinkling themselves with water in order to be fresher and more energetic for the evening. They fight hard, heroically, for life. Some are completely indifferent. Still living corpses, they move in order to avoid a beating, devour grass and sticky clay so as not to feel hunger, walk around in a stupor.

"All of us—crematorium. But all Germans will be *kaputt.* The war *fini*, all Germans—crematorium. All: women, children. Understand?"

"You understand, *Greco gut.* But it's a lie, there won't be a selection, *keine Angst*, don't worry."

I dig through the embankment. A light, handy spade does its work "by itself." The clods of wet earth yield easily and fly softly into the air. It is good to work when one has eaten a generous portion of bacon with bread and garlic for breakfast and washed it down with a can of condensed milk.

The Kommandoführer, a short, wizened little SS man in a disheveled shirt, is squatting in the meager shade of the stuccoed incubator. He has worn himself out sneaking around among the diggers. He knows how to inflict a painful blow with his riding crop. Yesterday he slashed me twice across the back.

"*Gleisbauer*, what's the news?"

I swish the spade and beat down the top layer of earth.

"Three hundred thousand Bolsheviks fell at Oryol."

"It's good, isn't it? What do you think?"

"Sure, it's good. Because just as many Germans died there. And the Bolsheviks will be here within a year, if it keeps on like that."

"You think so?" He smiles maliciously and asks the sacramental question: "Is it long until dinner?"

I pull out my watch, an old silver piece of junk with funny Roman numerals. I like it because it looks like my father's watch. I bought it for a package of figs.

"It's eleven."

The puny weakling stands up and calmly takes it out of my hand.

"Give it to me. I like it very much."

"I can't, because it's mine, from home."

"You can't? Then don't."

He raises his arm and hurls the watch against the wall. After which he sits down again in the shade and tucks his legs underneath him.

"It's hot today, isn't it?"

Without a word, I pick up the watch and begin whistling in a rage. First a fox-trot about jolly Joanna, then an old tango about Rebecca, then the "Varsovian" and Konopnicka's anti-German "Rota," and finally a repertoire of leftist songs.

I'm in the middle of whistling the "Internationale," repeating in my mind, "'Tis the final battle . . . ," when suddenly a tall shadow passes over me and a heavy hand falls onto the back of my neck. I lift my head and freeze. A gigantic, red, swollen face unfolds above me and the shaft of a spade hovers frighteningly in the air. An immaculate white-striped uniform is sharply outlined against the distant green of the trees. A small red triangle with the number 3277 sewn to the chest sways oddly and seems to grow before my eyes.

"What are you whistling?" the kapo asks, looking me straight in the eyes.

"It's some kind of international slogan, Kapo, sir."

"And do you know that slogan?"

"Well . . . just a little . . . from various places," I add warily.

"And do you know this?" he asks.

And in a hoarse voice he begins singing the communist *"Rote Fahne."* He throws away the spade handle; his eyes glisten uneasily. Suddenly he breaks off, picks up the stick, and shakes his head half contemptuously, half pityingly.

"If a real SS man had heard that, you'd be dead already. But that one . . ."

The puny weakling smiles broadly and genially from his place beside the wall.

"And you call this hard labor! You should have been in the Caucasus, like me!"

"Kommandoführer, we've already filled one pond with human bones, and how many were dumped here before this and how many went into the Vistula, neither you nor I can know."

"Shut your trap, you dog."

He stands up, moves away from the wall, and reaches for the riding crop he'd dropped.

"Take some men and go get dinner."

I throw down the spade and disappear around the corner of the incubator. From a long way away I can still hear the kapo's voice, hoarse and short of breath: "Yes, yes, they're dogs. Every last one of them should be killed. You are right, Kommandoführer."

I look back at them with hatred.

III

We go out along the road that passes through Harmenze. The tall chestnut trees rustle, the shade is even greener, but also somehow drier. Like dried leaves. It is the shade of high noon.

After we come out onto the road, we have to pass by a charming little cottage with windows framed by green shutters in the center of which are clumsily carved little hearts and white, partially drawn little curtains. Delicate roses of a pale matte hue climb beneath the windows and strange little violet flowers grow in miniature flowerpots. On the stairway with its little porch entwined with dark green ivy a little girl is playing with a large, surly dog. The dog, obviously bored, allows her to tug at its ears, and moves his head only to protect himself from the flies. The girl is dressed in a white little frock; she has sunburned brown arms. The dog is a Doberman with brown jowls, and the girl is the daughter of the Unterscharführer, the master of Harmenze. And this cottage with the little roses and dainty curtains is his home.

Before we come out onto the road, we have to cross a couple of meters of slimy, sticky mud, earth mixed with sawdust and soaked with disinfectant. This is to prevent us from bringing any infection into Harmenze. I carefully detour around this disgusting mess, and we crawl out together onto the road, where cauldrons of soup have been placed in a row. A truck has brought them from the camp. Each kommando has its own cauldron, marked with chalk. I circle around them. We got here in time; no one has stolen from us yet. We have to try it for ourselves.

"Good, take these five of ours; those two rows belong to the women, you mustn't cheat them. Aha, there it is," I declaim in a loud voice, and pull the neighboring kommando's cauldron over to our side and replace it with ours, which is half as full, and put new chalk marks on them.

"Take them away!" I shout loudly at the Greeks, who are agape at the procedure, which they understand completely.

"Hey, what are you doing exchanging those cauldrons? Wait! Stop!" yell the men from the other kommando, who are also coming to collect dinner, but are late.

"Who exchanged anything? Shut your trap, man!"

They come running, but the Greeks, dragging the cauldrons over the ground, groaning, cursing *putare* and *porka* in their language, shoving and urging each other on, disappear behind the barrier separating the world from Harmenze. I am the last to make it across, and I can hear the others, who are already at the cauldrons, hurling curses at me and lashing out at my family. But everything is as it should be: today I won, tomorrow they'll win, whoever comes first is the best. Our kommando patriotism never goes outside the bounds of sport.

The soup is bubbling away in the cauldrons. Every couple of steps the Greeks set the cauldrons down on the ground. They breathe heavily, like fish flung onto a bank, and stealthily lick from their fingers the sticky, hot goo oozing in thin streams from under the loosely fastened lids. I know the taste of it, mixed with dust, dirt, and sweat from one's hands, because I myself carried those cauldrons not so long ago.

They set down the cauldrons and look expectantly at my face. I walk over ceremoniously to the middle cauldron, slowly loosen the screws, for an endlessly long half-second hold my hand on the lid—and lift it. A dozen pairs of eyes grow dim with disgust: nettles. A watery, white liquid sloshes in the cauldron. On its surface float yellow globs of margarine. But everyone can tell by the color that underneath it lie stringy stalks of nettle, intact, not chopped up, with their rotten color and repulsive smell; that the soup is the same all the way down to the bottom: water, water, water . . . For a moment the world grows dark in the eyes of the men who are carrying it. I replace the lid on the cauldron. We carry the cauldrons down the hill in silence.

Now I cross the field in a great arc, walking toward Ivan's group, which is tearing up the surface of the meadow near the potatoes. A long line of men dressed in pasiaki stands motionless near the black earthen embankment. From time to time a spade moves, someone bends over, holds that position briefly, slowly straightens up, moves the spade and freezes in a half-turn for a long moment, in that unfinished motion, just like the animal known as a sloth. After a while someone else moves, waves his spade, and sinks into identically helpless stupefaction. They work with their eyes, not their hands. When an SS man or a kapo appears on the horizon or emerges from a niche where the damp shadow of fresh earth reigns, the man on watch scrambles out heavily, the shovels ring more animatedly, although for as long as possible they fly about empty, and limbs move as in a silent film, absurdly, angularly.

I come straight up on Ivan. He is sitting in his niche and carving decorations with a penknife into the bark of a stout pole: squares, squiggles, hearts, Ukrainian sayings. An old, respected Greek squats down beside him and puts something into Ivan's knapsack. I just manage to glimpse the white, feathered wing and red head of a goose with its strangely stretched-out neck, when Ivan, catching sight of me, throws his jacket over the knapsack. The lard in my pocket's gotten soft, and there's a nasty stain on my pants.

"From Pani Haneczka," I say abruptly.

"Did she say anything? Wasn't she supposed to bring eggs?"

"She told me to thank you for the soap. She liked it very much."

"*Khorosho*; very good. I bought it yesterday from a Jew in Canada. I gave him three eggs."

Ivan unwraps the lard. It's crushed, partly melted, and yellow. I feel nauseated at the sight of it, maybe because I ate too much bacon in the morning and it's still coming up on me.

"Oh, fuck! That's all she gave me for two pieces like that? She didn't give you any cake?"

Ivan looks at me suspiciously.

"You know, Ivan, she really did give you too little. I saw that soap."

"You saw it?" Ivan moves anxiously in the niche. "I have to go round up the men for work."

"I saw it. She did give you too little. You deserve more. Especially from me. I'll make an effort to pay you back."

For a moment we stare fiercely into each other's eyes.

IV

Sweet flag has grown up at the very edge of the ditch and on the other side, where a stupid, mustachioed guard with a couple of triangles on his arm marking his years of service is posted, grow raspberry bushes with pale leaves that look as if they are covered in dust. Murky water flows along the bottom of the ditch; some slimy, unidentifiable green creatures seem to have taken it over, and from time to time a wriggling black eel is scooped out together with the ooze. The Greeks eat it raw.

I straddle the ditch and drag my spade slowly across the bottom. I am careful about how I stand so as not to get my boots wet. The guard comes closer and watches in silence.

"What's going to be done here?"

"A dam, and then we'll clean out the ditch, sir."

"Where did you get such nice boots?"

My boots really are lovely: they are ankle-high with double, hand-sewn soles, decoratively stippled in Hungarian style. Friends of mine brought them to me from the loading ramp.

"I got them in the camp, along with this shirt," I reply, pointing to my silk shirt for which I paid something like a kilo of tomatoes.

"They're giving out boots like that in camp? Look at what I'm wearing."

He shows me his cracked, torn boots. The right one has a patch on the toe. I nod my head to show I understand.

"How about selling me your boots?"

I lift my eyes and look at him with infinite astonishment.

"How can I sell you camp property? How can I do that?"

The guard leans his rifle against a bench and comes closer to me, bending over the water, which reflects his figure. I reach for it with my spade and muddy his image.

"Everything is permitted, as long as no one sees. You'll get bread; I've got some in my haversack."

This week I received sixteen loaves of bread from Warsaw. Besides, for such boots you should get half a liter of vodka, that's for sure. So I smile empathetically.

"Thank you, but in the camp we get such portions that I am not hungry. I have enough bread and lard. But if you have too much bread, sir, then give it to those Jews who are working over there near the embankment. That one over there, who's carrying sod," I say, pointing to a skinny little Jew with bleary, tearing eyes. "He's a very decent lad. Anyway, these boots aren't any good, the sole's coming off."

There really is a crack in the sole. Sometimes I hide a couple of dollars in it, sometimes a couple of marks, at other times a letter. The guard bites his lips and looks at me, his brows knitted.

"What did they lock you up for?"

"I was walking down the street and there was a roundup. They caught me, locked me up, and brought me here. I'm completely innocent."

"You all say that!"

"That's not true; not all of us. My friend was arrested because he sang off-key; you understand sir, *falsch gesungen.*"

The spade, which I've been moving over the bottom of the muddy ditch all this time, catches on something hard. I scrape at it: a wire. I curse filthily under my breath while the guard, dumbfounded, looks at me.

"*Was falsch gesungen?*"

"Oh, it's a long story. Once in Warsaw, when they were singing church songs during Mass, my friend started singing the national anthem. And since his singing was terribly off-key, they locked him up. And they said they wouldn't let him out until he learned the notes. They even beat him, but nothing came of it; he'll almost certainly have to sit in prison until the end of the war because he's absolutely unmusical. Once, he even confused a German march with one of Chopin's marches."

The guard hisses something and walks off toward the bench. He sits down, picks up his rifle mechanically, and, fiddling with the lock, reloads it. He lifts his head, as if remembering something.

"Hey you, Warsaw guy, come here; I'll give you bread and you'll give it to the Jews," he says, reaching for his bag.

I smile as sweetly as I can.

The line we can't cross runs along the other side of the ditch, and the guards are allowed to shoot people at will. They get three days' leave and five marks per head.

"Unfortunately, we're not allowed to go over there. But if you wish, please throw the bread to me, sir, and I'll definitely catch it."

I adopt an expectant posture, but the guard suddenly puts the bag down on the ground, jumps up, and reports to the head guard who is passing by that "there have been no unusual events."

Janek, who's working next to me, a nice kid from Warsaw who understands nothing about the camp and, most likely, never will, is earnestly scooping out the ooze, depositing it carefully, evenly, on the other side, practically under the guard's feet. The head guard comes closer and looks at us the way you would look at a pair of horses who are pulling a wagon, or at grazing cattle. Janek smiles broadly at him and nods his head meaningfully.

"We're cleaning out the ditch, Pan Rottenführer; there's a lot of mud in it."

The Rottenführer stops and stares at the speaking prisoner with a look of amazement, the way you would look at a draft horse who had suddenly begun to speak, or a grazing cow who started singing a popular tango.

"Come here," he says to him.

Janek lays down his spade, jumps across the ditch, and walks over to him. Then the Rottenführer raises his hand and slaps him across the face with all his might. Janek rolls down toward the ditch, clutches at the brambles, and sails straight into the ooze. The water gurgles and I almost choke on my laughter.

Meanwhile, the Rottenführer says, "Who gives a shit what you're doing in this ditch?! You can do nothing at all. But when you speak to an SS officer you have to remove your cap and keep your hands at your sides."

The Rottenführer walks off. I help Janek crawl out of the mud.

"But why did I get hit? Why, why?" he asks, stunned, understanding nothing.

"Don't be in a hurry to volunteer," I reply; "and now go clean up."

We're just finishing up removing the ooze from the ditch when the Pipel arrives, sent by the kapo. I reach for my haversack, move aside a loaf of bread, some lard, an onion. I pull out a lemon. The guard watches me in silence from the other side.

"Pipel, come here. I've got it. You know who for."

"Great, Tadek. Listen, have you got something to eat? You know, something sweet. Or eggs. No, no, *I'm* not hungry, I ate at the manor. I got some omelet from Pani Haneczka. A terrific woman! Only she'd like to know everything about Ivan. But you know, when the kapo goes to the manor house, they don't give him anything."

"If he stops beating people, they'll give him something."

"Tell him."

"What good are you, Pipel? You don't know how to organize. Just look how some people can grab a goose and fry it in the barracks at night, while your kapo eats soup. Did he enjoy yesterday's nettles?"

The Pipel looks at me searchingly. He's young, but a very clever lad. A German. He was in the army, although he's barely sixteen. He was a smuggler.

"Tadek, just tell me straight out; after all, we understand each other. Whose trail are you setting me on?"

I shrug.

"Nobody. But pay close attention to the geese."

"Did you know that yesterday another goose disappeared, and the Unterscharführer beat the kapo in the face and was so angry he took away his watch? OK, I'm going and I'll keep an eye out."

We walk together, because it's time now for the dinner break. They're whistling fearfully from the direction of the cauldrons and waving their arms. People throw down their tools wherever they are. Spades stick up from the embankment. From every corner of the field exhausted men walk slowly toward the cauldrons, wanting to prolong the blessed predinner moment, the hunger they will satisfy in just a moment. Ivan's group is late, lagging behind the others. Ivan has stopped beside the ditch near "my" guard and talks with him for a long time. The guard gestures with his arm. Ivan nods. Shouts and cries urge him to hurry up.

Passing me, he blurts out, "It seems you won't reel in anything today."

"The day isn't over yet," I shoot back.

He darts a hateful, challenging glance at me.

V

In the empty incubator, the Pipel puts out plates, wipes the tables, and sets them for dinner. The kommando clerk, a Greek linguist, cowers in a corner, trying to look as small and inconspicuous as possible. His face, the color of boiled crab, with watery eyes that look like frog spawn, is visible through the kicked-in door. Outside, the prisoners are planted on a little square surrounded by a high earthen embankment. They're sitting in fives, by rows, and in larger groups—just as they were when they arrived. They sit with their legs crossed, backs straight, hands lowered to their hips. They are not allowed to move while dinner is distributed. Later, they will be able to lean back and stretch out on their neighbors' knees, but woe betide them if they should break formation. To the side, the SS men lounge in the shade of an embankment; they've nonchalantly laid their automatic pistols on their knees and are getting bread out of their backpacks and haversacks, spreading margarine on it attentively, eating slowly and festively. Rubin, a Jew from the Canada kommando, has sat down next to one of them and is quietly talking with him. He's taking care of business—for himself and for the kapo. The kapo himself, huge and red-faced, is standing near the cauldron.

We run with bowls in our hands like the most accomplished waiters. In absolute silence we hand out the soup; in absolute silence we forcefully yank the mess kits from hands that want to scrape up something more from the empty bottom, to prolong the moment of eating, to lick the bowl one more time, to stealthily drag their fingers over the bottom. The kapo has leaped away from the cauldron and into the ranks; he's noticed something. With a kick in the face, he knocks over a man who's licking a bowl; he kicks him once and then a second time in the belly and walks off, stepping on knees and hands, but carefully avoiding those who are eating.

All eyes are fixed on the kapo's face. Two more cauldrons: seconds. Every day the kapo delights in this moment. He is owed this complete power over people for his ten years in camp. With the end of his ladle, he points out who has earned seconds; he never makes a mistake. The better workers, the stronger and healthier, get seconds. A sick, weakened, wizened man has no right to a second bowl of water with nettles. It is forbidden to waste food on people who will soon be going to the chimneys.

Because of the office they hold, the Vorarbeiters are allotted two full bowls of soup with potatoes and meat, scooped up from the bottom of the cauldron. With my bowl in my hand, I look around indecisively, sensing someone's gaze fixed upon me. Beker is sitting in the first row; his protruding eyes are fixed greedily on my soup.

"Here, eat; maybe it will finally do you some harm."

He grabs the bowl from my hands in silence and starts eating greedily.

"Put the bowl down next to you for the Pipel to collect, or you'll get it in the mug from the kapo."

I give the other bowl to Andrei. He'll bring me apples in exchange for it. He works in the orchard.

"Rubin, what did the guard say?" I ask in a whisper, going around him toward the shade.

"The guard says they occupied Kiev," he answers softly.

I stop, astounded. He waves me on impatiently. I walk over to the shade, place my jacket under me to keep my silk shirt from getting soiled, and stretch out comfortably for a nap. We rest however we can afford to.

The kapo goes into the incubator and falls asleep after eating his two bowls of soup. Then the Pipel pulls a chunk of cooked meat out of his pocket, slices it onto his bread, and starts eating it ostentatiously in front of the eyes of the hungry crowd, accompanying the meat with bites of an onion, as if it were an apple. The men lie down in tight rows, one behind the other, cover their heads with their jackets, and fall into deep, restless sleep. We are lying in the shade. Across from us, a kommando of girls wearing white kerchiefs is lying down. They shout to us from afar and construct elaborate stories with signs. One or another man nods his head in comprehension. One of the girls is kneeling sort of sideways; her arms are straight up over her head, and she's supporting a large, heavy beam. Every minute or so, the SS man guarding the kommando lets out his dog's leash. The dog charges at her face, growling ferociously.

"A thief?" I wonder lazily.

"No. They caught her in the wheat field with Peter. Peter escaped," Andrei answers.

"Will she hold out for five minutes?"

"She'll hold out. She's a tough girl."

She doesn't hold out. She bends her arms, drops the beam, and collapses onto the ground, sobbing loudly. Andrei turns away and looks at me.

"You wouldn't have a cigarette, *Tadik*, would you? What a shame; that's life for you!"

Then he wraps his jacket around his head, stretches out comfortably, and falls asleep. I'm lying down to sleep, too, when the Pipel tugs at me.

"The kapo is calling you. Watch out; he's mad."

The kapo has just woken up; his eyes are red. He's rubbing them and staring into space.

"You."

He pokes his finger into my chest threateningly.

"Why did you give away your soup?"

"I have something else to eat."

"What did he give you for it?"

"Nothing."

He shakes his head in disbelief. He moves his enormous lower jaw like a cow chewing its cud.

"Tomorrow you won't get any soup at all. Those who have nothing else to eat will get it. Understand?"

"Fine, Kapo."

"Why didn't you make the four stretchers I ordered you to make? Did you forget?"

"I didn't have time. You saw what I was doing this morning, Kapo."

"You'll make them in the afternoon. And be careful that you don't end up lying on one of them yourself. I can do that to you."

"Can I go now?"

Only now does he look at me. He eyes me with the dead, empty gaze of a man torn out of deep thought.

"What is it you want here?" he asks.

VI

From under the chestnut trees a man's muffled cry reaches me. I gather up the wrenches and turnbuckles, stack the stretchers one upon the other, and call out to Janek, "Janek, take the box or mommy will be angry," and walk off toward the road.

Beker is lying on the ground. He's clearing his throat and spitting blood, and Ivan is kicking him wherever he can land a blow: in the face, in the stomach, in the groin . . .

"Look at what that snake has done. He's eaten your whole dinner! The damn thief!"

Pani Haneczka's mess kit is lying on the ground with what remains of the porridge. Beker is covered in porridge.

"I stuck his snout into the mess kit," Ivan says, breathing heavily. "You finish him off; I have to go."

"Wash the mess kit," I say to Beker, "and put it under the tree. Don't let the kapo catch you. I just finished making four stretchers. You know what that means?"

Down the road, Andrei is drilling two Jews. They don't know how to march properly, so the kapo broke two sticks over their heads and announced that they'll have to learn how. Andrei has tied a stick to each of their legs and is explaining as best he can, in Ukrainian: "You devil's spawn, you'd better learn, this is left and this is right, *links, links.*" The Greeks open their eyes wide and march in a circle, shuffling their feet over the ground in terror. A huge dust cloud rises high into the air. Near the ditch where the guard is stationed—the one who wanted my boots—our lads are working, "planing" the ground, delicately whipping it and stroking it with their spades, as if it were dough. They scream when people walk across it, leaving deep traces.

"Tadek, what's new?"

"Nothing; they've taken Kiev."

"Is that true?"

"A funny question!"

Yelling this out at the top of my lungs, I detour around them and walk along the ditch. Suddenly I hear a shout behind me.

"*Halt, halt, du, Warschauer!*"

And a moment later, unexpectedly in Polish, "Stop! Stop!"

"My" guard is running full tilt toward me on the other side of the ditch, his rifle lowered as if to storm my position. He is very excited.

"Stop! Stop!"

I stop. The guard climbs through the brambles, reloads his rifle.

"What did you just say? About Kiev? You are spreading political rumors here! You have a secret organization here! Number, your number, give me your number!"

Trembling with anger and outrage, he pulls out a strip of paper, spends a long time looking for a pencil. I feel something drain out of me. But I'm a little calmer.

"Excuse me; you didn't understand, sir. You don't understand Polish very well, sir. I was talking about the sticks that Andrei tied onto the Jews on the road. That's *kije*, sir, not *Kiev*. I said it was very funny."

"Yes, yes, sir. That's exactly what he said," a unanimous chorus confirms.

The guard aims his rifle at me as if he wants to reach me across the ditch with its barrel.

"You're crazy all the same! I'm still going to write you up as a political today! Number, number!"

"One hundred nineteen, one hundred nine . . ."

"Show it to me on your arm."

"Take a look."

I stretch out my arm with the number tattooed on it, confident that he can't see it from a distance.

"Come closer."

"I'm not allowed to. You can make your report, sir, but I'm not White Vanka."

A couple of days ago White Vanka climbed a birch tree that grew on the watch line in order to cut some branches for a broom. You can get bread or soup in camp for a broom. The guard aimed and fired; the bullet went through his chest at an angle and exited through the back of his neck. We carried the boy back to the camp.

I walk off in a bad mood, but Rubin catches up with me around the corner.

"Tadek, what on earth have you done? And what's going to come of it?"

"And what should come of it?"

"You're going to tell everything, that I'm the one . . . Oy, what have you done. How can you shout so loudly? You want to destroy me."

"What are you afraid of? We don't snitch."

"I know it and you know it, but *sicher ist sicher*. You, maybe you should give those boots to the guard. Don't you think he'll agree? *Nu*, I'll try having a little chat with him. So let it cost me. I've done business with him before."

"Oh, splendid; then he'll be able to report that, too."

"Tadek, I see blackness in front of us. You hand over your boots and I'll have a talk with him. He's a fine fellow."

"Only he's lived too long. I'm not giving him my boots; that would be a pity. But I have a watch. It doesn't work and the glass is broken, but that's what you're here for. In fact, give him yours, it didn't cost you anything."

"Oy, Tadek, Tadek . . ."

Rubin puts away the watch, and I hear a shout in the distance.

"Railway man!"

I race across the field. The kapo's eyes have taken on a menacing expression, and there's froth in the corners of his mouth. His hands, his enormous gorilla hands, are swinging, his fists nervously clenched.

"What did you trade with Rubin?"

"You saw, Kapo. You see everything, Kapo. I gave him my watch."

"Whaat?"

His hands start moving slowly toward my throat.

I freeze, terrified. Without the slightest movement ("He's a wild beast," the thought flashes through my mind), not taking my eyes off him, I burst out in a single breath, "I gave him the watch because the guard wants to report me as a political for carrying out secret work."

The kapo's fists slowly unclench and fall to his sides. His jaw drops slightly like that of a dog that is too hot. Listening to my answer, he waves the spade handle about indecisively.

"Go back to work. It seems they'll be carrying you back to the camp today."

At that very moment he makes an instantaneous move, leaps up to stand at attention, and removes his cap. I leap aside, struck from behind by a bicycle. I pull off my cap. The Unterscharführer, the boss of Harmenze, jumps off his bike, red with indignation.

"What is going on in this crazy kommando? Why are those men walking around there with sticks tied to them? This is work time!"

"They don't know how to march!"

"If they don't know how, then kill them! And do you know that another goose has disappeared?"

"Why are you standing there like a stupid dog?" the kapo snarls at me. "Andrei's got to teach them a lesson. *Los.*"

I fly down the path.

"Andrei, finish them off! Kapo's orders!"

Andrei grabs a stick and strikes one of them a hard blow. The Greek raises his hand to protect himself, lets out a howl, and collapses. Andrei places the stick on his neck, stands on both its ends, and rocks back and forth.

I quickly go on my way.

In the distance I can see the kapo and the SS man walking over to my guard and talking to him for a long time. The kapo gesticulates violently with the spade handle. His cap is pulled low on his forehead. After they leave, Rubin goes over to the guard. The guard gets up from the bench, approaches the ditch, then steps onto the dam. In a minute, Rubin nods to me.

"Thank the guard for not reporting you."

There's no watch on Rubin's wrist.

I thank him and walk back toward the shop. An old Greek, the one connected with Ivan, stops me along the road.

"*Camerade, camerade,* that SS man is from the camp, isn't he?"

"What of it?"

"Then there'll really be a selection today?"

And the gray, wizened Greek, a shopkeeper from Salonika, drops his spade and lifts his hands in bizarre exaltation.

"*Nous sommes les hommes misérables. O Dieu, Dieu!*"

His pale blue eyes are focused on the sky, which is just as blue and pale.

VII

We lift the cart. Filled to the brim with sand, it has come off the rails right at the junction. Four pairs of emaciated arms push the cart forward and backward, then swing it. They rock it, raise the front pair of wheels, set them on the rails. We place a spike under it, and the gondola is almost, almost back on the rails when suddenly we let go and straighten up.

"Assembly!" I yell, and whistle from a distance.

The gondola falls and its wheels dig into the ground. Someone flings down the useless spike and we pour the sand from the gondola right onto the junction. We'll have to clean it up tomorrow anyway.

We line up for *Antreten*. Only after a while do we realize that it's too early. The sun is still high in the sky. It still has a ways to go before it reaches the treetops on which it rests its nose at assembly time. It's three o'clock at most. The men's faces are anxious and questioning. We stand in groups of five, straighten out, tighten our backpacks and belts.

The clerk counts us over and over again.

SS men and our assigned guards are approaching from the direction of the manor house. They surround us. We are standing. At the rear of the kommando there are stretchers with two corpses.

There is more movement in the road than usual. The people from Harmenze are walking back and forth, made anxious by our early departure. But for the old camp inmates it's obvious: there will definitely be a selection in the camp.

Pani Haneczka's bright kerchief flashes by a couple of times.

The woman turns her inquiring eyes toward us. She puts her basket on the ground and leans against the barn, watching. I follow her glance. She is looking anxiously at Ivan.

The kapo and that runt of a Kommandoführer follow right behind the SS men.

"Stand apart from each other and raise your arms over your heads," the kapo orders us.

Everyone understands: a search. We unbutton our jackets, open our bags. The SS man is experienced and quick. He runs his hands over my body, reaches into my bag. Besides what is left of my bread, a couple of onions and some stale lard, there are apples, definitely from the orchard.

"Where'd you get these?"

I lift my head. It's "my" guard.

"From a package, sir."

For a moment, he looks me in the eyes ironically.

"I ate just the same apples after dinner today."

They gut our pockets and chunks of sunflowers, corn cobs, herbs, sorrel, apples fall out. Over and over, there's a sharp human scream: they're beating people.

Suddenly, the Unterscharführer walks into the very center of the ranks and pulls out an old Greek holding a large, stuffed bag.

"Open it," he says brusquely.

With trembling hands, the Greek opens the bag. The Unterscharführer looks inside and summons the kapo.

"Look, Kapo, our goose."

And he pulls out of the bag a goose with enormous, widespread wings.

The Pipel, who has also run over to the bag, cries out triumphantly to the kapo, "That's it, that's it. Didn't I say so?"

The kapo swings his stick.

"Don't beat him," the SS man says, holding onto his arm.

He pulls his gun out of his holster and turns to face the Greek, gesticulating eloquently with his weapon.

"Where did you get it? If you don't answer, I'll shoot you."

The Greek is silent. The SS man raises his pistol. I look at Ivan. He's gone absolutely white. Our eyes meet. He bites his lips and steps out of the ranks.

He goes over to the SS man, takes off his cap, and says, "I gave it to him."

All eyes are fixed on Ivan. The Unterscharführer slowly raises his whip and slashes Ivan's face once, twice, three times. Then he starts beating him on his head. The whip whistles, the prisoner's face is covered with bloody stripes, but Ivan does not fall. He stands there with his cap in his hand, erect, his hands alongside his hips. He does not bow his head; his whole body just sways.

The Unterscharführer lowers his arm.

"Write down his number and make a report. Kommando—march!"

We walk off with an even, military step. We leave behind a pile of sunflower seeds, a clump of herbs, rags and bags, smashed apples, and behind all of this, a large goose with a red head and wide-spread white wings. Ivan walks at the tail end of the kommando, with no one supporting him. Behind him, two corpses covered with branches are carried on stretchers.

As we walk past Pani Haneczka, I turn my head to face her. She is standing pale and erect, her hands pressed to her breast. Her lips tremble nervously. She looks up and glances at me. That's when I notice that her large black eyes are filled with tears.

After roll call they drive us into the block. We lie on our bunks, look out through chinks in the walls and wait for the selection to be over.

"I feel as though I'm to blame for this entire selection. That strange fatalism of words. In this accursed Auschwitz even a bad word has the power of coming true."

"Don't take it so hard," says Kazik. "Give me something to go with this paté instead."

"You don't have any tomatoes?"

"Not every day is St. John's Day."

I push away the sandwiches he's made.

"I can't eat."

They're finishing the selection in the courtyard. The SS doctor goes on to the next block, having come up with the correct total and checked the numbers of the men whom he's written down for selection. Kazik gets ready to leave.

"I'm going to buy some cigarettes. You know, Tadek, you're a sucker, because if someone had eaten my porridge, I would have beaten him to a pulp."

Just then, at the edge of the bunk, an enormous gray skull crawls out from below and embarrassed, blinking eyes gaze at us. Next, Beker's whole face appears, wrinkled and even older.

"Tadek, I have a favor to ask of you."

"Speak," I say, leaning down to him.

"Tadek, I'm going to the chimney."

I bend down even lower and look into his eyes from close up. They're calm and blank.

"Tadek, I've been so hungry for so long. Give me something to eat. For this last evening."

Kazik hits me on the knee.

"Do you know this Jew?"

"It's Beker," I answer softly.

"Here, Jew, climb up on the bunk and gorge. When you've stuffed yourself, take the rest along with you to the chimney. Climb up on the bunk. I don't sleep here, so it's all right if you have lice."

"Tadek," Kazik grabs my arm, "come; I've got a wonderful apple charlotte in my block, straight from my mother."

Climbing down from the bunk, he nudges me with his arm.

"Look," he whispers.

I glance at Beker. His eyes are closed and, like a blind man, he's groping for a board, so he can pull himself up.

LADIES AND GENTLEMEN, WELCOME TO THE GAS

The entire camp was walking around naked. True, we had already gone through delousing and had gotten our clothing back from the basins that were filled with Zyklon gas dissolved in water, which does a splendid job of poisoning lice in clothing and people in the gas chamber, and only the blocks that were still fenced off with wooden barricades had not yet received their clothes "ration," but both we and they were walking around naked—the heat was horrible. The camp was under a strict lockdown. Not a single prisoner, not a single louse would dare pass through the gate. The work of the kommandos had ceased. All day long, thousands of naked people spilled onto the roads and roll-call squares, sprawled next to walls and on top of roofs. People slept on boards, since the straw mattresses and blankets were undergoing disinfection. From the last blocks we could see the FKL; they were being deloused over there, too. Twenty-eight thousand women were stripped and driven out of their blocks; now they were milling about on the "free space," on the roads and squares.

Since morning, we'd been waiting for dinner, eating from our parcels, visiting friends. Time passed slowly, as it usually does when it's hot. Even our usual entertainment was missing: the broad roads to the crematoriums were empty. For a couple of days now, there had been no transports. Part of Canada was liquidated and assigned to a labor kommando. Since they were well fed and rested, they wound up in one of the worst kommandos, the one in Harmenze. An envious justice reigns in the camp: when a powerful person falls, his friends strive to make him fall as low as possible. True,

Canada, our Canada, doesn't smell of resin, as it does in Arkady Fiedler's prewar novel; it smells of French perfumes, but apparently there aren't nearly as many tall pines growing in that Canada as there are concealed diamonds and coins in this one, collected from all over Europe.

Right now, several of us are sitting on a bunk, swinging our legs in the most carefree manner. We divide up the ingeniously baked white bread, crusty, crumbly, with a somewhat annoying taste, but unlikely to go moldy for weeks. The bread comes all the way from Warsaw. A week ago my mother still held it in her hands. Dear God, dear God . . .

We pull out bacon, onion, open a can of condensed milk. Henri, large and dripping with sweat, dreams out loud about the French wine brought here by the transports from Strasbourg, Paris, Marseilles . . .

"Listen, *mon ami*, when we go to the loading ramp again I'll bring you some genuine champagne. You've probably never drunk any, right?"

"No. But you won't get it past the gate, so don't lie. Better you should organize some boots—you know, the stippled kind with a double sole. I'm not even going to mention the shirt you promised me a long time ago."

"Patience, patience; when the transports arrive, I'll bring you everything. We'll be going to the loading ramp again."

"Maybe there won't be any more transports to the chimney," I retort caustically. "You see how lax it's become in camp; no limit on parcels, beating is forbidden. You've been writing letters home, after all . . . People are saying all sorts of things about the regulations; you've been babbling yourself. Anyway, to hell with it, there aren't enough people."

"You shouldn't be talking nonsense . . ." The mouth of the fat man from Marseilles with a soulful face out of one of Richard Cosway's miniatures (he's my friend, but I don't know his name) is stuffed with a sardine sandwich. "You shouldn't be talking non-sense," he repeats, swallowing with effort ("go down, damn it!"), "you shouldn't be talking nonsense; there can't be a shortage of people or we'd all drop dead in this camp. We're all living on what they bring here."

"Not all of us. *We* have parcels . . ."

"You and your friend, and ten more of your friends, do; you Poles do, but not even all of you. But what about us Jews, or the Russians? And if we didn't have something to eat, what we've or-ganized from the transports, could you be eating your parcels so calmly? We wouldn't give them to you."

"You would, or you'd drop dead from hunger like the Greeks. Whoever has grub in the camp has power."

"You've got and we've got; what's there to quarrel about?"

Indeed; there's nothing to quarrel about. You've got and I've got; we eat together, we sleep in the same stack of bunks, our buksa. Henri slices the bread, makes a salad out of tomatoes. It tastes deli-cious with mustard from the commissary.

In the block, beneath us, people are milling about, naked, dripping with sweat. They shuffle around between the buksas in the passageway, next to the enormous, intelligently constructed stove, between the improvements that turn a horse stable (a sign still hangs on the door announcing *"versuchte Pferde,"* infected horses, must be placed separately there and over there) into a pleas-ant (*gemütlich*) home for over five hundred people. They nest on the bottom bunks in eights and tens; they lie naked, bony, stinking of sweat and secretions, with deeply sunken cheeks. Under me, on the very bottom, is a rabbi; he has covered his head with a piece of rag torn from a blanket and is reading from a Hebrew prayer book (we've got that reading matter here . . .), wailing loudly and in a monotone.

"Maybe we should calm him down? He's shouting as if he's caught God by the feet."

"I don't feel like climbing down from the buksa. Let him shout; he'll go to the chimney even sooner."

"Religion is the opium of the people. I love smoking opium," the fellow from Marseilles opines sententiously from the left; he's a communist and a *rentier*. "If they didn't believe in God and in life beyond the grave, they would have destroyed the crematoriums a long time ago."

"And why haven't you done so?"

The question is meant metaphorically, but the fellow from Marseilles responds.

"Idiot."

He stuffs a tomato into his mouth and seems to be on the verge of saying something, but he eats and keeps silent.

We had just finished our gorging when there was even more movement near the door to the block; the Muselmann jumped back and fled, running between the buksas, and a messenger flew into the block elder's hut. A moment later, the block elder made a majestic entrance.

"Canada! Antreten! Be quick! A transport's arriving!"

"Great God!" Henri screamed, jumping down from the bunk.

The fellow from Marseilles choked on his tomato, grabbed his jacket, screamed "*raus*" to the men who were sitting below, and they were already at the door. People were milling around on the other buksas. Canada was heading out to the ramp.

"Henri, boots!" I yelled in farewell.

"*Keine Angst!*" he yelled back from the yard.

I packed up our grub, strapped ropes around my valise in which an onion and tomatoes from my father's garden in Warsaw lay next to Portuguese sardines and bacon from "Bacutil" in Lublin (that was from my brother), mixed in with the most authentic mixture of dried fruits and nuts from Salonika. I tied the ropes, pulled on my trousers, and climbed down from the bunk.

"*Platz!*" I shouted, elbowing the Greeks aside. They made way. At the door, I caught up with Henri.

"*Allez, allez, vite, vite!*"

"*Was ist los?*"

"Do you want to go with us to the ramp?"

"Sure."

"So move! Take your jacket! We're missing a couple of men; I had a talk with the kapo." And he shoves me out of the block.

We stand in a row; someone writes down our numbers, someone at the head of the line yells "march, march," and we start running to the gate, accompanied by the cries of the multilingual crowd, which is already being driven back to the blocks with leather whips. It's not just anyone who gets to go to the ramp . . .

We've already taken leave of the men, we're already at the gate.

"*Links, zwei, drei, vier! Mützen ab!* Left, right, three, four! Caps off!"

Holding ourselves erect, with our hands held stiffly against our hips, we pass through the gate briskly, energetically, almost gracefully. A sleepy SS man with a large tablet in his hand counts us lethargically, marking off each group of five with his finger in the air.

"*Hundert!*" he calls out, when the last group of five passes him.

"*Stimmt!* it checks out," comes a hoarse cry from the head of the column.

We march quickly, almost at a run. There are a lot of guards, young men with automatic rifles. We pass every sector of camp II B: the uninhabited camp C, the Czech sector, the quarantine, we plunge in among the pear trees and apple trees of the morgue, the *Truppenlazarett*; amid unfamiliar vegetation that could have come from the moon, surprisingly overgrown during these several days of sunshine, we make an arc around some barracks, cross the line of the great *Postenkette,* reach the highway at a run—and we're there. Another thirty meters or so and we're among the trees near the loading ramp.

It's a pastoral platform, as is common at remote, provincial stations. A small square, framed with the greenery of tall trees, covered in gravel. Off to the side, near the road, a small, squat, wooden barracks, uglier and more ramshackle looking than the ugliest and most ramshackle of station buildings; farther on, great stacks of tracks, railroad ties, piles of lumber, parts of barracks, bricks, stones, cranks for wells. That's where goods bound for Birkenau are loaded—materials for enlarging the camp and sending people to the gas. An ordinary work day: trucks drive up, load up with lumber, cement, people . . .

The guards are stationed on the rails, the girders, in the green shade of the Silesian chestnut trees; they surround the platform in a tight circle. They wipe the sweat from their brow, drink from their canteens. The heat is extreme, the sun is at its zenith, motionless.

"Break ranks!"

We sit in patches of shade beside the rails. The hungry Greeks (a couple of them had sneaked in among us, the devil knows how) are poking about in the rails; one of them finds a can of jam, another, moldy rolls, half-consumed sardines. They eat.

"*Schweinedreck,*" a young, tall guard with wild, pale hair and a dreamy blue gaze, spits at them. "You're soon going to have so much to gorge on that you won't be able to eat it all. You'll lose your appetite for a long time."

He arranges his automatic rifle and wipes his face with a handkerchief.

"He's a pig," we repeat agreeably.

"Hey, you, fatso." The guard's boot lightly touches the back of Henri's neck. "*Pass mal auf,* are you thirsty?"

"I am, but I don't have any marks," the Frenchman replies with a professional air.

"*Schade*, too bad."

"But Herr Posten, doesn't my word mean anything any more? Haven't you traded with me, Herr Posten? How much? *Wieviel?*"

"One hundred. *Gemacht?*"

"*Gemacht.* It's a deal."

We drink the flat, tasteless water on credit—backed by the money and people who haven't arrived yet.

"Hey, be careful," says the Frenchman, flinging away the empty bottle so that it shatters somewhere down the rails; "don't take any dough, because there might be a search. Anyway, what the hell do you need dough for, you've got enough to eat as is. Don't take a suit either, because that raises suspicions about an escape attempt. Take a shirt, but only if it's made of silk and has a collar. And a sleeveless undershirt. And if you find something to drink, don't call me. I'll manage by myself, and watch out that you don't get it in the neck."

"Do they beat us?"

"Naturally. You have to have eyes in your backside. *Arschaugen.*"

The Greeks are sitting nearby; they move their jaws ravenously, like large nonhuman insects; they are greedily devouring the rotten lumps of bread. They are overwrought; they don't know what they're going to be doing. The lumber and the rails are making them nervous. They don't like lifting things.

"*Was wir arbeiten?*" they ask.

"*Niks.* Transport *kommen, alles* crematorium, *compris?*"

"*Alles verstehen,*" they reply in crematorium Esperanto. They calm down; they're not going to be loading rails onto the trucks or carrying beams.

In the meantime, it was growing noisier and more crowded on the platform. The Vorarbeiters divided up the groups, assigning some to opening and unloading the freight cars that would be arriving, sending others over to the wooden stairs and explaining what was going to happen. They were portable, capacious, wide stairs, like the ones used to provide access to a grandstand. Motorcycles kept roaring up, transporting noncommissioned SS officers besprinkled with the silver of their insignia—strong, fattened men with polished officer's boots and shining, boorish faces. Some of them arrived with notebooks; others had flexible cane switches. This lent them a businesslike, official look. They went into the canteen, because that pitiful barrack was their canteen, where they drank mineral water, Sudetenquelle, in the summer and warmed up with hot wine in winter; they greeted each other officially with arms outstretched in a Roman salute, and then cordially shook hands, smiled warmly, chatted about letters, news from home, their children, showed one another photographs. Some of them sauntered around the square in grand style; the gravel crunched, their boots crunched, the silver insignia glittered on their collars, and their bamboo switches whistled impatiently.

The variously striped crowd lay under the rails in narrow strips of shade, breathing heavily and unevenly; it chattered lazily in its own way and looked with indifference at the majestic men in green uniforms, the green of the trees, so close and out of reach, at the spire of a distant church from which the bells were being rung right at that moment for a belated Angelus.

"The transport's coming," someone said, and everyone stood up expectantly. Freight cars appeared from around the bend: the train was being pushed backward, the brakeman leaned out, waved, whistled. The locomotive let out a terrifying whistle in response, wheezed, and the train rolled slowly alongside the station. In its small, barred windows we could see people's faces, pale, crumpled, seemingly sleep-deprived, disheveled—terrified women and men who, wonder of wonders, had hair. They moved past slowly, staring in silence at the station. Then something began seething inside the cars and pounding on the wooden walls.

"Water! Air!" Hollow, despairing cries erupted.

People's faces leaned out the windows, mouths desperately gasped for air. Having caught a few swallows of air, the people from the windows disappeared, and others forced their way in to take their place and disappeared in turn. The cries and gasps became louder and louder.

A man in a green uniform, more sprinkled with silver than the others, twisted his lips in disgust. He took a deep drag on his cigarette, threw it away with an abrupt motion, transferred his notebook from his right hand to his left, and nodded at a guard. The guard slowly pulled his machine gun off his shoulder, lay down, and fired a round down the line of freight cars. It grew quiet. In the meantime, trucks were driving up, tables were placed next to them, the guards were stationed in a businesslike fashion next to the cars. The giant with the notebook gestured with his hand.

"Whoever takes gold or anything else other than food will be shot for stealing property of the Reich. Understood? *Verstanded?*"

"*Jawohl!*" we bellowed unevenly and individually, though with good humor.

"*Also los!* To work!"

The bolts clanged; the cars were opened. A wave of air rushed inside, striking the people like poisonous fumes. Packed together beyond belief, crushed by the monstrous quantity of baggage, suitcases, large and small valises, knapsacks, bundles of all sorts (for they had taken along everything that represented their former life, for they were supposed to be embarking on their future), they'd been cooped up in horribly cramped conditions, they had fainted from the heat, died of suffocation, and suffocated others. Now they crowded around the open doors, breathing like fish cast onto sand.

"Attention: Come out with your things. Take everything. Place all your stuff in a pile next to the train car. Hand over your coats. It's summer. March to the left. Understood?"

"What is going to happen to us, sir?"

They are already jumping down onto the gravel, anxious, in shock.

"Where are you from?"

"Sosnowiec, Będzin. What's going to happen?"

They repeat their questions stubbornly, looking earnestly into strangers' exhausted eyes.

"I don't know; I don't understand Polish."

It is the law of the camp that people going to their death are deceived until the final moment. It is the sole permissible form of pity. The heat is horrendous. The sun has reached its zenith, the overheated sky is shimmering, the air moves in waves, the wind that blows past us at times is like scorched liquid air. Already, our lips are cracked, we can feel the salty taste of blood in our mouth. From lying in the sun so long our bodies are weak and unwieldy. To drink, oh, to drink.

Out of the freight car pours a varicolored wave, loaded down, resembling a stunned, blind river in search of a new channel. But before they regain consciousness, assaulted by the fresh air and the fragrance of the foliage, their packages are already being ripped out of their hands, their overcoats pulled off; the women's handbags are ripped away, their umbrellas taken.

"Sir, sir, it's to protect me from the sun, I can't . . ."

"*Verboten*," is barked through clenched teeth, with a loud hiss. In back of us stands an SS man, calm, self-controlled, professional.

"*Meine Herrschaften*, ladies and gentlemen, don't throw your things around like that. You must show a little goodwill."

He speaks good-naturedly, but the slender whip bends nervously in his hands.

"Yes, of course, yes, of course," they answer in many voices as they pass by, and they walk more briskly beside the freight cars.

A woman bends down and quickly picks up her bag. The whip whistles, the woman screams, stumbles and falls under the feet of the crowd. A child running behind her squeals *"mamele"* in Yiddish—such a small little girl with tousled hair . . .

The pile of belongings grows bigger—valises, bundles, knapsacks, travel rugs, suits, handbags that open as they fall and spill out colorful, rainbow-colored banknotes, gold, watches; in front of the freight-car doors stacks of bread pile up, jars of varicolored marmalades and jams accumulate, heaps of hams and sausages swell, sugar spills onto the gravel. Trucks jam-packed with people drive off with a hellish roar amid the wailing and uproar of women crying for their children and the stupefied silence of suddenly forlorn men. They are the ones who went to the right, the young and the healthy—they are going to the camp. The gas won't pass them by, but first they will work.

The trucks drive off and return without a rest, as if on a monstrous conveyor belt. A Red Cross ambulance drives back and forth without a break. The gigantic bloody cross painted on the hood over the engine is dissolving in the heat of the sun. The Red Cross ambulance drives tirelessly: it's the vehicle in which the gas is transported, the gas with which they are poisoning these people.

The men from Canada, who are near the stairs, don't have a minute to catch their breath; they are separating the people for the gas from the people who are going to the camp; they shove the former onto the stairs, ram them into the trucks, sixty to a truck, plus or minus.

A young, smooth-shaven gentleman stands to the side, an SS man with a notebook in his hand; each truck is a checkmark, and when sixteen trucks drive off, that's one thousand, plus or minus. The gentleman is even-tempered and meticulous. Not a truck departs without his knowledge and his checkmark: *Ordnung muss sein.* The checkmarks swell into thousands, the thousands into entire transports which are referred to in shorthand as "from Salonika," "from Strasbourg," "from Rotterdam." Today, we're already speaking of this one as "Będzin." But it will receive a permanent name: "Będzin–Sosnowiec." The men who will go into the camp from this transport will receive numbers 131–132. "Thousand" is understood, but people will say it like this for short, "131–132."

The transports grow into weeks, months, years. When the war ends, they will count up the incinerated. They will calculate a total of four and a half million. The bloodiest battle of the war, the greatest victory of united and unanimous Germany. *Ein Reich, ein Volk, ein Führer*—and four crematoriums. But there will be sixteen crematoriums in Auschwitz, capable of incinerating fifty thousand a day. The camp will expand until its electrified fences bump up against the Vistula; three hundred thousand people clothed in pasiaki will inhabit it; it will be called *Verbrecher-Stadt,* "city of criminals." No, there will be no shortage of people. The Jews will burn, the Poles will burn, the Russians will burn, people will arrive from the west and the south, from the continent and the islands. People will arrive wearing pasiaki; they will rebuild the destroyed German cities, plow the fallow earth, and when they grow weak from their merciless labor, the eternal *Bewegung, Bewegung,* the doors of the gas chambers will open. The gas chambers will be improved, made more efficient, will be more cunningly disguised. They will be like the ones in Dresden, about which legends are already circulating.

The freight cars are empty now. A thin, pockmarked SS man glances calmly inside, shakes his head in disgust, eyes us, and indicates the interior.

"*Rein.* Clean it!"

We jump inside. Scattered in the corners among human feces and lost watches lie smothered, trampled infants, naked little monsters with enormous heads and swollen bellies. We carry them out like chickens, holding two in each hand.

"Don't take them to the truck. Give them to the women," says the SS man, lighting a cigarette. His lighter is jammed; he's very busy with it.

"Take these babies, for God's sake," I burst out, but the women run away from me in horror, drawing their heads down on their necks.

The name of God sounds strangely unnecessary, for the women with children are going onto a truck, all of them, without exception. We all know very well what that means, and we look at each other with hatred and horror.

"What, you don't want to take them?" the pockmarked SS man says reproachfully, as if surprised, and starts unfastening his gun.

"You don't have to shoot; I'll take them."

A gray-haired, tall woman takes the babies from me and for a moment looks straight into my eyes.

"Child, child," she whispers, smiling. She walks away, stumbling on the gravel.

I lean against the side of a freight car. I'm very tired. Someone tugs at my hand.

"Come; I'll give you something to drink. You look like you have to throw up. *En avant*, under the rails, go!"

I look up; a face is jumping around in front of my eyes, it's floating away, it's enormous, transparent, getting mixed up with the motionless trees which for some reason are black, with the overflowing crowd . . . I blink sharply: Henri.

"Listen, Henri, are we good people?"

"Why do you ask stupid questions?"

"You see, friend, a totally inexplicable rage is rising inside me against these people, that it's because of them that I have to be here. I don't feel the least bit sorry for them, that they're headed to the gas. May the earth open up beneath all of them. I could fling myself on them with my fists. But that's probably pathological; I can't understand it."

"Oh, on the contrary, it's normal, foreseen, and calculated. The ramp tortures you, you revolt, and it's easiest to unload your rage at those who are weaker. It's even desired that you should unload it. That's how a peasant mind works, *compris?*" the Frenchman says ironically, lying down comfortably under the rails. "Look at the Greeks; they know how to take advantage! They will devour everything that falls into their hands; one of them ate a jar of marmalade in front of me."

"Animals! Tomorrow, half of them will die from the runs."

"Animals? You, too, have been hungry."

"Animals," I repeat vehemently. I shut my eyes, I hear screams, I feel the trembling of the earth and the steamy air on my eyelids. My throat is completely dry.

The people flow on and on; the trucks roar like rabid dogs. In front of our eyes pass corpses carried out of the cars, trampled children, cripples stacked up together with corpses, and crowds, crowds, crowds . . . The freight cars roll in, the stacks of old clothes, valises and knapsacks grow, the people emerge, peer at the sun, take a breath, beg for water, go into the trucks, drive away. Again, the freight cars drive up, again the people . . . I sense the images merging inside me, I don't know if this is really happening or if I'm dreaming. I suddenly see tree foliage swaying along with the entire street, with the colorful crowd, but—it's the great avenue in Warsaw! There are noises in my head; I feel like I'm going to throw up.

Henri tugs at my arm.

"Don't sleep; we're going to load up the goods."

By now, there are no people. The last trucks are moving along the roadway in the distance, raising enormous clouds of dust; the train has left; on the emptied ramp the SS men are strolling in a dignified manner, the silver on their collars sparkling. Their boots are polished to a shine, their flushed faces gleam. Among them is a woman (only now do I realize that she was here the entire time)—

withered, flat-chested, bony. Her sparse, colorless hair is combed flat toward the back of her head and tied into a "Nordic" knot; her hands are concealed inside her wide trouser-skirt. She walks back and forth on the ramp, from one corner to the other, with a ratlike determined smile pasted on her dried-out lips. She hates feminine beauty with the hatred of a woman who is repulsive and is fully aware that she is. Yes, I have seen her already several times and re-member her very well: she's the Kommandantin of the FKL, she's come to look over her acquisitions, because a fraction of the women were placed away from the trucks, and they will be going on foot— "to camp." Our lads, the barbers from the Zauna, will relieve them entirely of hair and will get a great deal of pleasure out of these free women's embarrassment.

So, we load the goods. We lift heavy, capacious valises and strain to throw them onto the truck. There they are stacked in piles, crowded together, jammed in, slashed with a knife if possible, for the pleasure of it and in search of vodka and perfume, which pours right out on itself. One of the valises opens; suits, shirts, books tumble out . . . I grab up a bundle at random: it's heavy; I untie it: gold, two good handfuls—watchcases, bracelets, rings, necklaces, diamonds . . .

"*Gib hier,*" the SS man says calmly, holding out an open brief-case full of gold and colorful foreign currency. He closes it, hands it over to an officer, takes another one that's open and waits beside a different car. This gold will go to the Reich.

Heat, terrible heat. The air is like a motionless, white-hot col-umn. Our throats are dry; every word that is spoken causes pain. Oh, to have something to drink. Feverishly, just to get it over with faster, just to get to the shade, just to rest. We finish loading, the last trucks pull out, we diligently collect all the bits of paper from the track, rake up from the fine gravel all the foreign filth that arrived with the transport "so not a trace of this disgusting stuff should remain," and the minute the last truck disappears beyond the trees and we are walking—finally!—toward the rails to rest and drink our fill (maybe the Frenchman will buy something else from the guard?), a railwayman's whistle sounds from beyond the bend. Slowly, extremely slowly, the freight cars roll in, the locomotive emits its terrifying whistle, crumpled, pale, flat faces, seemingly cut from paper, with enormous eyes burning with fever, peer through the windows. Already the trucks are here, already there's a calm gentleman with a notebook, already the SS men have emerged from the canteen with their briefcases for gold and money. We open the cars.

No, I can no longer control myself. I brutally rip people's suitcases from their hands, tear their overcoats off them. Go, go, move on. They go, they move on. Men, women, children. Some of them know.

Here comes a woman, walking fast, she's rushing to get ahead, imperceptibly but feverishly. A little child, just a few years old, with a cherub's rosy, chubby-cheeked face, runs after her, can't catch up, stretches out its little arms, crying, "Mama, Mama!"

"Woman, carry that child in your arms!"

"Sir, that's not my child, sir, it's not mine!" the woman cries hysterically and runs away, hiding her face in her hands. She wants to hide, she wants to reach the ones who won't be going by truck, who will walk, who will live. She is young, healthy, good-looking; she wants to live.

But the child runs after her, complaining at the top of its lungs: "Mama, Mama, don't run away!"

"It's not mine, not mine, not . . . !"

Until Andrei, a sailor from Sebastopol, grabs hold of her. His eyes are blurry from vodka and the heat. He grabs her, knocks her down with a single sweeping blow; he seizes the falling woman by the hair and pulls her upright. His face is distorted with rage.

"Ach, you, you fucking Jewish bitch," he cries in Russian. "Running away from your own child! I'll give it to you, you whore!"

He snatches her up, with his large hand crushes her throat that is trying to scream, and hurls her onto the truck like a heavy sack of grain.

"Here! Take this, too! Bitch!" and he flings the child at her feet.

"*Gut gemacht*, that's the way to punish unnatural mothers," says the SS man who's standing near the truck. "*Gut, gut Russki.*"

"*Molchi!* Shut up!" Andrei mutters through clenched teeth and walks away from the freight cars. From under a pile of rags he pulls out a canteen that he's hidden there, unscrews the cap, touches it to his lips, then to mine. It burns my throat; it's pure alcohol. There's a roaring in my head, my legs buckle, I start retching.

Suddenly, from within this whole human wave that has been pressing on blindly in the direction of the trucks like a river propelled by an invisible power, a girl emerges; she jumps down gracefully from the train onto the gravel and looks around with an observant eye like someone who is marveling at something.

Her luxuriant blond hair tumbles onto her shoulders in a soft wave; she brushes it back impatiently. She runs her hands over her blouse reflexively, makes a slight adjustment to her skirt. She stands there for a moment. Finally, she tears her gaze away from the crowd and runs her eyes over our faces as if searching for someone. I seek her gaze unconsciously; our eyes meet.

"Listen, listen, tell me, where are they taking us?"

I look at her. There, standing before me, is a girl with wondrous blond hair, beautiful breasts, wearing a batiste summer blouse, with a wise, mature gaze. She is standing here, looking me straight in the eyes, and waiting. And over there is the gas chamber: collective death, hideous and repulsive. There's the camp with a shaved head, quilted Soviet trousers against the heat, the disgusting, nauseating smell of a filthy, scorched female body, animal hunger, inhuman labor and that same gas chamber, only an even more hideous, more repulsive, more horrifying death. Whoever enters here once will carry nothing, not even his own ashes, beyond the Postenkette, will not return to his former life.

"Why did she bring it, they'll take it away from her," I think involuntarily, noticing a beautiful watch with a tiny gold bracelet on her wrist. Tuśka had one just like it, only on a narrow black band.

"Listen; answer me."

I remain silent. She tightens her lips.

"I already know," she says with a touch of aristocratic contempt in her voice, tossing her head, and walks off bravely in the direction of the trucks. Someone tries to stop her; she moves away bravely toward the side and runs up the steps into an almost full truck. From afar, all I could see was her luxuriant blond hair, windblown as she ran.

I entered the freight cars, carried out the infants, threw out the baggage. I touched the corpses, but I could not overcome my growing wild terror. I tried running away from them, but they were lying everywhere; laid out in rows on the gravel, on the cement apron of the ramp, in the freight cars. Infants, hideous naked women, men twisted in convulsions. I ran away as far as I could. Someone struck my back with a whip; out of the corner of my eye I caught sight of a cursing SS man, I evaded him and mixed in with a group of men from Canada dressed in pasiaki. Finally, I crawled over to the rails again. The sun had dipped low over the horizon and was flooding the ramp with a bloody light. The shadows of the trees were eerily elongated; in the quiet that descends in nature toward evening a human cry sliced into the sky ever louder and more insistently.

Only from there, from under the rails, could the entire hell of the seething ramp be seen. There: a couple have fallen onto the ground, entwined in a despairing embrace. He digs his fingers into her body convulsively, clutches her clothing with his teeth. She is crying hysterically, cursing, swearing, until, stomped on with a boot, she emits a wheeze and falls silent. They're pried apart like pieces of wood and driven like animals into a truck. There: four men from Canada are lifting a corpse; it's an enormous, swollen woman; they curse and sweat from the effort, and kick out of the way stray children who are running around on the ramp, howling fearfully like dogs. They grab them by the neck, by the head, by the arms and throw them onto a pile, onto the trucks. These four can't manage to lift the woman into the truck. They call over others and through their collective intense effort shove the mountain of meat onto the bed of the truck. All over the ramp, huge, distended, swollen corpses are being collected. Squeezed in between them are cripples, the paralyzed, the smothered, the unconscious. The mountain of corpses seethes, bays, howls. The driver turns on the engine, drives off.

"*Halt! Halt!*" an SS man yells from afar. "Stop, stop, damn it!"

They are dragging an old man in a frock coat with an armband on the sleeve. The old man's head is banging against the gravel, the stones; he is moaning and wailing continuously, monotonously, "*Ich will mit dem Herrn Kommandanten sprechen* — I want to speak with the commandant." He repeats this with an old man's stubbornness all the way down the road. Flung into the truck, trampled under someone's foot, half-smothered, he keeps on wheezing, "*Ich will mit dem . . .*"

"Calm down, man!" a young SS man calls out to him, laughing out loud. "In half an hour you'll be chatting with the greatest commandant. Just don't forget to tell him *Heil Hitler!*"

Other men are carrying a girl who's missing a leg; they're holding her by her arms and her one remaining leg. Tears are rolling down her face, and she whispers piteously, "Gentlemen, it hurts, it hurts . . ." They fling her onto the truck, among the corpses. She will be burned alive together with them.

A cool, starry evening descends. We are lying on the rails. It's incredibly quiet. Anemic lamps are lit on the tall columns, beyond the circle of light.

"Did you exchange your boots?" Henri asks me.

"No."

"Why not?"

"I've had enough, man, absolutely enough!"

"Already after the first transport? Just think—since Christmas probably a million people have passed through my hands. The worst are the Paris transports; you always meet acquaintances."

"And what do you say to them?"

"That they're going to bathe and afterward we'll meet in the camp. And what would you say?"

I'm silent. We drink coffee mixed with alcohol; someone opens a tin of cocoa, mixes it with sugar. We scoop it out with our hands; the cocoa makes our mouths sticky. Again coffee, again alcohol.

"Henri, what are we waiting for?"

"There'll be one more transport. But it's not definite."

"If it comes, I'm not going to go and unload it. I won't be able to manage it."

"It's got to you, eh? Good old Canada?"

Henri smiles in a kindly way and disappears in the darkness. After a moment, he comes back.

"OK. Only watch out that an SS man doesn't catch you. You'll sit here the whole time. And I'll organize some boots for you."

"Leave me in peace with those boots."

I want to sleep. It's been night for a long time already.

Again Antreten, again a transport. Out of the darkness freight trains emerge, pass through the band of light and disappear again in the darkness. The ramp is short, but the circle of light is even shorter. We'll be unloading the cars one after the other. Somewhere the trucks are rumbling; they drive up to the steps spectrally black, illuminating the trees with their headlights. *Wasser! Luft!* The same thing all over again, a late-night showing of the same film: rounds are fired from automatic rifles, the freight cars quiet down. Only a young girl leans half her body out the window of a car, loses her balance, and falls onto the gravel. She lies there deafened for a moment; finally, she picks herself up and starts walking in circles, faster and faster, waving her arms stiffly as if doing exercises, gulping air noisily and wailing monotonously, shrilly. Starved for air, she's lost her mind. She gets on one's nerves, so an SS man runs up to her, kicks her in the back with his hobnailed boot. She falls down. He stomps on her, takes out his revolver, fires once, twice. She lies there, kicking at the earth with her legs until she's still. They've begun opening the cars.

I'm at the freight cars again. A warm, sweet smell bursts out of them. A human mountain fills the car halfway up to the ceiling— motionless, monstrously intertwined, but still steaming.

"*Ausladen!*" resounds the voice of an SS man emerging from the darkness. He has a portable floodlight hanging on his chest. He shines it into the car.

"Why are you standing there so stupidly? Unload!" and he swishes his whip across my back. I grab the hand of a corpse; its hand curls convulsively around mine. I pull away with a scream and flee. My heart is pounding, crushing my throat. Nausea crumples me immediately. I vomit, doubled over beneath the car. Staggering, I steal over to the stack of rails.

I lie on the good, cool iron and dream about returning to the camp, about my plank bed without a straw mattress, about a bit of sleep among comrades who will not be going to the gas during the night. Suddenly, the camp seems a kind of peaceful bay. Other people are dying all the time, but somehow one manages to live, one has something to eat, strength for work, one has a fatherland, a house, a girl . . .

The lights flicker spectrally, the wave of people flows on without end, confused, feverish, stupefied. These people think that they are starting a new life in the camp, and they're preparing themselves psychologically for a difficult struggle for existence. They don't know that they are going to die right now and that the gold, money, diamonds they have hidden with such forethought in the folds and seams of their garments, in the heels of their shoes, in their bodies' apertures, will no longer be needed by them. Professional, well-practiced people will rummage in their insides, extract the gold from under the tongue, diamonds from the womb and rectum. They'll tear out the gold teeth. They'll send them to Berlin in tightly sealed boxes.

The black figures of the SS men walk back and forth, calm and professional. The gentleman with the notebook in his hand makes the final checkmarks, rounds off the figures: fifteen thousand.

Many, many trucks have driven to the crematorium.

Now they're finishing up. The last truck collects the corpses laid out on the ramp; the goods are loaded. Canada, loaded down with breads, marmalade, sugar, smelling of perfume and clean linen, lines up for the return march. The kapo fills up a tea cauldron with gold, silks, and black coffee. It's going to the gate for the guards: they'll let the kommando pass without a search. The camp will live off this transport for several days: it will eat its hams and sausages, its preserves and fruit, it will drink its vodka and liqueurs, it will wear its linens, engage in trade with its gold and its bundles. Civilians will carry a lot of it out of the camp—to Silesia, to Kraków, and beyond. They will bring back cigarettes, eggs, vodka, and letters from home.

For several days the camp will talk about the Sosnowiec–Będzin transport. It was a good, rich transport.

When we return to the camp, the stars are starting to fade, the sky is becoming more and more transparent; it rises above us and the night is turning to dawn. It promises to be a fine, hot day.

From the crematoriums thick columns of smoke are rising and merging on high into an enormous black river rolling exceedingly slowly across the sky over Birkenau until it disappears beyond the woods in the direction of Trzebinia. The Sosnowiec transport is already burning.

We pass a detachment of SS walking with a machine gun to the changing of the guard. They walk evenly, one man beside another, one mass, one will.

"*Und morgen die ganze Welt . . . ,*" they sing at the top of their lungs.

"*Rechts ran!* To the right!" the command rings out from the head of their column.

We make way for them.

THE DEATH OF AN INSURGENT

Near the trench, across a narrow strip of meadow, lay a beet field. If you peered out over the brown wall of freshly excavated sticky clay, you could see green succulent leaves almost within reach and underneath them white mangels with pink veins, split open in the wet earth. The field lay on an uphill slope and ended against a wall of black forest that was blurry in the thin fog. A guard was posted at the edge of the forest. The funny sticklike barrel of a long, probably Danish, rifle jutted out from him like a lance. About forty meters to the left, under some rachitic plum trees, another guard was posted. He had wrapped himself tightly in a gray air-man's coat and pulled his forage cap down low over his ears and forehead; he surveyed the valley from under his cap as if peering into the bottom of a tank.

Farther up the slope, where the forest had descended in the form of groves of young willow trees, between an unexpectedly lively stream and a highway that sliced diagonally across the valley, enormous tractors dragging plows were leveling the earth that was being dug up by excavators and transported out of the pit in a huge number of carts pushed by human beings. It was dangerously noisy and crowded there. Men were pushing hand trucks, carrying ties and rails, ripping up turf in sheets to serve as camouflage for build-ings, followed by the tractor leveling the ground.

We were digging a trench in the bottom of this tank. The trench had been completed presciently in good times when the sun was shining and when there were plenty of ripe plums shaken

loose by the wind underneath the trees; during the rains it had begun to fill in again and was even threatening to collapse entirely,
since we had been ordered to dig it straight across to the pipes on
the wall and not, as they say, slantwise, for it hadn't been foreseen
that the Norwegians assigned to lay the pipes for the water supply
system would die in solidarity to the very last man by the time they'd
laid the first ten kilometers. So we had been hastily reassigned from
carrying rails and extracting the tangled steel rods that were lying
every which way in a pile at the station, and had been driven into
the bottom of the tank to repair the trench that ran indecently close
to the beet field.

"You'd think a trench like this, it probably means nothing," I
said to Romek, a former saboteur from Radom who had been laboring in German camps for the past two years to make up for what
he had ruined for them in Poland. We had worked together from
the moment they founded this lousy camp on the edge of a small
meadow beneath one of the Wirtemberg hills, and we'd achieved
a certain proficiency in digging trenches. He would smash the soft
earth into fine grains with a pickax, and I would hurl it onto the top
of the wall with the end of my spade. While he swung, gripping his
pick lazily, I leaned against the damp, cracked wall of the trench or
sat on my skillfully laid-down spade. While I swung, he took over
my function of supporting the trench. From a distance it looked
as if there was one man in the trench who was working slowly but
enthusiastically, and without taking a break.

"What of it, that it's a trench?" Romek continued the conversation, rocking without enthusiasm on his pickax. The ability to
conduct a conversation and drag it out for the entire day was almost
as important as food.

"It crumbled in on itself, and that's all. When we fix it, we'll
move on," he said, separating his words rhythmically with blows of
his pickax. "I hope not to be carrying rails or ties like those men

from the uprising. Working with a pick and spade, it will still be possible to hold out. But if you want to say something, then say it directly, and not in such a roundabout way."

He scanned the horizon. He had blue, almost bleached-out eyes and a good-natured, very thin face with sharply etched cheekbones.

"You can't even see the sun," he observed, disappointed. "What do you think? Is it going to rain?"

He crouched against the wall in a niche created by prescient hacking out of the clay. It was dry there and somewhat warmer. A blustery autumn wind was blowing over the trench, driving the restless, swollen rain clouds up above, but in the pit it was snug.

"The rain's nothing," I replied lightheartedly. "You think this is something new? Come on, this trench, when we started digging it, there were exactly one thousand of us old timers. Strong guys, every one of us with experience of not just any camp behind us. Many of us already knew the score."

Silent, I swung my empty spade a couple of times and tamped back the dirt that was spilling back down from the embankment.

"We worked at digging the trench, there was some sunshine, some rain, some earth falling back into the trench—and half of us were still alive. And out of those men over there," I indicated with my head the part of the trench beyond the bend where the rest of our group, the men from the uprising, were working, "I don't know if even half of them are alive. They said the corpse carriers got two loaves of bread each yesterday, because they carried out fifty corpses in a box. And one Jew drowned in the mud in the middle of the camp. That's why we stood so long at roll call yesterday. The soup in our block was already cold."

The former saboteur got up from his niche and grabbed his pickax.

"Not two loaves, not two; no, each corpse bearer got half a loaf and a little margarine as a reward. And you know, as for those insurgents, as you call them, I'm not in the least bit sorry for them. I didn't order them to come here. They wanted to themselves. Volunteers, they are. The war's almost over and they come here voluntarily to build a camp, to industrialize the country," he said bitingly, ending with a curse.

"They've probably cleaned out the entire trench, because I can't hear them quarreling over politics. They must have moved on. They've been working since early morning like fools. They think that Meister Batsch will give one of them a crust of bread."

"What do you mean? He will! Don't worry, our Croat will take a good look, he'll calculate, and then he'll give it to you as if it were a sausage! He has his own system; he knows how to goad people into working by not beating them but by luring them with crusts. He knows how to deliver a stinging rebuke, and you work, you fool. If you want to drop dead, wait for a crust. I prefer to eat less and not do anything."

"Together, two of them can earn a whole loaf, but they'll eat only a piece of crust," I agreed readily. "I think I'll go get some beets. We could do with a little something to eat, right? This is a good time, right now; the Meister's gone to the village."

"Sure; make a run for it. It's your turn. I got them yesterday and the day before. But watch out for the kapo; he's lurking near the excavator," Romek cautioned me. "Bring back at least two; maybe we can trade something. There's no shortage of fools. But don't give them away to anyone."

"As if I would! The old man will definitely come. After all, he prefers not to eat all his bread, and he's got to stuff himself with greens, as long as there's a lot of them. And he'll eat anything! Sow thistles and wild garlic, and parsley from the meadow. I'm telling you, he's going to kick the bucket."

I stuck the spade into the ground carefully so that if it fell it wouldn't get all splattered with mud, and crept stealthily along the trench between the puddles from the last rain.

The trick was that we had to pull the beets not from the field that was right under our noses, but from the other one, closer to the tractors and the uproar of the people pushing the carts loaded with earth, closer to the kapo, who was as nervous as a fish on a hook, and the guard who sometimes decides to shoot someone out of boredom. We were threatened with unambiguous punishments for taking beets, because was it the fault of the peaceful villagers of the Wirtemberg area that a gang of prisoners had unexpectedly descended on their land and spread out in small camps from Stuttgart all the way to Balingen in order to make oil out of rocks? As is, they'd already suffered enough; their crummy meadows had been torn up, their pastures placed under the administration of field factories, and the soldiers and foremen from Todt's Labor Army were rampaging as they pleased through their gardens and orchards, and even worse, among the fiancées of the absent natives who were at the front *zur Zeit.*

Around the bend in the trench, at a certain distance from us, a group of old men from the Warsaw uprising were working, dressed identically in pasiaki, though with certain individual variations. One had tucked his jacket into his trousers; another had an empty cement sack sticking out from under his jacket, an excellent protection from rain and wind; yet another had made use of roofing paper which he'd pulled over his body after tearing openings for his head and arms.

"Gentlemen, let me pass, God speed to you in your work," I said pleasantly. "And you, insurgent, you should take off that roofing paper. Didn't you see the beating the SS man gave that Jew because he found straw on him?"

"So, am I a Jew? Jews they can beat to death, but not Aryans. Anyway, worry about yourself. I'd be that smart, too, and would go around without roofing paper if I had three shirts."

"Sir, are you going to get beets?" the man with the soiled, once elegant, ankle boots asked me.

"So? And if I am, what of it?"

"You could bring one for us."

"Beets are bad for the stomach, mister. You'll come down with *Durchfall* and you'll drop dead in the blink of an eye. Isn't it better to survive than to die of dysentery?"

"Not if you want to eat. When you're hungry, you don't care very much about living," the old man said sensibly.

I took a good look at the old Muselmann. He'd tied a thick, patched-together rope around his jacket and stuffed it crudely with straw that stuck out from under the short collar which he'd turned up as if that piece of cloth made out of nettles and saturated with dampness could warm him. But it hadn't occurred to him to tuck his trousers into those once elegant ankle boots he'd worn in Warsaw. They were thickly coated with old, caked mud and a thick goo of newly added clay.

"Hey, old man, old man," I said contemptuously, "you don't know how to respect yourself. You've got to move around a bit, tidy up a bit, after all, the camp isn't a *pension* where they'll give you anything you want; you're not at home with your mama. If you'll brush the mud off yourself and move around just a little, you'll immediately do more for your health than by eating a slice of bread. If you eat only beets and in addition buy a cigarette every day for half a bowl of soup, what do you think will happen? That you'll hold out? They'll throw you into a box and cart you away, and that will be the end of you. You already look like a misfortune and a half."

"If you ate only a liter of watery soup and a slice of bread, you'd look just like us," the man covered in roofing paper interrupted the stream of my speech.

"So you think I eat more than you?" Frankly, I was offended. "It's just that I'm not accustomed to delicacies like you men from Warsaw. And I know how to respect myself."

"And who was it who carried out a canteen of soup from our block yesterday if it wasn't you? Perhaps you'll tell us — right?"

"Yesterday I sold a broom to your block elder, and he gave me a bowl of soup for it. All of us were working near the osiers. Did I prevent you from making brooms? You all were lying around comfortably at noon while I was braiding twigs."

"Yeah, yeah, I'm a smart guy. But will the block elder take something from me? He prefers to give soup away for nothing, to one of you from Auschwitz."

"If you sit in camp for a couple of years like all of us, then you, too, will be given a second bowl of soup everywhere," I replied, irritated, and ran over to the beets, cursing myself for the unnecessary delay.

Some hundred meters farther along, the trench made a turn toward the black rectangle of earth that had been torn up by the tractors and excavators. Just before the turn the embankment above the trench had been pushed to the side and two flat holes that served as firm footholds had been carved into the trench wall. Placing my foot into an indentation and clinging to the edge of the trench with my fingers, I pulled myself over the trench with great effort and, paying no attention to my jacket's getting thoroughly coated with mud, crawled cautiously among the beets. Here, with the beet leaves providing some cover, I felt a little safer. I selected the largest beet by eye, tore off its leaves one by one without undue haste, and pried it out of the ground. I looked around for a turnip but, aside from some cracked, white-and-pink beet tops, I couldn't spot anything else. So I got one more beet, slipped them both under my jacket, and, holding up a couple of leaves to shield me from the eyes of the kapo or the guard, started crawling back toward the trench. Finally, I slid down between the cracked damp walls and breathed a sigh of relief.

I cleaned my jacket and trousers with a wooden trowel that I took out of my pocket, scoured my hands and boots very carefully, and, supporting the beets under the hem of my jacket, quickly scampered back to my comrades. I was rather excited and was breathing like a hunted dog.

"Sir, give us one, give us a piece," the insurgents pleaded with me as I passed them.

"People, leave me alone!" I cried out almost in despair, clutching the hideously damp beet tops to my belly. "Go pull some for yourselves! There are beets growing over there for everyone! Am I the only one?"

"But it's easier for you, you're young!" said the one in the roofing paper.

"Then drop dead if you're old and afraid. If I'd been afraid, the grass would long since have been growing over me!"

"Then choke on it, you sonofabitch!" the man in the roofing paper screamed after me.

I squeezed through to the former saboteur. Romek was squatting comfortably in the trench, holding onto the handle of the pickax.

"No one's looking, so why try so hard?" he said very reasonably.

I pulled the beets out from under my jacket. The saboteur jammed the pickax into the bottom of the trench, dug out a little hole, extracted an invaluable item, a penknife, from some recesses in his clothing, and carefully peeled the beets, throwing the skins into the hole.

"You understand, once we went to deal with a certain village official not far from Radom," he said, cutting out the stringy parts of the beets that are unsuitable for a highly refined palate. "Jeżyny or Dzierżyny, the village was called something like that. We rush over there and surround his cabin, and Wilk" (in all of Romek's stories Wilk always played the leading role), "he crawls through a window into the cabin, and we're waiting for him to take care of it. But he doesn't do anything, just calls to me. I crawl in, too, you know, and look around because it's kind of dark: the official's lying in bed with his woman and doesn't want to get out. 'You have to come to an interrogation,' says Wilk. 'I won't let him go; interrogate him in bed,' the woman says. And the official's mum from fear. 'Shoot,' I say, 'right into them; it's rough, what one has to do for the Fatherland.' So the two of us shot the fellow and the feathers flew up to the ceiling. Do you think the woman started screaming for him? You guessed it! 'You so-and-so partisans,' she says, 'you've completely ruined my pillow and featherbed!'"

"That's all baloney," I declared, using my spade to tamp down the hole where I'd dropped the beet skins. "But what's the connection between the village official and beets?"

"There is one, and it's very big"—the saboteur handed me a sliced beet, which I immediately stowed in a pocket—"because in the old man's pantry we got hold of such a huge ring of sausage," and he drew an unbelievable circle with his arm.

"What kind of sausage, I ask you? Because I know a thing or two about smoked meats," the old man in the muddied, formerly elegant, ankle boots unexpectedly volunteered. He had quietly walked over to us and, leaning on the spade, had been listening reverently to the saboteur's little tale, following the slicing of the beets with no less reverence.

"What kind of sausage? Obviously, not half-smoked. Ordinary country sausage with garlic," Romek answered sullenly. "Definitely better than these beets. You can imagine that yourselves!"

He handed me a slice of beet and cut another for himself. They had the dull, biting sweetness of saccharine and caused an unpleasant wave of cold to flood the body. Which is why they were eaten cautiously and in small doses.

"Sir, give me a little piece, don't be like that."

The man in the ankle boots hovered above us with senile stubbornness.

"You should have pulled one for yourself," said Romek. "You'd like somebody else to stick his ass out for you just like in Warsaw, right? You're afraid to do it yourself?"

"How could I have fought in Warsaw when the Germans deported me immediately?"

"Go away, old man, go do your work and keep trying, maybe Meister Batsch will give you a crust of bread," I said mockingly, and when he didn't go away, incapable of tearing his eyes from the slices we were chomping on nonchalantly, I added impatiently, "Listen up, old man, beets are bad for the stomach. There's too much water in them. And you'll eat the entire thing. Don't your legs hurt?"

"Why should they hurt? They're only a little puffy," the old man said animatedly, pulling up the mud-splattered legs of his striped pants. From out of the mud-covered, formerly elegant, ankle boots, from fantastically wrapped cloths and rags, swollen, sickly white, almost blue calves emerged.

I bent down and pressed a finger against his skin. The saboteur scratched indifferently at the ground with his pick. He wasn't interested in swollen legs.

"You see, old man, my finger's pressing into your body as if it's kneaded dough. And do you know why? Water, nothing but water. When it travels from the legs to the heart, you're kaput. You mustn't drink anything, not even coffee. And it goes without saying that you shouldn't eat greens, either. And you want beets?"

The old man eyed his calf critically, then lifted his expressionless eyes to me.

"I'll give you a piece of bread, but in exchange for a whole beet," he said silently and pulled out of his pocket some bread wrapped in a filthy rag, about half the morning's ration, according to my instantaneous and professional evaluation.

The saboteur leaned on his pickax and clutched at his side with the other hand.

"You see, old man, you're always the same. It's the same thing with you every day. You should have taken out that bread from the first, and then launched into your prattling. So you've managed to hold out since morning," he added with a mixture of contempt, respect, and envy.

"Sure, it's necessary. With a beet like that a person can at least fill his gut. Give it to me quick, I've got to get back to work. We're talking and talking, and the others are digging for me back there."

"One gives bread for a fingernail, but for a beet one wants a whole hand," Romek said as a matter of principle. "So be it, just to keep you from whining."

He snatched the bread, placed it in the niche, then, taking the pieces of beet out of his pocket, reassembled them to demonstrate that there was no cheating involved and it was really a whole beet, not one that was missing a slice, and handed it to the old man, who gathered the pieces of beet into his jacket front and hurriedly walked off beyond the bend, dragging his spade behind him.

Then Romek reached into the niche, took out the bread, divided it fairly into two absolutely equal parts and gave me one of them. We both started gnawing at it, carefully mixing the bread with saliva and swallowing it slowly. Finally, Romek pulled two crushed, withered plums from his pocket. With a sly laugh he tossed me one of them. I caught it in midair.

"Observe: you have to have patience and be able to carry around your grub until the right time. I found the plums when we were going to the shed for our tools this morning. If only I could hold out with bread that way . . . But you would have eaten them immediately."

"Of course I would have," I agreed.

Again, without having to say anything, we got back to our former work system. He rocked back and forth on the pickax, crushing the rest of the clumps of earth that had fallen from the embankment, and I propped up the niche where it seemed to be slightly warmer than in the bare trench, maybe because the wind was blowing over the trench and here there was a bit of earth overhead, like a roof.

"You know, when I used to get packages in Auschwitz, I would drink the condensed milk immediately," I said dreamily. "I was never able to share it. And here I also eat my rations immediately. Have you ever seen me with bread? Eat it up, one-two-three, drink a bit of coffee, but not too much, and you can stand all day with your spade. The main thing is, not to work too much."

"The best system is to not carry food in your pocket. What's in your stomach can't be stolen by a thief, burned in a fire, or taken as a bribe. A person who picks at his food, divides it up, takes forever to eat, will soon drop dead. That's a Jewish system."

"Warsaw, too," I added, thinking about the just-concluded transaction.

"Warsaw, too," the former saboteur agreed.

He struck the pickax into the ground and leaned against the wall of the trench. The trench was narrow, but not proportionally deep. The damp earth gave off a corpselike smell of rotting grass. On one side of the trench rose the embankment, beyond the embankment the beet field stretched out, and beyond it, the tractors, the chain of guards, and the forest. On the other side there was a meadow on which grew a scattering of wild plum trees. The plum trees stretched in a line as far as the village that was situated completely in the valley, lower than the bottom of our tank. From our position we could see the spire of the church which rose up in the center of the village above a waterfall in a stream that was swollen in the autumn. And also the red roofs of houses descending lower and lower were visible. Farther on, a young spruce woods climbed up the slope of the hill. Beyond the woods lay our small, recently established camp in which, in the course of two months, three thousand people had died. A white strip of road was laid down from the woods, disappeared in the village, and flowed away along with the plum trees.

In the distance, the Meister, having left the road, was cutting diagonally across the meadow. In his brightly colored uniform of Todt's Army of Labor, he stood out against the wet green of the grass. He was a great specialist in the installation of water pipes, the carrying of rails, and the loading of sacks of cement, and also a splendid organizer—not matched even by us Auschwitzers—of all sorts of foods from the neighboring villages. He took care of his people, and he had twenty of us. Every day he collected bread crusts from his colleagues and distributed them to whomever worked most enthusiastically.

I grabbed my spade and began energetically throwing out the crushed earth. The former saboteur took his pickax and, moving a good two meters away from me so we shouldn't be seen standing together, raised his pickax high above the edges of the trench, allowing it to fall into the trench of its own weight.

"You were beginning to say something about the trench earlier, I think?" he guessed, when our silence had gotten dangerously long. It was important to converse all day long; then a person could lose track of time and have no chance to weave destructive daydreams about food.

"Say something! What was it?" And he swung the pickax again, taking care to let it flash above the trench.

"Because, you see, we putter around, digging so that a German can make a profit, first in Silesia, somewhere in the Beskidy foothills, then in Wirtemberg, then for a change on the Swiss border, and all the time one of our pals is dying, then they round up new ones, and so it goes, brother, in a circle. And there's no end in sight. And when winter comes . . ."

"Don't talk. Put your ear to the wall and you'll hear the earth rumbling from artillery. They're pounding them over there in the west, just pounding them . . ."

"They've been pounding like that for a month. And all that time we've had people dying, we've brought in lime, bricks, cement, rails, iron, and who knows what else, we've dug trenches, holes, we've laid tracks—and what does it lead to? We're getting hungrier and colder. And it's raining more and more often. A person held out somehow with the hope that he'd go home, but now? To whom? Maybe they're also digging holes somewhere like those insurgents of ours. But even if that's not so, do you think you'll know how to live? Or will you be afraid forever of who knows what terrors? Or are you going to steal with both hands, whatever comes your way, because what are you going to believe in? What's there to say; I've been thinking about food since morning. And not about some sort of splendid dishes like you read about in novels. Just my fill of bread slathered with butter."

"I don't think about what will be," the saboteur said sharply; "the main thing is to survive today. I want to go home to my wife, to my child; I've had my fill of fighting around the world. Surely you'll be better off than now, right? Or maybe you'd like this to go on till the end of your life." And he laughed derisively.

"Swing, swing your pick," I warned him. "The Meister's standing over the trench. Can't you see him?"

Pretending that we hadn't noticed him, we worked feverishly, seemingly absorbed in our conversation. I heaved out full, respectable spadesful onto the very crest of the embankment, groaning from the effort. Meister Batsch stopped above us for a minute, his hands behind his back, and looked on as if from an extraordinary height and walked slowly above the trench, the black of his tall boots glistening. The edge of his soldier's coat was thickly mud-encrusted.

"Kapo, Kapo," he shouted to me, standing over the group of insurgents. "Come here! Why is this man lying on the ground? Why isn't he working?"

The Meisters called everyone who could speak German "Kapo." The old Auschwitz hands found this very funny and even, to tell the truth, depressing, because after all, a kapo is a kapo.

I ran there through the trench. Beyond the bend, on the bottom of the trench, an old man sat bent over, the one with the mud-spattered, formerly elegant ankle boots, groaning and clutching his belly. The Meister squatted above the trench attentively, but looking the prisoner in the face from a distance.

"Sick?" he asked.

He was holding in his hand a rather large packet wrapped in newspaper.

Thin drops of sweat appeared on the frighteningly pale face of the old insurgent. His eyes were closed. His eyelids kept trembling. He must have felt hot, because he'd undone his collar. The straw had slipped out from under his armpits and was sticking up in front of his face.

"What is it, old man? So the beets did you no good?" I asked sympathetically.

His colleague with a pickax, the one in the roofing paper covering, cast a hate-filled glance at me and addressed Meister Batsch clumsily.

"*Krank.* He's sick, sick," he repeated with emphasis in the hope that the Meister would understand Polish. "*Hunger, verstehen?*"

"Yes, it's obvious," I added hastily. "He gorged on beets and now he's got stomach pains. He's only just arrived in the camp, so he doesn't know that vegetables are harmful. It's hard to cope with greed and hunger, Mr. Meister."

"Beets? From that field, eh? Oh, that's very bad. *Klauen*, right?" And Meister Batsch made the international sign for putting something stealthily into one's pocket.

"He's incapable of pulling that off!" I said with contempt. "He trades bread for beets every day."

Meister Batsch nodded to indicate that he understood and looked down sadly at the insurgent from the top of the trench, as if from the edge of another world. The old man's comrade, the one with the roofing paper, moved uneasily.

"Tell him, sir, maybe they can carry the man to the camp. After all, he's sick, very sick."

"Very sick?" I said, sounding astonished. "Then you've seen very little so far in this world. He can wait until evening. Don't you know, child, that no guard is going to leave here now? What is this, your first day in the kommando? And take off that roofing paper, or someone's going to hurt you. I've already told you once. Then later you'll complain again that we're not nice, that we don't warn you."

And I went back to my spade. The saboteur, profiting from the foreman's being occupied with something else, was squatting calmly in the niche, supporting himself skillfully on the pickax. When I grabbed the spade, he crawled out of the niche and also assumed a working posture.

"The old guy, right?" he guessed without much interest.

"He won't make it even till night," I answered. "I've already seen more than a hundred men like that. Swollen legs, Durchfall, and now he's gorged on beets. I see black before him."

"Again, one man fewer . . . I didn't order him to come here. They could have defended Warsaw once they began, right?"

"Certainly they could have. Besides, if they had gone to Auschwitz, no one would have kept an eye on them. They thought they were going to do labor. They rushed to do labor like a peasant to soda water."

Out of anger I heaved an entire lump of earth onto the embankment so that the handle of the spade bent.

"Why worry yourself about that one? If someone wants to serve the Germans, then good for him," said the saboteur. "In Auschwitz they cried that they aren't politicals, and every third one among them boasted that he had a Volksdeutsch uncle, so now they don't like it because they give them so little to eat. They arrived six weeks ago and they'd already like to get three bowls of soup!"

"Did you eat a lot more today than the ration?" I asked, interested. Food was a topic at moments of particular emotion.

"Whatever it was that I ate," the former saboteur from Radom bristled, "I ate it yesterday. The morning's bread ration and what was there to go with the bread?"

"Margarine and cheese," I prompted him.

"Margarine and cheese. Nothing the whole day. We sold the beet to the Jews in the evening. There was half a slice of bread for the two of us. And later in the evening also the soup for your broom. And then I got extra soup in the kitchen because I carried out the cauldrons."

"You couldn't come get me?" I asked regretfully.

"No, because I had to eat it in the kitchen. And today," he went on, "a slice of bread in the morning, a small square of margarine, then a couple of plums, then that bread again and a bit of beet. If it goes on like this . . ."

He broke off and took up his pickax. Meister Batsch was standing over us, silent. He glanced approvingly at the way we cooperated and our excellent work and tossed a tiny package wrapped in newspaper between us. Bread crusts spilled out under our feet.

"That's just what I was thinking about," Romek said energetically.

And he raised the pickax high over his head, making sure that it flashed above the edge of the trench, while I bent over eagerly to the ground.

THE BATTLE OF GRUNWALD

Across the broad, sunlit yard of the former SS barracks, as if at
the bottom of a deep well dug inside the stone walls of the surrounding buildings, the Battalion marched and sang, its dull, persistent
beat thudding against the concrete. Its forearms, cloaked in green
sleeves inherited from SS soldiers' jackets, rose energetically to its
waist and dropped toward the ground in an angry, unified sweep,
as if it were not the Battalion that was marching but a single multiplied person striding there, confident of its strength and hoarse
from singing. Only the varicolored legs of the Battalion, spattered
here and there with a bright splash of cheap felt clogs, disturbed the
military uniformity of expression.

Seen from on high, the Battalion resembled three green cater-
pillars with striped, pleated spines and an immobile torso; it circled
the yard stiffly, struck down by the trembling column of sunlight;
it passed a column of sturdy American trucks that was disgorging
from its insides, as from a sack of rags, its brightly colored contents
of people and baggage; it struck the concrete even more energetically under the slender, freshly painted flagpole because the colorful national rag was flapping on it in the wind as if on a fishing
pole; it slowed down near a pile of logs, young pine trees shed-
ding needles, benches, and chairs all readied for the evening bonfire; it made a sharp turn beside the once glass-enclosed assembly
hall in which patriotic SS meetings had been held until recently;
it crunched with its many feet on the glass from the thoroughly

smashed windowpanes; it broke off its singing in mid-word and entered as into a tunnel the gloomy jaws of the hall, fenced off from the square by its sharp sunny glare and the succulent, blackened greenery of the freshly cut branches. The blinding chalky serpent of dust that followed the Battalion curled up at the entrance to the assembly hall, turned gray, dropped to the ground, and, inflated by a chance puff of wind, swelled up, burst, rose up into the air and disappeared without a trace.

Sitting naked with my knee under my chin on a narrow, hard windowsill on the third floor of one of the walls surrounding the well of the courtyard, warming myself in the sunshine like a mangy dog, I stretched sleepily, yawned respectfully, and set aside the book I had organized from one of the officers' rooms—a story about the heroic, jolly, and praiseworthy adventures of Till Eulenspiegel and Lamme Goedzak.

"Chivalric soldiers," I said, turning around to face the room to give my back a turn in the sunshine, "the Battalion has marched to the church to attend the Mass. You have fulfilled your duty well to the Fatherland, which is everywhere in the world where you are. You are free to continue sleeping."

The room stank in a soldierly way of the stale, salty sweat of unwashed genitalia. Under the unpainted walls adorned with jingoistic Nazi slogans stood two rows of iron bunk beds; rough-hewn tables walked down the center, while under their legs a couple of backless stools hung around, and an enamel spittoon, as helpless as a lost child, roamed about. Narrow-striped lazy flies buzzed in the air and half-asleep men were breathing heavily.

"How did they march? Like an army? Because during drills they slouch around like a Muselmann in the mud," Cadet Kolka, who slept near the wall with the door, called out.

Huge and sinewy, he couldn't fit into his skimpy bed. Although he had quarreled with the officers during the distribution of German jackets and had decided to boycott the army, he never took off his cloth uniform; he lay in bed in it all day long, suffocating from the heat, and kicked his hobnailed boots against the iron bedrail, with each furious outburst scattering straw from the rotten mattress onto the lower bunk, onto the pallet on which I slept. He always kept his pimply face turned toward the window and, looking mindlessly at the sandbar of the windowsill, listened greedily to the singing and stamping of the Battalion.

"The Polish infantry marches well when Polish officers are leading it, to the glory of the Fatherland," I yelled, jumping down from the windowsill. My back was so heated up it felt as if someone had scrubbed it with red-hot pins.

"For six years in the camp they tramped around in groups of five and now that they've had a two-month rest, they're tramping around again — in fours, praise be to God and the Fatherland, and instead of kapos they have officers at their head. They'll learn to march, all right, but the cooks won't learn not to take grub from the kitchen for the Jewish women," I added, staring blankly into space.

"You're taking a jab at me, if I understand you correctly," the Chief Warrant Officer, who was reading a German book about the Katyń massacre,* growled surlily, and taking off his horn-rimmed glasses squinted at me with the sleepy eyes of a nearsighted man. He deliberately walked around in clinging, immaculate briefs, the muscular knots of his body gleaming. He was covered from head to toe with a faded tattooed design, like a dusty clay platter. On his

---

* In 1940 more than four thousand Polish prisoners of war, mainly reserve officers, but also officers in the regular army and policemen, were executed by the Soviet secret police in Katyń Forest, near the then Soviet city of Smolensk. Their mass graves were discovered in April 1943 by German occupying forces. The Soviets admitted their responsibility for the crime, and for the executions of at least sixteen thousand additional Polish POWs and political prisoners, only in 1990. Until then, the communist government of Poland had officially accepted the Soviet claim that the crime was committed by the Germans.

right thigh a thick, crookedly drawn arrow pointed to his groin, and a red inscription indicated unmistakably: "For Ladies Only."

"If someone has kitchen duty, he should watch out that no one steals. But the Warrant Officer watches to see if the cook will manage to steal for a pregnant Jewess," Stefan called out from the door. He was studying English and kept repeating vocabulary words in a whisper. He flung the book onto the table and walked over to the window, his heavy boots thumping on the stone floor.

"The sons-of-bitches are cooking on coal again," he said, sticking his head out the window. "They've got an electric stove, cauldrons, and everything they need for us, so what are they cooking on the little stove? Obviously, dinner for the officers. All us sufferers from the camps are supposed to be brothers, colleagues, but only for marching to Mass, and not to the cooking pot. And how do you like an inspector who knows this and reads picture books? If he crawled into a Colonel's ass he wouldn't crawl out unless it was from a Second Lieutenant's."

I snorted a short, approving laugh. The Warrant Officer sprang up on his bed, hit his head against the sharp corner of the upper bunk, emitted a stream of sexual vulgarities, stroked his thinning, stiff gray hair, and said with disgust, "Don't mess with me, you Bolshevik runt. If you don't like it, get out of the army."

His nipples, decorated with a couple of tattooed ears and dark blue drops mimicking eyes, quivered convulsively like a bunny's nose.

"They're stealing, they're stealing! Don't bark if you haven't caught them. A good dog doesn't bark; it catches and bites."

"Exactly, exactly; you, sir, should bite. You are a dog trained to catch. You hold the Colonel on a leash."

"Woof, woof," Stefan barked hoarsely and screwed up his little swollen eyes maliciously. His teeth, even and white like a dog's, glittered behind his nervously curled lips. He walked alongside the tables, as erect as if he were attached to the building.

The Warrant Officer got up slowly from his bed. Cadet Kolka stirred, interested, and removed his fist from under his head. The straw mattress rustled and straw fell onto the lower bunk. I wrinkled my brow disapprovingly.

From the yard came the choking sound of a truck preparing to depart. Suddenly, scraps of raucous conversation reached us and then fell silent, as if cut off with a knife.

At the same time, though, the sick Gypsy, whom I had nearly beaten to death in the struggle for a better place in the freight car during our transport to Dachau, sat up, groaning, in his bed, roused by the sudden silence.

"Oh, people, restless people, you're wanting to fight again," he whined, sniveling tearfully. "It's not enough for you that misery is beating you? But our Pole, our brother, is always stupid. He wants to drown his brother in a spoonful of water."

He pressed his blue, emaciated face into the pillow with a red-poppy design that he'd brought here from his nighttime raids of German farms. He'd been suffering from diarrhea for several days. He had stuffed himself with uncooked mutton. He lay motionless, patient as a sick animal. He preferred to die rather than go to the hospital, since he had memories of the hospital in the small Daut-mergen concentration camp.

The Warrant Officer sat down stiffly on his bed. He pedantically tucked in a protruding corner of his sheet, the only one, by the way, in this room. He drummed his toes nervously. He snatched up his book, noisily turned a couple of pages, and stared dully at the photographs of the graves in Katyń.

"There won't be a fight," I thought, disappointed, and leaned out the window.

Under the stone walls of the barracks, on narrow strips of lawn, between knocked-over garbage piles whose stench poisoned the entire yard, anemic little maple trees struggled upward and a red-flowering hedge had taken root right under the concrete. Higher up, above the spindly trees and the hedge, in the many rows of identical windows, scraps of various-colored linen hung from lines, and freshly painted wooden chests dangled from ropes, hung out to dry in the sun.

On the ground floor, where the prominents lived, was a row of smoothly glazed Venetian windows, immersed in succulent shade at the bottom and, at the top, in sunlight like golden paint. From the ground floor, from the upper stories, all the way to the garret, indefatigable radios blared hoarsely.

Outside the gate that was guarded by foreign soldiers, columns of trucks stretched out along the highway, a thin stream of bicycles flowed by, colorful summer dresses flashed among the abundant, firmly rooted, plane trees.

Out there was the world which we were permitted to enter as a reward for good marching, reporting a punishable action, cleaning up the corridor, for loyalty, for steadfastness, and also for the Fatherland.

And in the center wing of the building, on the third floor, where the kitchens of the Allach Central Military Command were located, from a small pipe, brown with rust, nonchalantly installed through a window vent, a delicate blue smoke filtered silently and stealthily dissolved in the air into a shimmering, exceptionally delicate trace.

"It's lovely out in the world, brothers," I sighed with feigned sorrow. "But what are you doing, man? You're sitting here locked up just like under the Germans; they won't give you a pass into the world because you're not capable of sucking up to them; you won't get out through a hole in the wall because they'll shoot. After all—you're a Häftling, an inmate from the camps! How can you sit there? If someone's son should bring him mutton or bring a German woman to him, then he can sit. And what do you say? Sit still, even though you're hungry and far from home. Just as long as they

don't steal! It would be easier if everyone was in the same boat . . .
But only for so long, only for so long . . ."

All this time I was looking at the Warrant Officer through narrowed eyelids. The Warrant Officer moved uneasily on his bed; his
lips trembled menacingly. But he didn't say anything. He pulled his
uniform out of the wardrobe and started to get dressed, wheezing
a little through his nose. He tightened his lips and looked at the
ground.

"You're probably going to the Grunwald Mass, sir?" Kolka
asked him indifferently from the other end of the room.

"No, Cadet. I'm going to the kitchen to check on things. But if
I don't find anything!" he muttered menacingly through clenched
teeth.

"You'll find something, Warrant Officer, you'll find something," Stefan hummed under his breath. "Just watch out that they
don't catch sonny, because who's going to feed you? The Colonel's
not going to bring you mutton."

"And what about you, Tadzio," Cadet Kolka stuck his legs out
through the bed rail, "aren't you going to Grunwald?"

"I don't feel like it. Maybe I'll go to the theater. It seems they're
preparing some surprises for the bonfire. What's interesting at
the Mass?"

"Go to the Mass," Kolka urged me languidly. He slipped his
hands inside his trousers and scratched attentively. "Go to the Mass,
then you can tell me what you wrote to the Editor for his rag of a
paper. Maybe he'll give you goulash. Goulash for supper today."

"He'll give it anyway. He gives me soup every day . . ."

"You could take a look at the girls . . . Wouldn't you like to see
the Archbishop?"

"What do we have in common?" I spread my hands apart
for emphasis. "Our life experiences are so different! He spent the
whole war somewhere out there in the world; you know what that

means—heroism and Fatherland, and a little bit of God. And we lived somewhere else, meaning, rutabagas, bedbugs, and running sores. He is undoubtedly well fed; I am hungry. He looks upon today's ceremony from the point of view of Poland; I view it as goulash and tomorrow's Lenten soup. I won't understand his gestures, and mine will be too ordinary for him; we both despise each other a little. As for *Grunwald*? Am I unhappy here on the windowsill? The sun is baking me, a fly is buzzing, it's pleasant to be talking with one's neighbor"—I bowed in the direction of the Warrant Officer—"and I can see everything as in a theater. In addition," I added sensibly, "it isn't here yet. The generals are only now arriving at the Mass with dignity and in good order, while above the generals floats the smoke and aroma of the dinner that is being prepared for them."

The Colonel was walking at the head of the column, in a uniform cut by local tailors in the English fashion from a blanket the color of withered leaves. Seen from a radically foreshortened angle, the Colonel resembled a massive block with a sun-polished head and stiff legs; he moved straight ahead, in a dignified fashion, making an effort to imitate an energetic, military pace. Beside him came the Major, wrapped in the virgin green of a German officer's uniform. He was gesturing at the Colonel with both hands, apparently explaining something to him in a sermonizing manner, maybe about the subversive agitation in the Allach Central Military Command. Behind them, like a throng of unruly children behind their teacher, a homogeneous herd of green and black jackets and gesticulating hands milled about, with red heads in forage caps liberally sprinkled with the national colors bobbing above them.

"Too bad the Germans didn't manage to destroy them, too!"

Stefan leaned against the windowsill in deep thought and looked out at the yard in a rage. His black hair, standing up on end, glistened like a dog's pelt.

"That kind of people will be with us until the end of the world. Poland, ah, Poland, for Poland. Just so long as we have two bowls of soup far away from her! How stupid I was, so stupid, stupid!"

He stepped back from the windowsill and slapped his forehead.

"After all, I saw it myself; I supported that rabble in the block, I fed them, stood up for them, stole grub from the stupid Gypsies."

"Don't boast, Block Elder," Cadet Kolka cut him off sharply, so that Stefan turned to face the room. "After all, we were in the same camp. When you stole, it was bread and butter for yourself, and for them soup, at most."

"And who gave them room in the block? Clean bunks, clean blankets, stuffed mattresses? Is that little? Would they have survived in a kommando?"

"The air would have been cleaner if they'd kicked the bucket," I added amicably, watching with amusement how Stefan—my former colleague, a Fleger from Birkenau, later an SS Laufer and a Pipel in a small kommando, who once, because I hadn't made way for him quickly enough, dealt me a serious blow to the face, who finally became block elder in the wealthiest Schonungsblock from which soup by the cauldronful and dozens of loaves of bread made their way into the camp in search of cigarettes, fruit, and meat for the block elder—how this Stefan was boasting that he had saved the lives of a couple of Polish officers from the Warsaw Uprising who now didn't want to repay him with as much soup as he desired.

"And do you remember," he continued bitterly, "what the Colonel was like in Allach? They brought him a coffee mill, he begged someone for a little wheat, sat down on a plank bed and—nothing, just the mill and baking pancakes. You understand, the world is crumbling, the SS artillery is firing into the camp, women are burned to a crisp, the villages are all burning, the guys have gone on a rampage with a knife, the Americans are coming, frenzy, fraternity of people, the end of the war! But for that one—it's about a coffee mill, pancakes, and he's running to the latrine. And already he's made himself into such an important person . . ."

I raised both my hands. Stefan fell silent, disconcerted. Then, taking advantage of the opportunity, I recited pathetically:

> Hierarchies are established,
> brother finally recognizes brother.
> Our Colonel, lord of the Curia,
> turns his mill, grinding flour.
>
> He received a second bowl of soup
> so he felt strong in his power.
> As for me, I am ready to serve,
> just give me something to eat.
>
> Colonel, take aim!
> Colonel, grind grain!
> Let's fight fire with fire,
> and create an army with a mess hall.
>
> For every battle won,
> Extra soup for everyone!

"That's how it was, you're right, Stefan," I praised him. "That's my poem, Warrant Officer. It's good, eh?"

The Warrant Officer was already all buttoned up. He fixed his calm gaze on me.

"I'm surprised at you, an intellectual," he said bitterly. "Such foolishness at a time like this . . . When we've been ordered to stick together and not to get into fights! Brawling will destroy us! We'll perish because of it!"

"In Katyń, eh? In Katyń? Are you disappointed, Warrant Officer?" Stefan barked venomously, going over to face the man. "You read your fill of books, lots of books, eat soup, grope a German girl, whatever you feel like doing . . . In Katyń, what?"

"Of course in Katyń, you bastard! Do you know what that means? Those are your beloved countrymen from the East, your Poland, you filthy reptile!" the Warrant Officer suddenly burst out, and also walked over to the table. He dug his knobby fingers into the black tabletop until his fingertips swelled with blood.

"So, you don't like Poland, right? You don't like it? You'd like a different Poland, Warrant Officer. One you can carry a banner in? So that sonny boy can go on raids at night and bring you girls? The Poland you're capable of building makes me want to throw up!"

"Then go to your own country; just go!" the Warrant Officer hissed through clenched teeth. His lips turned white and began quivering. "No one is keeping you here. Spy!"

"Don't worry, I'm going," Stefan started singing calmly. "I've got time. I'll just observe you for a while longer, I'll commit you to memory. I'll go and I'll be waiting for you, yes I will!"

Cadet Kolka sat down heavily on the bed and dangled his legs, scattering a bunch of trash onto my bed. He waved at me gaily and tapped his temple a couple of times, pretending to nod his head like an idiot. The black Gypsy groaned in agony into his pillow with the red-poppy design. I smiled at Kolka and shook my head in response, as if I were checking to see whether water was sloshing around inside it.

"Go to your Poland, to those Poles who created Katyń, go!" the Warrant Officer shouted, his face purple from passion.

"They did a good thing! Too bad it was just one time!"

The Warrant Officer scratched at the table, overturned it with a crash, and leaped at Stefan's throat.

In the glassed-in assembly hall decorated with freshly cut boughs the silvery tinkle of a bell could be heard. The small crowd, gathered in front of the hall, filed inside together with a priest in purple robes and, surrounded by a tight circle of black and green priests, steered themselves into the hall through the gala doors of headquarters, which was lavishly decorated in red and white.

"Hey, let's have some peace!" I squeaked and ran over to help Kolka disarm the combatants. "Don't kill each other, you sons of bitches! The Archbishop is on his way to perform the holy Mass!"

II

The Archbishop turned away from the altar. At his feet the gray heads of officers glistened above the arms of their chairs. Among the officers, in the first row, the President of the Committee sat as immobile as a statue. His massive, bull-like, close-cropped head emerged from a snowy collar arranged romantically à la Słowacki, and inclined solemnly toward the altar. Farther along, pushed ahead by the Colonel, the Actor was posturing in his chair. He felt ill at ease in his stolen civilian suit, which was too big and too stiff; he fidgeted nervously and flashed his eyeglasses inquiringly toward the audience, tightening his lips and tugging down his fleshy cheeks. Next to him, on the brown plush of her armchair, the Singer, about whom gossip had it that in the days of hunger before the war's end, all of Dachau had had a turn with her, poured out of her carmine dress. Now (the gossip continued) the Actor was having her. On her lap lay an American helmet liner. The First Lieutenant, the real commandant of the camp, was sitting with one leg draped over the other and chewing gum impassively; shining strangely from brilliantine, he had his eyes fixed dully on the Singer's thighs.

Behind the chairs, the mob crowded together, thoroughly covered the hall's windows, piously stared at the birch cross and the eagles cut out of paper and tacked onto the enormous national banners made out of sheets, and at the open doors in which ivy swayed and a gentle sky quivered. The mob watched in silence. The Battalion stood at attention beside the benches.

"When you're finished reading *Till Eulenspiegel*, give it to me," the Editor whispered. "Are you joining us for goulash? We're leaving early for the theater."

He dropped onto one knee and struck his breast with his fist.

"I'm coming," I assured him enthusiastically, slipping onto the ground.

The Archbishop took a look at the crowd at the foot of the altar and gave an imperceptible nod of the head. A priest from Dachau who had been standing near his chair with nothing to do hopped over and placed the miter on his head. The Archbishop adjusted it with an impatient gesture (apparently, it pinched him) and only then blessed us by helplessly spreading his arms wide. A faintly whispered prayer flowed over the hastily bowed heads.

On the other side of the concrete yard, on the narrow little strip of green beneath the anemic plane trees, the transport shaken out of the American trucks was setting up camp. The lawn was fenced off with various belongings on which nursing mothers who were faint from the heat immediately plopped down with their dark, wailing brats, and girls who were indifferent to everything sat, displaying their bodies through their translucent dresses. Men in sweat-soaked shirts stood watchfully near their bundles, wandered around next to the building, gaped at the assembly hall, while the more energetic ones went off to look at the rooms in which the transport was going to live.

"Aha, the poet. You're not at the Mass? You've run away from the national and divine mysterium? You're not building the foundation of the flagpole for the nation's flag, composed of the spirit of those who died on the field of battle and others?"

On a pile of suitcases, pillows, and quilts tied up with string sat a girl with unusual eyes. Instead of a cross, a peculiar, elongated capsule, like a small whistle, hung around her neck. Her strong, firm thighs were outlined under her batiste skirt. Her lovely legs flowed softly over a feather bed. Against them, straddling a suitcase with his tall boots, the Professor sat majestically, smiling at me ironically from behind his glasses as if from behind the wall of a trench. He must have noticed that my jaws were trembling with desire.

"I survived biologically. Now I am laying supports under the road to Poland. From spiritual lethargy I enter the living body of the nation," I replied evasively.

We both burst out laughing. We were quoting the choicest passages from the mimeographed pornographic-patriotic camp newsletter put out by the priest.

"This woman," the Professor gestured, accidentally touching the girl's legs, "has just escaped from the living body of the nation. The entire transport arrived from Pilsen. They walked out of Poland across the green border."

I raised my eyebrows thoughtfully. The girl flashed her teeth at me in answer. She rearranged herself on the feather bed. Her too heavy breasts jiggled under her blouse.

"From the forest bands?" I figured. Going from room to room in search of mutton, I'd listened to the radio from Warsaw. Between announcements of people seeking their family members they were constantly complaining about forest bands.

"The exact opposite. One of ours. A Jew. They fled. Like cows seeking better pasture. They attached themselves to us as if they were going after forbidden grain. But it's fallow land here, little lady!"

He leaned back, slapped her on the knee, and in full view trailed his hand over the girl's calf.

I offered the girl my hand. She squinted, perhaps from the sun which shone right into her eyes for a moment.

"Don't listen. That's the bitterness of a cow who has not found a better pasture even though she's wandered over half the world."

"We're from the same building," said the girl, "from the ghetto." She smiled, as if apologizing. "And now we've met again in the same building," and she pointed to the stones of the barracks, "an SS building."

"As if there'd been no war," the Professor added caustically and, delighted with himself, burst into raucous laughter. He wiped his wrinkled hands and brushed off his leather Bavarian shorts that were as stained as a butcher's apron.

"You should remember about the cows, you poet manqué," he added, and stared at his hairy knees.

"In order to see a better pasture?" the girl asked from her perch on the feather bed. With the tip of her finger, she stroked the man's hair. I tightened my mouth ironically, catching her oblique glance.

"No," the Professor answered reluctantly. "In order to have one's own pasture. And not to be an ambassador of one's herd in others' meadows."

"And where is our meadow?"

"In Palestine. In the Akko prison outside Jerusalem. I was held there for half a year for illegal emigration. During the war, ha, ha, ha," he barked a thunderous laugh, stood up, and without a word crossed the concrete yard toward the assembly hall. People were pouring out of it now that the service had ended, filling the yard, like a bowl, with noise. A swarm of eminences, surrounding the Archbishop with their jangling, flowed toward headquarters and vanished through the ground-floor doors of the apartment occupied by the Supreme Colonel.

"Over there is the living, ascetic body of the nation. The Polish mistletoe on the German oak." I waved my arm contemptuously in the direction of the square. "And yet, what power. Because we're fighting for an idea! And what about back there, in your Poland?"

I didn't walk away; my coarse cloth trousers were tickling my thighs insistently. The girl slid down gently from the feather bed and landed on the ground, rubbing her body against mine like a cat. Her too prominent bosom jiggled again underneath her blouse.

"Do you think I'm some poor passenger who's gotten off a streetcar in which half the people are seated and the other half are quaking? That it's because of the eagle's crown? You know those

Polish witticisms, right? Not at all!" she cried passionately. "That's not why at all!"

She reached energetically for her valise. When she bent over, her thighs flashed under her pink skirt. The transport started carrying its packages into the barracks in great haste. I grabbed up two bundles and, my boots striking the concrete with a masculine stride, dragged them upstairs. I kept my eyes on the girl's neck the whole time; loaded down with bedding, she shuffled along ahead of me. Some aunts or chaperones shouted at her in piercing voices, grabbed at the bedding with shaky hands, and pointed out the way.

We dumped our burdens in a room on the ground floor and ran out again to fetch the valises, shouting gaily and cursing under our breath. In the passageway I brushed against the girl again and caught her bemused glance.

In the large room which was to be occupied for a couple of hours, the men busied themselves with the half-caved-in doors, marking off a passageway with the smashed window and the mangled, piled-up plank beds. In this great room that was as dark as a cellar, thick dust rose all the way to the ceiling and choked our throats. The garbage was collected and thrown out through the smashed window of the corridor straight onto the heads of the men who had settled in at the rear of the barracks, men who, unconcerned about *Grunwald*, the fresh July day, or the threat of being punished for violating regulations, were sitting in groups near innumerable bonfires made from a couple of thick slivers hacked off from the plank beds and tables, and were cooking up all sorts of food—mutton stolen from a herd on the eve of *Grunwald*, kasha, soups, compotes—in saucepans, mess kits, soot-covered empty jam tins, and stolen aluminum pots; they were baking potato pancakes on rusty, red-hot sheets of metal, and using wooden trowels to stir boiling mixtures in all sorts of colors while blowing industriously on the flames. The smoke gurgled like thick, filthy sour cream that is just about to boil, puffed up, rose lazily from the ground, overflowed across the bullet-pocked wall onto the nearby meadow, wiping out the contours of the distant, flat woods that lay on the horizon, and like cream, encircled the dome-shaped plane trees beside the highway. The smell of raw meat cooking, mixed with smoke, tickled one's nostrils until one's stomach started churning. From below, from under the smoke as from the bottom of a pot, the gurgling of the cries and curses of the hungry people who were cooking for themselves could be heard. I pulled the girl away from the window and dragged her to the white, tiled washroom; filthy from the remains of food and shit, it stank like a latrine.

"So that's how you live," the Jewess said contemptuously, placing her hands under a stream of water. "Out front—*Grunwald*, and in back, cooking. I couldn't stand a single day here. No, I couldn't stand it!"

"You'd grow accustomed, lady," I replied, offended. "We're still under quarantine. Not quite concentration camp, not quite freedom. But it will be better, freer! We are a great power! A moral power!" I carried on rapturously. "But," I calmed down, "people want to eat. A man has to eat, he has to have women. People were hungry for so many years! For so many years they yearned for the moment when they'd eat as much bread as they wanted, when they'd have their first woman! These are fundamental matters. Not even *Grunwald* can help with that."

She shook the last clinging drops from her hands. She wiped her hands on the hem of her skirt. Her thighs flashed. We went out into the corridor. The automatic doors clanged softly behind us. They hadn't been destroyed yet.

"And after so many years in the camp aren't you yearning to walk out past these walls?"

She looked at me inquiringly as at a peculiar species of dog or cat.

"I'm not speaking about bread or," a slight tone of irony entered her voice, "about a woman. But simply going straight into the woods?"

"I'm afraid," I confessed sincerely, "because they've got guards posted. To have survived for so many years and then to die after the war—no, that's too grotesque. A person values himself twice as much."

"You're afraid!" She clapped her hands. "Ah, you're afraid!"

"And what drew you to . . . to foreign meadows, if not fear? You ran away from the Fatherland? To the mirage of the West? This is the West!" I pointed to the smashed window in which the smoke was curling. "We've all been afraid ever since there was peace."

The girl laughed mockingly. We were walking down the corridor, alongside the windows that faced the woods.

"Not fear at all! I ran away out of love. It's funny, oh, so funny!"

I pulled up my trousers which kept slipping down and crossed my bare arms across my chest. I was embarrassed by the pimples showing from under my tee shirt, but I hadn't been able to steal a shirt with a collar yet.

"For six years I was a Catholic, a Polish woman; I learned all sorts of commandments, attended church and confession regularly. My mother, before she perished in Treblinka, gave me a prayer book. I can see her inscription before my eyes to this day: 'For my beloved daughter, Janina, on the day of her First Communion, Mommy.' That was not my name. After all, I don't look like a Jew," she said with a certain degree of pride, looking for confirmation in my eyes.

In fact, she did not look like a Jew. She had blond, fluffy hair and a broad, somewhat flat face. Only her dark, deep eyes flashed anxiously.

"But you're an Aryan," I said, congratulating her.

Her eyes sparkled with gratitude.

"That's the terror. But where's the love?"

"There's love because I fell in love. With a Catholic. He was a communist and he didn't like Jews. There are so many like that in Poland!" she complained naively. "He loved me very much. I couldn't lie to him. I couldn't, right?"

I kept looking her straight in the eye with well-feigned sympathetic silence.

"He joined the army as soon as the Germans retreated. By the way, that was in Siedlce. I wrote him a letter to his field post office and ran away. It's very easy, oh so easy!"

"Without waiting for an answer?" I marveled.

She blushed like a peach and bit her lips.

"I was afraid that he'd write . . ." She stopped. "He was such a nationalist. And I . . . I couldn't keep it up any more! I didn't want to! I preferred to be called a Hymie, to see Poles avoiding me!"

A couple of men ran past, bumping into us, and disappeared behind a bend in the corridor. From somewhere outside excited cries reached us.

I took her by the hand. It was as warm and soft as cat's fur. Smoke from the windows seeped into the corridor and settled on the ceiling in narrow strips like a spider web.

"I can understand that very well," I said casually, mastering the trembling of my jaws with difficulty. "You are very brave. The bravery of terror. I would like to be that way."

And I burst out in one breath, "Would you go for a walk with me, outside the boundaries of the camp? They say there are pine trees there that give off the smell of summer, and I've never been there. I'd have probably run wild from my longing for space and would have headed out to the west or east. I'm reluctant to leave the books I've collected. But with you," I squeezed her hand confidentially, "I wouldn't go too far. It's safe."

I clicked my boots more energetically and pulled up my trousers with one hand. The dry, rough cloth stung like nettles. The cauldrons were already clattering in the corridors. Dinnertime was approaching. My stomach ached like a sore tooth. A cry came in from the courtyard. People ran down the corridor again and through the entrance door. Something must have been going on there.

"Tomorrow we're traveling on," the girl said, freeing her hand. "Who knows where to? A day in one camp, a day in another . . . New people, strangers, all the time. I'm disgusted by it!"

And suddenly she said almost in a whisper, "I'm terrified of going to Palestine. What do I have in common with Jews? To be a Jew by myself, privately—that's fine! But to live in a Jewish village, to milk cows, to check Jewish chicks for eggs, to marry a Jew? No, no," she cried out, as if I were urging her to do that. "Maybe I'll run away and study. But whatever I do, we'll never meet. No," she affirmed her own thoughts decisively, "we'll never meet. And it's a shame. Maybe I could fall in love with you?"

She smiled, amused by the expression in my eyes.

"Because you know how to listen. Just like Romek. He's the one from Siedlce," she explained abruptly.

I grabbed her by the elbow and turned her around roughly to face me. She almost touched me with her too prominent breasts. A wave of blood surged through my body.

"We'll never meet!" she bantered with me, and the corners of her mouth trembled, "but," and she lowered her voice, "it's better that way."

And when I released her, discouraged, she slipped out from under my arm.

"When do you want to go on that . . . walk?"

"After dinner, all right?" I whispered excitedly. "It will be easier when they change the guard. We'll go."

Again, a couple of men ran down the corridor. The last one turned around, waved at us encouragingly and called out, out of breath, "Go, take a look! A pacification action! Soldiers with rifles! Revolution!" and he clattered down the stairs.

The girl rushed to the door without giving me an answer. I ran after her. We ran down into the yard. A crowd was milling around in the doorway. In the middle of the square a wave of people was retreating, spreading out noisily at the sides in front of jeeps that were moving as slowly as boats, with soldiers standing in them, American soldiers, shaking their rifles threateningly. Suddenly, a shot rang out from the lead car. The crowd fluttered like a flock of startled ducks, responded with an ominous roar and fell silent, gurgling and running together to the chicken coop barracks. Immediately, all the windows filled with clucking human heads. The Major emerged suddenly from the headquarters door. He stood as if frozen at the sight of the soldiers, and then quietly retreated under the stairs on which the figure of the Archbishop shone with great dignity.

The girl's whole body was trembling. I pulled her toward me. Her too prominent bust yielded softly under my fingers. She cuddled against me trustingly.

"Beasts," she spat through clenched teeth; "ach, what beasts! I'd give anything to escape from here! Let's run away."

She covered my hand with hers. My empty stomach pinched me like a tight, painful shoe.

"It's because of those cooks," someone in front of us informed everyone. "They're the ones who sent the Americans. They've grown arrogant near their pots! They didn't want to tune the radio to London in the afternoons. The people make a lot of noise under their windows! Especially the one who cooks in the first kitchen; he became a cook in Allach, flung a bowl of potatoes at people. The guys rebelled. Only it has to be without any shouting. Grab him once, twice, twist the damn anti-Christ's neck and that's that. But is that possible with Poles?" And he lapsed into gloomy pensiveness.

"They gave it to them but good," someone else consoled him; "they won't get over it for a week. They're not going to come out of this camp alive, I'm telling you."

All the windowpanes on the ground floor were conscientiously smashed. In the shade-sprinkled interior of the rooms people circled around in the rubble of the furnishings, saving whatever they could. Sunlight, glancing off the helmets of the soldiers who were guarding the main entrance to the ground floor, blinded us. The soldiers waited, indecisive, while the jeeps turned back toward the gate.

Suddenly, from the door of the barracks wing opposite ours a group of men pressed tightly together emerged and, scuffling like a pack of hounds, moved across the empty square straight to headquarters. With head lowered like a butting bull, the Chief Warrant Officer led the way. Stefan was treading on his heels. He was holding a girl around the waist who was squealing and struggling to get away from him. Another man caught up with them from the side, grabbed her by the neck, shook her, calmed her down. The rest of them jumped up and surrounded those two and gigantic Kolka, who towered above everyone and was kicking ahead of him a man in a white apron, twisting his arm behind him. The soldiers rushed to meet them.

I squeezed my girl so hard that she cried out. I tipped her face to kiss her, but she pulled away angrily.

"What of it, after dinner," I said resignedly and, pushing aside the crowd, went out into the square.

"They're my friends!" I called out to her from afar.

She stood on tiptoe and raised her hand to her face, a little surprised, and a little as if on a railroad platform. I reached the fellows a minute before the soldiers surrounded us.

"Hey, Tadzio," Kolka thundered, smiling. "We've got a thief. We nabbed a whole sack of meat in the kitchen! And there's a German woman in bed in the cook's room! He didn't have time to let her out! Faster, beast!"

And he shoved the cook with his knee. The cook, seeing the soldiers, screamed with pain. A soldier ran up to Kolka, gurgling gutturally, and took aim with his rifle. But he didn't strike him.

On the steps in front of headquarters, between the Colonel and the Major, stood the Archbishop, looking at us with a kind, exhausted gaze. He moved his lips as if he was praying, but Stefan thought he was asking him something.

"Because he stole, Father, he stole food from his colleagues for the German woman! He stole and he committed adultery!" he shouted and, his bloodshot bruised eye flashing angrily, he shoved the girl onto the steps so that she fell on her knees. "And he won't let us listen to the radio! Your radio," he added rebelliously. "Not from Warsaw, from London!"

III

The editors' room was cozily decorated with wallpaper in a lyrical flower design. What remained after its orthodox inhabitants, the SS officers who either fell on the field of honor in the battle near the barracks, or fled to their families, or occupied the places in Dachau that we had vacated, was only a solid, two-door wardrobe, by some miracle not entirely ruined by Ausländers, who, almost as soon as they were released from the camp after the war ended, attacked the master-less barracks, smashed all the windows, the chandeliers, and the mirrors in the bathrooms and washrooms, thoroughly disassembled the movie camera, knocked out all the sprockets on the X-ray machine in the hospital, set fire to the trucks, motorcycles, and tanks in the garage, stole ammunition and blew up part of the barracks wall, broke up the more attractive mahogany living-room furniture, and, having mucked up the toilet bowls, went off singing their national anthems.

So there was a wardrobe, also a couch glued together from bits and pieces and covered with an imitation tiger skin, supporting a pile of trashy journalistic books discerningly collected from the rubbish covering the courtyard; the library, however, along with the hospital, pharmacy, cinema, and huge card file containing the identification cards and photographs of many tens of thousands of SS men, had been smashed into smithereens and thrown out onto the pavement.

I sat there, squeezed into a corner of the couch, staring mindlessly at a dark spot on the wall adorned with the evangelically bearded poet Cyprian Norwid, acquired who knows where.

From behind the partly open door the clanging of a cauldron reached us from the corridor. There, in the officers' rooms, even the Grunwald goulash was distributed without their having to line up and undergo inspection. Each officer took two or three bowls so as to have extra, for the evening. Because the bread was unpredictable, most often three hundred grams. Even for soldiers that was too little, not to mention for officers!

The Editor pushed his way inside, carefully protecting the two steaming bowls, fragrant with meat, that he carried in his hands. He shoved one at me.

"Here, eat and grow strong," he said curtly, but forcefully. He had perfected his diction, for he was a little bit deaf and lived with a captain, a former correspondent for a newspaper in Białystok, who was stone deaf. The two of them filled the room with anxious buzzing, like unruly beetles.

I dipped my spoon into the goulash slowly, carefully picking out the meat. I was no longer voraciously hungry. To celebrate *The Battle of Grunwald* we had each been allotted a liter of potatoes with meat and sauce.

"You know, I'd like to live in a room," I told the Editor, who shoved his typewriter and duplicating machine over to the window, sat down at the table, and started in on his food, vigorously and loudly smacking his lips. "So I could set out my books, hang up my trousers in a closet for the night, and in general sleep in a bed. Alone in a room; that's damn attractive!"

"Or in a twosome!" the Editor hooted.

"With this one?" I made a face.

"No, with a girl. You were eyeing one from the transport, I saw it!"

"Why are you surprised? After the camp, it's about time, right?"

The Editor had come to the camp from the uprising, straight from his young wife.

"Maybe I'll escape with her to the West."

He put down his spoon and looked at me out of the corner of his eye.

"What do you know," he said mockingly, "you and that escapee! You puppy, don't tell me you'd abandon your poems and books? Wouldn't you be afraid of the world? And what if you had to starve?"

Offended, I pushed away the bowl. I turned my face to the window. In the remaining fragments of its broken pane the sun was refracted into rainbowlike peacock sparks.

"Don't worry." The Editor got up from the table and stroked my face. "As you created me, Lord, that's what I am. And were you in that parade with the meat?"

"I was," I grunted reluctantly. "You could write about it. A sensation!"

"A real sensation takes place without the press, dear boy. Anyway, Father Tokarek wouldn't allow us to write about it. After all, we're a government newspaper!"

He broke off a small piece of bread and dipped it in the sauce.

"And did you manage to escape?"

"The soldiers let me out. You can walk through the world with English. I made it clear to the Okays that I hadn't meant anything, that it was an accident, I explained what it was about. They nodded. One of them even shook my hand. Do you know Stefan?" I asked. "He was block elder in the convalescent block."

"A communist? I was in his block. There were worse ones."

"Scum," I replied succinctly. "He beat people, served the SS just so he could become block elder and have his own room. When they threw him out into a kommando he became depressed. He couldn't last three days. He's no camp inmate."

The Editor nodded. He tipped his bowl and drank the sauce.

"One might say," he drawled in his Wilno accent between one swallow and the next, "that you disliked him a little."

"But he knew how to land on his feet, there's no denying that! They shouted at him that he was a communist and a bandit, especially the Colonel. But he said, 'Of course I beat people and I stole for the colonels and majors there. But today I won't beat or steal any more. They could all drop dead in the camps and I'd still help them.' There was some outcry!"

"And they didn't put him in prison, so I heard?"

"The American First Lieutenant gave him a choice of either being sentenced to the bunkier or separation from the camp. He couldn't do anything else because the Archbishop was listening in the whole time. Stefan took the German woman's arm, asked her forgiveness, and they left the camp together."

"In front of the Archbishop?! What a louse! The entire army has been compromised in front of him."

He licked his spoon, wiped the bowl with a piece of paper, threw the paper out the window, placed the bowl in the wardrobe, closed the wardrobe firmly, dried his lips with a handkerchief, put the handkerchief in his pocket, got the typewriter from under the window and put it back in its place, and then, ready to go out, announced, "You're going to the theater. There are two tickets. Janusz"—that was the other man, the deaf one— "went to play bridge at the Captain's. Someone has arrived from the Second Corps; he may be taking us to Italy. But not a word about this! Because everyone will want to go. Now they're playing cards. Nothing will move them, not the Archbishop and not even the show."

And he pushed me out the door, taking my book from my hands. He checked me out suspiciously while he did this. He didn't like anyone to take printed materials away from him on the sly. He locked the door carefully with a key, knocked on his neighbor's door, and vanished in the smoke that swirled near the closed window and carpeted the room like thick wool. Several bowls with leftover goulash in them were on the filthy floor next to some chairs. They had probably been set aside for the night. The Editor threw the key onto the table and walked out without saying a word.

In the courtyard, the preparations for the evening bonfire were complete. A solid, rectangular pile had been constructed, fortified with pitch-rich logs on the sides, and a German helmet had been planted on a post that protruded from the top of the pile, while two smashed German rifles without their locks were placed crosswise at the foot of the post. Benches, chairs, and armchairs surrounded the pile.

Although everyone was keyed up and waiting for the bonfire and the evening folk performances, the entire resident population of the barracks, except, of course, for those who were prowling around behind the sheds, guarding the halls against thieves, or were on trips outside the camp, moved over to a garage that had been transformed into a theater. The crowd stood in front of the locked theater gate, cursing and shouting threateningly, pushing against a policeman wearing a cardboard American helmet and with a national scarf across his chest. The policeman barred the way with pathetically extended arms.

"People, there's no room! Have pity, people! Come tomorrow! There'll be another performance of *Grunwald* tomorrow! Everyone will see it!" he shouted hoarsely, more and more hoarsely, until he crowed like a rooster, fell silent, and lowered his arms.

They shoved him out of the way, tore off his national scarf and trampled it. The crowd rushed the gate. It groaned, but the locks did not give way.

The Editor, amused, pulled me toward the other side of the garage, to a small door for the actors, saying, "For just an ounce of intelligence."

We slipped into the auditorium and instantly arranged the matter with the policeman who served as the theater's caretaker. I had the distinct impression that for a moment I was the equal of an officer.

We sat down right behind the generals, in the second row, on which a yellow light from the stage was still shining. The rest of the narrow and exceptionally long hall was sunk in blue-black darkness out of which people's attentive faces shone clearly. The threatening shouts of the crowd storming the theater reached us from outside, along with the creaking of the iron door they were attempting to force open. No one paid them any attention. Everyone was watching the stage.

For there, in the center of the brilliantly illuminated stage, draped in red and white and live greenery and propped up against the black box of a piano violently shaking with a patriotic melody, stood the Singer, an ample blonde in a Cracovian costume, flushed like a child at her birthday party, and crowned with a wreath of not quite ripe but already fading ears of corn. She held up her skirt with trembling fingers and raised her eyes innocently to the curtain, to the ceiling, to Heaven.

Surrounding her, several young people dressed in pasiaki were posed, holding up the ribbons of her bodice. I knew a couple of them: they had been Schreibers in the famous Allach camp. Their pasiaki fitted them like a glove; they must have been sewn especially for them while they were still in the camp. Others, in laborers' coveralls, were bustling around on the peripheries of the stage;

they were pushing wheelbarrows and carrying spades, picks, and crowbars around the Singer.

In the very front, almost at the edge of the stage, stood the fat, impassioned Actor; indicating the Singer with his hand, he was concluding this verse with pathos:

> . . . in the name of the Virgin,
> We are your children, O Poland, your soldiers and workers!

The horrific crash of the gate being breached and the triumphant shout of the crowd breaking into the overfilled garage merged with the raucous din of applause and the hysterical, patriotic screaming of the audience. When everything had quieted down a little and the sheet used for a curtain had again been drawn apart in order to reveal once again the flushed Republic and her lover, the Actor, whose eyes were fixed on her in a state of rapture, the Editor, who had finally settled down more or less on the edge of the bench, leaned toward me confidentially and bellowed out loud and with unfeigned satisfaction, "It's a shame that they didn't put a bed on the stage! What a gorgeous Republic! Well worth a sin!"

IV

"Tell me, why are you hanging around in this camp? Isn't there anything that draws you on?"

The girl bent over me tenderly. Her too heavy bust jiggled under her blouse. I was reflected in her anxious, opalescent eyes as a small, convex fragment of myself. I lifted my head and wanted to kiss her on her moist, parted lips. She knitted her brows and moved away.

"No, nothing draws me anywhere any more," I sighed lazily, and sleepily fell back onto the earth that smelled of moldy pine needles. "Anyway, you love only the man who stayed behind in Poland."

She covered my mouth with her hand.

Above us, the pine forest stretched up to the sky and soughed. The wind rustled as it brushed against the bark of the trees. The sun, splintered by the top of a pine tree, fell like a feathered arrow into the heart of the woods and lodged in the pale green grass, which, illuminated like the thinnest piece of gold, was full of the lazy smell of summer. An enchanting warmth emanated from it, as from the body of a woman. A stray beetle, a little bombardier, buzzed over us and landed on a mullein stalk.

"He's diving greedily into the conch, like a furry pup into a bowl of milk," I said indulgently.

"More like a child onto a windowsill," the girl observed. "Ah, how many of them I've had to play nurse to. I hate children!" she cried.

The startled beetle flew away, muttering angrily.

"Come!" she decided suddenly. "It's late. Look how dark the pines have become. Is it four o'clock? Five?"

She looked up at the tops of the pine trees that were immersed in a light stream of wind.

"Oh, how low the sun is."

She got up on her knees, brushed bits of pine needles off her dress, and smoothed her hair.

"Come," she broke off impatiently, pushing away my hands. "Come with me! Oh, come with me! I'm so frightened of Palestine!"

An asphalt road cut through the woods, fenced in by poplar trees. Couples, suntanned and in colorful clothes, were walking along it.

"You see, Nina," I broke our silence at the edge of the woods and grabbed her around the waist, "that's how the Germans live. I'd like to live like that, too. Do you understand? Without the camp, without the army, without patriotism, without discipline, normally, not for show! Not to receive soup from a cauldron, not to think about Poland."

"Well, that's just it," Nina took up the thread, "come with me to the West. I really am free."

"And the boy in Poland?"

"I'll forget about him."

"But you haven't forgotten yet?"

"I didn't have anyone else, so I haven't forgotten."

"You didn't?"

"These people with whom I've been traveling from Poland," she continued with some effort after a moment, "are strangers. I can break away from them. We'll go to Brussels. I have a sister there who's married to a rich Belgian. I'll study medicine."

The asphalt was burning under our feet. The towering poplars were afloat above the road, their canopies reaching all the way to the red walls and towers of the barracks, surrounding them with greenery like a bridge; they climbed upward, swelling with gold like a ripe apple, over the shingled roofs of the suburban housing estate, sparkling pink through the bluish smoke of the air as if through a silken shawl.

"Nina, stay with me," I said unexpectedly. "I am nothing here, but I'm going to become someone. I have friends who will help me, I have books that it's hard for me to abandon. I collected them so carefully. Do you understand? I'm afraid of taking risks; I've seen too much death to give myself up to be killed. Let others do that; why should I? I'm afraid of space, I'm afraid of people, because what am I after all? What rights do I have?"

I fell silent, seeking in my thoughts for the rights that belonged to me.

"None! Do you understand? None!"

I stopped speaking and looked into her face, as if seeking sympathy there.

"If we leave here, no one over there will give us food. Those black monkeys in white helmets can capture us at any crossroads and place us in an unknown camp where hunger will devour us."

"I'm not afraid," Nina said drily.

"But to have no ground under one's feet anywhere?!"

I broke off, searching for a suggestive metaphor.

"To be a tree without roots! To dry up!"

"Then you'll go back to Poland," the girl decided, and twisted her mouth contemptuously when I tried to stand up for myself. "You wanted me for one day only, like everyone."

"Everyone?" I whistled through my teeth.

"Yes, everyone!" she screamed. She stumbled. I steadied her by her arms. She pulled away violently and angrily.

"Everyone for whom I'm a Jewess! Do you see this?"

She touched the talisman in the shape of a whistle. Her fingers were trembling.

"You haven't asked me yet what this is, unlike the others. It's the tablets of Moses, the commandments in Hebrew. It's supposed to bind me to the Jews. But I'm neither a Jew nor a Pole. They threw me out of Poland. I find Jews repulsive. I thought there must be other people as well. But you're not a man, you're just a Pole. Go back to Poland!" she screamed venomously. "Go back to Poland!"

"Go back to Poland!"

I was terrified by a voice like that of a bird that suddenly flies up from underfoot.

In the tall, yellowish grass shone a black, close-cropped head. Stefan got up from the ground and bowed to the girl.

"Go back to Poland," he repeated. "Come with me. I'm going on foot."

"On foot? You're quite a guy," I marveled, brusquely.

"But where's the German girl?" I looked around suspiciously.

"She went into the bushes. Actually, I brought her back to her house."

He ran his hand over his hair.

"A lovely girl. Will you come with me?"

"You know, I would go, only . . ."

I hesitated. My cloth uniform scalded my entire body. Stefan squinted in the glare and looked at me with open contempt from under his lowered lids. He was twisting a dry twig in his fingers; it broke with a snap.

"Your books, your beloved books," he laughed bitterly. "Is that what you want to tell me? And that you'll be hungry along the way? And how will it become normalized? And I'll answer you: a skirt is holding you back, brother. You've bagged a skirt, eh? Bagged one."

His teeth glittered like a dog's. He held his hand up to his bruised eye.

"What do you have here besides this Jewess?"

"Let's go back to the camp," said Nina in a piercing whisper.

"You sir, you . . ." She clenched her fists. Her chin trembled violently. "You are like the SS!"

Stefan chuckled. He paid no attention to the girl.

"The camp is surrounded by the Americans," he said to me. "I wanted to go in and get my blanket. They didn't let me in. Tomorrow, they're going to take everyone out! Everyone!"

"You're crazy! The Colonel, and the Major, too? And the entire staff? And the priests, and the kitchens?"

"Go to the camp; you'll see," Stefan said. "I'll be waiting in Poland."

"They won't take people away; you're mistaken. After all, today is *Grunwald*."

"*Grunwald!*" Stefan burst out laughing, touching his bruised eye. "Go on with your *Grunwald*," he said ironically, and disappeared in the woods without saying good-bye. The branches of the fir trees swayed behind him as he passed.

"Let's go back to the camp," said Nina. She sighed heavily like a fish thrown onto the shore. "It's too bad; let's go back. Maybe we'll be able to get inside."

"We certainly will," I said, a little too eagerly.

I took her arm and led her along the road. She leaned in close to me. She was moving her lips soundlessly, as if saying something to herself. A stream of bicycles flowed nonstop along the surface of the asphalt.

The Germans were taking advantage of the hot summer afternoon. A man from the camp was sitting at the crossroads. He had placed two red suitcases in the shade so their lacquer wouldn't melt. He was fumbling in his open rucksack. A red kepi, the adornment of the Muslim detachments of the SS, had slipped down onto his ear. Its black tassel dangled with every movement of his head.

A line of people was moving from the camp all the way to the woods. They knew the openings and passages that were less guarded and were getting out of the barracks while there was still time.

We walked faster. The tops of the trees soughed as though the forest were walking in step with us. A couple of tanks were parked under a pile of dried-up bushes, and, just as neatly as if it were a dry goods store, artillery shells, German mines, and surrendered rifles were carefully lined up. They were guarded by an American soldier who was dozing in the heat.

Beside the road a column of trucks faced the camps with their narrow snouts that looked like they belonged to hungry rats. They were waiting for morning. Half-naked Negroes milled around among the trucks. They glistened with sharp brown sweat, looking as if they'd been sprinkled with copper. They shouted at us as we passed them. We planned to approach the barracks from behind, paralleling the road, then make our way over to them through the smashed gate that was blocked with piled-up rubble—a classic spot for transporting sheep. There was no one at the hole. On the other hand, in the corner, where the wall cast a modicum of coolness on the baked earth, beneath a tarpaper roof supported by a couple of sticks, a soldier was seated, dozing in the shade. He had set his helmet on the grass; his rifle was between his knees, and his chin touched his chest. At the second corner two soldiers were standing, their shirts unbuttoned, talking loudly and smoking cigarettes.

In plain view, we stood in the meadow in front of the gate like a pair of lost children in front of a witch's hut.

"Let's wait till it gets dark," I said, overwhelmed with anxiety. "Maybe they won't let us in. Let's go back to the woods."

She slipped out from under my arm and gave a short, contemptuous, snorting sort of laugh.

"You were in such a rush to see *Grunwald*, and what happened? Are you afraid again? Just wait, little one; follow me."

And before I could say something or make any kind of move, the girl smoothed her skirt impatiently, pulled her blouse down over her too heavy bust, and took off at full tilt toward the gate. She reached the rubble pile and started climbing it. At the top, a burst of wind clung tightly to her hips and ruffled her hair. She held down her hair with her hand, pressing against the wind. For a moment she turned her ironically smiling face toward me. She called out to me, but the wind blew her cry into tatters. I started running after her and then suddenly stopped. I raised my hand to signal to her; she turned away from me; I wanted to shout, but I remained silent.

The two soldiers who were smoking cigarettes turned around toward the gate, and one of them, lowering his rifle from his shoulder, called out laughingly at the top of his lungs, "*Fräulein, Fräulein! Halt, halt! Come here!*"*

"*Stop, stop!*" the other soldier shouted in a squeaky voice.

---

* Here and in the following paragraphs, italicized dialogue indicates that Borowski wrote the lines in English.

The soldier who was sleeping at the other end of the wall raised his head frantically and jumped up. He bent down, snatched up his rifle, which had slipped out from between his knees, placed it on his arm, tilted his head toward the right for an instant and—

The girl raised her hands to her throat in a defensive motion, as if she was suddenly deprived of air. She took one more step beyond the edge of the embankment and softly sank down behind it, as though she had started sliding down the bricks; she vanished behind the edge as if she'd been cast into a pit. Beyond the embankment, where the camp began, voices were raised, they merged into a babble, then grew into a scream. The two soldiers who had laughingly called to the girl threw down their cigarette butts, crushed them underfoot and raced over to the embankment. The sleepy soldier, the one who had fired the shot, slung his rifle over his shoulder with the barrel pointing downward, picked up his helmet from the ground, brushed it off, put it on his head and, whistling mindlessly, also rushed toward the gate.

I moved slowly onto the rubble pile, walked across it in front of everyone, and slid down beside Nina.

She had torn her cheek on a brick as she fell. A large blue fly had landed on her twisted lip, wet with a coating of fresh blood. Startled by my shadow, it flew off, buzzing. Her white teeth glistened lifelessly from under her lip. Her bulging eyes were growing dim like congealed aspic. Her hands, clenched convulsively in a defensive motion, lay heavily on the rocks. The last sign of life, her warm blood with its nauseating smell, seeped in a broad stain through her blouse that clung tightly to her too prominent bosom and dried up like rust at its edges. The little talisman in the shape of a whistle slipped sideways on her neck, hesitated a couple of times on its chain, and hung motionless. I removed a sharp, uncomfortable chunk of brick from under the corpse's head, gently gathered up her hair, laid her head on the soft limestone sand and, getting up from my kneeling position, carefully brushed the dust off my trousers. It was growing dark above me from the circle of people's attentive, silent faces. I elbowed my way with difficulty through the reluctantly yielding crowd. They let me pass and gathered even more tightly around the body.

In the courtyard fires were smoking under abandoned pots and mess kits. The wind twisted the smoke with a crunching sound, as if it was straw, and hurled it over the wall. Boards flung down from the attic onto the fire slipped noiselessly in the air, showed white against the background of the black windows, and landed with a horrific crash. A column of dust arose from the ground, slowly coiled over the ground, and collapsed. From a great distance a monotonous, muffled rustle of voices reached me as if from behind a wall. From between the dormitory blocks, from the street planted in young plane trees, from around the corner of the garage from which the long noses of the artillery protruded, covered with canvas, a small, funny-looking jeep leaped out, pushed by soldiers, slipped between the trees, raised an enormous cloud of smoke and dust, dug its wheels into the ground, and came to a stop, braking with a screech.

"*What's happened?* Why are these people yelling like this?"

The First Lieutenant leaned down to his driver. The driver moved his arm indifferently. I looked at the officer in amazement. In the silence surrounding us his voice sounded sharp and unpleasant like the ripping of cloth. The officer, meeting my glance, blinked and tightened his mouth. He stuck one leg out of the car and swung it hesitantly. The sun began to shine and then blossomed in his polished brown ankle boot. Two soldiers with machine pistols on their knees sprawled on the rear seat. The driver reached into his pocket, pulled out a pack of cigarettes, tore the colorful band, leaned over to the back, offering them a smoke. They lit up. A delicate stream of blue smoke floated near their faces and, snatched by the wind, vanished in the air. Without undue haste, I walked over to the car.

"*Do you speak English?*" the First Lieutenant asked rapidly. He moved his jaw indecisively, as if picking up speed, and all of a sudden started chewing.

"*I do,*" I nodded. My voice echoed in my head as if in an empty hall, and terrified me. I looked at the officer not as at a man, but as a distant, indifferent object.

The crowd was shielding the girl's corpse from view, but turned away and looked at the soldiers. My ears were ringing with noise like telephone receivers. Suddenly the wall of people moved, broke apart.

"*What's happened?*" the First Lieutenant repeated more sharply. He touched his foot to the ground. It seemed he would spring from the car. "Who has wronged these people? Why are they shouting like that? What happened?"

The soldier with the rifle, its barrel pointing down, emerged from the crowd, and the other two, who had been smoking cigarettes, followed him. But before the one who was walking in front could say something, I addressed the officer.

"*Nothing, sir.* Nothing happened," I soothed him, making light of things with a gesture and the polite submissiveness of my whole body. "Nothing happened. A moment ago they shot a girl from the camp."

The First Lieutenant leaped out of the car like a spring that is suddenly sprung. His face was momentarily suffused with blood and then turned white.

"*My God,*" he said. His mouth must have suddenly gone dry because he made a face and spat out his gum. The pink wad turned red in the dust of the road.

"*My God! My God!*" He clutched at his head.

"We here in Europe are used to this," I replied indifferently. "For six years the Germans were shooting at us, now it's you who are shooting. What's the difference?"

Across the low-lying dust, as across a shallow river, without looking back, I walked away with a heavy step into the center of the barracks, to my books, my cheap possessions, my supper, which had probably been taken by someone else already. The silence, like an inflated balloon, burst with a crash in my ears. Only now did I realize that the crowd was tightly gathered over the girl's body and, looking the soldiers in the eyes, had been furiously chanting the entire time:

"Ge-sta-po! Ge-sta-po! Ge-sta-po!"

The soldiers' hall was in ruins. On the tables and the floor the shattered shells of porcelain bowls glowed white in the thick darkness like dried bones scraped free of tissue. Straw mattresses, dragged from the beds, hung down helplessly, as if they'd been murdered. From the wardrobes, as if from opened, gutted bellies, rags flowed out and lay, crushed, on the ground. Piles of torn, smothered books crunched underfoot. A musty, corpselike smell as from a basement hung in the air, as if these rags, mattresses, shells, and books, battered and ripped apart, were still rotting and decaying.

The dark blue rectangle of a window, opened into the night, burst into bloom with a red flare like a gigantic flower. They were firing from a tall tower beside the gate. A gentle light flowed soundlessly along the window like fresh blood. The shadows swayed, wavered like shaken water, and rose upward.

Taking advantage of the light, I looked into the wardrobe. Everything the least bit useful had been taken; the rest was destroyed. On the bottom, I felt around in a pot of surviving potato pancakes. They rustled in my fingers like dry crumbled leaves.

The flare dropped onto the pavement, made a few hops, gave off a stronger red glow, and died out. It became completely dark. I walked over to the bed and groped it with my hand. My fingers ran over the coarse mattress. The blanket was gone. They'd stolen it. Deep in the hall someone groaned and moved on his bed. A piercing scrap of a whisper reached me, a stifled, broken giggle dissolved in a sudden crackling of straw. Then silence.

"Gypsy? Gypsy, brother, is that you?" I asked, greatly relieved. I moved away from the wardrobe and made my way into the depths of the hall, catching hold of the beds. Broken glass crunched under my feet.

"Gypsy, are you here?"

I halted, uncertain, and waited anxiously.

"Where else would I be since everything hurts like hell!" Gypsy groaned in the darkness. His straw mattress again rustled restlessly.

"That human race, what didn't they do! I wish I hadn't lived to see this. There was nobody, no one went for food . . ."

"Nobody brought supper?" I screamed in despair. I felt a sudden overwhelming hunger. I leaned against the table. I groped for the chair. I sat down.

"There's no supper," I repeated automatically. "And tomorrow there'll be a transport, and they won't give us food again."

"Nobody was here, no one took care," Gypsy said slowly and tearfully, choking in his words like tears. "They invaded the hall, smashed and stole everything. Pan Tadek, if you'd seen it, if only you'd seen it, your heart would have broken. They tore apart your books, they took Pan Kola's cigarettes. A Pole against other Poles. Oh, merciful God, have pity on us. And they took my boots. I was barely able to defend my suit. I had it under my head."

"You shouldn't have eaten raw mutton; if you hadn't, you'd also have stolen today. The boys are getting ready for a transport; it's no wonder they're stealing," I said mockingly. I gritted my teeth out of misery and kicked the skull of a bowl that was rocking under my feet. It rolled across the concrete with a clang.

"They're getting ready, they're getting ready; they should only get ready like this in their side," Gypsy cursed them, snuffling. "And Pan Editor came and he also collected your books from the wardrobe. He said you probably wouldn't come back and it was a shame to leave them. They'll come in handy for him because he left to join General Anders."

"The Editor? Who gave me soup? He left! So he really left! Without me!"

Again, I felt that I was hungry.

"And the Chief Warrant Officer is sitting in the bunkier and Pan Kola is also in the bunkier," Gypsy continued in a monotone.

A red flare again exploded against the dark blue sky; beside it, green, orange, and yellow blossomed, then fell to earth together as a bouquet. Gypsy's black face was covered with a corpselike neon light like mercury and then fell back into darkness.

"And people said that Pan Kolka and the Chief Warrant Officer will be sent to Poland as punishment."

"But Kolka wanted to go to Italy," I cried out in astonishment. "Well, then he'll meet up with Stefan in Poland. He's already squealing on them."

"And they smashed the Chief Warrant Officer's little chest, took his camera and his money. Oh my God, my God . . . They hid them underneath me . . ."

"Don't lie, don't lie, you lousy Gypsy, or I'll beat your mug again . . . You stole that money yourself. You watched Daddy hide it," the Warrant Officer's son called out from below. His bed began to creak from his passion.

"Oh, so you managed to come back?" I rejoiced politely. "Your daddy was worried about you."

"Let Daddy worry about himself, if he's stupid enough to fight," the Warrant Officer's son snarled. "I can take care of myself. I'm not going to be stupid, and I'm not going on a transport to Poland," he added carelessly.

"Did you bring something?"

"I did," he replied, "but not mutton. It's better than mutton. Listen."

He fumbled around and then an offended, female squeal emerged from the darkness. "I bought a Kraut. I pulled her through the hole. The cowboys I know were standing guard."

"You've got luck," I sighed jealously.

"You could have one, too, if only you went out. But all you do is sit with your books. It won't come by itself. You have to do it today."

"What about tomorrow? When there's a transport?"

"I'll talk about tomorrow tomorrow." He said the last word hoarsely, while yawning. "The boys won't give in."

"You think so?"

"Sure, they're getting ready to defend themselves," he assured me with certitude.

"Over there," he waved his hand in the direction of the court-yard that the flares were illuminating, "they're doing *Grunwald.* But we'll do something better. The boys have a lot of Brownings. And grenades, and rifles, and automatic pistols! Do you think there are flare guns only for *Grunwald?* When they set up at least two heavy machine guns in the attack and they start firing . . . What do you think? The Okays won't run away?"

He raised himself on his bed as if he wanted to stand up. But he only wrapped the girl in a blanket up to the top of her blond, fluffy hair, fell back onto the bed with a sigh, and slipped his hand under the blanket.

The sky was alight with all sorts of colors. A fountain of flares flowed through the air, fell into the depths of the darkness in flaming drops, splattered across the sky. The red roof of the barracks changed spectrally against the background of the motionless sky, which was flooded time and again with dark blue juice.

"They're doing *Grunwald,*" I said to the Warrant Officer's son. "They were supposed to repeat it tomorrow. Watch out they don't catch her tomorrow; it would be a shame."

"Oh, what a big worry." His voice shook a little, as if he was out of breath. "Let them catch her. Do you think I'll need her, or what? Maybe I'll go with her to join the boys and sit in the attic. There are hiding places there that the devil himself couldn't find. When the action's over, I'll come out, and everything will be fine, until the next time!"

"It seems the transport is supposed to go to Koburg," Gypsy spoke up. "How can I go when I'm so sick? Maybe they won't take me. You speak English, so ask the cowboys, will you, Pan Tadek?"

He lay there uncovered, breathing heavily like a dying beast. He fixed his eyes on me, glowing with reflections of the flares. They were uncannily glittery in his sunken black face, as if they were phosphorescent.

"How can you imagine that I'll concern myself with thieves? It's a pity that I didn't strangle you when we were on the way to Dachau; then you wouldn't have any problems today," I said contemptuously.

The Warrant Officer's son giggled and turned in his bed.

"I myself have to hide from the transport. Later, it will be easier to get some kind of position in the camp, like a provisioner or a secretary," I added calmly. "What else is there to do?"

"Go to *Grunwald*," the Warrant Officer's son advised me. "And when it's over, you can sleep here for the night. I'm going to cook the meat."

I got up from the table and, stumbling over the books, made my way to the door. Suddenly, it was opened from the other side, and from the black den of the corridor an angular, dark face with half-opened mouth flashed in the light of a yellow flare. The flare flowed downward, and the glittering eyeglasses were flooded with a rosy afterglow.

"Professor, it's you!" I screamed hysterically. I led him over to the table.

"Were you looking for me?"

The Professor was still wearing his leather Tyrolean costume. Colored shadows moved across his white knees with their sparse covering of black hair; they embraced his Bavarian shirt, climbed up his face and across the ceiling to escape through the window.

"I was," said the Professor. "I was supposed to be with you. I took the trouble to get you a good seat at the bonfire. It's beginning any moment now. Where were you all this time?"

He brushed his hands over his knees. He reached into his pocket. A crumpled, crushed cigarette twisted through his fingers and flared between his lips with a pale flame, driving its red into his mouth and settling with a weak reflex in the crevices of his face.

"To tell the truth, I don't know where I was," I said faintly. I lowered my head and stared at the floor. A woodcut ripped out of the heroic, jolly, and praiseworthy adventures of Till Eulenspiegel lay on the floor, and a girl with bare breasts playing a guitar rested against a wall.

"I was wandering somewhere in the camp. Does it make any difference? Comradely conventions? Here?! The day before a transport? In any case, after tomorrow we'll never meet again."

"It's a small world!" the Professor exclaimed. He drew on his cigarette. A fluffy clump of smoke gleamed with a rosy underbelly and flattened out under the ceiling after showing its blue back.

"Of course we'll meet. If not on this meadow, then on another . . . ," he returned to his favorite idea. "Only . . ."

He suddenly stiffened in the middle of a word.

"They shot her," he said after a moment, throwing away the rest of his cigarette. "They shot her at the gate. She'd gone for a walk."

"That neighbor of yours?"

"Yes, the one who came from Pilsen. My neighbor from my old building. When I left in September '39, she was still a child.

Sometimes, in the past, I would buy her little cakes. You know, the kind with cream inside. And a strawberry on top?"

He looked into my eyes, uncertain if I remembered them.

"I was a friend of her father's," he added in a tone of explanation. "And now, you see," he clapped me on the shoulder, "what a bosomy woman! I almost had her in my hand, I'd already felt her up, and what a misfortune . . ."

He reached into his pocket again. He dug around in it insistently. He didn't find anything. He gave a deep sigh and rested his head in his hands.

"What a misfortune!" he repeated, as if in a trance. "What's to be done?"

He was silent, shaking his head.

"Let's go to *Grunwald!*" he decided.

"I'm the one who was with her. I was with her in the woods," I said, surprising myself. "They shot her in front of me. And you're talking to me about *Grunwald* . . ."

I jumped up from my bed. The Professor lifted his head, moved heavily, as if emerging from water, swayed, and grasped my hands. A bronze deer, embossed on the strap that connected his suspenders, trembled in the light of the flares as if it were alive. On the Professor's bony face the lights merged and swelled, the red mixed in with green, together they moved toward his brow, floated up to the ceiling, and in their place came pink, blue, and yellow lights, and they settled under his chin, in the corners of his mouth, below his eyes, in the creases of his ears, like paints on a portrait. The Professor's face played with all the colors of the rainbow; it cracked open from the middle, swelled, the cheeks puffed out like glassy, changing bubbles, as if the Professor were choking on light. Suddenly, he emitted air with a whistle and, opening his mouth wide, roared an enormous, hooting laugh.

"Ha, ha, ha, ha! Ha, ha, ha, ha!" He choked on his laughter for a good minute, squeezing my hands more and more tightly, and the light immediately ran into his open mouth and whirled there in its many colors.

"Professor, please stop!" I shouted, tearing my hands out of his grip. "You've lost your mind!"

"And I thought I was going to sleep with her today. I arranged a supper. I even got hold of a sheet! Ha, ha, ha, ha! And you were with her! Youth, youth!"

His whole body shook with laughter, tall, thin, hideously colorful.

"And she was such an ordinary woman! I wanted her! Ha, ha, ha, ha!"

Suddenly he staggered, coughed violently, and bent over to the ground, wheezing. The whole hall, filled with lights, rocked like a ship. Colorful straw mattresses, tables, walls, bowls, books changed and whirled like brightly colored balls.

"You see, Professor," the Warrant Officer's son spoke up from his corner, "there was no point in falling in love in your old age. You didn't get the girl, but you got TB. And you won't be seeing *Grunwald.* Lie still, lie still, damn it," he added impatiently, and the bed began to creak.

"She's squirming around as if someone had poured tar into her."

"*Grunwald,* right, *Grunwald!*" The Professor straightened up. His face was covered with a Medusa-like glare, then died out with the last flare and turned gray as dying ash.

"Why don't you all go to *Grunwald!*"

Outside the window, in the darkness that had extinguished the flares, a red flame suddenly erupted, licked the black windows like a fawning dog, and rocked the darkness like a bell. The shadows of the trees lengthened until they topped the roof and swayed like candles.

"Why don't you all go to *Grunwald!*" the Professor crowed. He dragged me over to the window. "Look, sir, look!" he cried impatiently.

He turned around to the room. "All of you go," he importuned us. "Take the girl, let her see it, too."

I leaned out over the windowsill. In the black bowl of the court-yard around the trembling globe of the burning pile, which, beaten by the wind, was streaming like the mane of a galloping steed, the silent crowd was standing. Flashes of fire slipped over their faces and suffused them with blood that was immediately sucked out by the darkness. The dry boards burned with a clattering sound, and chips flew off into the darkness. The light from the flares grew subdued.

"Were you in the little church in the German settlement? No?"

The Professor had gotten control over himself. He spoke gravely, almost sternly. His face, dressed in darkness, had again become angular and exhausted.

"I go there every day. It's peaceful. Filled with God. To the point of overflowing. A miniature pulpit, tiny panes in tiny windows, a little altar, verses from the Bible on the walls. And under one of the walls there are little crosses, and on the crosses obituary notices, for SS men exclusively! Do you understand? And there are flowers under the crosses, tons of flowers!"

The red glare of the fire burned in his eyes.

"That's how the Germans honor their dead."

"And we?" I grumbled sadly. "Not a soul even notices when a man drops dead."

The Warrant Officer's son got up from the bed and shuffled over to the window, naked. The girl, wearing a nightgown, slipped behind him as silently as a spirit. Black Gypsy leaned on his elbow and looked out the window enviously.

"We?" the Professor repeated pensively. "We are right here among them. We . . . Look!" he screamed like a bird of prey, "look at the bonfire! That's what we're waiting for; that's *Grunwald!*"

Fresh pine boughs were thrown onto the pyre. The fire dimmed. It emitted thick, dirty smoke. The wind blew the smoke away, and the flame flared up toward the sky. A priest wearing a soutane emerged from the crowd. His white collar squeezed his red neck. The priest raised both his hands, as if bestowing a blessing. From somewhere in the depths of the darkness a man in an SS uniform was dragged out. His helmet fell clattering onto the concrete of the courtyard. The crowd erupted in laughter. The man's helmet was shoved back onto his head. The priest took him by the shoulders, maneuvered him with all his strength and, to the shouts of the crowd, shoved the man into the fire.

The face of the girl, who was standing next to me, turned gray as ash. Her eyes burned with horror like two coals. They faded, covered by her eyelids. She dug her fingers into me convulsively.

"*Was ist los?*" she whispered, her teeth chattering. I stroked her cool hand soothingly. She pressed against me with her whole body. A smell arose from her, striking my nostrils and drilling into my body.

"*Was ist los?*" Her mouth was twisted. She brushed the hair off her forehead.

"*Ruhig, ruhig, Kind,*" the Professor said gently. "Relax. It's an effigy of an SS man that's burning. It's our answer—for the crematoriums and the little church."

"And for a dead girl," I snarled through my teeth.

I reached behind me. The warm body of the girl adhered tightly to me, trembling from excitement and fear. She was breathing right into the back of my neck with her steamy, hot breath.

The Actor appeared before the crowd—fat, short, swathed in the fire's glow as in a red greatcoat, and while the priest kept shoving into the fire more and more effigies that erupted into columns of flame as if they were soaked in kerosene, he raised his arms, calmed the screaming crowd, with a single gesture of one hand divided the crowd down the length of the wide street, moved his head toward the dark roofs of the barracks, and gave a signal.

Cascades of flares exploded. The sky lit up like a Christmas tree, burst with Bengal lights, and fell in droplets onto the ground. Long volleys of automatic rifle fire resounded from the attics. The smoky shells flew across the sky in ash-colored trails, like a flock of wild geese. The crowd, enveloped in the flares' fire, lit up together with the entire courtyard, which swirled and whirled like a soap bubble driven by the wind.

"Let the dead bury the dead," the Professor said meditatively. "We, the living, should go with the living."

His cheeks, immersed in the crucible of the flares, swelled and burst again. Suddenly, the Professor started chortling again.

"The living with the living! Ha, ha, ha, ha! Ha, ha, ha, ha! The living with the living. Just like them, forever! Look!"

He stretched out his hand in the direction of the warehouse sinking into the murky darkness. From under its shadow, as if from under a gigantic shell half-opened with the blade of the fire, between the stone walls of the sheds, smeared with the shadows of trees, across the yard of the ex-SS barracks where, on the anniversary of the battle of Grunwald straw effigies of SS soldiers had been thrown onto the pyre, on the eve of a transport that was to destroy everything and scatter people irrevocably, the Battalion came marching, beating time dully, stubbornly, against the concrete, and singing.

The World of Stone

A Narrative in Twenty Pictures

A BRIEF PREFACE

To Jan Dobraczyński

The World of Stone is a single, capacious narrative composed of twenty independent parts. The author was testing the possibilities afforded by the form of the "short story," and considers that the attempt was not particularly successful. The form of the short story is similar to the form of a tight collar in that it restricts breathing. It weans one away from commentary and discussion, accustoms one to unity of plot, time, and place, and replaces the writer with a photographic apparatus.

Some of these short stories are merely realistic; some are trivial; others incorporate a polemic with other writers' authorial positions. The dedications, although not all of them, indicate to whom the polemics are addressed. Some of the dedications are only polite. I am not a positive catastrophist; I didn't know Kapo Kwaśniak, I didn't eat human brains, I didn't murder children, I didn't spend time in an isolation cell, I didn't attend the opera with Germans, I didn't drink wine in a garden, I don't indulge in infantile day-dreams—in short, I would feel very sorry if the stories in *The World of Stone* were treated as pages from the author's intimate memoir only because they are written in the first person.

I do not know whether this preface sufficiently justifies my short stories. I wrote them mainly to prevent various radical Catholics

---

Jan Dobraczyński (1910–1994) edited the conservative Catholic periodical *Dziś i Jutro* (Today and tomorrow), which published more than one hostile critique of Borowski's postwar writings and politics.

(and others, too), who are dependent on other people's grace and other people's money, from making demands on me.

THE WORLD OF STONE

For Comrade Paweł Hertz

For some time now an awareness has been growing inside me, like a fetus in a woman's womb, filling me with anxious expectation that the Infinite Universe is expanding like a cosmic soap bubble with unimaginable speed; a miser's prickly anxieties have been nagging at me whenever I think even for a minute that the universe is seeping into a void like water through one's fingers and that at some time, perhaps even today, or maybe not until tomorrow, or a couple of light years hence, it will evaporate irreversibly into that void as if it were constructed not of solid matter but only of transient sound. I should confess at the outset that even though ever since the war I rarely can force myself to polish my shoes and I almost never scrub the dirt off my trouser cuffs, that although it costs me a great deal of effort to shave my cheeks, chin, and throat every other day, that although I bite off my fingernails in order to save time, and seek neither rare books nor lovers, linking the meaning of my fate to the fate of the universe through this passivity—nonetheless, I have been leaving my house with great enjoyment recently on sweltering afternoons and going for long, lonely walks through the working-class districts of my city.

Paweł Hertz (1918–2001) provoked Borowski's antagonism with *Sedan* (1948), his collection of short stories exploring the shattering of the prewar intelligentsia under the onslaught of fascist ideologies.

I greatly enjoy drawing into my lungs deep drafts of the ruins' moldy dust, dry as bread crumbs, and, with barely masked irony, slightly tilting my head out of habit toward my right shoulder, observing the village women squatting beside their wares against the walls of bombed-out houses, the dirty children chasing a rag ball coated with mud among the puddles at night, and also the dust-covered workmen, stinking of sweat, who from dawn until nightfall are hurriedly hammering down the streetcar tracks—for I can see clearly, as if in a mirror, how these ruins that are becoming overgrown with grass, these village women with their flour-laced sour cream and their stinking dresses, the streetcar tracks, the rag ball and the children chasing after it, the barbells laid down beside the peat bog as well as the iron hammers and the muscular arms, the exhausted eyes and bodies of the workers, the street and the square behind it filled with wooden huts above which rise angry human voices and clouds driven by a swift wind—I see how all this suddenly blows away and drops, billowing, at my feet, like the reflections of trees and the sky in a stream flowing swiftly under a footbridge.

It seems to me at times that sensations I would call biological are congealing within me and growing stronger, impervious as resin. In contrast to years past when I used to look at the world with eyes wide-open in amazement and tread carefully along any street like a young tomcat on a parapet, now I insert myself indifferently into a bustling crowd and, absolutely devoid of emotion, rub up against the hot bodies of young girls, seductive with the nakedness of their knees and the deliberate piling up of their thick hair. I screw up my eyes and again take pleasure in seeing through my half-closed eyelids how a gust of cosmic wind drives the crowd all the way up to the crowns of the trees, stirs human bodies into a gigantic whirlpool, twists mouths that are open in terror, mixes the rosy cheeks of children with the hairy chests of men, wraps clenched fists in scraps of skirts, flings white thighs on top like foam from beneath which hats and fragments of heads entwined with the seaweed of hair peer out—and like that most marvelous concoction, that gigantic stew cooked up from the crowd, it floats down the street over the gutter and, practically gurgling, vanishes into nothingness as if it were flowing into a sewer.

There is nothing strange about the fact that, filled with scorn undergirded with mild contempt, I enter with human dignity into massive, cold, granite edifices. I am not accustomed to being thrilled by marble steps cleansed of burned remnants and covered with a red carpet which cleaning women, groaning from the effort, swat clean every morning; I pay no attention to new curtains or the freshly painted walls of a burned-out building. I slip indifferently into the crowded but cozy little rooms of important individuals and sometimes rather too politely ask for items that are too trifling, which truly belong to me but which—I know this, definitively—are not capable of preventing this world from swelling like the overripe fruit of a grenade and exploding, spilling dry, rustling ash instead of seeds onto a glass desert.

When, after a torrid day of dust and the smell of gasoline, refreshing darkness finally descends and changes the tubercular ruins into innocent decorations turning dark against the background of the ever denser sky, I walk back beneath the newly installed streetlights to my apartment, which smells of uncured whitewash and which I bought from a middleman for a large sum of money not registered in any treasury office; I sit down beside the windowsill, rest my head on my hand, and, lulled by the clatter of plates that my wife is washing in the kitchen alcove, I stare at the windows of the building across the way where one after another the lights go out and the radio speakers fall silent.

For another moment I still catch faint echoes from the street: a drunken song from the nearby cigarette kiosks, the shuffling of footsteps, the thumping of trains pulling into the station, the insistent, stubborn hammering of the night shift hurriedly laying the streetcar tracks already at the bend in the street—and all the more clearly I feel that an enormous disenchantment is welling up in me. I propel myself away from the window energetically, as if to snap a rope that restrains me; I sit down at my desk with the feeling that once again I have lost time irrevocably, I pull out of the drawer papers discarded long ago and, because the world has not yet blown away, today I take out clean sheets of paper, lay them out pedantically on the desk and, with my eyes closed, try to discover in myself a tender friendship for the workers on the streetcar tracks, for the village women with the ersatz sour cream, the goods trains, the darkening sky above the ruins, the pedestrians on the avenue and the new curtains, and even for my wife who is drying the dishes—and with a great intellectual effort I strive to catch the true meaning of the things, events and people I have seen. For I intend to write a great, immortal epic, a work that is worthy of this immutable, difficult world that is as if carved from stone.

A STORY FROM REAL LIFE

To Editor Stefan Żółkiewski

I thought that I would die. I was lying on a bare straw mattress, covered with a blanket that stank of the dried excrement and pus of those who had come before me. I was so weak that I had

---

Stefan Żółkiewski (1911–1991) was the editor, 1945–1950, of the Marxist literary weekly *Kuźnica* (The forge), which favored a broadly humanistic realism in opposition to Soviet-style socialist realism.

stopped scratching to chase away the fleas. Extensive bedsores had formed on my hips, buttocks, and arms. Stretched over my bones, my skin was red, and it burned like a fresh sunburn. I was disgusted by my own body, and I listened with relief to other people's death rattles. At times I thought I would choke to death from thirst. Then I would open my cracked lips and, dreaming of a particular mug of cold coffee, stare mindlessly at the fragment of empty sky that lay outside the wide-open window. The gray, corpselike smoke curling low over the roofs made it appear as if the weather was turning nasty. The tar on the roofs was melting and glittered like mercury in the sunlight.

When the flesh of my buttocks and back would begin to burn me like a live flame, I would turn onto my side on the coarse straw mattress and, placing my fist under my ear, lift my gaze expectantly in the direction of the swollen man in the next bed, a kapo by the name of Kwaśniak. On the table beside him was a mug of coffee, a partially gnawed apple, and a slice of crumbly bread. At the foot of his bed, hidden in a cardboard box under the sheet, green tomatoes sent to him by his thoughtful wife were ripening.

Kapo Kwaśniak didn't handle idleness well. He yearned nostalgically for his kommando, which was working in the women's camp. He was bored. His one entertainment, eating until he was full, had been taken away from him in the Krankenbau because his kidneys were diseased. His neighbor on the other side was a Jew, a violinist from Holland, who was dying alone from pneumonia. When he heard my mattress rustling, Kapo Kwaśniak invariably raised himself up on his elbow and screwed up his puffy eyes inquiringly.

"You've finally gotten enough sleep," he said angrily, barely concealing the impatience that was gathering in him. "Please tell me something else. A man is almost well, but he has to lie here like a Muselmann. There hasn't been a selection in a long time."

He wasn't satisfied with summaries of vulgar books, stories from adventure films, dramas from the grand repertory. He couldn't stand unbelievable narratives developed against a background of romantic works. But he became passionately involved in nonsensical sentimental themes as long as I could convince him that they derived from my own life. In fact, I had already dragged to the surface everything interesting that I had ever experienced: my aunt whose gamekeeper-lover played the guitar under her window in the evening; the live rooster from physics class which we'd locked into a wardrobe to spite our professor and now it had no desire to crow; the girl with sores in the corners of her mouth whom I associated, because of certain experiences, with the Polish September, etc. I also exhausted all my stories about my loves, regretting bitterly that there were only two. I was polite and I spoke the truth in the simplest words—nothing but the truth. But time passed very slowly, and my fever kept growing higher and my thirst more powerful.

"When I was in prison, a boy came to us in the cellar. He said a policeman had brought him. It seems the boy had been writing on a wall with chalk," I began slowly, licked my lips with my tongue, and narrated in an interesting abbreviated form the story of the boy with the Bible, a story that I repeated a couple of years later in a certain novella.

The boy had the Holy Scriptures with him, which he read all day long. He didn't speak to anyone and answered our comrades' questions briefly and curtly. In the afternoon, a certain young Jew returned to our cell from interrogation. He took one look at the boy and said that he'd seen him at the Gestapo.

"Confess," he added, "that you are a Jew just like me. Don't be afraid; here we're all friends."

The boy with the Bible said that a policeman had brought him here and that he wasn't a Jew. In the evening he was taken out with other men and shot in the courtyard.

"That boy, sir," I hastily concluded yet another true story, "was named Zbigniew Namokel and, as he said, was the son of a bank director."

Kapo Kwaśniak raised himself without saying anything and started fumbling for something at the foot of his bed. He extracted a tomato from his parcel and held it indecisively in his hands.

"That wasn't an incident from your own life," he said sternly, looking askance at me. "I've been lying here a little longer than you and, do you know what? He was here in this hospital, that Zbigniew Namokel of yours. He was suffering from typhus just like you. He died in the same bed you're lying on now."

He leaned back comfortably against his pillow and tossed the tomato from one hand to the other.

"You may finish my coffee; I'm not permitted to anyway," he said after giving it some thought. "But don't tell me any more stories."

He tossed the tomato onto my blanket, pushed the mug of coffee toward me and, lowering his head, watched with great interest as I fastened my lips to the liquid.

THE DEATH OF SCHILLINGER

In 1943 Senior SS Sergeant Schillinger was assigned the duties of Lagerführer—commandant, in other words—of the men's labor sector D in the Birkenau camp, which was part of an immense complex of larger and smaller camps scattered across all of Upper Silesia and attached administratively to the central concentration camp in Oświęcim, Auschwitz. Schillinger was a rather short and stocky man. He had a full, bloated face and hair as pale as flax, combed smooth so as to adhere to his skull. His eyes were blue and always narrowed; his mouth was tightly closed and his cheeks slightly raised in an impatient grimace. He paid no attention to his external appearance, and I never heard that he allowed himself to be bribed by the camp prominents.

Schillinger ran camp D vigilantly and with absolute authority. He rode his bicycle along the camp roads without stopping for breath, always looming up unexpectedly where he was least needed. He dealt blows heavily with his hand as if with a stick; he crushed jaws easily and beat men until they bled.

He was tireless in his vigilance. He often visited the other sectors of the camp in Birkenau, arousing a panicky terror among the women, the Gypsies, and the prominents in the Effekten-kammer—the wealthiest sector in Birkenau, where the riches of the people who were gassed were stored. He also oversaw the kom-mandos working inside the great Postenkette, suddenly inspecting the prisoners' clothing, the kapos' shoes, and the SS men's knap-sacks. He also paid visits to the crematoriums and liked watching as the people were shoved into the gas chamber. His name was uttered along with the names of Gerhard Palitzch, Ernst Kranken-mann, and many other Auschwitz murderers who boasted that they had each personally, with their own fists, sticks, or guns, managed to kill some fifteen thousand people.

In August 1943 the news that Schillinger had died in unex-plained circumstances circulated in the camp. Various supposedly authentic, but entirely contradictory, reports about the incident were passed along. Personally, I was inclined to believe a Vorarbeiter from the Sonderkommando whom I knew and who, one afternoon as we sat together on a bunk where he was waiting for his share of condensed milk from the Gypsy camp's warehouse, told me about the death of Senior Sergeant Schillinger. What follows is his story:

"On Sunday after the afternoon roll call, Schillinger drove up to the crematorium yard to visit our boss. But the boss didn't have time because the first trucks from the Będzin transport had just arrived. You yourself know, brother, that unloading a transport and ordering them to undress and then driving them into the chamber, it's hard work that demands, if I may say so, great tact. Everyone knows very well that until the people are sealed inside the gas chamber, it's not permitted to stare at their belongings, to poke around in them, and it's especially not permitted to fondle the naked women. You understand, brother, the very fact that the women are ordered to strip together with the men is a real shock for people from a Zugang. So we employ a system of great haste; we pretend that there's a spate of work in the so-called bathhouse. In fact, we really do have to hurry in order to have time to gas one transport and clear the chamber of corpses before the next one arrives."

The Vorarbeiter rose, seated himself on a pillow, dangled his legs over the buksa and continued his story after lighting a cigarette.

"So, you see, brother, we had a transport from Będzin and Sosnowiec. These Jews knew very well what awaited them. The boys from the Sonderkommando were also nervous; some of them come from those parts. There had been incidents when relatives or acquaintances arrived. It happened to me, too . . ."

"I didn't know that you're from that region. I couldn't tell from your accent."

"I graduated from normal school in Warsaw. About fifteen years ago. Then I taught in the Będzin academic high school. People told me I should go abroad, but I didn't want to. Family, you understand, brother. Well, that's how it was."

"That's how it was."

"The transport was anxious; you know, they weren't merchants from Holland or France who were thinking about setting up a business in camp for the Auschwitz internees. Our Jews knew very well.

So there was a whole bunch of SS men, and Schillinger, seeing what was going on, pulled out his revolver. Everything would have gone as intended, but Schillinger took a liking to one body—and really, it was classically built. Probably that's why he came to visit the boss. That's when the naked woman suddenly bent down, scooped up a handful of sand, and threw it into his eyes, and when Schillinger, crying out in pain, let go of his revolver, the woman grabbed the gun and shot him several times in the stomach. In the square, panic erupted. Naked people rushed at us, screaming. The woman shot one more round at the boss and wounded him in the face. Then the boss and the SS men fled, leaving us alone. But, thank God, we figured out what to do. We drove the transport into the gas chamber with sticks, screwed the door closed, and called to the SS men to drop in the Zyklon. After all, we'd had a little practice."

"Sure, *ja*, of course."

"Schillinger was lying on his stomach and scratching the earth with his fingers in pain. We lifted him up and, without being especially careful, transported him to a truck. The whole way there he kept groaning through clenched teeth: '*O, Gott, mein Gott, was hab' ich getan, dass ich so leiden muss?*' Which means, 'O, God, my God, what have I done that I have to suffer so?'"

"So the man didn't understand to the very last," I said, shaking my head. "What a strange irony of fate."

"What a strange irony of fate," the Vorarbeiter repeated pensively.

In truth, what a strange irony of fate: when shortly before the evacuation of the camp the Jews from the Sonderkommando, fearing execution by a firing squad, staged an uprising in the crematoriums, set fire to the crematorium buildings, and, after cutting the wires, started fleeing into the field, several SS men shot them down with machine gun fire, all of them, to a man.

THE MAN WITH THE PACKAGE

To Adolf Rudnicki

Our Schreiber was a Jew from Lublin who came to Auschwitz as an experienced camp inmate from Majdanek, and since he had discovered a close friend in the Sonderkommando, which exercised great influence in the camp due to the riches it extracted from the crematoriums, he immediately pretended to be sick and without any difficulty went to KB zwei—which is what the special dedicated hospital sector of Birkenau was called for short (from Krankenbau II)—and once there, he immediately was given the splendid role of Schreiber for our block. Instead of turning earth over with a spade all day long or carrying sacks of cement on an empty stomach, the Schreiber performed clerical work, which made him the object of envy and plots of the other prominents who also assigned their friends to functions. He escorted and brought back the sick, took charge of roll calls in the block, prepared patients' charts, and participated indirectly in the selections of Jews, which, during the autumn of 1943, took place every two weeks almost like clockwork in all the sectors of our camp. The Schreiber was charged with conducting the sick to the Waschraum with the help of the Flegers, from where trucks drove them away at night to one of the four crematoriums, which were still functioning in shifts. Finally, sometime in November, the Schreiber contracted a high fever; to the best of my recollection it was from a chill; and because he was the only sick Jew in the block, he was marked down at the

---

Adolf Rudnicki (1912–1990), a Jewish writer associated with *Kuźnica*; known for the psychological realism of his prewar novels, he was among the first to begin writing about the Holocaust, although he himself never experienced the camps, having survived the war under an assumed identity. Borowski disdained the way in which Rudnicki romanticized the suffering and deaths of the camp victims.

first selection *zur besonderen Behandlung,* for special handling—in other words, for the gas.

Right after the selection an older Fleger who was referred to as block elder out of politeness, set off for Block 14, where almost everyone was a Jew, in order to work out a deal whereby we would deliver our Schreiber to them ahead of time, thus ridding ourselves of the unpleasant burden of conducting him personally to the Waschraum.

"We'll *verleg* him *auf vierzehn, Doktor, verstehen?*" he said after returning from Block 14, addressing the head doctor, who was seated at the table with a stethoscope in his ears. He was very carefully tapping the back of a newly arrived patient and writing up his chart in his calligraphic hand. The doctor waved his hand dismissively without interrupting his work.

The Schreiber was sitting on the top bunk with his legs tucked under him, attentively tying string around a cardboard box in which he kept dainty Czech boots that laced up to the knee, a spoon, a knife, a pencil, and fats, rolls, and fruit that he had received from the sick men for various Schreiber services, just as almost all the Jewish doctors and Flegers in the KB did; after all, unlike the Poles, they did not receive any packages from anyone. Furthermore, the Poles in the KB who received help from home also took both tobacco and food from the sick.

Across from the Schreiber an old Polish major, held in our block for several months for unknown reasons, was playing chess with himself, having stopped his ears with his thumbs; beneath him, the Nachtwache relieved himself lazily into a glass bed urinal and then immediately buried himself in his quilt. In the back rooms people were coughing and bringing up phlegm; pork fat was crackling loudly in the stove; it was stuffy and steamy, as it always was toward nightfall.

The Schreiber slid down from his bed and picked up his package. The block elder handed him his blanket roughly and told him to put clogs on his feet. They left the block; through the window we could see the block elder removing the blanket from the Schreiber's shoulders in front of Block 14, taking back the clogs, and patting him on the back, and the Schreiber, dressed only in a nightshirt now, which was being blown by the wind, entered Block 14 accompanied by another Fleger.

Only toward evening, while rations, tea, and packages were distributed in the rooms, the Flegers began taking the Muselmänner out of the blocks, tearing off their blankets and slippers, and leaving them in front of the doors in groups of five. The SS man on duty appeared in the camp and ordered the Flegers to form a chain in front of the Waschraum; in the blocks, in the meantime, people ate their supper and dug into their new packages.

We could see through the window that our Schreiber came out of Block 14 with his package in his hand, lined up in his place in a group of five and, chased by the Flegers' shouts, dragged himself to the washroom along with the others.

"*Schauen Sie mal, Doktor!*" I called out to the doctor. "Look at that!" He removed his stethoscope, walked over to the window with a heavy step, and placed his hand on my shoulder.

"He might have shown a little more sense, don't you think?"

It was already growing dark outside; we could see white shirts moving in front of the block; the people's faces were blurry; they walked to the side and disappeared from our field of vision; I noticed that the lights were on above the wires.

"After all, an old camp inmate knows very well that in an hour or two he'll go to the gas naked, minus his shirt and minus his package. What an incredible attachment to one's remaining property. He could have given it to someone else, after all. I don't believe I would . . ."

"Do you really think so?" the doctor asked indifferently. He removed his hand from my back and moved his jaw as if he was probing a cavity with his tongue.

"Forgive me, *Doktor*, but I don't think that you . . . ," I said casually.

The doctor came from Berlin; he had a wife and daughter in Argentina and often spoke of himself as *"wir Preussen"* with a laugh in which the painful bitterness of the Jew mingled with the pride of a former Prussian officer.

"I don't know. I don't know what I would do were I going to the gas. Probably I, too, would take my package with me."

He turned toward me and smiled facetiously. I noticed that he was very tired and needed sleep.

"I think that even if I were going to the chimney I would certainly believe that something would happen on the way. I would hold onto my package like someone else's hand, you know?"

He walked away from the window, sat down at the table, and ordered another sick man to be pulled out of his bed; he was preparing tomorrow's Abgang of cured patients going back to the camp.

The sick Jews filled the Waschraum with howls and groans; they wanted to set fire to the building, but none of them dared to touch the SS orderly who was sitting in a corner with his eyes closed and was either pretending that he was napping or actually napping. In the early hours of the night the powerful crematorium trucks drove up to the camp; several SS men walked in, the Jews were ordered to leave everything in the Waschraum, and the Flegers started throwing them naked into the vehicles until great heaps of people piled up on the trucks, crying and cursing, illuminated by the floodlights, and rode away from the camp, desperately holding onto each other so as not to fly off onto the ground.

I don't know why later on people in the camp said that the Jews on the way to the gas sang a heartrending Hebrew song that no one could understand.

SUPPER

We were all waiting patiently for total darkness. The sun had already set behind the hills; on the freshly plowed slopes and the valleys covered with patches of dirty snow, shadows were settling and growing steadily denser, full of milky evening fog, but on the drooping, rain cloud–distended underbelly of the sky there were still pink streaks of sunset. The gusty, darkening wind, saturated with the odor of thawing, sour-smelling earth, drove the clumps of clouds in front of it and, like an icy blade, penetrated to the very marrow; a lone piece of roofing paper, ripped by one of the stronger gusts, clattered monotonously on the roof. A fresh but piercing cold was blowing in from the meadows; in the valley, the wheels of freight cars grated against the rails, and locomotive whistles moaned. A damp twilight was descending; hunger grew ever more painful, and on the road traffic was slowly dying out. Less and less frequently, the wind carried scraps of conversation from over there—the cries of carters, the intermittent rattling of carts harnessed to cows lazily shuffling their hooves over the cinders on the path. The clomping of wooden clogs on the asphalt grew more distant, and the throaty laughter of the village girls on their way to a Saturday party faded away.

Finally, the darkness thickened sufficiently, and a light rain started falling. The violet lamps, swaying on their tall posts, cast a dim light on the tangled black branches of the roadside trees, the glittering roofs of the guardhouses, the emptied road shining like a wet belt; the soldiers marched past beneath their glow and disappeared in the darkness, and the sound of gravel crunching under their feet drew closer and closer.

Then the Kommandant's driver aimed the flattened beam of headlights shielded by a hood at the passageway between the blocks, and the block elders escorted twenty Russians dressed in pasiaki out of the washroom, their hands tied behind their backs with barbed wire, and drove them across the embankment; they were made to stand on the stones of the camp street, facing sideways to the crowd that had been standing motionless, with bared heads, for many hours, suffering silently from hunger. The Russians' bodies, flooded with the sharp light, melted into a single block of flesh encased in prison uniforms and covered with shadow; every wrinkle, swelling, and pleat of the cloth; the cracked soles of their well-worn boots and the taps on their heels; the dried lumps of red clay on the hems of their trousers; the thick seams of the crotch; the white threads weaving through the dark blue stripes of the uniforms; the drooping lobes of their buttocks; the tensed hands with the white fingers clenched in pain, with drops of clotted blood in the creases of their knuckles; the strained tendons on their wrists, on which the skin was blue from the rusty wire digging into it; the bare elbows, drawn unnaturally together by another wire—all emerged clearly from the darkness, as if frozen. The backs and heads of the Russians blurred in the dark, only somewhat whiter, because the shaved backs of their necks shone from under their jacket collars. The elongated shadows of these people lay on the road, on the barbed wires twinkling with dewdrops, and were lost beyond the wires on the slope of a hill that was overgrown with sparse, dessicated, drily rustling rushes.

The camp Kommandant, a grizzled, weather-beaten officer who had come to the camp from the city especially for this evening, walked through the beam of light with a tired but energetic step and, standing to the side, confirmed that the two rows of Russians were at the required distance from each other. Now the affair proceeded quickly, but not as quickly as a chilled body and hungry stomach would have wished, having waited for seventeen hours for half a liter of soup that was probably still tepid in the barrack cauldrons.

"Don't think this is trivial!" the very young Lagerältester cried, moving out from behind the Kommandant. He held one hand behind the lapel of his prominent's jacket, sewn from black cloth especially to fit his figure; in the other, he held a willow riding crop, which he rhythmically slashed against the tops of his boots.

"These people are criminals. I don't have to spell it out for you. They're communists, right? The Kommandant has ordered me to explain that they will be punished as an example, and as the Kommandant says . . . Well, boys, I advise you, pay attention, right?"

"*Los, los*, we're in a hurry," the Kommandant said in an undertone to an officer in an unbuttoned greatcoat. He was leaning with his hips against the fender of a little Skoda, lazily pulling his glove off his hand.

"It won't dare last long," the lieutenant in the open coat replied. He brushed himself off carelessly with his fingers and smiled with the corner of his mouth.

"*Ja*, but the whole camp will be deprived of today's dinner," the young Lagerältester shouted. "The block elders will take the soup back to the kitchen, and if even a liter is missing, I'll be missing myself, right, boys?"

A deep sigh flew through the crowd. Slowly, slowly the rear ranks started slipping toward the front; it became crowded next to the road, and a blessed warmth flowed from backs warmed by the men crowded against them, ready to jump.

The Kommandant motioned with his hand, and from behind his little car SS men holding rifles in their hands emerged in single file and, obviously experienced at this, lined up behind the Russians, each behind his man. It was impossible to tell from looking at them that they had marched back from the kommando together with us, had already had time to eat their fill, to change into freshly pressed dress uniforms, and even manicure their nails; they pressed their fingers around the gun stocks and the blood turned their evenly trimmed fingernails pink; evidently, they were getting ready to go into town to a party with girls. They loaded their weapons with a crash, rested the stocks on their hips, and touched the barrels to the shaved necks of the Russians.

"*Achtung! bereit, Feuer!*" said the Kommandant without raising his voice. The rifles clicked, the soldiers hopped back one step so that the shattered heads shouldn't splash them. The Russians swayed on their feet and collapsed with a smacking sound like heavy sacks, coating the stones with blood and pieces of splattered brains. The soldiers flung their rifles onto their shoulders and left hurriedly for the guardhouse; the corpses remained provisionally stretched out under the wires; the Komendant got into his Skoda accompanied by his suite, and the car, belching clouds of smoke, moved in reverse to the gate.

Scarcely had the grizzled, weather-beaten Kommandant managed to drive away without mishap than the silent crowd, which had been pushing more and more insistently toward the road, exploded in a gloomy clamoring, fell like an avalanche onto the bloodied stones, roiled noisily over them, and, driven apart by the blows of the block elders and Stübe elders, who had been summoned from the entire camp, dispersed stealthily among the blocks. I was standing somewhat to the side of the execution square and couldn't make my way there in time, but when we were driven out to work the next day, a Muselmannized Jew from Estonia who was carrying pipes with me assured me earnestly all day long that a human brain is really so delicate that it can be eaten without being cooked at all, absolutely raw.

SILENCE

They caught him in the German kapos' block at the very moment when he had already placed his leg across the windowsill. They pulled him onto the floor without a word, and breathing hard from hatred dragged him onto the camp's side road. There, tightly surrounded by the silent crowd, they began strangling him with scores of greedy hands.

Suddenly, warning shouts passed from mouth to mouth starting from the camp gates. Along the main camp road soldiers with weapons were running, bent forward, avoiding the groups of people dressed in pasiaki who were blocking their access. The crowd fled from in front of the German kapos' hut and hid in their own crowded, fetid, noisy blocks. On the smoking stoves people were cooking all sorts of food stolen during the night from nearby Bauers; they were grinding grain in hand mills on and between the bunks; they were pulling out the veins from meat on table tops; they were peeling potatoes and throwing the skins right onto the ground; they were playing cards for piles of stolen cigars; mixing batter for pancakes; greedily devouring steaming kasha and impassively killing fleas. Stifling, sweaty smells seethed in the air, mixed with the stench of food, smoke, and the steam that formed drops on the roof rafters and dripped monotonously like light rain onto the men, the furnishings, and the food. People crowded near the door; a young American officer with a lightweight helmet on his head entered the block and looked around companionably at the bunks and tables. He was wearing a beautifully pressed uniform. The revolver in his open holster was suspended on long straps and kept slapping against the young soldier's thigh. The officer was accompanied by an interpreter with a yellow armband inscribed with "interpreter" on the sleeve of his civilian suit jacket and by the president of the Prisoners' Committee, who was dressed in a white summer jacket, evening-dress trousers, and tennis shoes. The men in the block fell silent and looked attentively into the officer's eyes, leaning out of the bunks and lifting their heads from their cooking pots, bowls, and mess kits.

"Gentlemen," said the officer in English, removing his helmet, and the interpreter immediately interpreted sentence by sentence, "I know very well that after what you have experienced and seen, you harbor a deep hatred for your torturers. We, soldiers from America, and you, people from Europe, have fought so that law should rule over lawlessness. We must respect the law. You should know that all guilty people will be punished, in this camp and in all the other camps. You now have an example: captured SS men have been used to bury the corpses."

"Of course, we could go to the square behind the hospital. They haven't brought them all out yet," whispered someone on a lower bunk.

"Or to one of the shelters," another replied in a whisper. He was sitting astride the bunk with his hands digging into the blanket.

"Shut your trap! Are you in a hurry? Listen to what the officer is saying," a third man who was lying across the same bunk said in an undertone. They couldn't see the officer because he was blocked from view by the closely massed crowd which was gathered on that side of the block.

"Colleagues, our commander gives you his word of honor that all the camp criminals, both SS men and Häftlings, will be justly punished," the interpreter said.

Applause and shouts echoed from all the bunks. With gestures and laughter people tried to express their liking for the young man from across the ocean.

"That's why the commander asks you," the interpreter continued in a somewhat hoarse voice, "to be patient and not to commit lawlessness, because that will only come back to haunt you; just transfer the swine into the hands of the camp guard, okay?"

The block responded with a single prolonged shout. The commander thanked the interpreter and wished the prisoners a good rest and a quick reunion with their loved ones. Accompanied by friendly chatter, he left the block and set off for the next one.

Only after he had made the rounds of all the blocks and returned to headquarters in the company of soldiers did we pull that guy from the bunk on which, wrapped in blankets and smothered by our bodies he lay tied up, his face shoved into the mattress; we dragged him onto the concrete floor next to the stove and, to the accompaniment of the heavy, hate-filled wheezing of the entire block, we stomped him to death.

ENCOUNTER WITH A CHILD

Having found the gouged-out opening in the embankment behind the barracks that they'd been seeking for days, the two of them cautiously crept under the barbed wire, protecting their eyes with their sleeves and scraping their backs on the gravel. They tumbled down the embankment, turned over onto their bellies, and, supporting themselves on their elbows, crawled into the tall grass that was illuminated by the red glare of the setting sun. Under the corner tower an American soldier sat inside a guard booth that was plastered with yellow signs warning OFF LIMITS; his helmet liner and automatic rifle lay beside him on a bench. Immense drops were falling from the boards of the tower, striking dully into the ashes of the dead nighttime campfire.

When they determined that they were a safe distance from the wire, they sat down on a hillock and carefully brushed the clumps of sticky clay from their pasiaki and used knives to scrape off the brown stains from their knees and elbows. Finally, they got up on their feet and started moving with easy strides through the soaked meadow in the direction of the road, making a large arc around the camp from whose terrain the blue smoke of evening fires rose and the crash of broken boards and the voices of thousands of people could be heard.

"The wind's blowing toward us, you can smell the corpses," said the taller one, who was carrying a bundle, when they walked around the field in front of the hospital, filled with corpses lying between cords of wood. He had a swollen, pockmarked face and was an albino. His thin hair stood up stiffly on his skull like fur. A strip of shaved skin ran down the center of his head. The too short sleeves of his camp jacket revealed his sinewy, freckled, hairy arms.

He sniffed. "They didn't have time to burn them."

"That's obvious," said the shorter one.

His voice was hoarse; every minute or so he spat through his knocked out teeth. He was covered with a black stubble down the shaved center of his head. Dark, winding paths could be seen in the silver plush of the grass, wet from the recent rain.

He added matter-of-factly, "Look, they've already gone ahead of us. They're heading for the train cars."

"Don't worry about it, there'll be enough for you," the taller one said.

They descended to the road under the elongated shadows of the chestnut trees, in the direction of the neighborhood of private homes on the other side of the railroad tracks on which stood rows of freight cars without locomotives.

The valley was surrounded by a black spruce forest behind which the copper sun was sinking. At the edge of the forest, on the valley bottom among gardens in bloom, in the darkening greenery, lush, luxuriant, shiny with tiny pellets and needles of silver rain, single-family houses with small round columns spread out before them as clear as daylight, their rosy plaster shining. The sky above the valley was transparent, airy, as if made of silk, and slowly contracting with cold. Only along the forested mountain slopes thin gray patches of fog were descending and dispersing among the spruce trees.

"There are your freight cars; eat your fill," said the shorter one. They passed a field of new potatoes and came out onto the railroad track. The cars were open, filled with bodies that had turned blue, placed in orderly fashion with their feet toward the doors. On the top lay a layer of children, swollen and white like starched pillows.

"They didn't have time to burn them," said the taller one.

They jumped across the signal wires and crawled across under the car.

"That's obvious," said the shorter one.

They looked each other over and smiled, their lips tightly closed. They jumped across the next signal wires, slid down the embankment, and, zigzagging between the gardens, made their way down to the very bottom of the valley, to the officers' houses.

The colony, built by prisoners' hands for the highest officers of the camp and their families, was empty, and were it not for the beautifully kept gardens, the windows veiled with the whitest of curtains, and the smoke rising to the sky from the chimneys, it would have seemed that it had died out.

They walked down the main avenue and turned onto a side path next to the woods. The sun was still shining through a gap in the mountains; at the edge of the shade beside an isolated villa a woman in a flowered robe was relaxing in a lounge chair. Next to her, a curly-haired little girl in a blue frock was playing with a doll in a lacquered carriage.

They stopped on the path and looked at each other through half-closed eyes. They smiled at each other without stretching their lips. They lifted their gaze to the child's head, embracing it tenderly and carefully with their gaze as if with their hands. Then their eyes found the sharp corner of the villa, fenced off from the path by a patch of lawn, and again they glanced at the child. The taller one took a step forward, and then his shadow fell on the woman's legs and slid upward toward her breasts.

The woman lifted her bulging eyes and half-opened her mouth. Her upper lip was drawn up like a rabbit's. Catching her glance, the two lads smiled more broadly and, swinging their hips in camp fashion, began moving unhurriedly toward the child.

THE END OF THE WAR

Beside the plane tree–shaded highway loomed the naked concrete massif of the barracks building. A great heat was baking the air, drying it into ash. Smoke rose from openings in the attic; it stank of mutton stock. On the grass plots beneath the windows shards of glass crunched; scraps of books lay scattered around; helmets clattered as they were kicked around; sacks of white, acrid powder that dispersed in the air burst with a loud pop, like puffballs; rotten ribbons of soldiers' black ties flew out of the windows along with tables, bunks, and wardrobes, striking the ground with dull thuds as if they'd landed on a belly. American trucks manned by bored soldiers, elegant in their apparently brand-new uniforms, roared through the gate and expelled onto the concrete of the courtyard swarms of men in torn clothing, women with plaid kerchiefs on their heads, children, bags, and bundles, brought here from the surrounding camps, factories, and farms. The crowd spread out lazily in the square, kindled large fires to cook their dinner, and with a dull hatred set up housekeeping inside the barracks, methodically knocking out the windowpanes, smashing mirrors, chandeliers, and porcelain, destroying the hospital, cinema, and warehouse equipment, scattering throughout the courtyard books from the library and stacks of party identity cards discovered in the archive, demolishing room by room, suite by suite, corridor by corridor, toilet by toilet, floor by floor, the dwellings of their jailers; in the meantime, the trucks returned to the highway wailing and choking, drove alongside the provisional camp for SS men who were working all day long in the town's ruins under vigilant but decent guards, then took off at full speed to the collection point for a new load. Smiling Negroes nodded cordially from behind the driver at passing German girls. The girls smiled reservedly and looked after the column of trucks for a long time.

Right next to the barracks, separated from the SS camp by the highway, was a suburban workers' housing estate. Little cottages with chalk walls covered with young ivy and pink roofs beneath a cobalt sky glistened amid lush greenery; luxuriant chestnut trees shed succulent spots of shade on them. At their little windows veiled with tiny curtains, sunflowers bloomed vigorously; bean stalks twined around supporting poles; anemic little rosebushes drooped over the gates, their peach-colored petals trembling in the silence. In a raspberry thicket, on porches and in arbors, flashes of women's bright dresses could be seen; flowers, jostled, swayed on their tall stems. A dachshund was barking in a squeaky voice; men in suspenders were working in the garden; children, lost in thought, were walking along the road, rattling sticks along the picket fences.

Deep inside the settlement, in front of a small paved square surrounded by a flowering hedge, was a little church. Its steps were made of gray stone, almost brown in the shade that slanted across them; grapevines spilled down from the roof, swaying like green icicles, a simple cross of black marble among them; there was a verse over the iron doors, chiseled in Gothic letters in the stone. A gentle, soothing smell of flowers from the church garden hovered in the quivering air. Above the church, a twin-engine bomber flew past with a whine and a crash; its silver underbelly glistened as it made a turn and it vanished behind the trees, leaving behind a ringing silence in one's ears.

The stone interior of the little church was cozy and cool like an arbor. The steep vault that resembled hands held together in prayer was adorned with gold and purple branches of ornaments. In the round stained-glass windows, bright sunlight broke into the colors of the rainbow and settled on the walls of the church as on a glass globe. Over the altar, covered with a white cloth, from behind tall flowers, an angel with a brass trumpet leaned out of a painting, puffing up its chubby cheeks and supporting with its hand a sky-blue garment streaming in the wind. In the center of the church, leaning against a round pillar, a round little pulpit, light as a box of chocolates, stood on a wooden post. The stalls were also made of wood polished by a human hand. Little cushions for kneeling hung on hooks in front of the benches.

One wall of the church was empty, colorless, and raw. The benches had been moved away from it; a carpet was spread over the floor, which was covered with cut and potted flowers — roses, nasturtiums, gladioli, carnations, lilies, peonies, myrtle, and tulips; the flowers throbbed with color and mesmerized with their fragrance. Wax candles burned evenly and calmly, undisturbed by anyone's breath. Against the wall stood wooden crosses furnished with small plaques and enameled photographs. Simple, polite soldiers' eyes looked out from the photographs; the men's mouths were tight with seriousness, iron crosses shone black on their breasts, and on their collars the silver insignia of the SS glittered. The inscriptions explained that these were sons and brothers and husbands and fathers who had fallen in the distant steppes of Russia and the mountains of Yugoslavia, in the deserts of Africa and everywhere else, and that their mothers and sisters and wives and daughters are praying for them, and hold them in memory, and may God grant them a happy, eternal life.

"INDEPENDENCE DAY"

To Kazimierz Koźniewski, political commentator
A filthy man, black from the smoke and soot that was pouring down his glistening, blood-engorged face along with his sweat, was bustling about industriously in a shell-damaged large room in the attic of the barracks that had belonged to the Germans and, swearing coarsely, was attempting to fan a slow-burning fire by blowing on it violently. The iron stove, hauled here from a German Bauer, was missing its stovepipe, and every time he blew on it, it emitted a milky puff of smoke that dispersed through the room like a thick fluid. On the rusty stove top round pancakes made from potato flakes were baking in a row.

A tall, distinguished-looking gentleman wearing a white-and-red armband appeared in the smashed doorway. Entering the smoke, he choked violently and coughed.

"Get out of here, friend!" he cried mockingly. "That's enough fire! Are you going to burn down the entire barracks? Haven't you heard about the ban on cooking in secret? Well? A true Pole doesn't act like this! *Go on!*" he screamed in English, quite impatiently.

The filthy man got up from the fire, wiped his face with his sleeve, looked askance at the distinguished gentleman, and, calmly scraping the burned matter off the stove top, replied, "Give me more to eat, you son of a bitch, and then I won't cook. Do you think I like the taste of it? Here, try some!" and he thrust a steaming, rotten-smelling pancake under his nose. "See? Don't worry; if you didn't steal, I wouldn't cook. You're gobbling our butter by the spoonful, but you resent my pancakes?"

Kazimierz Koźniewski (1919–2005), active in the underground Home Army as a courier between occupied Poland and London, in the years immediately following the war published sensationalized stories about the conspiratorial underground movements.

"Listen, my friend, don't you insult me," said the gentleman. "The smoke here stings something awful! Wouldn't it be better to spend some time in the fresh air?"

"Someone who devours our share and brings meat to Jewesses also savors the taste of fresh air. But I'm fine right here. If it stings someone, he's free to leave."

The man with the armband on his sleeve grabbed the filthy man violently by the lapels of his jacket, dragged him away from the stove, and said through clenched teeth, "We'll see if you won't be better off somewhere else!"

At the same time, another man with an armband appeared on the room's threshold, a stocky man with a low forehead and a square jaw; he walked into the smoke without hesitating.

"What a bitch," he said to himself in a singsong voice.

A moment later, all three of them left the smoke. They disappeared around a bend in the corridor, leaving behind the unextinguished fire and unfried pancakes. They descended the stairs together, but their paths diverged on the ground floor. The tall man with the armband set off down the corridor to the left, having first told his colleague, "My friend, be so kind as to conduct him to the gate and inform the master sergeant that he wanted to beat up a policeman; in the meantime, I'll go grab us some bread and kielbasa. It seems there are forms for going abroad; we'll have to organize a couple just in case."

The stocky man responded, wrinkling his forehead so hard that it disappeared under his close-cut hair, "I can manage it, pal. Don't you worry. And you, you turkey, don't you try and escape, or I'll break your bones."

He jerked the filthy man by his twisted arm. The filthy man cursed like a sailor. They crossed the concrete yard and reached the gate. There was a bunkier in the building near the gate. On the small square in front of the bunkier an American soldier standing ramrod stiff was raising an American flag on the flagpole. Several

soldiers had dropped their baseball and the rubber gloves they wore
to catch with and were saluting ceremoniously. Before the others
could disappear into the building, the soldiers had returned to their
interrupted game.

In honor of Independence Day the master sergeant had freed
all the criminals in the bunkier; the filthy man was the first brought
in after the amnesty. He was led to an isolated cell and left alone
for a week. The man squatted on the stone floor and looked at the
courtyard through the narrow slit of an open window. It was getting
on toward nightfall. The trees looked dark blue, and the air was contracting with darkness. Courting couples were strolling under the
trees. They were cooks who bought their girls with food stolen from
the kitchen. The filthy man stood up, pulled a piece of a pencil out
of his pocket, wiped it on his trousers and, puffing out his cheek with
his tongue, painstakingly wrote in block letters on the uneven wall:

Two times in the bunkier:

*21 September 1944–25 September 1944, for sabotage while work-
ing in the German KL Dachau, for frying potato pancakes.*

*4 July 1945—for violating regulations in the American collec-
tion camp for former Häftlings from KL Dachau, for frying potato
pancakes.*

Then he signed with a flourish and, propping his elbows on
the windowsill, looked out enviously at the courtyard where the
girls were strolling with the cooks.

OPERA, OPERA

After a brief overture the plush curtain rose again. The golden
glow of the floodlights flooded the stones of the prison courtyard,

which was surrounded by gloomy plywood walls. A theatrical sharp shadow concealed the entrance to the cellars from which the dull thudding of people's feet reached us, skillfully enhanced by the orchestra's basses. The conductor, in black tails, stood with his side toward the stage, which was lit from below with a corpselike wax light. His face was yellow, and his half-open mouth and sunken eyes were dark blue, as if they were dried out. His hands shook and trembled poetically to the music's beat, like branches in a blustery wind. The singer, dressed as a man, was huddled in a corner of the prison wall. The jailer, who was standing next to her, was wearing a cloak that hung down to his knees, had a false bald patch on his head, and was holding a bunch of real iron keys.

I leaned back in my seat and rested my elbow on its cloth-covered armrest. My nostrils trembled instinctively. The sweetish smell of hair mingled with the acrid odor of skin, the fragrance of powder, and lavender. I felt a woman's warm breath near my cheek.

"How beautiful," I whispered, full of admiration for the involuntary contrast of subtle shadows and lights that played over the auditorium, the orchestra and the stage.

"*O ja, das ist wunderschön,*" the woman whispered back eagerly. She turned her head toward me and smiled tenderly. She had glassy, pearly teeth. One of her eyes seemed to be filled with fog; it lent her face a tinge of eternal embarrassment. I looked at her through half-closed eyes, slightly wrinkling my forehead.

"*Bist du vielleicht böse?*" she asked in a whisper, suddenly anxious. She fluttered her eyelids and stroked my hand with the tips of her fingers. Rows of people's heads—women's, soldiers', and clerks'—were leaning out of the semidarkness at our feet. In the loges, officers' gray faces with their sallow eye sockets shone brightly against a backdrop of black curtains.

"*Aber wo? Warum soll ich denn?* Why should I be angry?" I pulled a chocolate bar out of my pocket and gave it to the woman to nibble on. She broke off a square; I slipped the rest back into my pocket. The tinfoil rustled drily in my fingers like shredded newspaper.

The conductor dropped his arms and the music became softer, almost silent. Footsteps rose from the basement and, amplified by the cellar's echo, carried throughout the theater. A moving weariness, terror, and yearning could be felt in them. The music rose spasmodically and immediately fell silent. And at that moment, from out of the damp pit a writhing cluster of bodies crawled through the cellar door and snaked like sticky plasma into the center of the courtyard, in full sunlight. Seemingly forged together to form a single chain, covered as if with a single rotten rag, the cluster lifted a single—or so it seemed—terrifyingly blind face to the sun and stretched out dozens of bare, nightmarishly white arms to the sky. And suddenly it whispered in a sepulchral whisper: "*Sonne!*" and together with an explosion from the orchestra it erupted in gigantic sobbing: "Sun, Sun!" A visible shudder ran through the auditorium, sweeping over my body, too. After a moment the music grew softer and the actors froze in somewhat theatrical ecstasy in the very center of the courtyard. Finally, the singer performed an aria, and after she finished singing, the jailer with the keys started moving nervously near the wall. The cluster of bodies writhed like a trampled worm and, escorted by the jailer's baritone, slipped through the cellar door and vanished into the basement.

The woman looked at the stage with wide-open eyes. She leaned forward, dug her fingers into the armrest. Catching my watchful gaze, she smiled helplessly.

"*Bist du vielleicht böse?*" she asked in a fearful whisper. Her breasts rose as she sighed. Her extreme décolleté revealed a deep, white furrow between them.

"*Aber wo? Warum soll ich denn?*" I replied, moving my eyes over her tightly encased abdomen.

The curtain fell slowly; the officers, soldiers, Allied clerks, society ladies, students, and young women rewarded *Fidelio*, the prisoners, and the jailer with stormy applause. The conductor gave a deep bow, brushing his long hair away from his brow. The curtain rose again. The woman looked at my green SS jacket with its overly long sleeves with room to grow in that I had acquired when we left the camp, having handed in my pasiaki, the shirt made out of nettles, and my underwear. Her lips moved, but I didn't catch the words. She said more distinctly, *"Bist du böse?"*

"Nee, warum soll ich denn?" I replied, smiling. "Why should I be angry?" I placed my hand on her hip, slid it all the way down to her groin, and dug my fingers into her with such force that the woman's whole body jerked upward; the back of her neck was jammed into the headrest, and between her convulsively tightened lips her glassy, pearly teeth flashed, clenched in pain.

A JOURNEY IN A PULLMAN CAR

The teacher leaned his head out the window of the Pullman car. The train was rumbling over a switch and was being shunted onto a different track between freight cars carrying wood, machines, and coal. At the semaphore it started braking and sounding its whistle.

"We're getting there," said the teacher.

"Yes," I answered.

"I have to go to the children," said the teacher.

He swung his legs off the berth, rubbed his eyes, and stretched.

"Since we crossed the border you've been lying down the whole time. Isn't lying down boring?"

"Lying down isn't boring," I answered.

"We'll probably leave the children at the station. They can wait there for their parents," said the teacher. "The train will be empty when it goes on. This drudgery will be done with."

"Repatriation was pleasant," I said, getting down from the bed.

"Very," said the teacher.

He left the compartment and slammed the door. The train was moving more and more slowly. It switched to yet another track, whistled, and stopped under the semaphore. On the next track, freight trains packed with people, cattle, and equipment, and decorated with withered greenery, were stopped. Cows thrust their skinny faces through the open doors; bony horses stood in the middle of the car. Iron stoves were giving off smoke inside the cars. Women in wide skirts bustled around the pots. A couple of men were washing up in front of the door, rinsing their hands with water that they held in their mouth. Chickens wandered apathetically under the wheels of the freight car, pecking at the muck. A barefoot girl was carrying an armload of hay for the cows. Her long braids bounced against her back. The wind carried over an animal and human stench from the freight cars.

The teacher reentered the compartment. He glanced out the window and placed his hand on my arm.

"Well?" I asked.

"We're settling in," said the teacher.

"Yes," I replied.

The teacher began whistling through his teeth and climbed into the bed. He settled in comfortably and wrapped himself up tight in a blanket.

"I was there among them," he said, and sighed. "Oh Lord, Lord."

"Yes," I answered.

"They've been traveling for two whole months already. They've been stopped here for four days. And no one knows . . . ," said the teacher. He turned his face to the wall.

"Yes," I answered.

The train hooted and moved. The wheels rumbled over the switch. The train passed cisterns, flatbeds, and empty freight cars and pulled into the station on the main track.

The station platform was elevated above the town's street and was crowded with people. Travelers were sitting on the stairs next to their bundles. They were wearing wrinkled clothing and were exhausted. A railway workers' band in black uniforms stood near the barrier. The conductor signaled with his baton and the band started playing the national anthem.

"Oh, Lord," said the teacher, not turning away from the wall.

The girls from the school went up to the train and handed out bouquets of carnations through the windows. Women dressed in white and wearing little nurses' caps carried hot cocoa in porcelain mugs and fresh buttered rolls down the length of the train. The tubercular children, brought here by Pullman car, crowded the windows, smiled at the band, and clapped their hands.

"So that's that," I said, and stepped away from the window. I stretched out on the bed and, placing my hands under my head, stared mindlessly at the ceiling.

MY ROOM

I live in a room in which there are two burned-out windows. One of them is fitted with solid, though somewhat rusty, bars. On the sill of the other window there's a demijohn filled with cherry liqueur and a piece of crumpled needlework.

Among the furniture that was placed on the rotting floor immediately after the city's liberation, the most valuable piece is a cabinet because, squirreled away on its top shelf, are: a tin of American sardines, two tins of biscuits, and an officer's rubber raincoat purchased in a certain DP camp for eight packs of Camel cigarettes. On the middle shelf is a Continental typewriter that cost exactly thirty dollars. Probably the one who made the most profit on it was the money exchanger from the hotel with the familiar face of a fellow Varsovian. On the lower shelf are four pairs of socks and half a kilo of tomatoes in a sack.

Spiders crawl across the ceiling.

I can't stand the solid daybed hauled here by my thrifty family because, just like the camp bunk, it is crawling with fleas and bedbugs. When in the evening it looks as if there will be no rain overnight, I take my pillow and two shaggy Canada blankets, the property of a certain block elder in the Allach camp, and go to sleep in a public garden which is full of lovers and drunken militia men who fire their rifles at the moon.

After the day has dawned I sit at my round mahogany table, obtained from the apartment of a slain German, and, stifling in the heat, write until sunset. At the same time, I scratch my body incessantly; it burns as if it's being roasted over coals.

A girl in a black dress fusses over the glowing iron stove and sings. Her small rosy face is obscured in a frame of pretentiously pinned up hair.

The girl dozes on the bed in the other corner of the room. Every day she cooks my dinner and, having placed bread, tomatoes, soup, and potatoes on the table, stealthily carries a full plate of soup out the door and runs up the stairs with it to a certain young unemployed man who can't find appropriately convenient work.

Because it's with him that she lives, and not me.

SUMMER IN A SMALL TOWN

For Wojtek Żukrowski

High above the pitched roofs of the small town an enormous redbrick church stood on a hill among linden trees. Its stone stairs rose steeply from a base overgrown with the lush grass of the mountain on whose slopes goats grazed voraciously right up to the wrought-iron church gate that, wide-open, led into the gloomy abyss of the church, which was saturated with the damp smell of medieval walls. The church was adorned with two pointy towers covered in gray roofing paper. On the peak of the left tower a slender gold cross flashed in the sunlight; on the right, in memory of Peter's devotion, the builders had placed a black metal rooster that turned in the wind on its tall rod.

A narrow street wound gently along the side of the hill and, making a wide arc around the church, led to the town square on which an itinerant four-pole circus had set up. A loudspeaker installed on the peak of the circus tent blared the free melody of a love song; a colorful carousel revolved in time with its beat, as did the swaying swings. A garish crowd moved raucously among the booths, where exotic beasts were displayed in cages: a camel, a llama, and a jackal, and laughing girls crowded impatiently around an organ-grinder with a parrot that used its beak to draw lots predicting fortune or misfortune from a box. A warm wind caressed their faces and ruffled the cloth of the colorful umbrellas shading the flower stalls and the little tables for games of three-card monte. The square was enclosed on three sides by the ruins of burned-out buildings.

Wojciech (Wojtek) Żukrowski (1916–2000), Catholic writer and journalist; author of a 1946 collection of wartime stories, *Z kraju milczenia* (From the land of silence).

On the fourth side of the square, huddled against the severe walls of the church, stood the rectory. It was a two-story building the color of ripening raspberries, topped with a slightly moss-covered violet roof. At the level of the second story the house was surrounded by a gallery in extraordinarily delicate, one might almost say Mauritanian, architectural style. Green shutters shielded the windows of the rectory from the sun that lit up the roofs and the walls of the building, shone right through the branches of the weeping willow at the front of the porch, and flooded with light the garden that was in bloom in front of the rectory and that had recently been enclosed inside a picket fence.

Between bushes of overripe raspberries and currants a young, rosy-cheeked priest in a soutane fastened up to his neck was strolling along a garden path. The young priest was reading a leather-bound book attentively, holding it right up to his eyes and gently moving his lips; he paid absolutely no attention to either the noise or the laughter of the crowd wandering among the fair booths, nor to the clapping and cries of delight which greeted the tightrope walker in a black leotard who was performing on the square to advertise the circus, nor to the hoarse song from the loudspeaker. Only, from time to time, he lifted his tired eyes from the book and, clasping his smooth, yellow-tinged hands over his stomach, straightened up and turned his rosy, rather chubby-cheeked face, adorned with a kindly half-smile, toward the gallery on the second story that was extraordinarily delicate, one might almost say Mauritanian, in its architectural style.

Along the second-story windows shielded by green shutters, beneath the slightly protruding roof of the delicate, Mauritanian galleries, weighing down a thick white rope, pieces of women's underwear were hanging, transparent and airy, in a semicircle of various colors (sea green, carmine, bright blue, and black): shirts, panties, pajamas, and stockings—they were swaying gently on the rope, nudged by the warm wind, as if worn by somebody.

THE GIRL FROM THE BURNED-OUT BUILDING

I leaned over the bridge railing out of curiosity, firmly holding on to the cold iron of the guardrail to keep it from crushing my chest, and shut my eyes for a moment. The air still smelled of summer rain, but it was already beginning to shimmer in the sunlight and steam like warm breath rising from the heated stones and brushing against the skin of my legs. Invigorating beech-tree breezes rose from the river, gained strength, and weakened; they glimmered faintly like breaking waves, and from time to time the winey odor of rotting leaves slipped between them like a flash on the water. True, I was holding my nose in fear, because there were trucks clattering down the asphalt roadway, emitting the sickening stench of exhaust fumes that mixed with the smell of damp dust, soaked up the marshy effluvia of the gutters, and completely choked out the gusts of river wind.

The burned-out building; the red, almost brown, bricks that seemed to have rotted from the top and were covered with eczema patches of plaster and dark blue water stains; inside its empty interior, the thin pipes of chimneys that had been totally consumed by fire; illogical openings in the wall for unnecessary doors and windows—everything tangled in the voracious ivy that had eaten its way into the walls and crept along the cornices; the rusty, tattered netting separating the building from the street; near the building, an asthmatic, pale poplar tree, silver from the rain and shattered by a shell—observed from above from the arcades of the bridge—looked miniature and fragile, as insignificant as a child's toy.

Beyond the walls a broad field spread out, overgrown with luxuriant, fluffy grass that was faded like the old upholstery of the green couch that once stood in the burned-out building; rainbow-colored shards of smashed panes sparkled in the grass. Here and there flakes of fresh rubble showed rusty red; the vegetation hadn't managed yet to completely swallow a recent pile. A street with contorted lampposts, excavated from the collapsed buildings and not yet frequented by pedestrians, inscribed an arc around it while on the slope of the escarpment fantastically luxuriant trees were growing, frothy with leaves, heavy and weighted into the ground; grass climbed rapaciously along the slope and stung one's eyes with its sharp greenness; among the trees, screened by the bushes, stood tanks painted the color of withered leaves, and models of fighter planes glowed white. On the yellowish sand beneath the escarpment artillery guns of various calibers were placed on public display. Two-wheeled peasant carts clattered over the cobblestones of the bridge, loaded with bricks and lime; above the building, above the field, the escarpment, and the carts, clusters of clouds with lilac and pink underbellies rolled across the sky, blossomed, and withered in the wind like flowers forced into bloom.

From the arcades of the bridge I brooded mistrustfully over this landscape, and against my will I almost expected that when I opened my eyes the grass growing over the pile, the iron grating daubed with iron oxide paint, the tanks, airplanes, and artillery of every caliber placed there on display, those two-wheeled carts, the apathetic horses, the carters, their bricks and lime—all would disperse in the wind and in their place would return fragile, thick bushes filled with the rustling of leaves and the twittering of birds; the desiccated trees would turn green, the burned-out building would fill with people, and, leaving the warped, eternally stuck door ajar, a girl in a navy blue cape would emerge from the nonexistent corridor and raise her pale, intense face toward the sky. The girl would walk along the paths beside the hedge, vanish between the bushes as gracefully as a nimble animal; in the evenings, when the sky was sparkling and slippery as ice, the moonlight settled on her figure or the swaying shadow of the poplar enfolded her, the heavy perfume of night-scented stock or the severe cellar smell of springtime earth accompanied her or the dried leaves rustled under her feet, and bits of ice crunched like glass; she emerged from around the corner of the street and, squatting under a pillar of the bridge, we ate potato soup or borscht or the thin kasha gruel intended for my supper, greedily gulping down the burning liquid; on how many paths, streets, in how many interiors the figure of that girl remained; how many times did I feel the coolness of her blood-red lips, the close warmth of her body; how many times did I peer in the darkness at her tawny face, painfully absorbed in the rhythm of her body; a boy's love and a woman's jealousy; tenderness and relentlessness; separations and returns; childishness and maturity; streets, sidewalks, doors of buildings, people, images of the sky, parks noisy with shadows, full of her white hands; folk toys in percale colors, rains, suns, trees, and air—all are filled with images of her, more enduring under shut eyelids than the camouflaged tanks among the greenery, the whitewashed airplanes and the various-caliber guns displayed on the yellowish sand for people to gawk at.

I opened my eyes, which were still filled with a long-vanished landscape, and, dragging one foot after the other, heavily descended the stone steps of the viaduct with its stench of urine and mud, all the way down to the sidewalk on the street. I glanced at the half-naked workers on the side street who were carrying out bricks from the ruins and dropping them beside the wooden gutter; I glanced at the wagons with bricks, drawn by exhausted horses; I took in at a glance the grassy field, the desiccated trees, the escarpment, and the poplars on the escarpment—a landscape to which I was once attached—and finally, furrowing my brow intently, with an energetic stride I set off for the city center. As I walked past the burned-out building on which the ivy was spreading, the wind blew up from the field and I sensed in my nostrils, as if it were alive, a sweetish puff of air that seemed to emerge from the very depths of the foundations, from the scattered rubble of the cellars, the faint smell of a decomposing body.

But my sense of smell had deceived me since, as I learned by chance, the girl had been buried in the rubble on a different street and in a different building, and furthermore, half a year after her death her relatives had exhumed her and buried her, *lege artis*, in a cheap cemetery on the outskirts of the city.

AN ADVANCE

The man was short and somehow exaggeratedly animated. His voice was thin, singsong, almost womanly, and when he smiled, tiny droplets of sweat appeared on his face, which was as round and smooth as a suckling babe's. The man slid along the corridor floor and, pointing out the door to his office with his chubby hand, invited me by miming with his cheeks and mouth as well as by the fluid bending of his body to go inside and wait for him. I had scarcely had time to settle into the leather-upholstered chair and slide the sole of my sandal over the shaggy carpet a couple of times and also scan the room to see whether a new picture had been hung up between the windows on the one wall that wasn't covered with kilims, when the man slipped into the office ever so softly, shut the door discreetly, and with a skill acquired, as I thought maliciously, through persistent practice, sat down behind his mahogany desk in his director's armchair.

"No, no, no, no!" he shouted after a long moment of silence with perfect but perhaps excessively affected diction.

I removed the briefcase from my knees, stood, straightened up to my full height, bowed stiffly and walked out of the office on tiptoe, looking at the ceiling the entire time.

"I am very happy that despite all obstacles you are walking into the future with your head up!" the man said, smiling. He had floated out of the room right behind me, slid agilely down the corridor and disappeared inside a room across the hall that was jammed with pine desks and chairs and full of silent, concentrating clerks.

"That man ought to have struck me as antipathetic," I thought, mechanically stroking the iron railing on the stairs. "And yet, he looks very appealing. Obviously because," I thought as I kept descending, "contrary to the habits of short people, he doesn't hold his head up high and doesn't try to give himself significance in relation to tall people by putting lifts on his heels."

Only after I had gone down the two flights of stone stairs did I suddenly realize that I, after all, am a lot shorter than he is.

A HOT AFTERNOON

For Józef Morton

The sun lay dead in the naked sky like a dried-out bone. The overheated air stood over the earth like a column. The asphalt was melting in the roadway and smelled of baked tar. Ministerial

---

Józef Morton (1911–1994), during the war, fought with the underground communist People's Army; his fiction, which includes a focus on his characters' erotic lives, explores life in rural Poland during and after the war.

limousines rode over it without even a rustle. Behind the limousines fine dust rose and fell back on the leaves like silver rust.

Over the eczema plaques of the trampled earth ragged children were running around, kicking a ball made of rags, shouting hoarsely and spitting out the dust from their throats. Their faces were puffy and flushed with blood from their exertion. Inside the goal between a pile of clothing and a poplar tree that had been shredded by a shell, a boy was standing with his legs wide apart, his hands resting on his thighs. The goalie's knees were scraped, but the blood had already dried on his skin.

The game was just ending as I left the street and walked across the dried-out grass, drawing closer to him. Quarreling noisily and tossing the rag ball from hand to hand, the boys walked off into the shade. The goalie rubbed saliva over the wounds on his knees, picked his clothes up off the ground, and followed the others.

"Oh, what a shameless girl," he said as if offended, stopping near me and pointing his chin in the direction of the dried-up hedge that was growing under the ruins. A wild grapevine was climbing up the walls of the burned-out buildings; it twined its whiskers around the stone caryatids and flourished on what remained of the balconies and galleries. In the shade of the trees, on the damp lawn, people were settling down in family groups. The men lay half-naked on blankets; they were breathing heavily and were pale and gone soft like cooked fish. Their women slept with their faces in the grass, next to crumpled newspapers, bread wrappers, and egg shells. Other men, with their jackets off, were playing cards in closed circles and keeping an eye on the children who belonged to them, who were playing with a pink ball and chasing each other, laughing, among their parents.

Beyond the circles of the families, though, in the very center of the sun, right on the dried ground beside the hedge, a lone girl in a flowered dress under which she wore no underwear was lying helpless, like a felled post. She had turned her fat, sweat-covered face greedily to the sun, drawn up her knees, and audaciously and enticingly spread her fat white thighs.

"Indeed, what a shameless girl," I replied cordially, nodding in agreement, and placing my hand on the boy's shoulder, started looking at her greedily—just like him.

UNDER THE HEROIC PARTISAN

For Jarosław Iwaszkiewicz

In the beer garden Under the Heroic Partisan, among the tables and benches of unfinished wood set into the ground, slender, uneven poplar trees were growing. Their ragged crowns, delicate as bird feathers against the twilight sky, were absorbing the purest blackness. Amid the treetops cumulus clouds were drifting slowly across the sky like ice floes on sluggish water.

In a corner of the beer garden a wooden shed which housed the buffet had been built onto the wall of the neighboring apartment building. The young miss behind the counter had her hair pinned up artistically; she had a frightened face, a décolleté modestly adorned with a holy medal, fat hands, and gnawed fingernails. The waiter had a rosy bald patch that got darker along with the sky and a pencil behind his ear; he wound his way gracefully among the tables, benches, people, and poplar trees. On the other side of the stone balustrade girls who didn't have money for an entrance

---

Jarosław Iwaszkiewicz (1894–1980), poet, prose writer, and editor of the periodical *Nowiny Literackie* (New literary works) in which *The World of Stone* first appeared. Borowski attacked Iwaszkiewicz in print, asserting that the war had not left a deep enough imprint in his writings.

ticket peered into the garden. A cow on a rope lead was walking
down the street on its way back from pasture, slapping its hooves
noisily against the pavement, its heavy udder swaying.

"I'm telling you, those women are definitely lesbians," my wife
said insistently. Smoking one cigarette after another, she was staring through narrowed eyes at the dancing couples. I almost never
danced with her since she was stronger and taller than me.

"Lesbians in a provincial town? That's very touching," I said,
smiling. "Let's drink a bottle of wine in their honor."

In the green plywood shell which smelled of musty dampness,
musicians in shirtsleeves were performing a sentimental tango.
The shadows of the shell and the evening blurred their figures; the
setting sun's glare, reflected off the white wall of the theater adjacent to the garden, cut the accordion player's face in half. He was
standing at the edge of the stage and, running his fingers over the
keys, tilted his head curiously, as if trying to catch the sound of the
people's movements. His protuberant eyes were, obviously, blind.

At the blind accordion player's feet the small-town crowd,
as colorful as if shaken out of a bag of rags, was swarming on the
oak dance floor. Individual couples would emerge from inside the
crowd, trip over the edge of the floor, and disappear in the bushes. A
demobilized officer in a black beret wrapped his arm right around
the neck of a petite woman, bending his legs in their stiff sapper's
boots that reached halfway up his calf. A boy with close-shaven
hair, wearing sport trousers, pushed away his older partner at arm's
length as she attempted to snuggle close to him; they took mincing
sideways steps, attentively moving their feet to the swing rhythm.

But the most beautiful dancing was performed by the two lesbians. The woman dressed as a woman was wearing purple sandals
and a dress with red hearts and green maple leaves; her blond hair
fell smoothly onto her shoulders. She had a rose pinned to her bosom; she had faint dark circles under her eyes. In the arms of the
woman dressed as a man she bent like a flower in a breeze, antici-

pated with her body every move of her man, understood every flut-
ter of his hand, every variant of his turns; she brushed against him
happily, her hip against his; her tiny feet glided along the parquet
right beside the black shoes of the woman dressed as a man. She
looked into his eyes with unspoken surrender; her blood-red lips
opened lasciviously, revealing tiny, sharp, predatory teeth.

The woman dressed as a man was wearing a loose jacket dressed
up with a polka-dot bow tie and a white carnation in the lapel. Her
wide sailor's trousers could not conceal from an onlooker's eye that
her hips were wide, good for giving birth. Her small shoes with their
pointed toes betrayed the fact that the foot connected to the rhythm
did not belong to a man. That man had blond, wavy hair, cut above
the nape of the neck, and a delicate face with subtly outlined lips.
He steered his partner among the crowd cautiously and with a sure
hand; he knew how to slip into every gap, danced as freely as if
there were no one else on the dance floor. He looked into the eyes
of his woman with an indulgent half-smile, and when the dance
ended, the woman pressed his hand feverishly to her breast. They
left the dance floor pressed close to each other.

In the meantime, it had grown completely dark in the garden.
Lights like golden balls swayed in the wind among the trees. The
black shadows of the trees moved soundlessly over the ground.
The poplar leaves trembled and their illuminated backs twin-
kled; the wind bent them down, drowned them in shadow and revealed their black underbellies. The sky was dark blue, almost blue-
black; the smell of human sweat mingled with the fragrance of the
linden trees that grew in the park on the other side of the street.

The lights came on in the music shell. On the dance floor it
was even more crowded; the lamp cast a strip of light onto the edge
of the floor boards. The dancing crowd emerged from the dark,
floated across the strip, and disappeared in the shadow. At the head
of the crowd, on the back of a wave, the two lesbians glided through
the strip. The woman dressed in a man's suit suddenly stopped

dancing, excused herself to her friend with an embarrassed smile, and walked off into the depths of the garden under a shadowed poplar tree.

We couldn't believe our eyes. When the lesbian finally entered the circle of light, buttoning up her fly with a characteristically male gesture, we were finally convinced that she was a man.

DIARY OF A JOURNEY

> . . . fascist, you mortal enemy of mine.
> *Adam Ważyk*

Leaving the Renaissance cathedral in which a triptych by Titian, more smoke-covered than the windows, hung just beneath the vault above the main altar, which had been pushed away from the wall for the convenience of tourists, we ambled over to the city archives that were housed next door in the city hall from where, after glancing at scores of Arabic, Turkish, Latin, and Slavic documents sealed with enormous wax seals and colored initials and even with sketches, we set off at a leisurely pace along the main street of the old city. The street was populated with little statues and a noisy crowd of patients from the spa, who were taking advantage of the Mediterranean autumn that was just like our summer; it was paved with stone paving blocks that had been bleached white by rain and

---

Adam Ważyk (1905–1982), a prominent figure in Poland's prewar avant-garde movement, was an experimental poet, short story writer, and novelist. During the war, he became a fervent adherent of Stalinism as an antidote to Nazism. His wartime and early postwar writings conformed to the strictures of Soviet-style socialist realism. The phrase "fascist, you mortal enemy of mine" is from Ważyk's wartime collection of poems, *Serce granatu* (Heart of a Grenade, 1943).

sun; it climbed from the port's barbican that protruded into the sea and still protected the entrance to the jetty all the way up to the city gate, which was built on a slight incline. This gate separated the old quarter of the city, enclosed within a thick medieval wall, with houses crowded right beside each other, with little streets and alleyways so narrow that one could stretch out one's arms and touch the walls of the apartment houses that faced each other across the roadways—a quarter that smelled of soup, of wet laundry flapping on clotheslines above the streets, that was full of feral cats and skittish, dirty children; the gate separated that old quarter from the new district, which was built up along an asphalt boulevard with *pensions* and hotels concealed among luxuriant palms, orange trees, myrtles, cypresses, and stone pines, and which was replete with attentive waiters, call girls, and shoeshine boys. Both districts extended across the slopes of a limestone hill on which the occasional agave or cypress tree grew and whose summit was crowned with the gleaming white, menacing forts of Illyria dating from the Napoleonic era, while lower down the slopes, set into the city walls, were the gray, round cupolas of the German bunkiers of Nazi Croatia.

Since there was time until dinner, we walked at a snail's pace, stopping in along the way at goldsmiths' shops filled with subtle folk art made of fake silver; or we ogled the tall girls dressed in black dresses down to their ankles, with gold fringe on their bosom, as they strolled in the street, swaying like ships, proudly concerned only with themselves. These were women from the surrounding villages, the most beautiful women of the South, the products of peasant women consorting with blue-blooded tourists. At least that is what the city guide assigned to us by the city administration assured us was the case. I have to admit that in our long and varied journey through six republics, nowhere had we seen such beautiful girls, although to be sure, some of them were slightly disfigured by syphilis.

Finally, we reached a stone bench and sat down on its sun-warmed sandstone, marveling at the open sea, sea-green and emerald, rather silvery from the wind, and breaking with a crash against the rocks at our feet. Behind our backs a delightfully colorful miniature trolley rang its bell among the palm trees and started climbing up the hill; on the next bench sat a sunburned woman in a flowered summer dress holding between her knees a child who was playing with the red coral necklace that hung from her neck; from the sea came almost steamy breezes smelling of seaweed; seagulls were circling in the pure sky and dropping down onto the waves. It was warm and quiet, a good season for oranges to ripen.

"Are they writing about us in the newspaper?" a Member of the Delegation asked. "In Lubljana they devoted an entire article to us."

"Come on, let's go in to dinner; we're going to be late again," said another Member of the Delegation.

"Stop going on about the food," said the first man. He turned around at the sound of a bell; the trolley was coming downhill. "Primitive like that customs officer Rousseau."

I started looking through the newspaper, scanning the headlines of its modest little articles and notices. Unfortunately, on the fifth page of the paper (it was *Borba*, "The Struggle," from 11 November 1947) reprints of photographs from some English newspaper momentarily caught my attention. The first one showed a bare, stony field. In the field, face to face with a row of soldiers in English uniform, at rest with their guns at their feet and standing sideways to the viewer so that the camera took in clearly only the white cuffs and the belt of the first soldier and a large ammunition bag for a tommy gun hanging on his chest, stood a row of people among whom I made out the silhouette of a woman and a man in striped trousers.

The second photograph showed a detail from the first: the man and the woman. The man was very slender, really young, almost a head taller than the woman. He was wearing a jacket over a pajama top. His pajama collar was open like that of a polo shirt. The man was beginning to go bald; he had sideburns and a neatly trimmed moustache. He was standing erect, his left hand curled tightly into a fist; one might think that his lips were tight and narrowed and his forehead wrinkled. The girl was dressed in a bell-shaped coat and wore on her head a turban (colorful, as far as could be discerned from the photo) that held down her luxuriant hair, which was piled up stylishly over her forehead. Her head was slightly inclined toward her shoulder; a tiny cross showed red on her bared neck, or maybe it was only a drop of printer's ink. The girl supported herself on her left leg; the right one was somewhat bent at the knee, as on a person who has grown tired from standing for a long time. Her lips were drawn into a little pout, as if she was cold. The man's right hand and the girl's left hand dangled helplessly from their bodies because they were tied together. The girl was twenty-five years old and was named Eftimia Paza; the man, whose surname was Vaskekis, was a schoolteacher and he hadn't had time to get dressed.

The third photograph showed a soldier in an English uniform, his legs apart, bending over the corpses of people. Below the photographs was a caption explaining that these were Greek fascist troops executing suspects, and that the soldier in the third photo was turning over the bodies of the condemned with his heel and finishing off those who were still moving.

"No, there's nothing about us," I said, after looking through the entire paper. "Only that today's my twenty-fifth birthday. That's apparent from the date. The newspaper's a day late."

"That's really interesting," the Member of the Delegation said ironically. "Let's go in to dinner already," the other Member of the Delegation said, nervously gnawing his red moustache, which had not been trimmed for a month now and was falling onto his upper lip.

We stood up and walked at a lively pace to the hotel where we were served: a selection of *hors d'oeuvres variés* and *caviar de Cladave, crème de volaille, dindonneau rôti, charlotte russe,* and the Serbian red wine called *dingač,* along with "Turkish coffee."

A BOURGEOIS EVENING

For His Excellency Stanisław Dygat

My passions are books, smells, and thoughts, or rather, somewhat infantile erotically tinged fantasies before falling asleep. When I open both windows wide in the evening in order to let into my room the nauseating odor of the blossoming linden trees that grow on the other side of the street and, without extinguishing my night light, lie down on my bed—or rather, on my daybed—on a crackling, starched sheet, I slip my hands under my head, shut my eyes partway, and, observing through my fine, half-narrowed lids the rustling flight of a moth, I abandon myself to my thoughts. It's true that I experienced a lot during the past war, and I tell my friends with a certain pride that one day I saw twenty-eight thousand naked women, and in the course of a year well over a million people of both sexes and all ages going to the gas, and sometimes I even suggest enthusiastically that images of those human crowds follow me insistently—that, for example, I still hear human screams in my memory, the squeals of children, and the cowardly, subservient silence of the men—and that often I think I'm really smelling the nasty stench of putrid female blood mixed with sweat, and the

---

Stanisław Dygat (1914–1978), prose writer, author of sarcastic postwar stories about ineffectual "intellectuals" who are incapable of positive action.

damp, greasy odor of burning people, and yet I have to say that in my lonely contemplative moods, especially before sleep, I am not in the habit of reaching for that material. What usually happens is that, bored by watching the trembling shadow of the dancing moth on the gray ceiling, I close my eyes tight and then underneath my eyelids varicolored, kaleidoscopic geometric figures immediately appear: rectangles, irregular polyhedrons, circles, and spots of light, and also lines, stripes, pinpricks, moving clusters of vertical lines that rise up to the tops of my eyelids, grow smaller or larger, change their color and shape, combine, disappear, divide, and separate, finally escaping to the back of my head, and in their place new spots and lines float up from the bottom of my eyelids. I must confess that I am interested in them only in passing, since they function as a bridge to my real thoughts.

What I think about is women. Real and imaginary women with whom, obviously, I experience incredible emotions, experiences, and delights. During the war, when I was a lot younger, I thought about girls my own age, who seemed to me marvelously beautiful and perfect. I didn't understand at that time how ugly are sharp knees, skinny elbows, narrow, angular hips, and pointy breasts. Only now do I understand that a certain woman my own age with whom I came to experience love a couple of years ago (and whom I still recall today in a sentimental fashion), truly eager and devoted, was, however, as rough and hard as the bark of an oak tree.

Now, having overcome the shyness of first youth, in the evenings I reach in my thoughts for mature women, experienced and bold. I have stopped liking in my fantasies girls whom I would have to initiate into love. This probably derives in large measure from my being, in reality, fearful and extremely awkward, and I'm always at risk of experiencing difficulties.

If someone were to assume, however, that in my thoughts I aim at reaching a climactic image by a direct route, he would be mistaken. On the contrary: I construct an entire narrative around it, a complex intrigue, often borrowed from fragments of books I've read, whose ranks I rearrange on my shelves every so often. I create closed, but only lightly sketched, stories, and I think out in detail only individual images. I add the transitions between the images as a single sketch, almost as the intent of my thoughts. I hurriedly outline the characters, arrange the conflicts, add (as fits the circumstances) criminal or noble traits, equip my body with the qualities or defects necessary to compose the image, indicate where the action will take place in a couple of cinematic summaries in order to speed things up, constructing it out of elements seen that day, out of remembered interiors, objects, figures, and events, but although I tug at the narrative impatiently as if turning the pages of a fascinating book, I can never come in time.

True, I hold my hands over my ears, but I can still distinctly hear that the rustling in the bathroom is about to stop. Next, one door slams and then another; I can hear the sound of soft slippers on the floor, the swish of silk pajamas. When the night light finally goes out, the quilt is lifted, and the daybed's springs creak, I open my eyes in the darkness, and, still rather dissatisfied that my thoughts have been interrupted almost at the very moment of the climactic act, I turn over energetically and take my young wife into my arms.

A VISIT

I was walking at night, the fifth man in the row. A bronze flame from burning people was flickering in the center of the violet sky.

In that mild darkness I had my eyes wide open, and although the blood from my bayonet-pierced thigh bathed my body in warmth

that intensified to the point of pain with every step, and from behind, through the thick, hasty stamping of men's feet I caught the
delicate, apprehensive footsteps of the women (among them a girl
who once was mine was also walking), I can recall nothing from
that night other than what I saw with my wide-open eyes.

That night I saw how a half-naked man, steaming with sweat,
having fallen onto the cinders of the camp loading ramp from a
cattle car in which there was no more air, reveled in the fresh, cool
darkness, ran over to another man and, throwing his arm around
him, started feverishly insisting to him, "Brother, brother . . ."

Yet another man (in the struggle for air he'd been smothered
in the freight car, next to a slit in the wall), lying in the shed on a
pile of steaming bodies, suddenly kicked with all his might at the
thief who was bending over him and who was pulling off his foot
an almost new officer's boot made out of box-calf and no longer
needed, after all, by the dead.

For many days afterward I saw how men cried over a pick,
a spade, or near a lorry. How they moved rails, sacks of cement,
concrete posts for a fence, how they painstakingly evened out the
ground, smoothed the walls of ditches with shovels, erected barracks, guard towers, and crematoriums. How they were devoured by
scabies, phlegmon, typhus, and hunger. I saw others who collected
diamonds, watches, and gold, and buried them deep in the earth.
Still others attempted out of snobbery to kill as many people as possible and to possess as many women as they could.

Ah, but I also saw women who carried beams, pushed carts and
wheelbarrows, and built dams on ponds. Also, those who sold themselves for a slice of bread. Those who could afford to buy a lover—
for silk shirts, for gold, and for jewelry stolen from dead people. I
also saw a girl (who once was mine) covered with sores and bald,
but that's my private affair.

All these people who, because of phlegmon, scabies, and typhus, and also because they were too thin, were going to the gas

chamber, begged the nurses (who were loading them into the crematorium trucks) to look and remember. And to tell the truth about man to those who haven't learned it by experience.

Now I look out a window covered by a wild grapevine, beyond which is a building burned all the way to the sky; farther on, the rockslide of a classical gate with an intact amphora on a column; banal, fragrant, blossoming linden trees and a sky floating past in the form of clouds toward a horizon of ruins on the far side of a glittering river.

I sit in someone else's room among books that are not mine, and, writing about how I saw the sky, other men, and women, I keep thinking that the only one I could not see was myself. A certain young symbolic-realist poet speaks of me with scathing disparagement, saying I have a concentration-camp complex.

In a moment I shall lay down my pen and, yearning for the people I saw then, think about whom I should visit today: the almost smothered man in the officer's boots who is now an engineer at the municipal electric works, or the proprietor of a splendidly prosperous bar, who once whispered to me, "brother, brother . . ."?

The others are visited by those who, digging around in thoroughly rotted human ashes mixed with earth, search diligently for lost gold.

Uncollected Stories

Before and After Auschwitz

THE BOY WITH A BIBLE

The warden opened the door. A boy entered the cell and stopped on the threshold. The door clanged shut behind him.

"What did they lock you up for?" asked Kowalski, a typesetter from Bednarska Street.

"For nothing," the boy replied, and ran his hand over his shaved head. He was dressed in a threadbare black high school uniform. A coat with a sheepskin collar was draped over his arm.

"What could they lock him up for?" said Kozera, a smuggler from Małkinia. "He's still a puppy. And most likely a Jew?"

"You shouldn't say such things, Kozera," Szrajer, an office worker from Mokotowska Street, spoke up from his place against the wall. "The boy bears no resemblance."

"Don't jabber; he'll think that only bandits are locked up here," said Kowalski the typesetter. "Sit down, lad, on the straw mattress. There's no point in thinking."

"He shouldn't sit down there; that's Mławski's place. He might be coming back from interrogation at any moment," said Szrajer from Mokotowska Street, in whose house they'd found illegal news sheets.

"What's going on with you, old man; are you completely mad?" Kowalski the typesetter marveled. He moved over, making room for the boy. The boy sat down and placed his coat on his knees.

"What are you looking at? It's a cellar, that's all it is. You haven't seen one before?" asked Matula, who, pretending to be a Gestapo agent, had worn tall boots and a leather jacket and requisitioned pigs from peasants.

"I've never seen one," the boy blurted out.

The cell was small and low-ceilinged. In the darkness, moisture shone on the cellar walls. The filthy, warped door was covered with dates and names carved on it with penknives. A bucket stood next to the door. Two straw mattresses lay against the wall on the concrete floor. People sat hunched over on them, their knees touching.

"Take a good look," Matula laughed. "You won't get to see this just anywhere."

He arranged himself more comfortably on the mattress.

"Are you still taking?" he asked.

"I'm taking." I took a card. "For myself."

He took three cards. He looked at them.

"It didn't work out. Enough."

"Twenty."

I laid out the cards.

"I lost," said Matula.

He brushed dust off his knee. His riding breeches still had sharp creases.

"You win the bread. But I still say the cards are marked."

There was the clacking sound of switches in the corridor. A faint light began to glow under the ceiling. A dark blue piece of sky and a fragment of the kitchen's roof remained caught in the small window under the ceiling. The grate in the opening was completely black.

"What's your name, boy?" Szrajer the office worker asked. In addition to the news sheets, they had also discovered some receipts for money collected for the organization. He hadn't moved from the mattress all day, and he kept chomping with his dentures without letup. His ears stuck out even more from hunger.

"What does it matter what my name is?" the boy said dismissively. "My father is a bank director."

"In that case, you are a bank director's son," I said, turning to him.

The boy was sitting bent over a book. He was holding it close to his eyes. His coat was neatly arranged on his knees.

"Aha, a book. What kind of a book?"

"The Bible," said the boy, without lifting his eyes from the book.

"The Bible? Do you think it's going to help you here? It will help you like a hole in the head," Kozera the smuggler spoke up from near the door. He was walking from wall to wall with big strides, two steps forward, two steps back, turn in place. "One way or the other, it's a bullet in the head."

"Like whose?" I said, taking a card from Matula again. "Twenty-one."

"I wonder who they'll take out of the cell today," said Szrajer from Mokotowska Street. He was always expecting to be shot.

"Again?" Kowalski the typesetter said angrily.

"Deal me another," said Matula the Gestapo agent. His gun had jammed during his last requisition. "Risk-shmisk, a person has to live."

The cards were made out of the cardboard from a parcel. The numbers had been drawn with a chemical pencil by those who were here before us. Each card was marked.

"Nothing will happen to him," I said, shuffling the cards. "He'll sit here for a while, daddy will cough up the dough, mommy will smile at whoever needs to be smiled at, and they'll let the boy go."

"I don't have a mother," said the boy with the Bible. He brought the book even closer to his eyes.

"There, there," said Kowalski the typesetter and placed his hand heavily on the boy's head. "Who knows if we'll still be alive tomorrow?"

"Again?" said Szrajer the office worker from Mokotowska Street.

"Don't worry about anything," I said to the boy. "The main thing is people shouldn't be worried about you. That's the worst. When did they arrest you?"

"They didn't arrest me," the boy answered.

"You weren't at the Polizei?" Kozera, the smuggler from Małkinia, asked, astonished.

"No," the boy answered. He laid the book down gently and put it into his coat pocket. "I was caught in the street."

"There was a roundup today? On which street?" Szrajer the office worker at whose place they'd found news sheets and receipts asked him anxiously. He had two daughters who attended high school lessons. He hoped he'd be getting a food package from home.

"Something's not quite right," said Kowalski the typesetter. "If there was a roundup, they would have brought a whole bunch of people here and not just him. We would have heard something."

"Can you see the gate through this hole?" I said, indicating the window under the ceiling with my head. "All you've got is the roof of the kitchen and a piece of the workshop."

I showed my cards to Matula the Gestapo agent.

"Nineteen."

"What do you mean?" said Kozera, the smuggler from Małkinia. He was transporting lard to the Generalgouvernement when he was caught in a classic spot on the border. He stood near the door and looked out the window. "You can see more from the door. A guard with a dog is patrolling near the kitchen. They're unloading the potatoes for tomorrow."

"Again I've got nothing," said Matula, throwing his cards onto the mattress. "I have no luck. They'll definitely be coming for me. Because why else would they have transferred me here? Only for a bullet, right?"

"Did you think it was to set you free?" Kozera the smuggler replied.

He was pacing with long strides from the mattresses to the door and back.

"Ah, well," Matula said, sighing. "Maybe I'll win. If not, then tomorrow's bread ration is yours."

He started dealing out the cards made from the cardboard from a parcel.

"If they come for you today, why should I count on your bread ration for tomorrow?"

I stretched out my hand.

"Give me the cards."

"I was caught by a policeman on Kozia Street," said the boy.

"A blue policeman? Me, too," said Kozera the smuggler.

"An ordinary policeman. And he brought me here."

"Right to the gate? Through the ghetto? Not true," said Szrajer, the office worker from Mokotowska Street.

"He brought me in a hansom cab. He said it's very late, or else he would have taken me to the Polizei. So he delivered me to the gate," said the boy, and smiled at everyone.

"He had a sense of humor," I told the boy. "You were probably writing on a wall with paint?"

"With chalk," the boy answered.

"Did you have to draw?" said Kowalski, the typesetter from Bednarska Street. "The janitor of that house is going to have work to do because of you. If I were your father . . ."

He stroked the boy's completely shaved head.

"Kowalski, so why were you printing a news sheet on Bednarska Street?" Kozera the smuggler asked. He was walking from wall to wall with long strides.

"I wasn't printing a news sheet. I was on my way to buy an ottoman."

"At the underground printing press, eh? Nothing."

I handed the cards to Matula the Gestapo agent.

"It suited you like a French ducat does a streetwalker's palm. That's Shakespeare, typesetter Kowalski."

"One more time, and I'll win," said Matula, and started shuffling the cards.

"Enough. Two rations are already mine."

I pushed away the cards.

"I wound up here just as innocently as you," said Kowalski, the typesetter from Bednarska Street.

"You know very well that I only went to look for my fiancée because she hadn't come home in two days."

"At a gunsmith's, eh?" Kowalski the typesetter laughed.

I leaned over toward the boy and touched him.

"Will you give it to me later to read for a while?"

The boy shook his head no.

"Anyway, how could I have known?" said Kowalski the typesetter. "After all, the ad was on a pole."

We fell silent. The faint light burned under the ceiling. We were sitting on two torn mattresses. In the corner beneath the window, with his head on his knees, sat Szrajer, the office worker from Mokotowska Street, whose two daughters attended secret high school classes. His ears were sticking out more and more. Matula the Gestapo agent, who went around making requisitions, sat with his back to the door, shielding the cards he'd spread out on the mattress. On the other mattress sat Kowalski, the typesetter from Bednarska Street, who had been buying an ottoman in an underground printing shop. Next to him sat the boy who wrote with chalk on walls and read the Bible. Kozera, the smuggler from Małkinia, was pacing from the mattresses to the door and back.

The door was black and low, full of scratched-in names and dates. Beyond the black bars of the broken window a red fragment of kitchen roof sparkled and the violet sky shone brightly. Lower down was a wall, and on the wall, the vertical shapes of guard towers with automatic weapons.

In the distance, beyond the wall, were the uninhabited buildings of the ghetto with their blank windows in which down from torn pillows and feather beds fluttered.

Szrajer the office worker raised his head from his knees and looked at the boy with the Bible.

The boy was reading again, holding the book close to his eyes.

Steps could be heard in the corridor. The iron plates covering the floor reverberated. Cell doors started clanging.

"Finally, they're coming," said Kowalski the typesetter, who was listening at the door together with Szrajer. "I wonder how many new ones there are."

"There's never a shortage of these goods. No need to smuggle. They'll come on their own," said Kozera, the smuggler from Małkinia.

"But there's profit to be had in that they'll say what's happening in the outside world," said Matula, who used to go about requisitioning and was waiting for his death sentence to be carried out.

"You were out in that world just two weeks ago," said Szrajer the office worker. "Did you know a great deal about what was happening?"

"But I don't know if two weeks from now I'll still be in this world," Matula replied.

"Then why do you care what's happening? You'll still get a bullet in the head, right?" said Kozera.

"But if the war were to end soon, maybe they wouldn't shoot me?"

"A Polish court would also pop you for robbery," said Kowalski the typesetter.

"And it will award you the Cross of Merit for buying an ottoman."

The cell door opened again. In walked Mławski, who had been taken to interrogation. The door crashed shut behind him.

"How's it going, boys?" he asked. "Today I was scared shitless. I thought I was going to stay there all night. They came for me in a different car."

"The trees must be in bloom already, eh? People are walking around in the streets as if everything's normal? Right?" I asked, turning over the cards in my hand.

"Didn't you see it for yourself when you were driven here? People are living their lives."

"Here's soup for you." Kowalski the typesetter handed him a bowl with his supper. "They ate your lunch soup."

"They gave us pea soup with bread for lunch. The grub's not bad there. On the other hand, the heating is deluxe," said Mławski. He was standing near the straw mattress, using a spoon to cut his soup, which had congealed like aspic.

"How did it go? Can you sit?"

"What happened to me there? Nothing much. Just the narrow cell, the 'streetcar.' I knew the interrogator. He used to do business with my father in Radom. You know what it's like, don't you?"

He was taking his time spooning up his soup.

"I like this fermented rye soup. Sometimes it tastes good even if it's cold. Just like at home. There's a lot of potatoes today."

"I told the food trusty that it was for you. He scooped it up from the bottom," I answered.

"And what did the interrogator say?" Szrajer the office worker asked, the one at whose home they'd found a news sheet and receipts.

"He didn't say anything," Mławski replied irritably. He put away the bowl under his mug and took off his coat. "I got slapped across the face because of your coat. A piece of glass fell out from the lining. Were you planning on slitting your wrists, or what?"

"Just in case," I answered, and tucked the coat under my back. He had borrowed it from me for his interrogation because he was afraid that at the Polizei they'd take away his almost new leather jacket. Mławski sat down near me.

"You know," he whispered, "I suggested to my father that he should become an informer. What do you think?"

"What does your father think?" I asked.

"Father agreed. What else could he do, tell me?"

I shrugged. Mławski turned to the boy with the Bible.

"You're new, eh? I think I saw you at the Polizei, right? Weren't you sitting with me in the streetcar?"

"No," the boy said from behind his Bible. "I wasn't in any streetcar."

"He says a blue cop caught him on the street and brought him to the prison by hansom cab," Kozera said to Mławski from his position near the door.

"I'd put money on having seen you at the Polizei," Mławski said to the boy, "but since you say a policeman caught you . . . It's odd, but maybe it did happen."

We were silent. Between the sky and the black grating a spring evening lay, illuminated from below by the prison streetlights. Szrajer was sitting with his face in his hands; his ears were getting more prominent from hunger and stuck out between his hands. Kozera was pacing from the door to the mattresses and back again. The boy was reading the Bible.

"Will you play a game of twenty-one?" Matula asked me. "We're sitting here like stumps. Maybe I'll win back my losses?"

"Lay off the cardplaying," Szrajer said without lifting his face. "You'd gamble away your own mother. You . . ."

He fell silent. Shifted his dentures.

"He's spoken. The intellectual from the news sheet," said Matula.

"Will you play?"

"Get up for roll call instead. The food trusty's already trembling," said Kowalski, the typesetter from Bednarska Street.

We got up from the mattresses. We lined up in a row, faces to the door.

"The Ukrainian's on duty today. But maybe he'll be calm," I muttered to Mławski. He nodded.

The door to our cell was opened. A short, fat SS man with a square red face and thinning blond hair stood there. His mouth was tightly clenched. He had gleaming tall boots on his crooked legs. He had a 7.95-caliber pistol in his belt. He was holding a whip. Behind him stood the tall Ukrainian with the keys. His wore his black forage cap jauntily tilted onto one ear. Next to him stood the food trusty and the Schreiber, a short, withered Jew, an attorney from the ghetto. The Schreiber was holding documents.

Szrajer from Mokotowska muttered a few memorized words in German. Such and such a cell, containing such and such a number of prisoners. Everyone present.

The red-faced Wachman counted carefully with his finger.

"*Ja,*" he said. "*Stimmt. Schreiber,* who from this cell?"

The Schreiber lifted the paper to his eyes.

"Benedykt Matula," he read, and looked at us.

"God help me, boys, they're going to shoot me!" Matula whispered loudly, Matula who'd gone around dressed up as a Gestapo agent requisitioning goods.

"*Los,* get out, *raus!*" the Wachman yelled, and grabbing him by the throat with one hand, shoved him out the door and into the corridor. The door opened wide.

Farther along the corridor fully armed Wachmen were posted. Their helmets shone gloomily in the dim glow of the light bulb. They had grenades tucked in their belts.

The Wachman turned to the Schreiber.

"That's it? Should we go on?"

"No, not everyone," said the Schreiber, a Jew, an attorney from the ghetto. "One more. Namokel. Zbigniew Namokel."

"Present," said the boy with the Bible.

He walked over to the mattress and took his coat. At the door, he turned around to face us. But he didn't say anything. He walked out into the corridor. The cell door crashed shut behind him.

"Roll call's over at last! One more day! Two people gone! Give us another day!" shouted Kozera, the smuggler from Małkinia.

"We've got a lot more of them," Kowalski said dully. "A boy existed; the boy's no more."

He squatted over the shit bucket.

"Piss, lads, we're laying out the mattresses. So nobody steps on anyone's head later. Hurry up, make the beds while it's still light."

We started laying out the mattresses.

"It's a pity he didn't leave the Bible," I said to Mławski. "There would have been something to read."

"He's got no need of the Bible now. But I did see him today at the Polizei, I swear it," said Mławski. "What could he have done, such a little kid? And why did he lie about a policeman catching him on the street?"

"He looked like a Jew, so he probably was a Jew," Szrajer said from his place under the window. He was already settling down on his mattress and was groaning as he wrapped his coat around his feet. He was lisping, because he had removed his dentures. He wrapped them in a piece of paper from a parcel and slipped them into his pocket.

"In that case, what did he need the Bible for?"

"He was definitely a Jew. Otherwise they wouldn't have taken him to the firing squad," said Kowalski, lying down on his side next to Kozera. "Although they took Matula, too."

Mławski and I lay down together. We covered our feet with his leather jacket and the rest of our bodies with my coat. I burrowed my head into its soft fur collar. A pleasant warmth emanated from it.

A damp cold blew in from the broken window. The sky was completely black by now. The space between the sky and the window, lying on the level of the earth, was filled with a golden light. All the prison lights were on. Faint, twinkling stars shone through their glare.

"It's beautiful in the world, brother, except that we don't exist in it," I said to Mławski under my breath. We were lying close to each other so we'd be warmer.

"I wonder," he whispered to me; "did they take my father?"

I turned to him and looked into his face.

"It came out today that I'm a Jew," Mławski said.

The interrogator had recognized him. They had done business together in the ghetto in Radom.

"Then they would have taken you, too," I said in a whisper.

"No, not immediately; I'm of mixed blood. My mother was a Pole."

"But if your father's supposed to be an informer? They're not supposed to take you."

"God grant that he is. That would be good."

"Shut your traps for the night," said Kozera, sitting up on his mattress. "Do you want to do punishment exercises before you go to sleep?"

We stopped talking and began drifting off. From somewhere close by there was the sound of a hollow, dull shot. Then another. We all sat up on our mattresses.

"It seems they didn't take them out to the forest. They're shooting them here, next to the prison," I said under my breath and started counting: "Fourteen, fifteen, sixteen . . ."

"They're shooting them across from the gate," said Mławski. He was squeezing my hand with all his strength.

"He must have been a Jew, that boy with the Bible. Which shot was for him?" said Kowalski the typesetter.

"Lie down and sleep," Szrajer, the office worker from Moko-towska Street, lisped. "My God, lie down and sleep."

"We have to sleep," I told my comrade.

We lay down again, covering ourselves with the leather jacket and the coat. We huddled even closer together. A biting cold was blowing in through the window.

I look at the calendar hanging on the door of the Stube. 15, Freitag, Juni. I remember the year myself: 1945. The Stube is filthy and it stinks. Twenty bunk beds, almost never made—the lairs of free people. On the table, which is covered with filthy paper, are unwashed bowls full of garbage and reddish-pink roses. Having nothing to do, I wander from corner to corner, unable to find a spot in these gigantic stone SS barracks among the fresh greenery of early summer. Anno Domini 1945, one and a half months into the American era, one and a half months of moral torment.

The enormous barracks yard, concrete, clean, like everything German. In the gigantic hall with its semispherical roof, Polish and American banners are hanging; an eagle straddles them and there's a rather strange piano, taken from some church. Actually, from Dachau.

Over the gate is an American flag; inside the gate, American soldiers are guarding the new Europe's order. All around the barracks are posters: "Whoever attempts to go out will be shot." "Under quarantine."

Yes, we were prisoners. We had walked the roads of many camps: Auschwitz, Lublin, Dachau, Buchenwald; we had been extricated from the very depths of the war. We lived for years having nothing of our own, not even ourselves. We have been living for months now possessing nothing of our own. Not even ourselves.

But back then we had a fatherland. Today, we have none.
The new American age.

Yesterday, they distributed jackets—new ones, formerly German, military. The three of us, Kolka, Stefek, and I, don't get any.

"How is it, Warrant Officer, that it was only our Stube for which Sury named the names of those who shouldn't get any?"

"The lieutenant said that you gentlemen don't attend exercises."

"Aha, and would you know if Sury was paid for all those clothes?"

"No, not for all of them. Anyway, I don't know; inquire for yourself."

Kola is lying on the bed, unable to cope with his height. The heat, the lack of anything to do, and homesickness have broken him completely, but he lifts his head.

"Listen, Tadek, hop over to Sury. You haven't had any conflict with him yet, go ask him."

"I'm on my way."

"Wait a minute." He gets up from the bed with difficulty (he sleeps above me; I've got plenty of garbage from his straw mattress on my blanket), walks stealthily into the corridor.

"Resolve the matter politely with him, you understand; ask him straight out who is not supposed to get a jacket?"

"You think it's the warrant officer?"

"Definitely; he's the one who ratted to the colonel about the Stube's unhappiness with the grub."

Lieutenant Sury lives in a side corridor, in the officers' quarters, two men to a room, with wallpaper, furnished. A radio, a desk, a lamp; you could hear a pin drop in the corridor. There's a business card on the door. But I don't find Lieutenant Sury. "So 'suristic' of him," as Jakub says maliciously.

My priest has a square face with a broad jaw and flat lips. But the smile on those lips is wide and full, without any "buts": as if the world were simple and unambiguous. It doesn't have the instinctive defensiveness that characterizes each of us and places its stamp on our faces, posture and movements . . .

My priest has no uncertainty or worries. Rather, "the high school will open in September," "there will be English-language classes, they'll last about three months," "we're starting a Latin class . . ." As if Freimann—a symbolic name—were not an SS barracks near Munich or "North Munich" but simply a seminary in Warsaw. As if we weren't living from day to day with ever-increasing yearning and despair in our hearts. My priest has a full smile and a square face. He gestures forcefully, as if he wants to pour into us, to force into us, these alien sounds. We are seated at tables, assorted people, assorted smiles, assorted despairs: clean-shaven priests, gentlemen with Spanish goatees, young men . . . We repeat in unison, in English: *The teacher is going to the door* . . . We are beginning our life as émigrés . . .

A man with an armband that says "Camp police" crossed the yard at a clip in the shade of the young linden trees that grow in single file along the barracks street. He made it just in time. At that very moment Jewish women were carrying something wrapped up in a blanket out of our kitchen. The man with the armband wanted to fulfill his duty, but the cook beat him. The Jewesses with the bundle got away.

Soup—watery, without potatoes or meat. In the winter of 1945 they made better soup in KL Dautmergen. "Daily rations for each man: 299 grams of meat." "And potatoes?" "300." We have neither meat nor potatoes in the entire cauldron. They steal. All the military and civilian men, the committee and the police, the cooks and the Jewesses. But in the officers' rooms they don't just distribute a liter of soup. There, they call out, "Who wants soup?" KL Auschwitz 1943. KL Freimann—1945. Political prisoners. Cadres of the Polish Army.

Jakub got hold of some Polish newspapers. From the Jews, no doubt, because only they have any. Anyway, they're the only ones with whom he maintains contact. The poet Jan Lechoń's *Polish Weekly* from New York. Courageous words addressed to Churchill. A firm position on the state of Poland's independence. A firm position against totalitarianism—of any kind. Also, the poet Kazimierz Wierzyński, polite as always. An émigré poetry is being born that will not yield to the poetry in Poland. But we, have we matured to their level?

Today's the day that the fifth partition of Poland is being carried out in Moscow. Precisely today: O, Poland, known as "the inspiration of nations."

16 VI. Life is most burdensome for people who say *vita brevis*. Time drags on like an unbearable nightmare. Sometimes I think about death.

22 VI. The warrant officer has been assigned the job of inspector. "Sir, I shall catch them today. Please look below out the window: do you see?" Smoke was coming out of an iron pipe protruding through a window. "What on earth are they cooking over there?" "But that's the kitchen!" "Yes, but the stove's electric." The warrant officer runs downstairs.

I go to the English lesson; when I return, the "kitchen master" is standing next to the colonel, who is writing up a report. "How many kilograms of meat are thrown into a cauldron?" "I don't know; there was a cauldron and a half of meat." "Aha. And how much lard?" "I don't know." "And you also don't know about other products?" "Please, Chief Warrant Officer, I came here, I sat on the table and I watched. How am I supposed to know, Chief Warrant Officer, tell me yourself, how much meat is supposed to be thrown in? Do I have a scale or something?" "But how much of that meat did you eat up, friend?" Kolka asks from under the window. "O, good Lord, o, holy Mother of God, as if I need that piece of meat. That I should have lived to see such a day, that . . ." "I'm writing you up! How can it be that an entire cauldron of meat has been privately fried up and you knew nothing?! You're going to the bunkier for seven days."

The dark, haggard man looks uncertainly into the warrant officer's face. His eyes glitter as they do in a man who has been experiencing hunger for a long time. The warrant officer's body is strong and hirsute. He's sitting there almost naked, brown and glistening. His son has set off by bicycle to organize, as they say. The warrant officer was a boxer in Warsaw.

22 VI [*sic*]. Adam has gotten fat, his normally pale complexion is bronzed; he looks very handsome in his American shirt.

"Listen, Adam, what's going on?" "Fuck off; how am I supposed to know?" "And personally?" "I'm sitting with the women! I'm telling you, yesterday Pietrek wanted to use a rope on her."

"Take away the car." "What, when I'm getting stockings for it every day? I'll take it away when they stop giving me."

22 VI [*sic*]. The warrant officer comes back. "I reported to the major." The major shouted, summoned the lieutenant, the sergeant major, the kitchen commissar.

"And shit came of it," said Kola. "Because I hadn't collected a corpus delicti from the kitchen." "You should have brought me a pot with meat in it and taken it over to the major." "For the major to eat?" "What do you mean, eat?" "Well, what is an officer capable of who distributes his word of honor left and right?"

24 VI 1945. Seven men have been killed in a span of three days, and one prisoner has been wounded. Two were caught by Germans while stealing a heifer and were stabbed to death; four were killed on returning to camp, and the following communiqué was issued about one man: "Intercept him at night and hide him . . ."

I wanted to go for a walk. At the gate, a pass. A tall American with widely spaced eyes stops me: "*Zurück . . . Sagen Kameraden, das ist verboten,*" and points at my tee shirt. Someone standing to the side adds, "Put on a jacket, damn it . . . It's forbidden to go out without a jacket." I come back totally drained of my good humor. Maybe I should take up Greek? It's good for the nerves . . . Or think about Tuśka, my fiancée?

24 VI 1945 [*sic*]. Polish toilet paper; brand name: "Monte Cassino."

At a ceremony honoring the fallen, the dead, the murdered, the killed, those gassed in the crematorium gas chambers, a woman dressed in Polish national garb, with a wreath of ears of wheat on her head, was led out onto the stage, surrounded by several young people, former political prisoners dressed for the occasion in work-ers' coveralls; they milled around with wheelbarrows and spades. "It's a shame they didn't put a bed on the stage. A fine broad . . ."

The colonel is dressed in a uniform sewn from a blanket and tailored according to the English fashion; his face has grown raptur-ous, fat, you'd never recognize his former self . . .

The Braunschweig punishment camp. Every day people drew lots in the Stube to determine who would die the next day because the Kommandant wouldn't allow overcrowding in the camp and transports were arriving at the camp every day. In the morning, those who had drawn death would stand separately and go to work separately. Around noon they were rounded up onto trucks: sometimes they were hanged, sometimes shot . . . At the end of 1941.

To share one's pay with the kapo . . .

A guard earned five marks for killing a prisoner. In Auschwitz, three days' leave and a monetary reward.

Returning from work, the prisoners carried rocks into the camp . . .

It's almost two months since the sturdy lads in the deep helmets walked up to the wire fences of Allach, smiling emotionally at our tear-soaked faces. I squeezed the hand of a bleary-eyed Frenchman, shouting into his ear, "*Ils sont, camarade!* Comrade, they're here." They liberated us from the Germans, these sturdy, kindhearted boys. But who will liberate us from these sturdy, kindhearted boys?

The boys are sturdy, that's true, and they have deep helmets. They were very polite with us, as was appropriate for the liberators of "inmates of the concentration camps." But they, too, have traditions, you see, that are identical to those of the Germans: bunkiers, guard posts, near starvation rations . . .

This entire great war, friend from Chicago, probably happened so that you could cross the salt waters, fight your way through Germany and, having made it to the wires of Allach, share a Camel cigarette with me.

And then you were pulled away for guard duty so that you could guard me and we wouldn't have any more conversations. You remind me of an SS man. And I must remind you of a prisoner, because you search me and address me discourteously. And your murdered comrades are silent.

In the window blackened by the night, two worlds are reflected, equally unreal: the distant lights of the street lamps and the illuminated windows of the neighboring wings, seemingly suspended in the darkness, and the fragment of the room in which we are sitting. The wall, yellow, is perfectly reflected in the window; even its bluish, ultramarine hue is more strongly accented. Nothing else is visible. But we can sense it perfectly: it is calm and warm. A summer night on the outskirts of Munich.

The breathing of men as they sleep—how varied it is! Each man has his own sleep and his own way of breathing. A young boy from the forests of Radom breathes heavily, covered with his blanket up to his mouth; the warrant officer breathes cautiously, clings to his pillow, and, although it's a hot night, pulls up the blanket, nervously arranges himself, like a man who is forcefully driving sleep away, then again lies as still as a corpse. He is eavesdropping.

Our first cultural act after regaining our freedom was the publication of three clerical leaflets; our first expression of a Polish *raison d'état* was handing back the country to the protection of St. Joseph, and dedicating both a candle to God and its unburned stub to the devil—in other words, trying to serve two masters at the same time, because after all, Stalin's first name is Joseph . . . Anyway, the example comes down from the top: *The Polish Standard*, a periodical published in Paris (do you remember how feverishly we ripped it from American hands in those first days?) can find no other way out of our political difficulties, suggest no political position, other than prayer.

We are incapable of speaking Polish, we are incapable of thinking in categories of some sort of raison d'état, we are incapable of living according to the most primitive rules of collective life.

When the first printed Polish word appeared, I was astonished and horrified. The word was as splendid and flowery as the head of Bottom's ass crowned with Titania's flowers. As a sweet, wistful reminder of a Polish phrase, I shall bring back to our country "the fundament of the staff of the national standard, composed of the spirit of the fallen and others." Who can forget this glorious bugle call?

Jesters from a Shakespearean comedy. Only, they have excellent control over the language. It's we who are incapable of speaking Polish.

We are incapable of living according to the most primitive rules of collective life. This is the spiritual Muselmannization of the Polish intelligentsia: we are incapable of divvying up lard without drawing lots, bread without drawing lots, sausage without drawing lots. But we dream, we insist, that we will be more successful at sharing our country justly than others!

FATHERLAND

Obviously, I thought, were it not for me, working in the kommando would make him swell up from hunger. The men from the uprising were actually intelligent and thoroughly resourceful fundamentally, but they were growing accustomed to death too easily; they had been taught that it is beautiful to die for the Fatherland. Among us, in our small, hard camp, they were like frightened bunny rabbits; toward the Germans, they were as disgustingly accommodating as toilet seats; among themselves, as greedy as worms for every bit of carrion; and when they were on their own, they had no idea what to believe in, they were as dazed as a child on a merry-go-round. When our boys pulled their leather boots off their feet and drove them barefoot into the mud and snow, they imagined that the sky was about to fall. They were losing their ability to comprehend the smiling logic of the world, and so they were dying peacefully. When they boasted of their ignorance, I thought immediately about the gas chambers.

"I've always had that proverbial woman's luck (you won't believe me, of course), but after all, I've only stumbled once in my life. I survived this whole stupid regime abroad; however, right before the war, I don't know why myself, I decided to leave Turkey and return to my husband," a woman who was snuggled in the corner of the purple, plush-covered bench was explaining politely.

"What did she say now?" the young soldier with an albino's white hair and red, freckled cheeks, wanted to know. His legs in their carefully pressed trousers were stretched out against the plush.

Out of boredom, he was combing his hair with his big hands, which were covered up to the wrists with colorless fur.

"She regrets that she returned to Germany," I interpreted for the soldier. The woman looked at the albino from under her long lashes and wrinkled her round nose, its shadow wandering over her face as she smiled. The train slowed down on the curve, stopped for a moment under a semaphore, and pulled, clanking, into the station.

"I don't regret that I came here; war's a very interesting thing," the albino, who was wearing an American uniform, remarked. He spread out an illustrated weekly magazine on his knees, and after taking a good look at the legs, thighs, and breasts of a girl lounging in an unambiguous pose on its two glossy pages, rolled it up and gave it to the woman. She thanked him and started mechanically looking at the pictures.

"Wouldn't you really like to go home?" I asked the soldier.

The platform was almost empty; evacuees, driven away from the express train by military police in white helmets, shuffled over to a freight train without a locomotive that was standing on a siding. The darkening cloudless sky shone through the ribs of the station lobby's burned-out roof.

"In Europe there are white girls, a lot of white girls, you know," the albino said, and stretched out his muscular, sweaty hand. "Look at what blue nails I have."

"What's he saying now?" the woman asked anxiously, locking and unlocking on her belly her slender suntanned fingers with bands of lighter skin from the rings she used to wear.

"He's saying he's a Negro and he likes white girls a lot," I interpreted for the woman. I didn't need to find an outlet in daydreams, I thought; it was necessary to trust one's herd instinct. It was necessary to go along with the entire camp; German villas were wide-open for liberated camp prisoners; the women washed their feet for them out of fear and went to bed with the former prisoners on demand. The stupid and the sensible were equally starved. But the stupid raped peasant women they happened upon, and brought onions and meat to the camp. The sensible stole clothing, watches, and gold, and mistresses showed up on their own. Why, then, did I drag myself mechanically around the camp, mocking both the one and the other? Was I expecting some kind of morality? If I'd enriched myself, then I could be making use of my capital now; after all, I'm one of the sensible ones. For years on end I dreamed of liberation, and when it came, I was as flustered as if I were impotent. If I'd only been able to describe it!

"Tell them they should pay for your services in this erotic transaction," a man from Warsaw said in Polish. He was sitting comfortably in the other corner of the compartment, his legs spread out lazily, and was looking out at the empty corridor. He yawned with boredom, took some cigarettes out of a pack, and held them out to the woman. She felt around in the cigarette case with her fingers, and, having selected the one she wanted, not too firm and also not too crumbled, she asked for a light. The car swayed, and the train, finally emerging from the demolished station, moved slowly alongside the burned-out railroad workshops. Rusted, warped railroad tracks stuck out between half-destroyed walls; bent metal sheets, burned through, lay in piles, and shells of locomotives that had been exploded by bombs towered over them. Near the walls and along the railroad track there was a green meadow riddled with bomb craters in which murky, filthy water had collected. The train rode across a high viaduct from which one could see a red city that looked as if it had been flayed, and then, gathering speed, it emerged onto a railway embankment beyond the outskirts of the city.

The albino with the blue nails took a pack of cigarettes wrapped in cellophane out of his pocket, broke the seal, tapped his finger on the bottom of the pack, dug out one cigarette and offered the rest to the woman.

"I like her; she's not as persistent as the ones in France," the soldier said, and encouraged her with a gesture to take them. The woman put the cigarettes in her pocketbook and shrugged her shoulders with joyless sympathy. Her feet were propped on the radiator pipes; her legs were graceful and in thin stockings that lent a darker color to her skin, as if she were suntanned.

"Beautiful, really beautiful," I said seriously to the woman, making an explanatory gesture. She had wide lips, painted red in the American fashion, and fine, gray, cozy wrinkles under her eyes, which gathered around her nose when she smiled. Her blond hair fell onto her shoulders in gentle waves. She was dressed unfashionably and seductively; she wore a light blue shaggy coat and under it a see-through pale pink embroidered dress, without any décolleté, as was the style in Germany during the war, with navy blue silk that clung tightly to her body shining through it.

"You'd better leave that woman alone," the albino with the blue nails said impatiently, understanding my gestures. It was becoming hotter and hotter in the compartment from the radiator. The albino unfastened his wool shirt and displayed his hairy, freckled chest under it, as white as the skin underneath a woman's brassiere.

"Naturally you like them," the woman confirmed with understanding. "Before the war, I was a classical dancer, but now . . . Maybe I'll perform in the American officers' casinos. But you know, my husband . . ."

I have been born again, I thought; I can begin to live again. From my former life I still have my name, the number on my left forearm, a German uniform, and experience. Now, I could get together a little bit of money if that guy would really let me in on it. I'll live with him for a couple of months, then I'll cross the border into France or go to Italy to join the army; transports are leaving all the time by truck across the Brenner Pass. I could enroll in a university in Paris, Bologna, or Rome. So why, then, have I sat here for so many months? I should have left immediately when we were still being welcomed with open arms and open pockets. And have I already gotten to know this country and this people so well that I can leave them now? I won't be able to describe them faithfully; I always construct characters and landscapes from the same elements; I could make up a short, uncomplicated list of them. True, I could just as well have lied, using the eternal devices that literature has grown accustomed to using to support the pretense that it is expressing the truth, but I don't have the imagination for that. Besides which, I also thought, I don't know either Italian or French.

"Are you going to take her?" I asked the albino in the unbuttoned shirt.

"Oh, I don't know yet; I only have two days of leave and I'd like to, but I don't know of any private room in the city, a *Zimmer*, understand," the albino answered, and went back to his magazine. His right cheek was flushed; you could see the white design from the plush headrest stamped into his skin.

"Soldier, I have a room," the man from Warsaw said in awkward English and blocked the aisle with his legs.

A thin, hunchbacked man with gold spectacles, dressed in Tyrolean fashion, opened the compartment door and said, "Ah, but there's room here with you."

"You, go out," the albino said, looking indifferently at the man in the gold spectacles.

"*Der Herr* says there's no room in the compartment," I translated for the thin man.

He looked at my German uniform and said in a soft voice, without any sign of impatience, "You understand that my wife is seated in this compartment."

"You just found her now?" I asked ironically.

"Ah, what can you know? I was looking for her through the whole train," the man said.

"Why doesn't he leave?" the American soldier asked and, placing two fingers in his mouth, let out a long, piercing whistle, like a locomotive coming round a bend. Equally piercing whistles answered him from the neighboring compartments.

"I beg you, please don't say anything to him," the woman said with feeling. She extracted from her bag the cigarettes that she'd gotten from the albino and gave them to the man. She implored him, "Peter, go away, really go. You think you're . . ."

The man stretched out his hand, but the American soldier took the cigarettes out of the woman's hand and said firmly, "No!"

"You can see, it's occupied," the man from Warsaw said indifferently, and slammed shut the door to the compartment. The train rode through a bombed-out station, passed long chains of burned freight cars and crowds of people with bundles waiting on the platform, and again emerged onto the embankment that cut through the valley. In the valley, darkness was descending, and we looked down at the patches of dark grass as if from a moving cloud. The hilltops burned with a western, metallic glow; in the hollows lay stony coarse violets and reddish snow, and lower down, on the gentler slopes, grapevines shone red, while small cottages, enveloped in a gentle evening mist, glowed dimly in the light from the sun as it set behind the mountains.

She ought to have survived, I thought; if only they sent her to work for a Bauer. The German countryside didn't kill people immediately, although it sucked and devoured a person alive like a spider. If she wound up with a stupid or greedy farmer, she might have contracted tuberculosis, syphilis, or a child. What about a factory? She had never really grasped what physical labor is like, and carrying German rails and cement had already killed more than a million people, even those familiar with work. Most likely, she died in the city, but if she survived, she was probably sent to a camp; after the uprising, transports of women passed through Auschwitz and Ravensbrück.

"Ask her why she gave him the cigarettes," the soldier said angrily. He stood and lifted down from the luggage rack a shiny briefcase with a Gothic monogram. He pulled out a thick choco-late bar, broke it, offered some to the woman and put the remainder into his pocket. The briefcase was stuffed with canned goods, bis-cuits in translucent wrappings, and two bottles of French wine.

"The stranger asked me for cigarettes," the woman lied and looked at me inquiringly.

I translated her words faithfully for the soldier and added, "Do you have a lot of cigarettes? Or maybe you know someone among your acquaintances who'd like to sell some goods?"

The albino rummaged in his briefcase and extracted a crushed pack in cellophane. He unwrapped it and offered it to us. I said that I don't smoke. The man from Warsaw took two, winking, slipped one into his jacket pocket and crushed the other one indecisively between his fingers. Now the train was traveling near an airport, which was situated on a plain nestled against a sparsely forested mountain slope. Endless rows of four-engine planes, their motors covered, stretched across the field. In wooden huts raised up on tall stilts, sentries were walking back and forth, back and forth. The train passed tents and buildings at the edge of the airport and en-tered a terrain of wetlands overgrown with reeds.

"Tell him that I'll buy any quantity of cigarettes, gold, cameras, postage stamps, and, you know, in general," the man from Warsaw said. The soldier listened attentively, wrinkling his white eyebrows.

"I followed right behind the front-line troops, so I do have a few things," he replied. "Will you find me a room in the city?"

The man from Warsaw smiled broadly and pulled a piece of paper and a fountain pen from his pocket. He began to explain the route to the soldier, making use of some dozen English expres-sions that he had learned from trading with the army. The woman and the soldier bent over the paper attentively. I went out into the corridor, slamming the compartment door behind me. The train thudded and rocked rhythmically. Only the fleeting telegraph poles and the landscape revolving on an invisible axis indicated that it was moving extremely fast. Inside the compartment, the man from Warsaw leaned back more comfortably against the plush, covered his head with his coat, and began to nod off. The albino with the blue nails sat down next to the woman and placed his hand on her knees. The woman twisted her head with annoyance, but didn't protest more violently than that. I lowered the window. I felt a damp, cool wind on my face mixed with the suffocating, oily smoke from the locomotive spreading out across the field like sticky down.

I wonder, I thought, if all women smell alike. They use different perfumes and wear differently cut dresses, but does an ordinary female body bathed in hot water always smell the same? In the summer, the Jewish women smelled of stale blood; they wore padded Soviet uniforms and then they went to the gas and smelled like burned fat. If she went to a camp, I followed my thoughts, she almost certainly didn't survive the evacuation. Of course, they might not have discovered that she was Jewish; fortunately, the Talmud doesn't require that women be circumcised; after all, how could it be done? But in Ravensbrück right before the war's end Aryan women also went to the gas. She could have had swollen legs or scabies; she could have gotten chilled and contracted dysentery; she might simply have become very thin, she was always worried about keeping her figure.

The German with the gold-rimmed spectacles emerged from the next compartment and came down the corridor, somewhat stooped and walking with a slight limp.

"Would you by any chance have a cigarette, friend?" he asked, stopping near the window with his back to the compartment.

"I'm from a camp," I said to the German. I gave him a friendly smile and patted my pockets.

"Yes, we're all well off now," said the German. He said that he is a technician by profession and that now he has to do physical work; during the war he was enrolled in the party. That's of no help now to either him or his wife. He spent three years in the west building fortifications, but he took shrapnel from a bomb; they had to operate on his leg and groin.

"That doesn't help us either," he added with a faint smile.

I'll have to wait and get rich, I thought. I'd like to describe what I experienced, but who on earth will believe a writer who uses an unknown language? It's as if I wanted to convince trees or stones. Anyway, I wouldn't be writing out of love of the world; I'd write out of hatred, and that's not popular. I wonder what I would do if I found out that she is alive after all? I don't know, I thought cautiously; too often in my mind I undress women whom I see on the streets.

It was already completely dark when the train pulled into our station. The few streetlamps shone with a yellowish glow on their high poles and didn't illuminate the road at all. The station buildings covered the platform with an even darker shadow.

People's shouted greetings, footsteps, the shuffling of packages on concrete, and the railroad workers' whistles all could be heard on the platform. Soldiers were jumping noisily out of an American express train, throwing their military bags onto their backs and climbing the stairs to the embankment that separated the train station from the city located high above it; they loomed up for a moment at the top of the embankment, brightly illuminated by a streetlamp, and then immediately disappeared in the darkness. Their youthful laughter, shouts, and whistles reached us from far away. The man from Warsaw jumped straight down onto the ground from the car and took his small suitcase from me. The American soldier with the blue nails carefully lifted the woman down from the high step and took his briefcase from her. She slipped her hand under his arm, and, calling good night to us, they clomped up the wooden stairs and disappeared behind the embankment with the other people.

"We don't have where to sleep today," the man from Warsaw said with satisfaction. "We'll go to a certain friend of mine, only it stinks a little of broads at his place, you know?"

"Did you make a deal with the cowboy for your room?" I asked as we crossed the platform. We handed our tickets to a controller wearing a cap with official stripes and headed for the stairs.

"The main thing is to establish contact and trust with someone," the man from Warsaw said coolly.

"Why did you give it to him for nothing?" I said angrily. "We ought to have taken her, a completely fresh woman, though maybe getting a little stout."

"Didn't you see that she's older?"

"Of course, I like older women!"

"How could I know, my dear, you've always insisted on the opposite," the man from Warsaw said, surprised.

"You always know only what's convenient for you," I said belligerently. The locomotive whistled and the express moved on. The brightly lit windows of the cars slipped past the platform, the burned-out buildings, and freight cars, and vanished inside the trench.

"Man, if only you'd put together some dollars, you'd have so many of them here! You wouldn't have enough life or desire!" the man from Warsaw said, shrugging his shoulders dismissively. We walked slowly over the gravel. Right near the steps we passed a cripple who was dragging a large backpack and a suitcase and supporting himself with a Tyrolean walking stick. He hopped up the stairs clumsily, lifting his stiff leg.

"Did you by any chance notice, gentlemen, which way my wife went?" he asked when we emerged onto a dark street that ran among the ruins.

"No, we didn't by any chance see her," I answered.

I thought: I really like these deserted German cities, slowly decaying like carrion in the wind and sun. Whoever has smelled crematorium smoke can appreciate the beauty of the cellarlike smell of German ruins that no one has touched. I like these people who, waiting for what will happen as if for trains that pass them by, wear out their old clothes, ideas, women. I could wander without rest through the burned-out streets of these cities and constantly experience anew many hours of happiness. Does there still exist in this world another country that could be more of a fatherland to me?

"Of course, I did see your wife," the man from Warsaw said haltingly. He walked on a couple of steps in silence, then added, "She went off with the Negro. What a woman! *So eine Frau!*"

He laughed maliciously and bent his elbow as an expression of his admiration for the woman.

"A pity," said the cripple. He crossed the road with us, stepping heavily under the trees, dragging his leg over the withered, rustling leaves.

"A pity," I answered.

"You wouldn't by any chance have a cigarette?" the cripple asked the man from Warsaw.

"I don't by any chance have a cigarette," the man from Warsaw answered patiently.

"Good night, gentlemen," said the cripple, touching his hand, in which he held his walking stick, to the brim of his Tyrolean hat with its white bit of edelweiss.

"Good night," said the man from Warsaw.

The German with the gold-rimmed spectacles turned away and, dragging his leg, started across the street. I called after him in a singsong voice, "Good night, good night!"

The man from Warsaw erupted in a high-pitched giggle. I started whistling loudly and out of tune until the echo carried down the empty street. I rubbed my hands together maliciously and struck him a blow across his shoulder blades with the flat of my hand.

THE JANUARY OFFENSIVE

I

Now I will relate a short, instructive anecdote that I heard from a certain Polish poet who, accompanied by his wife and his mistress (a classical philologist by training), set off on a journey through West Germany in the first postwar autumn in order to write a series of reports from inside that incredible and at the same time comic melting pot of nations, seething and boiling dangerously in the very center of Europe.

West Germany was swarming with starved, stupefied, terrified hordes of people who smelled danger everywhere, not knowing how long, why, and where they should be grazing, chased from town to town, from camp to camp, from barracks to barracks by stunned, awfully young American boys who were equally terrified by what they had found in Europe, who had come like apostles to conquer and convert the continent, and who, having finally settled down in their zone of occupied Germany, started solemnly instructing the distrustful, recalcitrant German burghers on the rules of the democratic game of baseball and instilling in them the fundamentals of free self-enrichment by trading cigarettes, chewing gum, condoms, crackers, and chocolate for cameras, gold teeth, watches, and girls. Raised in a cult of success that depends solely on shrewdness and courage, accustomed to calculating a man's value according to the sum of his earnings, these strong, athletic, frank, and open boys, full of optimism about life and a joyous expectation that the main chance will always be sent by fate, with their pure thoughts as fresh and neatly worn as their uniforms, as rational as their occupations, and as decent as their bright and simple world, nurtured an instinctive, blind contempt for people who hadn't managed to preserve their wealth, had lost their businesses, positions, and occupations, and had fallen to the very bottom of society. In contrast, they behaved respectfully and with understanding toward the polite, tactful Germans who had preserved their culture under fascism, and the beautiful, muscular, jolly, friendly German girls, as good and as kind as sisters. They weren't interested in politics (the American intelligence agency and the German press took care of that for them); they believed they had done their job, and they yearned to return home, a little out of boredom, a little out of nostalgia, and a little out of fear about their jobs and that chance of a lifetime.

Thus it was very difficult to extricate oneself from this carefully guarded and marked mass of the "displaced" and to make one's way to a larger city and into freedom so as to begin a normal, private life after joining a patriotic Polish organization and getting linked up with the black-market chain, and then, having acquired an apartment, a car, a mistress, and official passes, to climb higher and higher in the social hierarchy, moving around Europe as in one's own home, feeling like a free and complete human being.

After liberation, considerately isolated from our surroundings, we vegetated for all of the fair, fragrant month of May in the filthy DDT-powdered barracks of Dachau; then, Negro drivers transported us for the summer to military barracks, where we lazily lay about in a large common room, edited patriotic news sheets, and, under the leadership of our elderly religious colleague who had an almost mystical mind for business deals, traded whatever came to hand and thought up ways of legally getting outside the walls. After two months of such nightmarish and amusing efforts that they ought to be described separately someday, the four of us moved into a small room of the dynamically functioning Polish Committee in Munich, in which we established an Information Agency, and then, thanks to our camp certificates, three of us, politely and in accordance with the law, succeeded in getting a comfortable, four-room apartment vacated by an activist in the former Nazi Party who had been evicted for a certain period, told to stay with relatives, and advised to leave some of his furniture and religious images for us. We brought over the rest of the furniture and a bookcase from the committee, where they were not being used. Our leader made contact with UNRRA officials and the London-based Polish Red Cross, busied himself with distributing American packages in the camps, returned to his prewar artistic activity, started paying us a regular stipend, and, having settled down permanently in a stylish Bavarian villa located in the park district of the city, drove to see us in a magnificent, official, freshly repainted Horch automobile.

II

At that time we were confirmed émigrés, and all four of us longed to escape as quickly as possible from the destroyed, locked-in ghetto of Europe and to move to another continent where we could live in peace and become rich. For the time being, we participated enthusiastically in locating our families and people we loved. One of us was searching for his wife from whom he'd been separated in the Pruszków camp after the evacuation of Warsaw and from where he was sent to a camp in Germany; another, for his fiancée, no trace of whom remained after Ravensbrück; the third, for his sister, who had fought in the uprising; the fourth, for a girl whom he'd left, pregnant, in the Gypsy camp when in October 1944 he walked out of Birkenau in a transport to Gross-Rosen, Flossenburg, Dachau; all four of us, swept up in the universal fever, were searching wholesale for our families and our closest and less close friends. Despite this, however, we welcomed with feigned warmth all arrivals from our country, no matter if they were defectors or official envoys, but in reality we greeted them with repellent distrust, suspiciousness, and caution, as if they were infected with typhus. The envoys were dealt with by the intelligence service of the Holy Cross Brigade, which sent the information it gained directly to Italy; the defectors sank without a trace into the nameless crowd of displaced persons and not infrequently emerged after a while as local kings of butter, stockings, ground coffee, or postage stamps, and often assumed positions of trust over former Nazi factories and firms, which was the highest level of advancement.

Overwhelmed, however, with understandable curiosity, and yielding in part to the charm of the fame that surrounded the poet in our country, the three of us invited him to be our guest for a couple of days, along with his wife and his mistress. At that time we were working in the office of the Red Cross, editing, printing, and distributing by post interminable notices of people searching for their families, so that our apartment was empty in the morning; in the afternoon we would go down to the river to sunbathe and swim; in the evening, we worked assiduously on our book about the concentration camp whose publication, anticipated fame, and wide sales were to help us escape from the continent.* The poet, accompanied by his wife and his mistress (the classical philologist), rested up from the rigors of their journey for several days in our landlord's bourgeois, mahogany conjugal bed (having gathered his strength he later showed an unexpected liveliness, became thoroughly acquainted with all the corners of the destroyed city, penetrated the secrets of the black market, and got to know firsthand the complicated problems of the polyglot mass of deportees); bored, he

---

* This is a reference to *Byliśmy w Oświęcimiu* (We were in Auschwitz), jointly written by Janusz Nel Siedlecki, number 6 643 (dates unknown), Krystyn Olszewski, number 75 817 (1921–2004), and Tadeusz Borowski, number 119 198 (Munich: Oficyna Warszawska na Obczyźnie, 1946), in which the first two stories in the present volume first appeared.

read a couple of fragments of our book and took offense at its being
saturated with such profound and hopeless lack of faith in man.

The three of us began arguing heatedly with the poet, his silent
wife, and his mistress (a philologist by training), insisting as we did
that in this war morality, national solidarity, love of one's fatherland, a sense of freedom, justice, and human dignity had dropped
off man like a rotten garment. We said there is no crime that a
person won't commit in order to save himself. Having saved himself, a person commits crimes for ever more trivial reasons, then he
commits them as a duty, and then from habit, and in the end—for
pleasure.

We derived pleasure from telling them many stories from our
hard and painful camp life that had taught us that the entire world
is like a camp: the weak work for the powerful, and should they not
have the strength or the will to work—let them steal or die.

"The world is not ruled by justice or morality; crime is not punished nor virtue rewarded; both the one and the other are forgotten
just as fast. The world is ruled by power, and power derives from
money. Work never has meaning; after all, money is not earned by
work but is plundered with the help of profit. It we are not able to
make the most profit, then let us at least do the least work. A moral
obligation? We don't believe in either the morality of man or the
morality of any kind of system. Books and devotional items were on
display in the shop windows of German cities, but the crematoriums were emitting smoke in the forests.

"Certainly, one might escape from the world to an uninhabited island. But is that really a possibility? So let no one be surprised
that instead of Robinson Crusoe's fate we choose to hope for a fate
like Ford's. Instead of a return to nature, we choose capitalism. Responsibility for the world? But can a man in a world like ours be
responsible even for himself? We are not to blame for the world
being evil, and we don't want to die in order to change it. We want
to live; that's all."

"You want to escape from Europe in order to discover humanism," said the poet's mistress, the classical philologist.

"Above all, to save ourselves. Europe is lost. We are living here from one day to the next, protected by a fragile dike from the gathering flood around us which, when it comes, will soak the vestments, wash away factory deeds and conference protocols, inundate private property, power, the black market, and the police — it will strip off man's liberty like a piece of clothing. But who knows what man will be capable of if he wants to defend himself? The crematoriums have stopped functioning, but their smoke has not yet settled. I wouldn't want our bodies to be used for kindling. And I wouldn't want to be a stoker. I want to live, that's all."

"Understandably," said the poet's mistress with a faint smile.

The poet listened attentively, in silence, to this short discussion, walked around the bedroom taking large steps, nodded his head both at what we said and what his mistress said, smiled like a man lost in another world (his analytical and visionary verse was famous for that posture before the war, as well as for the length of his narrative poems); finally, over a supper which was prepared by his silent, attentive wife and lavishly watered with the fatherland's colorful vodka that opens the hearts of Poles without regard to their gender, religion, or politics, the poet, crumbling bread in his fingers and throwing little pellets of it into the ashtray, told us the following anecdote that I repeat in a shortened version.

III

When in January the Soviet armies broke through the front on the Vistula in order to advance to the Oder in one giant leap, the poet, together with his wife, his children, and his mistress, a classical philologist, was living in a large city in southern Poland where, taken in after the uprising by a doctor friend of his, he was sharing the man's professional apartment in the municipal hospital. One week after the start of the offensive, Soviet tank detachments, having defeated the enemy near Kielce, unexpectedly crossed the little river that protected the city and, along with their accompanying infantry, but without artillery preparation, struck at the city's outskirts starting at midnight, causing panic among the Germans who were busy evacuating their bureaucrats, documents, and prisoners. The fighting lasted throughout the night; in the morning, the first infantry patrols and the first Soviet reconnoitering tanks appeared on the city streets.

The staff of the municipal hospital, like all the inhabitants of the city, looked with mixed emotions at the filthy, unshaven, drenched soldiers who, neither hurrying nor slowing down, lost in thought, were trudging on to the west. Then, through the narrow, winding streets, clanking tanks raced past followed by phlegmatic, sleepily moving cloth-covered supply trucks, horse artillery, and field kitchens. Only from time to time, when the Soviets were informed that some lost and determined Germans who hadn't had time to escape were still hiding in a cellar or a garden, did the soldiers silently slide down from the trucks and disappear into a side street. They would come back out immediately afterward and the column roll sleepily onward.

In the hospital, after the initial deathly silence and astonishment, movement and commotion reigned from early morning; wards and bandages were prepared for the wounded soldiers and city inhabitants. Everyone was in a fever and aroused like ants in a disturbed anthill. At one moment, a nurse burst into the chief doctor's office, out of breath, her large bosom heaving, and cried out, "You deal with this yourself, doctor!"

She grabbed him by his sleeves and led him into the corridor. The doctor, alarmed, caught sight of a young girl sitting on the floor against the corridor wall, dressed in a soaking wet uniform from which water dripping off it was creating a filthy stain on the sparkling linoleum. The girl was holding a Russian automatic rifle between her widespread knees; a soldier's rucksack lay next to her.

She lifted her pale, almost transparent face, concealed under a Siberian fur cap, smiled at the doctor with an effort, and got up from the floor with difficulty. Then everyone saw that she was pregnant.

"The pains have got me, doctor," said the Soviet girl, picking her rifle up from the floor. "Do you have a place where I can give birth?"

"It will be found," the doctor answered, and joked, "You'll be giving birth instead of going to Berlin, eh?"

"There'll be time for everything," the girl replied gloomily.

The nurses fussed around the girl, undressed her, and put her to bed in a separate cubicle. They hung up her clothing to dry.

The birth took place normally; the child came into the world healthy and screamed so loudly that it could be heard throughout the hospital. For the first day, the girl lay peacefully and occupied herself exclusively with the child, but on the second day she got out of bed and started getting dressed. The nurse ran for the doctor, but the girl dismissed him with the curt observation that it was none of his business. Putting on her uniform, the Russian girl swaddled the child in a sheet, wrapped it in a blanket, and fastened it onto her back Gypsy fashion. Taking leave of the doctor and nurses, she picked up her rifle and rucksack and walked down the stairs to the street. On the street, the Russian girl stopped the first presentable passerby and asked him directly, *"Kuda na Berlin?* Which way to Berlin?"

The passerby, startled, blinked dumbly, and when she repeated her question impatiently, he understood and pointed in the direction of the route along which trucks were driving without a break and columns of soldiers were walking. The Russian girl thanked him with an energetic nod of her head and, throwing her rifle over her shoulder, started out for the west with a strong and confident stride.

IV

The poet finished his story and observed us intently, without smiling. But we were silent. Then, having drunk the health of the young Russian with our next shot of fatherland vodka, all three of us said unanimously that this tale had been artfully constructed. But even if the poet had really heard about a Russian girl who gave birth in the municipal hospital, then the woman who had thoughtlessly set off to join the January offensive carrying her child and an automatic rifle had unnecessarily exposed the highest human values to destruction; she was certainly no humanist.

"I don't know when a person is a humanist," the poet's mistress said. "Is it humanism when a person who is locked up in the ghetto dedicates his life to forging dollars for purchasing weapons and producing grenades out of canned-food tins, or is it humanism when a person escapes from the ghetto to the Aryan side in order to save his life and read Pindar's *Epinica?*"

"We admire you," I said, pouring her the rest of the fatherland vodka. "But we're not going to imitate you. We are not going to forge dollars; we prefer to earn real ones. Nor will we produce grenades. There are factories for that."

"You don't have to admire me," the poet's mistress said, and emptied her glass. "I escaped from the ghetto and sat out the whole war on my friends' daybed."

After a moment, she added with a faint smile, "Yes, but I know the *Epinica* by heart."

V

Then the poet purchased a used Ford in Munich, hired a chauffeur, and taking our families' addresses and requests for our friends, he set off for Poland via Czechoslovakia in the company of his wife, his mistress (the classical philologist), and his trunks. In the spring, two of us also returned to Poland in a transport, bringing with us books, clothing made from American blankets, cigarettes, a bitter memory of West Germany, and distrust of our own fatherland. One of us found and interred the body of his sister, who had been buried in rubble during the uprising; he enrolled in architecture school and now produces plans for the reconstruction of destroyed Polish towns; the other, in typical bourgeois style, married his fiancée, who was found after the camp, and became a writer in his country, which is beginning to fight for socialism. Our leader, the priest of capitalism, a member of an influential and wealthy American sect that genuinely believes in the reincarnation of the soul, the self-annihilation of evil, and the metaphysical influence of human thought on the deeds of the living and the dead, cashed in his automobiles and, having bought a great many rare stamps, expensive cameras, and valuable books, traveled to another continent, to Boston, in order to make contact there, in the capital of his sect, with his wife, who had died in Sweden. Our fourth friend crossed the Alps illegally and reached the Polish Corps, which had been evacuated to the British Isles and was housed in military barracks in labor camps. Before our departure from Munich he asked us to visit his Birkenau girlfriend in Warsaw, the one he'd left pregnant in the Gypsy camp. He had learned from a letter she'd written him that their child entered the world healthy and that, like all babies born in the camp, it was killed with an injection of phenol, but that its mother, waiting to be gassed along with hundreds of the sick, was saved by the January offensive.*

---

* The present translation restores Borowski's original version of "The January Offensive" as published in the journal *Odrodzenie* (Rebirth; 1948:5). Editorial changes of a political nature, intended to emphasize Borowski's disdain for capitalism and efface any criticism of the new order in Poland, were introduced into the text when it was prepared for publication in the 1954 edition of his selected works. In that revised version, a triumphant note was introduced into the final sentence: the infant born in the concentration camp is not killed with an injection of phenol; rather, it survives, along with its mother, to live on (presumably) in the radiant future made possible by the arrival of the Red Army.

AN AUSCHWITZ LEXICON

The distinctiveness and exotic social characteristics of the milieu, the intermingling of many language groups, the official German language—all these elements came together to form a peculiar camp language which, like the language of the underground opposition, awaits its codifier. We append here the meaning of a number of terms used in Auschwitz that may make it easier to understand certain parts of the text.*

ABGANG—A group that moves from one block to another, from the hospital to the camp, from the camp to the hospital; also a single individual. "Today, an *Abgang* of thirty people left our block." "How many *Abgangs* do you have?"

ANTRETEN—A line-up. Camp life consisted of two moments: when the prisoner walked alone and when he walked in a

---

* This glossary of terms, not all of them actually used by Borowski in his stories, was appended to *Byliśmy w Oświęcimiu*. In the two stories he contributed to that volume, "Here in Our Auschwitz . . ." and "The People Who Were Walking," as in all his concentration camp stories, Borowski treats these terms as if they belong to the standard Polish lexicon, subjecting German words and camp neologisms to the rules of Polish spelling, phonetics, and grammar. In an attempt to mimic Borowski's representation of a language forced to assimilate alien words and concepts, the translator has opted for inconsistency. For example, because Borowski "de-Germanizes" all words containing *Kommand-* by using only one "m"(as their Polish equivalents are spelled), here the translation reverts to German spelling but pairs it with English endings when possible, such as adding *s* to form the plural. For *Pfleger*, however, Borowski's spelling, "Fleger," which spits out the alien sound of the initial consonant cluster, is followed.

crowd. "Don't you hear, it's time for *Antreten?*" "We're going to *Antreten.*"

APEL—The daily evening head count in the camp. A sacred, daily activity. Also, the head count of a block in relation to the camp head count. "Let's go to *Apel.*" "'Does your *Apel* agree?' the *Blokowy* asked the *Schreiber.*"

ARBEITSKOMMANDO—A labor unit. Every prisoner was attached to a kommando with the exception of those who were confined to a punishment cell or lying in the hospital. "How're you doing in your new kommando?" "I have to change my kommando or I won't make it."

BAD LAGER—Each newly opened *Lager* (camp); a prisoner's nightmare. For example, Flossenburg.

BIG LAGER—Real camps, such as Auschwitz, Dachau.

BLOK—A camp barrack, or block. In the so-called Old Auschwitz they were solid, multistory buildings constructed by prisoners. In Birkenau, almost without exception, they were wooden horse stables. Every prisoner was assigned to a particular block in which he had to appear for the head count, or *Apel*. Kommandos occupied assigned blocks. *Prominents* slept in blocks which they were free to choose for themselves. "Get moving to *Apel* from the *Blok!*" "*Blok* 6 to delousing!"

BLOKOWY—The highest-ranking prisoner in a block, the block elder; he was in charge of maintaining order in his block, supervised the distribution of food, packages, etc.; he was responsible for making sure the *Apel* came out right. Other occasional tasks: looking for escaped prisoners (within the greater *Postenkette*), meting out corporal punishment at official executions, etc. Surrounded by an aura of criminality (some had on their conscience several thousand murdered prisoners), in time they limited themselves to the convenient function of representing the block to the SS, leaving their real power to the *Schreiber* and the *Sztubowy*. The block elders from Birkenau's

Kwarantanna were famous, especially the Poles (e.g., number 1825 Franek Karasiewicz).

BUDA—A small room for the block elder or the *Schreiber*, constructed at the front of the block. Usually very luxuriously appointed (on an absolute scale). Of course, it was impossible for prisoners in the block to enter there.

BUKSA—Also referred to as a plank bed. A three-story structure for sleeping. Because other structures (and the space for them) were lacking in the block, it was the place where a person took care of all his activities (other than excretory functions): eating, killing lice, scrubbing mud off himself, writing letters home and—*organizing*. The bottom and second floors of this structure resembled a sloping drawer; one had to lie flat in them. On the top, it was possible to stand, sit, hang up clothes on the rafters, so they were occupied by the so-called better guests.

BUNKIER (Polish for bunker)—A hiding place dug into the ground by prisoners who were planning an escape. Also, a cement cell in which a prisoner "arrested" in the camp for some crime (engaging in trade, a torn blanket on his back as protection against the cold, an escape attempt, an illegal letter) was made to stand, the nape of his neck touching the ceiling, for long weeks, day and night. Also, the protected post for the camp guard, what the English call a pillbox. "As long as there's a *bunkier*, it's possible to escape." "Yes, but when they catch you, then it's the walled-in *bunkier*." "Of course, they've built up *bunkiers* around the camp. How will you get past them at night?"

CHIMNEY—Synonym for crematorium and for death in the gas chamber. "Why are you rushing like a Jew to the chimney?"

DAW—*Deutsche Abrüstungswerke*, a difficult kommando assigned mainly to disassembling airplanes shot down over Germany. A classical place for escape attempts. "The siren is blaring; probably someone's escaped from the DAW again."

DURCHFALL—Diarrhea, dysentery, the classic camp sickness, the terror of all prisoners. In the great majority of cases, uncured and incurable. Everyone battling *Durchfall* was left entirely to his own resources. This battle is one of the unwritten epics of Auschwitz. "Don't drink the water or you'll get *Durchfall.*" "The best thing for *Durchfall* is bread burned to charcoal."

EFEKTY—Originally, the warehouse for the prisoners' private belongings. Later, also an entire separate camp sector; in its blocks lay (and rotted) riches collected from the transports going to the crematorium. "Bring me a nice-looking shirt if you're in *Efekty.*"

FLECK—Spotted typhus, the third classic Auschwitz sickness. Until April 4, 1943, everyone who was sick with typhus went to the gas chamber without exception. In many people's memory typhus is connected with the person of Dr. Zentkeller, an indefatigable stalker of lice and typhus-sufferers who were hidden by their *Fleger* friends in other, nontyphus hospital blocks.

FLEGER (German *Pfleger*, Polonized spelling)—A paramedic in the hospital; the *Fleger* was more or less equivalent to a *sztubowy* in the camp. "*Fleger*, water!" "A *Fleger* is more important than a doctor."

FUNKCJA (Polish for function)—A good position in the camp (not in a kommando!), not necessarily officially good (a block elder's *Pipel*, a runner, a *Fleger* in the hospital, etc.). "The boy's got luck; he's made it to a *funkcja.*"

GASKAMMER—The gas chamber. A couple of million people passed through a couple of small Auschwitz halls and exited "in the character of smoke through the chimney," as it was ironically described in the camp. Because each larger concentration camp had its own gas chambers and crematoriums, there must have been hundreds of them. The architecture of the twentieth century! "The entire transport went to the gas." "Why worry, either way we're going to the gas."

GONG—A wake-up call, the signal for work, for *Apel*, for sleep. "Get up, fine guests; it's already past the second gong."

GYPSY—The Gypsy camp. Gypsies from all over Europe who were interned in Auschwitz rapidly lost all the rights and appearances of rights of interned people and fell victim en masse to hunger, filth, disease and barbaric treatment by the SS and the camp staff. "I'm going to the Gypsy." "There's nothing like what's at the Gypsy, brother."

HOLZHOF—The famous *Muselmann* kommando; the wood warehouse.

KANADA [CANADA]—The symbol of camp well-being. Also, the kommando that worked with the transports arriving at the camp and the gas. "Now, there's Canada in the camp; you should have arrived earlier, then you would have seen something." "Canada is going to the ramp."

KAPO—A prisoner in charge of a work group. He kept an eye on the work, distributed the soup, rewards, and blows. He had unlimited power over the prisoners. A kommando's goodness was measured mainly by whether its kapo was good (although there were fundamentally bad kommandos, *Weichseldurchstich*, and fundamentally good ones—for example, working in the women's camp). As a rule, each kapo had his own hut in the field, a place for rest, sleep, barter, drinking bouts, and collusion with the SS, as well as the well-known relations with their *Pipels*. "If the kapo says so, you have to do it." "I'll tell the kapo that you don't want to work."

KOMMANDO—A labor detachment with its own kapo and an SS man in a supervisory position (*Kommandoführer*), working on a defined task or in a defined place.

KRANKENBAU—The hospital, the famous KB.

KRÄZE [SCABIES]—The fourth classic Auschwitz sickness. Often, entire infected blocks went to the gas (e.g., from the FKL). "You've got *Kräze?* Smear yourself with tea."

LAGER—A camp (understood: concentration).

LAGERÄLTESTE—The camp leader.

LAGEREK—A disdainful name for a small camp.

LAGROWIEC—A concentration camp prisoner.

LEICHENHALLE—The camp mortuary where the daily harvest was placed in model order (corpse next to corpse, in layers, heads facing feet, tall on top of tall). Every corpse had a death certificate; before being transported to a crematorium, the corpses were placed in a row on the camp road beside the hospital so that the number tattooed on the left arm was clearly visible for the SS man who checked the identity of the dead. In the evening, the corpses were loaded onto a truck with a raised platform; in front of the crematorium they were spilled out automatically; the rest was the job of the Jews in the so-called Sonderkommando—and of the fire.

LITTLE LAGERS—Camps of several thousand people each.

MELDUNG—Denunciation; a penal report. The system of informing was intricately developed among the prisoners, especially where it wasn't simply a matter of tearing off a piece of blanket, smoking a cigarette during work, or not washing one's bowl— such matters were also laden with consequences, but *Meldung* was linked to long-ago scores among the old numbers, profitable functions, women, gold concealed in the rafters.

MILIONER—A person with a number in the tens of thousands. "How many tens of thousands do you have in your number?"

MILIONOWCY—Prisoners with higher numbers, e.g., 119,000, 170,000, etc. The old numbers referred to these men as *milionowcy;* it more bitterly expresses disdain and contempt based on "what *we* have seen."

MUSELMANN—A man who is completely destroyed physically and spiritually, without the strength or will to keep fighting for life, usually with dysentery, abscesses, or scabies, as ripe as can be for the chimney. No explanation can convey the contempt with which a *Muselmann* was treated by his colleagues in the camp. Even prisoners who take delight in writing camp autobiographies are reluctant to admit that they were "also" *Muselmänner* at one time.

NUMER [NUMBER]—Each prisoner had a number tattooed on his left forearm. Russian prisoners of war had special numbering on the left side of the chest (from 1 to almost 12,000). The Gypsies also had their own numbers; the women had their own numbers. Jews often had letters beneath their number and a Jewish triangle; in individual cases I saw a six-sided star. The numbers were consecutive, with none skipped (it was different in Lublin, for example). "Do you have a number sewed on?"

OLD LAGER—A camp that has been in existence for a long time; usually good. Also, the camp of justice—Buchenwald.

OLD NUMBER—A low number indicating a prisoner who's been there for a long time. The source of honor and respect from other old numbers and young numbers, too (prisoners who arrived at the camp later, also referred to as *milionowcy*). Appointment to the best camp functions, extraordinary capacity for camp life, camp patriotism. "What do you, *milionowcy*, know about the camp?! Ask some old number (!), he can tell you what he lived through."

ORGANIZACJA [ORGANIZING]—Acquiring the means of survival beyond one's ration, no matter how: either honorably (from the SS kitchen, from *Efekty*, from the ramp) or dishonorably (from one's colleagues' rations). An *organizator*, a person accustomed to this way of life, often had powerful wealth and always enjoyed the full respect and envy of the camp.

PASIAKI—Gray-and-blue-striped camp clothing made of a special material (people said it was from nettles). Well-cut *pasiaki*, made to fit the figure, were a sign of well-being, of *funkcja*, and the strong self-esteem of the prisoner wearing them. [From a Polish word meaning stripe.]

PHLEGMON—An intramuscular abscess, the second classic Auschwitz sickness; as was the case with *Durchfall*, for many years people who had it were destined for the gas chamber.

PIPEL—A boy at the service of a block elder or a kapo. Usually a youngster rescued from a Jewish transport. The female equivalent was a *kalifaktorka*.

POST—An SS guard. *Blokführers*, that is to say, those who supervised the interior life of the camp, were sent off "to *posts*" for transgressions (trade, relations with women, etc.)—if they were caught.

POSTENKETTE—A chain of guards surrounding the camp or a worksite. A small *Postenkette* was posted at night near the camp's wire fences. A large *Postenkette* was posted during the day (day and night in the event of an escape), surrounding the camp at a radius of several kilometers.

PROMINENT—Or "better guest": a prisoner in a good position, having all spheres of influence open. Clean, elegant, well fed on sardines, "campified." A term with a slight tinge of contempt. No one referred to himself as a *prominent*.

REWIR—The hospital, but only in the slang of the women's camp, which didn't use the expression "KB."

ROLLWAGE—A cart pushed by people. On the grounds of the camp there were no draft animals. For transporting soup, bread, clothing, excrement, corpses, from the camp to the hospital, people were used.

SCHUTZHÄFTLING—A "protected" (political) prisoner, locked up just in case. An official camp designation (with the addition of a number).

SELEKCJA [SELECTION]—The selection of *Muselmänner* for the gas. It occurred more or less regularly every two weeks, although there were periods (for example, the summer of 1944) when, because the crematoriums and gas chambers were overcrowded, selections were not carried out in the camp.

SŁUPEK—A rope is drawn between a prisoner's arms, which are tied behind him, and he is pulled up by a gear in a post or, when special equipment is lacking, simply across a transverse rafter in the block. He hangs like that for an hour or two. His arms come out of their sockets, the tendons rupture. The entire operation is called *słupek* [from the Polish word for post].

SONDERKOMMANDO—A special kommando composed exclusively of Jews, working in the crematorium while people are gassed and burned. "Who should have gold if not the Sonderkommando?"

STÓJKA—Standing during a protracted head count. The longest *stójka* in Auschwitz: two days. [From the Polish imperative meaning "stand!"]

SZPILA—An injection of phenol to the heart, with which *Muselmänner* were put to death during the first years in Auschwitz. "They all went to the *szpila*." [From the Polish word for stiletto.]

SZTUBA [STUBE]—A large room or part of a block. "I'm in the sixth block, third *sztuba*, on the top *buksa*."

SZTUBOWY—The "Kommandant" of a *sztuba*. He distributed food, saw to the cleanliness of the *sztuba*, and, it goes without saying, did not go out to work with the kommando. Unlimited power over a prisoner.

TOTENMELDUNG—The death certificate filled out by the hospital or, if the death occurred in the camp, by the block elder. It gives the time and cause of death. In the certificates for gassed prisoners: "transferred for special processing."

TRAGE [BARROW]—A stretcher. Also, a box for carrying bread. Also, wheelbarrows for moving earth.

TRUPPENLAZARETT—The SS hospital located inside the great *Postenkette*. It remained unfinished until the end of the camp.

UNTERKUNFT—The camp storerooms, warehouses, the name of a kommando.

VERNICHTUNGSLAGER—An extermination camp. Apparently, an official designation for Auschwitz.

VERTRETER—The block elder's deputy. Actual authority in the block (during the period when the block elders represented a block).

VORARBEITER—A kapo's assistant; what the English call a foreman.

WASCHRAUM—Essentially, a washroom. However, it often served other purposes. The *Waschraum* in Old Auschwitz was the arena for boxing and wrestling matches. The *Waschraum* in Birkenau was the place for performances organized in the hospital during one period, and for the entire time the hospital was in existence it was the collection point for Muselmänner who were brought to the *Waschraum* after selections from all the hospital blocks. At night, they left in trucks for the gas.

WHAT THOUSAND ARE YOU?—Hundreds weren't distinguished, as is characteristic of mass gatherings.

WINKEL—A colored triangle identifying the type of crime, worn in front of the camp number on the left side of the chest. "He has a red *Winkel*, but he's worse than a criminal."

YOUNG NUMBER—A prisoner newly arrived from prison; contemptuous and rash.

ZAUNA—The bathhouse, the delousing chamber. Because belongings brought by the transports and used by the prisoners were also deloused in it, the people who worked in the *Zauna* had everything, from gold to books. The women were shaved (to their bare skin) and disinfected exclusively by men.

ZIELONY [GREEN]—An SS man. Used relatively infrequently.

ZLAGROWANY—A man who thinks only in the categories of camp life and acts according to camp morality. "You're completely *zlagrowany*." [A German-based Polish neologism meaning "lagerfied," "campified."]

ZLAGROWANY NARÓD [LAGERFIED PEOPLE]—The masses collected in the camps.

ZULAGE—A supplemental ration for workers. "There's a *Zulage* today; it will be easier to hold out until dinner tomorrow."

ZYKLON—The gas used in the gas chambers. In 1944, in order to reduce expenditures, the dose for each gassing was reduced. Death, instead of taking five minutes, took from fifteen to twenty-five minutes, according to the Jews from the Sonderkommando. This gas was produced by a private German firm.

Tadeusz Borowski (1922–1951), a Polish poet and participant in Warsaw's underground resistance to German occupation, was arrested and sent to Auschwitz in 1942. He emerged after the war as a writer of short stories that portray the concentration camp social order and, later, stories about the postwar world he reentered through a DP camp near Munich. Borowski's Auschwitz stories, translated from Polish into many languages, have long been recognized as literary classics.

Madeline G. Levine is Professor Emerita of Slavic Literatures at the University of North Carolina–Chapel Hill. Her many literary translations include Ida Fink's *A Scrap of Time and Other Stories* (honored with the 1988 PEN-America translation award), Miron Białoszewski's *A Memoir of the Warsaw Uprising*, and Czesław Miłosz's *Beginning with My Streets* and *Legends of Modernity: Essays and Letters from Occupied Poland, 1942–1943*. For her translation of Bruno Schulz's *Collected Stories*, Levine received the Polish Book Institute's 2019 Found in Translation Award.

Timothy Snyder is the Richard C. Levin Professor of history at Yale University, where he is responsible for east European history. His studies of the Holocaust, *Bloodlands* and *Black Earth*, have received a number of awards. An illustrated edition of his political pamphlet *On Tyranny* will be published later this year. He is completing a philosophical book on freedom.